RIGHTEOUS CORRECTION?

RIGHTEOUS CORRECTION?

Simon J Stephens

Copyright © 2017 Simon J. Stephens

The moral right of the author has been asserted.

Apart from any fair dealing for the purposes of research or private study, or criticism or review, as permitted under the Copyright, Designs and Patents Act 1988, this publication may only be reproduced, stored or transmitted, in any form or by any means, with the prior permission in writing of the publishers, or in the case of reprographic reproduction in accordance with the terms of licences issued by the Copyright Licensing Agency. Enquiries concerning reproduction outside those terms should be sent to the publishers.

Matador
9 Priory Business Park,
Wistow Road, Kibworth Beauchamp,
Leicestershire. LE8 0RX
Tel: 0116 279 2299
Email: books@troubador.co.uk
Web: www.troubador.co.uk/matador
Twitter: @matadorbooks

ISBN 978 1788033 503

British Library Cataloguing in Publication Data.
A catalogue record for this book is available from the British Library.

Printed and bound by CPI Group (UK) Ltd, Croydon, CR0 4YY
Typeset in 11pt Minion Pro by Troubador Publishing Ltd, Leicester, UK

Matador is an imprint of Troubador Publishing Ltd

Prologue

The knock at the door wasn't unexpected. I knew that I'd been living on borrowed time and that events would catch up with me sooner or later. I had everything prepared as much as possible and anything that needed to be hidden was as well-hidden as could be, given that my home was barely more than six feet wide and consisted of just under forty foot of living space. It was late at night that they called, just before midnight, so I knew it wasn't another boater asking for some help or telling me that my mooring ropes had come loose. Similarly, no near neighbour would knock quite that loud on steel doors.

As a morning person, I was already in bed and sleeping when they came, which left me a little off guard, but they were quite patient as I threw on the clothes I knew would have to see me through a few wearisome days. Of the few outfits I had, there was little doubt in my mind that one I'd pre-prepared for going away was appropriate on that night. It wasn't anything special, simply practical, decent clothing, comfortable enough to wear for a few days and with pockets loaded up with the tobacco and cash that were my minimum living requirements. If they were going to take me away, I figured I could at least go with a few home comforts. The rest of it, I was happy to leave behind. I'd had a good run and there had to be an end to it at some point.

PART ONE

Chapter One

Up until the day that I experienced the loss of everyone that I loved, the most challenging thing that I had had to deal with in my life had been explaining to people that my first name was Zipoly. Over time, I'd got used to this but every new relationship began with the inevitable explanation of why I carried this name. Maybe it would have been easier if there were some heroic reason, but the truth was that my parents had dug this name out of a Scrabble bag. It was either Zipoly or Waduut, so it could have been worse. Fortunately, Zipoly reduced nicely to Zip, which in itself isn't too radical a name to carry with you.

It was my name that first got me talking to my future wife when were both starting out at university. Everybody needs something that makes them stand out from the crowd and what better than a catchy nickname like Zip and the mystery of the story behind it. Her name was a more ordinary Francesca. But that was the only thing that I found ordinary about her and I knew from that first moment of our meeting that we would be destined for a future together.

There are some who say that you should have the experience of a string of lovers before you settle down, but I lost my virginity to Francesca and never craved the touch of another woman since our first night together. She wasn't quite so innocent, having grown up as a clergyman's daughter and as such, had felt almost duty bound to rebel. However, after that first time with each other, she too would remain forever faithful. I remember that night very clearly, not least because the date was a very memorable thirty-first of December nineteen ninety-nine, the last day of the old millennium. We were both in our first year at Liverpool University and had regularly passed each other by on the way to the library or at the refectory, but we'd never had cause to stop and get to know each other. Fran was by far the brighter one of us and was studying veterinary medicine, whilst I was limping along on a social science course. She was also the most committed and to my mind there was nothing that was going to stop her graduating and realising her dream career. I had no such goal, other than getting through my degree and then seeing what came up.

We met that December by accident in a pub off Hope Street, and for the first time, forced mainly by a too-close New Year's Eve proximity, we found ourselves making small talk. This led on to a lengthier conversation and, as happens with true love, we just clicked. We shared the same sense of humour, the same love of classic English literature and of course, a degree of mutual attraction. One thing led to another and despite my nervousness we ended up in bed together at her flat as the last of the fireworks confirmed that we had entered the New Millennium without the anticipated breakdown of the technological age.

I knew that I wasn't her first, although at the time I didn't confess to her that she was mine. I think she probably guessed though and was, to coin a phrase, 'gentle with me'. From that moment on, we were an item and the University years rolled by with our bonding more and more, and inevitably living together and marrying. Despite her still having four years of study left, we married on my graduation and I started work in the offices of a local sanitaryware business, trading tutorials for toilets. This was not my chosen career path, but the money was good and I found myself to be particularly adept at selling some of the more complex waste management and plumbing solutions that the business offered. My aptitude in this most unexpected field led to my progressing through the ranks to become a territory manager by the time that Fran began her first work placement in a local veterinary hospital. That would have been in the late Summer of 2006.

To the outside world, we had a lot going for us and, to be honest, we wouldn't argue with this. We had a house, cars, disposable income (despite still paying down our student debts) and on top of all this, we had each other. Family life outside our closed circle of two was limited only to Fran's parents over in Yorkshire, as my own parents had long since passed on and my brother was somewhere off the radar down South, if indeed he was still alive. Whether it was the age gap between myself and the rest of my limited family, or simply my own insularity that led me to consider myself alone in the world, I'm not sure. Jim, my more traditionally named brother was a generation ahead of me and I had appeared as an unwelcome accident to parents who were in sight of retirement. Having been accepted by them, I grew to love Fran's parents almost as much as I loved her, but they were never imposing and we probably only saw each other a few times a year. They were busy enjoying life in a pre-retirement collection of village parishes, and we were wrapped up in each other and in planning the brood of children that we wanted to share our lives with.

The first of these came along on a cold, wet November evening in 2009. We called her Jessica and we instantly became that sort of new parent who believes that they have given birth to the only baby ever to have been born. She was our world and I was fortunate enough to be able to step away from work for her early years to look after her full-time whilst Fran opened her own practice in a pet superstore down in the Midlands. I knew the area well, having travelled extensively in the pursuit of ever larger contracts, so the move into Staffordshire was relatively straightforward even with a baby in tow. The house we bought backed onto the canal which provided the three of us with hours of simple pleasure whether feeding the local wildlife or waving to the boats as they passed by.

Our second child, Daniel, arrived two years later, at which point we decided that our ambition to spawn a larger brood was probably not the best way forward, so I had the necessary operation and we stuck at two. One of each was the ideal for us and with each other to allay the challenges of being an only child, we knew that they were children born to a promising and privileged future. Fran was quite stern with them and insisted on an almost Victorian standard of discipline, but always with the best intentions. I, however, was as soft as custard and was probably less of an adult guide to them than a fellow playmate. On the odd occasion that this caused tension between Fran and I, it was obvious that the fault was mine and I yielded without argument. And deep down I knew that the kids understood and respected Fran's firmer hand as it supported them, secured as it was by a mother's unconditional and unremitting love.

There was only one thing that we now felt was missing from our lives. Having watched the passing traffic on the canal over the years, we hankered for a narrowboat to fill up the mooring space at the bottom of the garden. I'd been fortunate enough to pick up some consultancy work after Jessica's first birthday, and with Daniel's birth, was able to carry this on at home on a part-time basis. For the most part though, I reverted back to house-husband mode with the boat that we bought becoming my home-working project. She was a little beauty; a genuine 1979 Springer 30 footer, in bright red and with most of the original interior still in place. The engine had been changed at some point in her history, but other than that she was as close to the original as you could get. Records indicated that she had been over-plated multiple times in her life, but that Springer moustache had lasted the years and so too had the upper structure.

As somebody who was effectively banned from doing any sort of do-it-yourself around the home, my patience not matching my ambitions, the boat gave me the opportunity to have a crack at renovation without too much fear of sinking her or setting her on fire. Despite my limited patience, I soon got to grips with some of the basics of boat maintenance and not before time, as we had in fact been sold a bit of a wrecker. That lovely original interior was held together by nothing more than multiple layers of paint, and every piece of woodwork that I presented the drill to collapsed into a dusty and rotten heap. Despite this, I had never felt more satisfied than rocking away on board this boat, building a new interior and tackling wiring, gas pipes and occasionally a dab of welding.

The kids loved being on the boat as I worked away, Daniel nestled in the unfortunately named coffin-bed at the rear, whilst Jessica played with her toys or chattered away to me at a million words a minute. When it went smoothly, I'd often find myself finishing off what I was doing only to find the two of them fast asleep together. At other times, when niggling problems occurred and my stress levels got the better of me, Jessica would joyfully shout, "Daddy done a rude!", as the words escaped my mouth before I could stop them. We had a pact between us that she kept, for the most part. Every rude word I said procured her a sweet treat, provided that Mummy didn't get to hear that word from her lips. Needless to say, this helped me check my language and I grew calmer in my work as I became that bit more competent and less expectant of a quick result.

Fran prospered at work, gaining a reputation amongst the local farmers as something of an expert on livestock, whilst the children flourished in our small piece of England by the water. As they got that bit older and the boat became habitable, they took to boating as naturally as if they had been born on the cut. With the veterinary practice well established and when Daniel was old enough to be squeezed into a life-jacket, we escaped to the water pretty much every weekend and were able to forget the madness of day to day life, as we discovered remote spots all around the local canal network.

From our home mooring in the commuter village of Weston, we could travel on the Trent and Mersey towards Stoke, stopping in either the rural tranquillity of Burston or the busier town of Stone, where the kids never ceased to be excited at the prospect of working through the locks. Heading the other way, we would be at Great Haywood junction within an hour or so, from which we could embrace the vast open space of Tixall Wide, head further on into the M6 blighted Penkridge, or choose to drift down to what was to become our favourite location, Wolseley Bridge. The attraction of Wolseley Bridge, despite being beside a main road, was that the towpath allowed for the kids to run wild on the wide and safe towpath, whilst we fired up the barbecue. If we had time, we moved further along the Trent and Mersey to Fradley, where there was more activity to keep the youngsters entertained and a great pub to keep me quiet. Like many a young couple, we talked and dreamed about living aboard, but with the children and work commitments this was only ever a pipe dream. Despite changes to the management of the waterways that seemed to be conspiring to make this a much harder dream to aspire to, there were still plenty of people out there who had made that lifestyle choice and who would never return to bricks and mortar. We still loved the trappings of modern life a little too much and with young children it wasn't really practical, but these 'water gypsies' we met certainly had a peace of mind about them that made us bank this thought as a retirement dream. As long as those liveaboard boaters continued to maintain this uniquely English way of life, despite the challenges they faced, we saw no reason why we shouldn't join them in the years ahead. For us then, although an unreachable goal at present, that retirement dream would sustain us and help us cope with the pangs of envy we felt as boats drifted past our garden on balmy Summer evenings.

Then it all went a bit wrong.

Chapter Two

Fran's parents had invited us to their fortieth wedding anniversary celebration and, as it was Jessica's half term, we decided that we might as well make a bit of a holiday of it. After visiting them we had booked a log cabin in the Dales, complete with sauna and hot tub, in which we fully intended to shake off the end-of-Summer blues. After much deliberation, and understanding the financial burden imposed on the clergy, we decided to treat them to a special gift for their anniversary and I managed to source, at a ridiculously low price, one of my ex-employer's company cars. They didn't know anything about this surprise and we hoped that they would forgive us the indulgence.

We therefore set off in two cars, heading up the motorway with Fran in our four by four and me following behind in the more practical and certainly more comfortable executive saloon. Aside from being almost an essential for her work, Fran loved the Land Rover and the feeling of security that it gave her. Because it was our day to day family vehicle as well, it had been fitted with television screens in the back, so the contest as to who the kids would travel with was really no contest at all.

Accompanying the children was the latest addition to the family, a retired greyhound called Spurt. It had been my idea to get a dog, but she was an instant hit with all the family and we'd spent the last few weeks walking her late into the evenings, discovering while we did so, that the few remaining dog-friendly pubs along the towpath were a great place to stop and rest. When we decided to get her, we were a bit worried that Spurt might curtail our boating, but those fears proved to be groundless. From her first step on board, she loved being on the boat as much as we did and she just about managed to fit in the bed with the rest of us.

It was Spurt's face, tongue lolling out and steaming up the back window, that was my main view as we travelled North. For all they may have loved me, I knew that the rest of the gang in front would be happily engaged in a series of stupid car games and that any thought of me was far from their mind. We did however have a few hands-free chats as we progressed, more to keep me from being bored than to remind them of the wit and wisdom of their father.

To be honest, I didn't mind being on my own in the car. I had racked up a lot of miles in my time as a travelling salesman but I never got bored with driving. I'm no car fanatic or speed freak, but I do enjoy the isolation of being in a moving box with the world passing by outside and only my own thoughts or my music collection to keep me company. On that day it was Johnny Cash who accompanied me. Amazing to think that he still had a huge fan base so many years after his death, but he was one of a kind and his music and voice are as timeless as a Mozart piano concerto or a Beethoven symphony. I was lost in a world of my own, but fully conscious of everything going on around me, locked into that automatic processing mode so loved by psychologists. There was the usual build-up of road freight on the inside lane, whilst both Fran and I opted for the slowest car lane, leaving the outer two for those who were in more of a hurry.

It was about half-way through our journey that I had to swerve suddenly to get out of the path of a black sports car that slipped over into my lane as it overtook. A quick glance at the driver showed him to be busily sorting through paperwork as he drove, whilst simultaneously trying to speak to someone on some sort of mobile device that seemed to balance on his wrist. He had no idea that he had caused me to swerve and honking the horn would have been futile, since he was already way out ahead and parallel with Fran, several cars ahead. The outside lane backed up and I saw his brake lights flash on and off as he impatiently waited behind the row of cars that had the nerve to slow his journey down.

I'd seen it all on my travels and I no longer got stressed about driving, since fate usually intervened at whatever speed you were travelling and I was much happier letting the racers try and outwit fickle circumstances. Whenever I'd known that I was due to travel on a notoriously busy route, I'd always chosen to leave very early in the morning, which usually meant me arriving an hour or so early, but there were always cafes to grab a coffee at while I waited. This guy was something else though, having drawn level with Fran, he flashed the car in front of him and drove bumper to bumper with it as they passed our four by four. At that point, a siren went off and an unmarked police car revealed itself to those in the outside lane. Our friend in the sports car failed to hear any of this and continued to try to push further ahead. With the unmarked car behind him, he must have had a momentary jolt of common sense and looked back in his mirrors only to see the flashing blue light.

His reaction was exactly what one would expect; a knee-jerk reversal of his speeding to manoeuvre back into the inner lane and help the police car on its way, certain as he was that it couldn't be wanting to stop him. I braked hard to keep out of his way, but realised too late that he was drifting across in front of Fran's vehicle, which he clipped on the front bumper as he passed. The occupants of the police car saw this and instantly slowed but they, like myself, could only watch as a terrible scene unfurled before our eyes.

Over time, I've related the sequence of events that followed to many people and always without variance since they remain forever fixed in my mind, as permanent as any tattoo. The black sports car corrected itself and sped off, seemingly oblivious to the impact, meanwhile, Fran's car started to fish-tail and I knew that she was struggling to keep it under control. Helpless to do anything, I watched as that fish-tailing built up a momentum that swung the rear of the car into the path of a lorry that was coming down the inside. There followed the squeal of brakes, the honking of horns and the clatter of metal on metal as the two vehicles made contact and the four by four was flipped in the air. I watched it all. The flight of Fran's car, its landing back on the tarmac on its roof and then its unrestrained slide towards the pillar of a bridge. If there was any saving grace to this, it was simply that the vehicle stayed facing forwards and I was spared the sight of the faces of its occupants as they headed towards that steel-reinforced block tower of concrete.

With a final slap, the moveable and immoveable met and the unchangeable forces of nature went to work to tear the vehicle apart on impact. I stopped dead in my lane and, ignoring the vehicles around me, ran to scene.

Can any words describe what I saw? My wife was dying in the driver's seat. The twisted metal piercing her beautiful face and that body I so loved were testimony enough to her not having any chance of survival. I ran to her and she mouthed words to me that bubbled in her mouth as they mixed with blood and saliva.

"The kids?" she whispered, "Zip, the kids."

"They're fine," I told her, justifying the lie as I knew these were her final words.

"I love you," she said, struggling to get the words out, "I love you all."

"Love you too," I whispered, but the words were too late to pass into a living body.

Behind the body of his mother, Dan remained in his seat. At least, what was left of him did. They would only find his head much later, after the wreck had been recovered and prised apart. Frantically searching around, I saw Jessica's dress further on up the embankment and ran towards her with the briefest flicker of hope in my heart. Had I not recognised that flowery dress she so loved, I might easily have thought that she was nothing more than another piece of wreckage, but it was her alright. At least, what was left of her.

I wiped the mess of blood and grass from her face and tried desperately to find a pulse of life in her. But those wide open eyes that stared at me told me that she too was gone. In her hand she still clutched the ragged and tattered teddy bear that went everywhere with her and which had joined her on her final journey. I lay my head across her chest and wept.

The police were joined quickly on the scene by the other emergency services who frantically tried to make sense of the carnage but who had quickly reconciled themselves to this now being a clean-up job rather than a rescue. They found me on the embankment and led me away to one of their vehicles where they checked me over and tried to offer comfort where none could ever be found.

Death is a difficult bed-fellow, even in circumstances where his appearance is expected and timely. Witnessing the work of death on those you love and being there as their life is extinguished, in a time and a place and a manner that could never be anticipated, is a pain that is beyond description. All that I had loved and everything that I held precious lay broken, bloody, destroyed and dead all around me. The shock kept the tears and the screams back. Not just for that moment but for many days to come. When the feelings came though, they came with a force that seemed to tear the heart out of my body, whilst every tear-drop bathed my flesh with a thousand agonised tongues of bitter fire. Nothing would be the same from that moment on.

Chapter Three

At some point or other in our lives, I think we all spend some time imagining how the funeral of a loved one will pan out. This doesn't make us morbid or mentally unstable, although I suppose that dwelling on the vision, or even looking forward to it, is probably not healthy. When it's imaginary, it seems all too easy to construct the perfect send-off, complete with appropriate music, plentiful numbers of deeply upset guests and that perfect requiem speech. When it happens for real, those plans and dreams seem to vaporise and it is not a situation anyone truthfully wishes to experience. Then again, the truth of the matter for me was that I seemed to be a spectator at the event, and now remember only brief snippets of that day when my family was consigned to the dust.

The funeral took place just as Autumn was giving way to Winter. The trees had shed their leaves and the air had a distinct chill to it. It was a church-centred burial, and not simply because that was the expectation, given Fran's family background. The two of us were believers and, despite not being anything like regular churchgoers, that belief was an almost unspoken element of our relationship: it was there, but it didn't command us in our daily life. The children had both been christened and we got involved in some of the activities of the local church, mainly because, as one of the local vets, Fran was fairly well known in the village and had difficulty escaping the call to help at fetes and with the annual pantomime. Under the circumstances, the vicar did a pretty good job as far as I can recall, faced as he was by a building full of distressed and confused mourners who were trying get to grips with a good God who could watch over the death of innocent children.

My semi-detached isolation from events was nothing to do with my own inner strength but was instead the result of the powerful anti-depressants that caused most of my higher functions to be switched off. They were prescribed to me to help me get some sleep, but I knew that they would do more than that. And, to be honest, I didn't really care that they would dull the part of me that needed to feel the full impact of my grief. So it was that I got through the service, endured the follow up at the crematorium and mingled amiably with all those who had come to be a part of this most tragic of days.

It surprised me just how many people were there for the service. Of course, the event had been well reported and was the talk of our village for quite a while, but even still, Fran had more friends, relatives and well-wishing contacts than I had ever imagined. There were youngsters there who came to pay their respects to the nice lady who had dressed their pony's wounds, and there were local farmers too, who may not always have agreed with Fran's approach but whose livestock still enjoyed the benefit of her treatment regimes. I was pleased that Fran had been able to serve in some way and I'd never had an issue with her being the professional in our partnership, nor was I ever jealous of her being the career person in our relationship. Her success had meant that my joy had been greater in spending more time with the children and if that meant that I worked less outside the home and more on domestic chores, then so be it. We'd had a good life together.

It was this theme of service that the vicar chose to talk about. Fair play to this man of the cloth, as somebody who knew Fran quite well and who had christened our children, it can't have been an easy day for him. Of the little I remember, snippets of his sermon come to me every now and then. He talked about the brevity of life and our need to make the most of every day. He touched on the myriad small duties that we could all perform to make a difference. And he talked about justice and the need for us to reconcile what had happened to an innocent, when so many of the guilty walked away. It was that that I remembered most, maybe not with the acceptance that the vicar had wanted it to engender, but as the flicker of a new flame that seemed to have been ignited in me. A flame that would flare up in the future and forge me into a new creation.

I was aware that some people felt that it was cold-hearted of me to choose the anaesthesia of anti-depressants to carry me through the mourning process. What they didn't know was that the reality was quite different. The drugs took a little of the edge off things but I was less out of it than anyone knew. My only way to cope though was to choose the path of distanced silence over sentimentality because cold facts simply couldn't be dressed up with patronising words. How else was I to sit in front of the three coffins that contained the broken remains of my wonderful family? We all cope in different ways I guess and who are any of us to judge another's mourning?

Fran's parents were a lot more understanding even in the face of their own grief. They allowed me to do what I felt was right and never criticised me for keeping my own counsel and standing half-removed from so much that was going on.

Truth is, I didn't really care what other people thought. The things that we cremated that day were nothing more than the shells of the people they represented, and the dust that we scattered was no more than that. Neither Fran nor myself were into this idea of leaving behind gravestones and plots that would only fade and crumble over time, but I yielded to her parent's wish that a small memorial plaque be erected at the church. It wouldn't be something I would make a beeline to visit as it held nothing for me. My choice was to concentrate on remembering the life we had together, rather than the stillness of our separation.

I stayed on the pills for longer than I really needed to. They gave me a solid crutch to lean on, even if I knew that they might be impeding my healing. I only came off them three months later when the inquest date had been set. Not that I relished facing that hearing. I had to be fully myself for it though. This was something I had looked forward to and if justice was going to be done then I wanted the whole me, not a shadow of what I am, to be there to witness it.

The driver of the car that had caused the accident was being interviewed by the police less than an hour after it happened, not because he had voluntarily come forward, but because the plethora of CCTV cameras that lined the motorway and surrounding roads had tracked him to his workplace. Not only had he been the cause of this tragedy, but he had also failed to stop at the scene. A fact that I knew would do little to endear him to a general public who I felt were on my side. Off the record, the police had also advised me that this wasn't the first time that he had been spoken to about his driving. All in all, it looked good from my side and I have to say that I harboured a very deep urge to see this man pay heavily for what he'd done, even considering what I would write to him as he languished in his prison cell.

I was surprised when they told me that they had let him go pending further investigation, but not unduly concerned as I felt confident that when they'd gathered all the evidence he would be made to pay for his actions. I didn't hear anything more from them until the inquest, at which they presented their evidence, holding back on any further action until the coroner's verdict was recorded.

Chapter Four

The inquest was worse than the funeral. It was always going to be the hardest obstacle to face for a number of reasons. Firstly, I was off the happy-pills and fully aware of what was going on about me and, secondly, because it was the final closing of the book on the past. Most importantly though, it was the day of justice that I had waited so long for.

On the 12th December, whilst the first snow of the year lay turning to slush around the court room steps, the inquest began with a stark, factual, presentation of the evidence that reduced those I'd held so dear into medical parlance. The lead doctor outlined the specifics of each of their injuries, gave a cursory lay-man's explanation as to how those injuries had come about and then concluded with a summary cause of death. I struggled a bit with this but managed to stay composed even when every part of me wanted to scream out that the cause of death was nothing more and nothing less than the selfish act of a selfish fool shoving their car into a concrete pillar. Nevertheless, I understood that, as with the law, the medical profession was one with a duty to deliver facts unencumbered by emotion.

Once the bare facts of the outcome had been detailed, it was the turn of the police to outline their own take on the matter. I looked across to the public gallery at this point and saw my family's killer sitting there looking a lot less concerned than I expected him to be. Worse than that, he seemed to sense me looking at him and I saw the faintest of smiles on his face as he caught my eye. Deep inside, I felt a stirring of dread as I looked back to the police spokesperson taking the stand.

Anybody interested in reading the full details of what was said can look up the inquest record. I certainly never intend to. Nor do I need to as I remember more than enough of what I heard that day. In short, the police had investigated the accident, held long and exhaustive interviews with the driver and had come to the conclusion that they concurred with the driver's statement that he had panicked on seeing the police car in his mirrors and had swerved back into his original lane in order to help them proceed in their duty. To add insult to injury, they then detailed the numerous allegations that I had made against his driving and tore them apart one by one.

"Whilst it has been alleged," the police representative explained to the court, "that the driver of the impacting vehicle was preoccupied in handling some form of mobile device, we have established no evidence of this and are assured by the said driver that he would never endanger the public by driving whilst distracted."

"Similarly, ", he continued, "we can find no other witness to collaborate a report of the driver recklessly drifting out of his own lane, or of his being aggressive towards those vehicles behind which he was travelling. The driver of the impacting vehicle has expressed immense regret at having been responsible in some way for this tragedy, and has accepted a fine and penalty points for leaving the scene of the accident. In his defence, it has been sufficiently proven that his claim to not have felt the impact is valid, as his vehicle was fitted with the latest in high-absorbency front and rear bumpers. We have asked the manufacturer of this vehicle to review the use of these bumpers in the light of this event. Further to this, it has been noted that the driver has been accused before of other driving offences but it is my duty to advise that none of these have ever been proven and they must therefore have no bearing on this case."

I was too stunned to say anything. Even the righteous anger that was to drive me on into the next year, remained silent within me, and all I could do was sit staring at the coroner, hoping that he would see the truth behind my eyes. Of course, he had to go with the recommendation of his superiors and a verdict of accidental death was duly recorded on the three members of my family.

There was so much that I needed to say. I'd done my research and I knew what this guy was capable of: stopped twice for being over the limit, caught reading paperwork whilst driving at well over the speed-limit and most poignantly, being involved in a collision with a cyclist leading to their death. I knew that in each case he had employed the best of lawyers to defend him, but surely the police had to take some of this into account? Here now, was my opportunity to set the record straight, as the coroner asked me if there was anything that I wished to say.

"Yes, there is," I replied, standing shakily to my feet, "yes, there is."

"That man," I continued, pointing to the driver, "caused the death of my family. That much has been accepted today. However, this has been attributed to an unavoidable accident in which he almost appears to be a victim himself."

The coroner rose to his feet and I knew that he was trying to stop me saying anything else. At the same time, the driver's lawyer looked my way and shook his head, mouthing to me to be careful.

"I will not be silenced," I shouted, "and, frankly, I don't care what repercussions may follow, but I will state publicly, here and now, that I know what happened that day and that man is guilty of killing my family. If justice has failed today, then it will be seen to be done one day."

The police officer who sat next to me pulled me back down to my chair and, before I knew what was happening, had ushered me out of the hearing and into a nearby corridor.

"Look," he said, "I know how you feel, but you can't act like that. You've just opened yourself up to prosecution for slander and threatening behaviour. I can't say whether anything will come of it, but for now, you need to get yourself away from here and I'll do what I can to cover for you. Please, just go now."

I knew he was right and I did as I was told, leaving the hearing via a fire exit before walking the long way round to my car. Whatever was said after I'd left, I think I do owe that policeman a favour, as he seemed to diffuse the situation and prevent any action being taken against me.

As it happened, I didn't return to my car that afternoon, choosing instead to go for a couple of pints in the first pub that I passed. It was quiet in there and the beer was good, so I switched my phone off, grabbed the daily paper and worked my way through the list of guest ales. A couple of hours later I took a taxi home and was barely across the threshold when the doorbell rang. Hoping that this meant only a brush off for the local Jehovah's Witnesses or the receipt of a parcel, I opened the door, but unfortunately it was neither. The woman who stood there, I pegged at mid-thirties and noted that her dress had a certain elegance that complemented her figure well. Of all my first impressions though, I could see straight away that she was a member of the press.

"Mr Hardacre?" she asked.

"That's a reasonable assumption," I answered, weariness very evident in my voice, "and I'm guessing that you are not here to ask my opinion on the latest trends in household spending. So, I'll save you the bother and say, inquest, travesty, no further comment."

I was just about to close the door but she gave me a look that made me pause and which provided her with just enough time to make an appeal to me.

"Yes," she said, "I am from the press. But please hear me out, there's a little more to it than that."

"My name is Jean Carter," she continued, producing a photo-identity that I gave the briefest attention to, "I work for the Sentinel and yes, of course, if we can talk about the inquest then that would be great, but I really need to talk to you about Jim Slater."

She knew just how to get my attention and I felt my stomach churning as she mentioned that name. Jim Slater, Managing Director of Quadra Audio and erstwhile killer of my wife, my children and my dog.

"Ten minutes," I whispered to her, opening the door to let her in, "as you'll appreciate, I'm not really in the mood today. And I want to see any copy if you're here for a story, especially in view of the fact that I may be slightly under the influence just now."

As the day still had a fair amount of sunshine on offer, I showed her through the lounge and into the large conservatory that we had built recently to make the most of the view of our garden and the passing boats. We sat opposite each other. I poured myself a decent shot of whisky, choosing not to extend the courtesy to my guest, then I told her to go ahead.

"Thanks," she said, "I really do appreciate this, and I hope that we can be of help to each other. Firstly, if I may, can I just run the situation at the inquest by you. It's fine if you don't want to say anything, but I can assure you that our reporting of events might well surprise you in its sympathetic tone. I've got all the details of the hearing that I need, but I would just like to discuss your final speech."

"There really isn't anything to discuss," I told her, "You were there, so you heard what I had to say and, however the police may feel about it, that remains my position. That man killed my family. You'll never publish that and I know that I may still face court proceedings for saying it, but I will never change my opinion. Now, I don't say that he did it deliberately or that he set out that day with any intention of harming anyone, but that doesn't change the fact that his selfishness caused the accident. The police know all about his reckless driving but because nothing has ever been proven, he is as innocent as you or I. And I'm supposed to believe that justice has been served today? Report what you like on that, but please don't tone my comments down in any way. I know what happened and I know what he did."

"I'm not here to defend Mr Slater," she leaned towards me, "In fact, quite the opposite. Firstly, on the record, thank you for clarifying your side of things, none of which surprises me and which, as I've already assured you, we will report as favourably as we can without risking a libel action. Now, off the record, the hidden agenda of my calling in person on you. I agree with you completely about that man."

"Of course," she continued after composing herself a little, "this is not the view of The Sentinel, so, for now, we need to keep this to ourselves. The fact is that I reported on the death of that cyclist who Slater ran over. Without going into the gory details, that was another accident that didn't have to happen. I'm convinced that Slater was over the limit on that day, but he just scraped through the breathalyser by the time he got to the police station. In short, you're not the only one to have suffered at his hands and I wanted you to know that."

"Which leaves me where?" I asked, anger rising in my voice, "Am I supposed to thank you for highlighting even more of the injustice of this case? Why come to me with this? You know my opinion, and you know my thoughts on what happened and now you tell me that I'm right. Well, sorry, but I knew that already and I'm not out to earn any sort of reward for my knowledge, I just want to see justice done. It hasn't been, it won't be and no amount of wishing for a different outcome will bring it about or bring my family back. There's nothing more to be said."

I was just about ready to ask her to leave when the doorbell rang again. I muttered a curse and she got up to go, but by that time I was at the window and could see a police car parked in my drive.

"Please," I motioned her to sit down again, "stick around. I'd like you to be here with me for this conversation."

A couple of minutes later I came back with two police officers who looked particularly uncomfortable and who had clearly drawn the short straw in being asked to come and see me. They say that the older you get, the younger the police look, but in this case there was no disguising that neither of these officers had been in the force for very long. Their worried looks grew even tauter as they saw the reporter sat there.

"If we could speak to you alone Mr Hardacre?" one of them tried to say, but I was having none of it.

"No, if you have anything to say to me, then I'd prefer it if Ms Carter were here with me. Now, go on, get it over with."

They looked at each other clearly trying to get their act back together, before the slightly taller one of the two began:

"The thing is, that we've been asked to come and see you with regards to your comments at the inquest today."

"Not," his colleague intervened, "that this is a formal interview at all. However, we do need you to take our conversation seriously."

"Okay," I gave them my nicest smile as I replied, "but shall I just save you the trouble because I pretty much know that you are here to advise me that my comments at the inquest were both threatening and slanderous and that I need to be very careful in my use of language or I may face some form of cautioning or prosecution. How's that for a summary?"

Thrown off their guard like that, they stumbled for a long minute before confirming that, yes, this was why they were there.

"Well," I said, "thank you for your concern. I presume that this word of warning is not off the record, so I look forward to reading about it in The Sentinel."

I looked across at the reporter who nodded and smiled.

"As for my own actions," I continued, "let me tell you that if a similar situation ever comes up I will neither tone down my approach, nor be backward in coming forward. I know what Slater did and I know that he has somehow avoided a prosecution for manslaughter. I can't prove anything, nor am I in any position to avenge his actions. However, I stand by my position that I hope to see justice done to him and soon, and in such a way that he pays the price for his crime. Now, please leave, or, if you're not happy with what I've said, arrest me. Or better still, get out there onto the roads and do a bit of proper policing rather than harassing the victims of your incompetence."

Needless to say, they were happy to be given the option to leave and did so as swiftly as possible. As I was seeing them off Jean Carter appeared behind me and indicated that she too would leave now.

"Thanks again for your time, Mr Hardacre," she held out her hand and I shook it, "I'll e-mail my article to you before publication, but I'm sure that you'll be okay with it. I don't know that there is anything else we can do, but I agree with your sentiments entirely on seeing Slater bought to justice. That visit from the police was very timely and I think we can make a nice play even sputtered once. Maybe I should have had more faith in it. The exhaust threw out a nasty black cloud for the first few minutes but even that cleared once the engine had warmed a little. I'd get it serviced soon, but at least I knew it worked and, when I put her in gear I could feel the propeller start to push against the mooring ropes. It was good. All that time left alone and unloved and still she was ready to cruise.

As I pottered around inside the cramped cabin, digging into drawers and cupboards to check for damp and to remind myself of what we had on board, I began to realise just how comfortable I felt in this confined space. Although I was at the bottom of my own garden and the sound of the main road could still be clearly heard, there was a reassuring sense of isolation and peace all about me. Maybe this was what I needed to break out of my malaise. After all, the big old world out there may not be where I wanted to be, but on the canal you were in that strange place of being part of the bigger scene but always half a world away. We'd never cruised far from home, due to work commitments, but even on the short journeys that we'd made, we'd moor up somewhere and feel that we could have been a million miles away from home. Now I was free to go wherever the canals and rivers could take me and that idea appealed to me greatly.

Returning to the house, I looked around at all the accumulated possessions that we'd filled the place with, and I realised that if I was to spend more time on the boat then I'd have to live with a lot less than I had been used to. But the reality was that all this stuff that surrounded me hadn't even been used for the past six months or more. How much of it could I live without? It didn't take me long to come to the conclusion that most, if not all of it could go. I fished out a pad and pen and started to make some notes, beginning at first by listing all the items we had and ticking them off as necessary or surplus. Then I realised that I was approaching this the wrong way, threw that first list away and started again on another: what exactly did I need to keep me going? Clothes, soap and shower gel, food, money, coal, books and booze. That was all I could come up with. The clothes were already on board, as were the basics of everything else apart, of course, from perishable foods. It wasn't like I was going trekking in the Amazon, so, as long as I had access to money I could buy anything else as I went along. And wouldn't it be great to be self-contained like that?

I cracked open and demolished a bottle of Merlot then decided to sleep on things, but that whole night I kept waking up with a real sense of anticipation and a new hope for the future stirring in me. There was, after all, nothing to stop me simply heading away from it all. Apart that is from the trappings of living in a modern home with all the luxuries of space, electricity, running water and central heating. Aside from the kitchen, I was only really using the lounge and conservatory to read in and my bedroom to sleep in. The boat had all of these, albeit a little smaller than I'd been used to. If I translated smaller to cosier, then it sounded so much better. As for utilities, there were service points all over the canal network and if we'd managed for weekends why not a week? And if a week, why not a month?

When I woke up the following morning, my mind was made up. Not only would I move onto the boat, I would also sell the house and everything in it. Radical, yes, but it was only stuff and all of it was replaceable if I changed my mind. I could live for years just off the proceeds of the house and that still left me with a bulging bank account that wasn't doing anything. Whether I did it for a few months or for the rest of my life, the time to start was now, and if I didn't move quickly doubts might start trying to draw me back into those four walls. I picked up the phone to the estate agents and started the ball rolling.

It took nearly two months to get rid of everything in the house but time flew by as I embarked on this cathartic process, ridding myself of all that had signified my past life. That was a life that was gone now, never to be relived. All the possessions that I had were laden with potential sentimental value, but if I kept reminding myself that they were in fact nothing more than inanimate objects then selling them or giving them away presented no problems. There were a few things that I allowed myself to keep: a picture of Bambi from Jess's bedside table, a couple of Dan's treasured model cars and a few pieces of jewellery that Fran had particularly loved. The rest of it went and by the time the house sale was completed, the new occupants were able to take possession of an empty building.

There were some who criticised my approach to things. Fortunately, I had little contact with other people so I avoided their judgements. I can understand where they were coming from though and realised that yes, there was a certain coldness about what I was doing. But it felt right at the time and I have had no regrets since. I'm not the sort of person who can live in the past, and when that past has such bitter memories as mine held, I'm sure there are many who would agree that, for me, the best way into the future was with a clean break. What that new future held, I didn't really know, nor was I totally convinced that I wouldn't be back on dry land again in a short while. But that didn't matter as this was an opportunity to at least try a new way of life and to ensure that whatever the future held it wasn't corrupted or twisted in any way by the past.

So it was that on the 1st May 2017 I handed over the keys to the house, walked the short distance down the garden and loaded the last of my limited belongings onto the boat. I looked back at the old place, whispered a final goodbye to all those memories of Fran and the children and untied the ropes that bound me to the past. I pushed the boat off, stepped aboard and slid the engine into gear. And I was off, heading at three miles per hour into what truly were unknown waters.

Chapter Seven

Mere words are insufficient to describe my feelings in that first month of living on board the boat. To the casual observer, I was no more than another individual making their home out of what was essentially an over-elaborate bathtub on a three-foot-deep ditch in the English countryside. To me, I was a liberated man, freed from the chains of all the complications of modern living. The freedom, the peace and the tranquillity of this lifestyle were beyond my highest expectations. Even the daily routines that still needed to be completed were a joy in their simplicity and a welcome reminder of the basic necessities of life. But, beyond all this and the greatest surprise to me as I took to the waterways, was the experience of meeting the people who shared this lifestyle.

Of the many populist words so recently used to excess in Britain for almost the last decade, community and austerity must be the two most dominant. What so often passes for either of these is but a bare reflection of what the words actually mean and is so often a corruption at best, or at worst, a lie. Our austerity, to previous generations, would have been unimaginable luxury and our community is based more on division than communion. But on the canals, community is real: it is a complex and varied mix of diverse personalities, all joined by the thread of wanting to be that bit apart from the mainstream, and every one, with a story to tell and a hand to lend to a fellow boater. As to austerity, when you are living in twenty foot of accommodation, working with two hundred litres of water and with what is nothing more than an over-elaborate plastic bowl for a toilet, only then can you begin to understand the value of things and the sheer luxury afforded to even the poorest in our society. Not that poverty is a requirement to live on the canals: I met the wealthiest of people and the poorest; the smartest and the most intellectually challenged; the young and the old.

I didn't travel far from familiar territory in that first month. Our house was near to the junction of the Staffs and Worcester canal and the Trent and Mersey at Great Haywood in Staffordshire, which, fortunately is possibly the best part of the canal network to begin exploring. In a vague 'inverse triangle' I was able to travel out towards the industrial heartlands of Wolverhampton and Birmingham in one direction, in another direction, up through the rural beauty of Staffordshire towards the Potteries and in the third direction out towards the breweries of the East Midlands.

Believe me, a month is not enough to explore this area and every place needs visiting multiple times in both directions if all the hidden local gems are to be discovered. There were odd days when I'd find a nice mooring spot near to a friendly and 'proper' pub and choose to stay there for a little while. At other times, I drifted into less attractive areas, felt the hint of threat as my way of life clashed with my terrestrial neighbours, and couldn't wait to move on. I was sometimes alone in the middle of a field, with nothing to keep me company at night but the hooting of owls and the soft whisper of traffic in the far distance. Other times, I was in town centres and the boat was lit up all night by supermarket floodlights.

Having nothing of any value worth stealing was liberating, as it took away any worries that I might have about leaving the boat alone while I explored the local area. It would have been nice to have had a dog with me to share my long walks, but I knew that such a commitment wasn't appropriate at this time. I was enjoying freedom like I'd never enjoyed it before.

When we had been a couple, the thought of going out to a pub for anything more than a meal or a quick drink on a sunny evening was completely alien to us. The norm was to spend our evenings at home, chill out in front of the television or do any combination of the myriad time-wasting activities that modern life presents. The boat, the children and the dog had all changed this a little but we remained primarily home birds. When I was on my own on the boat though, although enjoying my own company like never before, I discovered the joy of the English pub for the lone traveller. Not only did a visit to a new pub offer me the chance to plan a decent explorative walk along the towpath, it also opened up for me a world of exciting potential and curiosity about who I might meet. I'm not a naturally gregarious person, indeed, at times I often think of myself as being shy. For that reason, as well as the obligatory pouch of tobacco, I would always carry a book with me, just in case the weather prevented me from sitting outside. Both the smoking and the reading gave me something to do whilst enjoying a drink and stopped me from looking like some weird predator lingering on his own in a hostelry. On most occasions though, within a few minutes of being at a new pub I was getting into a conversation with a complete stranger and thoroughly enjoying my dip into their lives. For all that social media might allow the individual in this day and age to present to the world an image of their personality, it is over a pint of decent bitter that real lives and real experiences create the timeless bond between humans. These are conversations when barriers can be let down and where there is little fear of having to maintain a long-term commitment and friendship, and where the truth is the only option since the face always gives the game away.

The conversations would usually start with a brief comment about the weather, following which, the topic of boats would normally find its way in. Either the people I met were fellow boaters, locals who remembered what things used to be like along the cut, or alternatively, they would be a diverse mix of individuals from that other world beyond the canals who were drawn to the waterside for a time of relaxation and reflection. I met them all and I learnt the most important lesson of all about people when I came to the realisation that for all our lives may be nothing more than a fleeting shadow of dust, they remain a part of an unseen and complex web that makes us all relevant to the human experience.

What I also learnt from my meeting people in pubs, was the hidden history of things both close to my towpath home and in the wider world in general. In Weston, where I began my new life, I discovered from a local I met, that the nearby Ingestre Church is the only other religious building, after St. Paul's Cathedral, to have been designed by Sir Christopher Wren. I also discovered, from a fellow boater aged over ninety, that British bombers had dropped a toilet as part of a bombing raid on Berlin during the second world war. I was told about the great rock stars of the seventies who gathered in nearby pubs and informed of the 'ring' in Little Haywood that may have inspired Tolkien during his recuperative stay in that village. I passed by a large house complete with swimming pool and, after commenting on the ridiculous honking of car horns as they passed over the bridge, discovered that it was this noise that drove a very famous pop star's mother away from that same house. And I heard tales of love and loss, success and failure, fear and prejudice and every other human experience in-between. I didn't have a television on board, but who needed one with all this stuff going on?

After leaving Weston, I'd initially headed up through a few locks, past the villages of Salt, Sandon, and Burston, then on into the historic town of

Stone. Now, this account of my life is not a tourist guide to the area, but what happened to me in the time I spent discovering this hidden world has shaped much of my future and changed me in ways that mean it can't be ignored. These are all real places, accessible to anybody, and even to this day I visit them regularly and would encourage others to do so. The essence of our canal network may essentially be nothing more than a water-filled ditch that links the major cities of the country, but there is so much more to it than this. It is a bastion of sanctuary and escape from the world that races by, often within sight, and it is a place where the soft swell of water courses gently through the most beautiful natural landscape. It is also a stunning example of the labours and ingenuity of our recent ancestors who, faced with the opportunity to embrace the industrial revolution, did so in a way that transformed this small island nation. For all our celebration of modern technology, how many of the things that we honour now will remain in use and unchanged two hundred and fifty years later? Sit outside the pub in Stone and that's what you witness.

Arriving at the town and mooring below the bottom lock, I felt a certain sense of comfort about being in a populous area where I was able to enjoy the comforts of nearby shops. Breaking away from four walls and a car was not going to be instantaneous but I already felt myself being distanced from the chaos of the mainstream world. In Stone, I was also able to stock up on books from the more than plentiful charity shops, carrying on my commitment to broaden my reading experience and not caring too much if a book at fifty pence was barely readable. It frustrated me a little that this town, so important in the history of the canals and often referred to as the birthplace of the canal network, was in decline. Yes, there were lots of boats, but there wasn't the celebration of history that I would have liked to have seen, nor did the busyness of the canal seem to reflect in the prosperity of the town. I did however find the best pub in which to while away the hours and work my way through a constantly changing stream of guest ales. There were also sanitary facilities and water here, so I was able to wallow in the shower and eat as much as I liked without worrying about filling up the toilet cassette. It amazed me how quickly I was adapting from being somebody who loved to wallow in the bath and who visited the loo at home several times a day, to being in the position of measuring out every drop of water that I used. With the electrics running wholly on solar power, I also felt like I was as 'back to nature' as it was possible to go, although I did have the money to eat out whenever I liked and treat myself to anything that I wanted. Funnily enough, I didn't really want for that much.

Retracing my journey back from Stone, I headed past Great Haywood junction on the Trent and Mersey and moved slowly down past Lord Lichfield's estate, into Little Haywood, where I picked up that nugget about Tolkien. I was also shown, by an ex-lockkeeper, a buried stone that sits just above Colwich lock and which is marked simply L and L with a line between. This is the exact halfway point being Leeds and Liverpool via the canal, he told me. I moored up at Wolseley Bridge for a few days and, to this day, I can still say that there is no spot on the canals where I feel happier than at this place. The sunsets at night are absolutely stunning, whilst the beauty of Cannock Chase offers the best backdrop imaginable. Add to this a superb curry house, decent pub and a wetlands conservation park, and you get the ideal location. That said, the main road that runs alongside and over doesn't make for the quietest of spots and there is an awful lot of shooting that further breaks the silence. Then of course, for me, there are also the memories, but they are fading now.

From Wolseley, I headed out towards Fradley Junction and Alrewas, before turning back towards Great Haywood again. To have made this journey by car would have been an hour at tops, but I had burned up nearly a month and I still had so many things that I'd missed. At this point, I calculated that to cover the whole network of UK canals and do justice to everything that was in or around them, would be the work of a lifetime. Once I knew this, I knew also that it would be the work of my lifetime and that I never had to go back to that madness that existed half a world away.

With that in mind, I took the third leg of my journey and headed out along the Staffs and Worcester canal towards Wolverhampton, which would keep me busy for another few months, at which point I planned to enter Autumn by doing my whole journey over again.

Chapter Eight

Despite the agony of the grief that I still carried over the death of Fran and the children, that first Summer on the boat was a time of peace and happiness that I still fondly recall. I may have some sort of social disease that causes me to be a little detached and cold, but I wasn't going to let Slater take another life and was determined that my few days on this Earth would not be wasted in thoughts of what might have been. I believed that my family were in a better place and if the tables had been turned I would certainly have wanted them to move on in life and make the most of the situation. At some point during that Summer, probably as the second anniversary of my tragedy loomed, I decided that I was allowed to draw a line under the past and look forward to a new future. I was happy on my own and, despite the occasional day of wanting some female company, I was certainly not interested in tying myself down into another relationship. This was my time, my opportunity and there remained some sort of future for me.

The old boat was the source of many a long conversation with other boaters and towpath users alike. It was surprising how many people recognised the boat as one of Sam Springer's huge output and who could recall that their own first boat had been built by him. There are still plenty of them about to this day, with their distinctive 'moustache' on the bow, and although they were the budget boats of the day, they are the ones that have been kept on the water the most. Springers are as historic as any of the old working boats to my mind as they represent the transition of the canals from the working past to the new leisure age. They are no frills boats that do a job and that continue to bring new people out onto the cut. Little did I know that my passion for what Sam Springer had done in his day would lead me to a similar project in the future. But that's for later in my story.

The smoky and raw water cooled engine was less positively received. It didn't run very cleanly and had a habit of emitting bursts of dry black smoke when the water pump missed a beat or two. Still, it worked for me, but I could see where they were coming from and there were times when

I thought that a replacement might be the best option. I even considered turning her into an all-electric boat, chuckling to myself at the thought of the reception that this would get me from the traditionalists. There was a time, in the nineteen eighties, when the future was going to be all electric for narrowboats and there was a lot of planning and talk about having charging stations along the way, but this never happened. As with the Springer side of things, this was also something that would inspire me in the years to come.

Whilst I loved that old boat and everything about it, there was something about her that did become an issue and which I couldn't really change. She was that little bit too small for me to live on comfortably. Okay, so I didn't need an awful lot of space, but having to make the bed up every night was a bit of a bind and I'd started to accumulate a number of books that I wanted to keep rather than return to the charity shops or leave in facilities blocks. On the day of the second anniversary of my family's death, I made two important decisions. Firstly, I committed to living on a boat for the foreseeable future, and secondly, I decided that to do this, I would need to replace the boat. Of all my possessions, that boat was the only one that was a tangible reminder of the life I'd lived previously and the times that I had shared with my wife and kids. Putting all sentiment aside, she was simply too small for me now and the logical thing to do was to make her available for another family to enjoy.

They say that planning and buying a boat is a long-winded and challenging process. Having had six months' experience of living aboard however, I was pretty certain of what I wanted from a new boat and so felt confident that the whole transition would be fairly straightforward. The old boat went into a marina to be sold under brokerage, whilst I hired a mobile home for a month or so, in order that I could visit boat-builders and check out what was available on the second-hand market. My criteria for buying was simplicity and reliability. Unfortunately, neither seem to be mainstream criteria on decent narrowboats, so it took me a little longer than I anticipated. With hindsight, I would simply have gone to a boat builder and ordered a new build to my specification, but, as they say, hindsight is a lovely thing. I therefore narrowed down my choices to either cancelled new build orders, or basic shells with only the minimum of internal fittings.

I had to forego any notion of an all-electric boat if I was to go for a bigger one, but there were hybrid engines out there which fitted my requirements. It was whilst I was investigating this aspect of propulsion that I came across my new home. She was an ex hire-boat that had been gutted by vandals, before making her way to a boat yard pending a decision on her future. Although there had been an apprentice working in the yard, who blasted the shell back to steel and then painted the hull, he had left a few months back and she had been sitting on hard-standing since then, without an engine and with an uncertain future. Whilst most boats looked pretty much the same to me, this one had a bit of character about her, was in need of some tender, loving care and happened to be available in a boat yard where they could have her fitted with a hybrid engine within a fortnight. I checked her out, haggled a bit over the price, shook hands with the owners and paid for her. I now had my new home, although with just a basic shell, new windows and a new engine, she was a little bit too basic to live on. Making sure that I resisted the urge to splash out on the bells and whistles that I could easily have afforded, I listed my essential requirements and paid to have a simple gas cooker, 12 volt electrics with a battery bank and solar panels, a plain kitchen sink with drain and a cartridge toilet to be installed. Oh, the luxury!

This only left one thing for me to do, and that was to decide what she was to be called. Believe me, that was a long and difficult process. I started with the obvious choices of naming it after the family, but something about the constant reminder that this would give me held me back from that line of thought. Then I went through all the usual and predictable witty names and puns, but decided that I couldn't live with another 'Narrow Escape', nor any of the humorous plays on words that so many owners thought so original. 'Wine Down' 'Meander' and 'Piston Broke' may be witty for a moment but they would have wound me up after a while. No, I wanted something that meant a little more to me, but that was anonymous enough that I didn't have to explain it to every passer-by. I also wanted a name that whispered meaning when it needed to and provoked some thought to anyone who read it. This led me to thinking of, 'New Hope Arising', and something about this phrase struck a chord with me. So that's what I called her.

As her stripped down shell had been fully water-proofed and painted in multiple layers of undercoat with a matt black top coat, I didn't feel the need to have her professionally painted according to some complex scheme that would need regular maintenance. I simply ordered her name in vinyl graphics, applied them myself while they were fitting the engine, then waited in the motor home whilst they put her through the final checks and launched her into the water.

On the first of December 2017, they handed me the keys. She was the right boat for me and although she was all but empty inside, somewhere in those steel walls she seemed to have absorbed some of the character and history of all those hundreds of people who had enjoyed their holidays on her. The purging by the vandals had cleansed her, but all traces of that part of her history were now gone. She was a little naked but that was perfect for me as I had decided that my Winter project would be to fit her out as I wanted. This, despite my lack of experience in what was potentially a very complex project. If I kept things simple, I reckoned, then how difficult could it be? It was to prove a little more challenging than I had imagined.

Having secured a mooring for the Winter in the same boat yard where she'd been purchased from, some of the time pressure was taken off me as they had reasonable facilities for visitors on site. The wet-room could wait, as it would never be up to the standard of their showers, and, with a few pubs within walking distance, all serving decent food, the galley could wait as well. Besides which, there was a holiday park nearby where I could rent myself a chalet for a few nights if I felt the need for a bit of luxury.

Keeping the boat in the yard was the best decision I had made as they had the people and the equipment on hand to help me out. I was able to seek out a great deal of advice, on top of which, the amount of unsolicited help that came almost every day helped add to my store of knowledge. Of course, there were times when it was a bit too much but I listened anyway and carefully filtered the useful from the useless. I wasn't too proud to ask for help, and it was great to have others to call on, but there were times when I was bombarded with just a little too much wisdom from the more experienced boaters.

Once I'd sorted out the basics of the fit-out, I moved away from the yard and into the adjoining marina. Since there were restrictions on boaters to do any major work on their boats whilst on their moorings, I found myself drifting into a pattern of spending the weekend on my moorings, planning what needed doing. I'd then order any materials I'd need to be delivered on the Monday, load them onto the boat and then take her out onto the cut where I'd work on her until Friday afternoon. This gave me the contact I needed with the outside world but at the same time, the freedom to spend most of my time concentrating on new challenges without disturbance. They weren't always enjoyable times, as the shadow of darkness quite often drifted over me, especially when things weren't going according to plan. At these times, I'd find myself dwelling on the pointlessness of so much of what I was doing as I didn't have anyone to share it with, or, worse still, on my own arrogance and vanity in thinking that I could even begin to undertake such a huge project with my limited experience and even more limited abilities.

That was when I'd find myself opening the red wine and wasting days, sometimes weeks, simply sitting alone in the camping chair that, along with a mattress, was the only furniture on the boat. Because the first task that I'd successfully completed on-board was the installation of a new log burner, I was able to while away many hours just watching the flames flickering behind the glass door, and letting my thoughts wander over the deepest existential questions and the most trivial distractions. Whilst I was still drinking far more than any government guidelines would ever recommend, I was eating more healthily and the work on the boat had started to trim away a lot of the excess weight that I'd put on in those first months of crawling from pub to pub.

Corny as it may sound, I used that New Year to resolve to get myself fitter and to shift from smoking to vaping, whilst committing to not just walk the towpath but to run and cycle along it as well. This not only got me more into shape, but I also found that it was a great way of releasing pent up energy and channelling my more negative thoughts into more positive activities. The alcohol stayed with me though, but I did moderate it as much as I could, given that I still enjoyed canal-side pubs and meeting new people over a pint or two.

Throughout the Winter and into the following March, I cut, trimmed, shaped and fitted what must have amounted to several tons of timber, and the result was a pretty good boat interior for an amateur. Having researched how she would have looked like in her hire-boat days of the nineteen eighties and nineties, I paid homage to the boats past by using varnished tongue and groove throughout, and by avoiding the simplified modern lines of so much contemporary furniture. It had been a long time since I had worked with wood at school, but as I became more patient and less results-driven, I found that I had a bit of a talent for carpentry. Mortise and Tenon joints began to appear in place of the areas where I'd simply drilled bits of wood together, whilst harder woods came to life as I carved them into new shapes and spent hours treating them and polishing up the grains. As I think is inevitable with fitting out a boat, I wasted both a lot of time and a lot of material, either by completely messing the work up, or more usually, because I changed my mind about how I wanted things and ripped out what I'd done to replace it with a new piece. There was a fair bit of electrical work that I had to teach myself to do, but as long as I kept things on twelve volts, I found this pretty straightforward.

Slowly, New Hope Arising transformed from being an empty shell into a functional and attractive home on the water, and it was a delight for me to show off my work to the few visitors that I allowed on board. This naturally led to some requests for work on their own boats and with one thing leading to another, I approached that Spring with the potential of a new career looming up ahead of me. This was confirmed when the guys at the boat yard asked if they could use me on their own boats, offering at the same time to tie me up with a master carpenter they worked with who would see me through an apprenticeship. Okay, I may have been a bit old to be the trainee, but this gave me the opportunity to gain accreditation in a profession that I could carry with me as I travelled about the waterways.

Part of me was reticent to embark on a new career, but the voice of reason triumphed as I understood that working as a craftsman would give me the freedom to live as I wanted and to make a contribution in some way. I didn't have to be beholden to a nine to five existence and I could create things that would look beautiful whilst serving a purpose for other people. I could pass boats and look in their windows and say to myself, 'I made that', and I could change the way that people thought about boat layouts, as some of my ideas were slightly off-centre and challenged many pre-conceptions about narrowboat design.

I let them talk me into it and spent the whole of that year at the same marina, finishing off my own boat and learning the basics of proper craftsman carpentry, as well as a host of other boat related skills. As I was there anyway, I pushed myself through learning about electrical systems and gas installations, as well as getting myself qualified as a helmsman. I steered clear of engines though. They would have added years to my training and I had never really been that interested in them. Had I carried on in this vein, within another couple of years, I could have been a fully qualified boat-fitter, doing something that I really loved and taking a new direction in my life that veered far away from my degree studies or my experience in selling sanitary wares.

Chapter Nine

There's a lot to be said about prudently planning the direction that you wish your life to take. There's also a lot to be said about being open to trying out new things and living more in the present. I've experienced both and as somebody who has seen all my initial plans destroyed, I am now much less rigid about any longer term goals. Much as I was loving working on boats, and even considering settling down into this as a career, to have done so would have cost me just that little bit too much freedom. So it was that I finished at the marina in February 2019, two years after giving up terrestrial dwelling, to set out on a lengthy investigation of the whole English canal network. There were just too many parts of it that I hadn't seen; too many potential possibilities for broadening my horizons; and, most likely, too much energy driving me to a new challenge. If I was truly to do justice to such a project, it was obvious that I should do it when I was young and fit enough, although I had begun to realise with the number of couples in their eighties that I met, that simply living on the canals seemed to be a good way of lengthening life expectancy.

The guys at the boat-yard were very understanding and didn't try to prevent me making this move. My carpentry skills had developed nicely and, although he wasn't able to sign me off on my apprenticeship, the Master Carpenter I had worked with was happy that I could take on any work that I was offered. I'd learnt enough about the rest of boat-building that I could hold my own with any repairs that would need doing, and also offer a helping hand to other boaters. With money in the bank, I didn't need to earn a living, but doing some useful work whilst on my travels was not something I would shy away from.

It was after just a month of this new adventure, as I was taking my time exploring the beautiful Caldon Canal, that I settled down one evening with Thomas Hardy and a glass of red. I'd only been reading for a few minutes, when I realised that I hadn't checked my e-mails since leaving the marina. Truth be told, I had very few contacts and even less reason to waste my time surfing the web, so I rarely switched on the 4G box that opened up the world to me. It had been a long time since I'd had a smart phone, as they kept falling in the cut and were costing me a fortune. The cheap and cheerful brick that I used for my few calls was all I needed, and it afforded me a lot of peace in its inability to do anything other than act as a telephone. My old faithful computer whirred slowly into life, connecting to the Wi-Fi box as soon as it had fully booted up. The AOL mail address that I had, had been mine since University days, but it had long since stopped filling up with inane semi-conversations from old acquaintances or dodgy offers on medicines: perhaps even the spam computers thought that I had dropped off the planet. I was surprised then to see the e-mail that was first in the list of my unread missives. More surprised at the name though, Jean Carter, the Sentinel reporter whom I hadn't spoken for a long time.

Opening up the file, I read the following:

'Dear Mr Hardacre
If at all possible, could you make contact with me.
There's something we need to discuss.
Best Regards
Jean Carter'

This was followed by a landline and a mobile number.

Checking the rest of my e-mails and replying to the few that needed a response, I went back to that initial message and stared again at it. Jean Carter was a name from what seemed like a long distant time ago. She was a link with a past that I thought that I had moved on from. Now, seeing her name again, memories of the events that drew us together flooded back and I fell into a deep and dark place.

There was something foreboding about that e-mail, but I wasn't going to jump right in and make the call straightaway, especially not when my mind was elsewhere. All I could think of were Fran and the children, the dog that never had a chance to be a full part of our lives, and the atomisation of every dream that I had ever enjoyed. The bottle of red disappeared, to be followed by half a bottle of a single malt whisky that I'd been given in lieu of some drawers I'd fitted. Whisky and I are not good bedfellows so I never bought the stuff myself, but that night it seemed the right medicine, fuelling my melancholy and helping me fall into a pained and purgative sleep that would scourge me and make me remember so much of what I had coldly turned away from. My family wouldn't have wanted me to live in the past, but I had moved too far away from their presence as part of my history and I realised that this did them a disservice. Their deaths were facts. Nothing that I could do could bring them back. Yet, the experience of their deaths left me with something that shouldn't have simply been ignored and perhaps I should have used that experience for better aims.

The following morning, I woke to a crisp, cloudless sky and stood on the deck of the boat looking out over the splendour of a stunning sunrise. The fresh air hit me and the coffee that usually did the trick failed to stop me suffering something of a shaky morning-after. Bobbing back into the boat, I threw a few rashers of bacon into a pan and toasted some bread. The bacon sandwich did the job that the coffee had failed to do. Then I remembered what had led me to last night's troubled sleep.

Forgetting the early hour, I called the mobile number I had written down for Jean Carter, and waited. It went to voicemail after ringing half a dozen times, so I left a message and waited. She rang back within five minutes.

"Mr Hardacre," I could hear the sleep in here voice, "sorry I missed your call, it's a bit early for me."

"No problem," I answered, "and please, let's drop the Mr Hardacre thing. Call me Zip."

She apologised, but I knew that she was going to face the same challenges that everyone else does before they get used to calling me by that name.

"Look," she continued, "I really want to have a talk with you, but don't want to elaborate over the phone in detail. Is there any possibility that we could meet?"

"Of course," I replied, "I'm not exactly snowed under at the moment so whenever you want. You'll have to come and see me though, as my only mode of transport has a maximum speed of four miles per hour."

"I'm living on a boat," I told her, "I'm on the Caldon Canal just now. Can you get to Leek?"

"That would explain why you're not easy to get in touch with," she said, "but, yes, Leek's fine. I know it's short notice but is today possible?"

I confirmed that this was fine, and gave her the address of the pub that I had found yesterday, just ten minutes' walk away. We agreed to meet for lunch and were just saying our goodbyes when I remembered something.

"Just one thing," I asked, "can you give me something of heads-up on what this is about?"

Her answer shouldn't have surprised me.

"Not what..." she replied, "...who. Slater."

A cold dread washed over me as I ended the call. That name attached itself to the face that had sneered at me when the cause of my family's death had been established in law. And that name stirred up a hatred in me that I didn't want to feel, but which was impossible to restrain.

As it was mid-week, there were very few people in the pub that lunchtime, so we were able to find a quiet spot by the fire, where we settled down after ordering drinks and simple food from the lunch menu. June was looking older than I remembered her to be, but she had a certain class to her and managed to pull off that mature but desirable look. Not that I was thinking of her in that way. We started by talking about general things, catching up on what we had done since we last met, and drifting into a few random, related topics. She thought that there might be a nice human-interest story in what I had done, but I declined her offer on that score, preferring my anonymity. The food arrived and we continued the conversation in a similar vein as we ate, but when the plates had been removed and we had fresh drinks in front of us, I challenged her with the reason for our meeting.

"So, come on then, what are we really doing here?"

She paused, took a long draught of her drink and replied.

"Okay, I suppose I need to lay my cards on the table and tell you what's happened. It's Slater, I'm afraid, he's done it again."

"You what?!" I interrupted her, shocked at what I was hearing, "you mean he's killed someone else?"

"I'm sorry Zip," she said, "I wasn't sure if you'd heard or not, but yes, another car crash and this time an elderly couple. The husband died at the scene, the wife is in a coma, not expected to pull through."

"When did this happen?" I asked.

"A couple of months ago, just before Christmas."

"And you kept it from me for until now, for what reason?"

"I didn't keep it from you" she looked at me with a hint of hostility in her eyes, "I didn't think that you'd be interested, or that you'd want the past dragging up again so soon. Besides which, how was I supposed to know that you'd opted to jump off the rollercoaster and were hiding away on the canals?"

"So why now then?" I asked.

"Because he's walked away again," she whispered, "Another 'victim' of a tragic accident and not his fault at all."

The silence between us said everything. I didn't know what to say but she was clearly steeling herself to take the conversation further. Words can't describe the mixed emotions that flooded over me: the anger that there were more victims of this insensitive demon, and the sadness for another family devastated by his actions. I felt the tears welling up in my eyes and rose to leave.

"Well, thanks for telling me."

"No," she said, standing up and taking hold of my arm, encouraging me back to my seat, "that's not why I'm here."

I was confused now and less comfortable with what was happening.

"Tell me quickly then and without all this gentle preamble," I whispered, "Just what is it you are here for?"

"Justice," she answered, "I want to see justice done. And I don't know what to do."

"You see," she continued, "this is the third time that I've written up the stories of people whose lives have been ended by that man. If he was a serial killer, he'd be locked away for life, but there he is, back on the road again as if nothing had happened. They gave him six points on his licence and they fined him £300. I forget what the minor offence was. But that was it. £300 for two lives. It makes me sick."

She paused and rummaged through her handbag for some tissues to dry her eyes, then she continued: "I went to my Editor for support. Asked if we couldn't look into this whole Slater thing in a bit more detail. He didn't want to know. Worse than that, he warned me off pursuing it any further. He started on about libel and all that stuff but I think they may know each other. Either way, I wasn't allowed to do anything."

"Go on," I said.

"Well, I couldn't leave it there. So I confronted Slater myself. I tried the softer tactic of seeing him as somebody who, through no fault of their own, had been involved in a series of tragic accidents. I know, it sounds absurd, but the only way I could get close to him was to mollycoddle him as a victim."

"I don't know how you could do that," our voices were both low now, "I couldn't bear to be in the same room as him."

"I agree," she said, "but it was the only way."

"I arranged to meet him at his house, and when I got there his wife and three little kids were so pleasant to me. They act like the sun shines out of his backside. We started talking and I made copious notes, then, after about an hour, I started prodding. I asked him if he perchance felt any responsibility for the lives he'd ended. Well! You can imagine how that went. By the end of the day I'd been physically removed from his house and then electronically removed from The Sentinel. My Editor sacked me by e-mail immediately after he'd heard from Slater's solicitors."

I couldn't believe what I was hearing.

"Welcome to the club then," I said, "another of Slater's victims. What are you going to do for work?"

"Oh," she waved off my concern, "that's not an issue. I'm not desperate for money, and I can get work hacking around most of the dailies. It's not the sacking that gets me. As I said before, I'm looking for justice."

We stopped talking and I sat thinking. Okay, so justice may be an honourable ambition, but what is justice? For all its faults and, despite the way it had failed me in the past, I am proud to be a part of a nation that is built on the best concepts and institutions of justice in the world. If that system errs on the side of caution and allows people like Slater to continue to take lives, then I'd rather have that than innocent people being deprived of their freedom, or punitive penalties destroying additional lives. Then I began to wonder just why Jean Carter had contacted me.

"Have you spoken to the other victims about this?" I asked and she just shook her head.

"So why," I continued, "have you decided to come to me?"

She looked at me with a hint of fear in her eyes, as if she knew what was coming.

"Look," I said, "I may feel exactly the way that you do about Slater. I think the whole situation stinks. And I am one of the real victims of his selfish arrogance. But that doesn't justify me being a vigilante. What did you want me to say to you today? That I would go and stab the git and see how he likes it? That I'd inflict some equivalent punishment on him, maybe abduct and murder his wife? No, I'm sorry, but justice is as justice does and in this case, whatever our feelings may be, the process has let him go free."

"But I just thought…"

"Never mind what you thought," I struggled to keep my voice down, "this whole thing is out of control in your mind and you need to stop and think. You're not happy with what's happened, well, believe me, I've got more reasons than you to be unhappy about it, but revenge isn't the answer. You came to me because you thought, and to some extent you were right to do so, that I would be so fired up by all this that I would go after Slater. Well, I'm not your hired assassin, I'm sorry. Now, I'd like to say that it has been a pleasure, but it hasn't. Goodbye."

I stormed out of the pub and back to the boat, chewing over in my mind all of the events of that lunch time and thinking on the audacity of this woman in trying to recruit me for her crusade. No wonder they'd fired her. No wonder Slater saw right through her. Arriving home, I lit the fire and let another bottle of red ease me back down from my anger. This was why I'd packed it all in and run off to the cut – people are so damn difficult to live with. Fortunately, the Caldon is not only beautiful, it is also peaceful and the quiet of that evening managed to silence many of the demons singing in my head.

Chapter Ten

It would be fair to say that I am probably not the most pragmatic of people; to me, black and white rarely have any gradations between them. Unfortunately, this can lead me to being a little too dogmatic at times, and see me abandoned, standing on principles that may be laudable, but which are less than realistic. When I woke the morning after meeting with Jean, there was a hint of regret in my heart about my behaviour, even though this was offset by an anger that she had wanted me to act in a way that I couldn't do.

For days, my mind was in a turmoil. The safe and peaceful life that I had found for myself seemed to be threatened at every angle, and I couldn't shake the thought of Slater still being out there, carelessly racing across the country with reckless abandon. But revenge was not the answer. Aside from the practicality of how that revenge should be shaped, there remained the question of the morality of it. Injustices were done, had been done in the past, and would continue to be done in the future. As a nation, we had systems and procedures in place to minimise injustice which, by their nature, had to allow for the guilty to walk free if so required.

Jean was wrong to pursue her personal mission against the instruction of her boss, and Slater couldn't be blamed for her losing her position. She had refused to let it drop and had to endure the consequences. Slater too, was an unknown quantity to us in many respects and our contact with him had only been brief. Were we right to paint him as the Devil incarnate when to others he was possibly a loving husband and dedicated father? My searching the internet for the details of this latest 'accident' had yielded very few details other than that it was likely that Slater was culpable to some degree, and indeed, had been punished to an extent. What remained a mystery was the unseen aspect of the event, and all I had for reference there was my own experience. I couldn't talk to the victims and the road had been fairly empty at the time so there were few eye-witnesses. The bottom line was that I had to accept what had happened and try and remove myself as much as possible from the situation.

That wasn't as easy to do as I imagined though. On the one hand, I still felt guilty about the way I had dismissed Jean in such an off-hand way, and on the other hand the scent of injustice remained a stench to me. Hard as I tried, I couldn't shake off the feeling that something needed to be done. It didn't seem fair that I had been drawn back into the real world in such a harsh and bitter way, and yet, it was a reality check for me to understand that for as long as I walked this little globe, I could never escape its challenges if I was to enjoy its pleasures.

A week after our first meeting, I called Jean to apologise and to arrange to meet with her again. She was a little bit off with me, but agreed to meet nonetheless and so we again found ourselves sitting in a pub with drinks in hand. I needed to draw a line under this situation as soon as possible and decide one way or the other what the right thing to do was.

"Tell me," I asked, "what exactly do you envisage in this search for justice against Slater?"

"Truth be told," she chose her words carefully, "I don't know. It's not a personal vendetta, I can assure you, but there are at least three families out there, one of them yours, that he has destroyed. My concern is less about vengeance for what has been done, as concern about what could potentially happen in the future."

"Go on," I said, beginning to understand a little more about where she was coming from.

"Look at it this way," she tried to explain her thinking to me, "There are threats out there that people have no issue with taking action against. We all rail against smokers and the effect they have on innocent people, and nobody bats an eyelid about legislating to prevent accidents, whether that's through speed limits, safety testing or whatever. The argument is that this is all about prevention. Closing the stable door before the horse bolts. But here we have Slater who clearly should not be in a position to drive, and yet he is out there and could kill again."

"My point, Zip," she continued, "is that both you and I know there is a chance that Slater will be involved in another accident and we might have to read or write about another death or serious injury. Now, legally, we are not in any position to do anything about this, other than maybe talking to the guy and trying to change his way of thinking. Quite frankly, I think that's a dead end. So, do we just sit back and take the stance that it is beyond our control or do we take a moral position and act?"

More drinks were ordered and we moved outside to the smoking area to carry on our conversation. I may have moved to vaping for the most part, but there were times when a cigarette was in order.

"I'm not sure what to say," I said, "I understand where you're coming from but we don't do vigilantes in England. Look at the paedophile baiters out there, are they in the right when they hound people off their estates? And, who makes us the moral majority? Surely, keeping to the law of the land is more of a moral stance than acting against that law."

She nodded in partial agreement.

"And," I continued, "then there are the practicalities. What action do you envisage taking? And how do we avoid being caught and punished? If, of course, that's what you want, because, believe me, I certainly don't intend to waste my life as a martyr to a cause I'm not certain about. And finally, what is the morally right position? I'm not a Bible-basher, but I believe in God and He says that vengeance is His. How do I square that circle?"

"Again," she answered, "I don't know is the only answer I can give you. I agree that forgiveness is freedom and yes, we have a moral code that we need to live by, but I could also quote an eye for an eye. What I'm talking about here is an acknowledgement that the justice system has been at fault, and nobody can argue that it is perfect, and that there may be a place for some sort of righteous correction to injustice."

"Righteous correction?" I liked the term, "But again, what is righteousness? It's just too far off my radar to think about, that's all. However, just for arguments sake, in this instance, what would be the righteous correction for Slater?"

"I've thought about this long and hard," she answered, "and I think that somebody needs to stop Slater driving. It's as simple as that. I also think that he needs to be made aware of the pain and suffering he has caused in order to bring him to that place of acceptance of whatever happens to him. Does that make sense?"

"Sort of," I replied, stubbing out my cigarette and immediately beginning to roll another, "but it goes against your eye for an eye. If you're right, then surely Slater has to die? And I'm sorry but murder is not on my agenda. And I can't get it into my head how we do something and get away with it. As soon as something happens to Slater, the first place they will look is to his victims. I don't know much about the cyclist he killed or their family, but I do know that I would be prime suspect in this. How do we resolve that?"

I couldn't believe that I had become so immersed in this conversation that I was seriously considering Jean's proposal, but that's how it was and we continued talking for the rest of the afternoon. To give her credit, she'd thought this thing through in a lot of detail. So much detail in fact that I began to see that it might work. When we parted, we agreed to meet the following week and make a decision one way or the other.

On returning to the boat, I chose to distance myself as much as possible from what we'd talked about and give myself some breathing space. The days were still fairly short and the weather was a little drab, so I resolved to only cruise for a few hours each day and to work on the boat in the afternoons. As I wanted to keep something of a clear head, I also took the radical step of not drinking anything until the evening. I drifted down through Staffordshire and back to my favoured haunt of Wolseley Bridge, catching up with fellow boaters and enjoying the cheerful feeling of the canal coming back to life after Winter. I was at peace with myself, but still hadn't decided what to do.

By the day before my next meeting with Jean I still hadn't received the guidance that I had hoped would come my way. I was torn between stepping away from the whole thing and making the most of the new life I was forging for myself, or taking the radical step of becoming a criminal. It should have been a simple decision. It wasn't. Every argument against taking action was sound, correct and just the right thing. But the thought of another victim suffering at Slater's hands kept coming back to me. If the family of the cyclist had stopped Slater driving, then my family might still be alive. If I had acted against Slater, instead of running away, then that elderly couple would still be alive (I'd just found out that the wife had died). But who appointed me as any sort of moral crusader? I have a gut feeling for justice and what is right, but I'm no moral philosopher nor academic.

The question always boiled down to motivation. Was I wanting to act to punish or prevent? If it was punishment, then it was wrong. If prevention, then it was a different matter. Would I break the law to intervene in a situation where a life was in immediate danger? Yes, I would. Were lives in immediate danger in this instance, or was that just me trying to justify a certain route? Believe me, I searched hard and long for the answer.

Chapter Eleven

The police caught up with me at Gas Street Basin in Birmingham. I wasn't surprised to see them as I'd seen the press coverage surrounding our friend Slater, and now that we all had to carry transponders as part of our boat licensing terms, I would never be difficult to find. There were two of them. Both male, my age, and obviously used to working together. They were twins in attitude if not in looks as one was sporting a thick head of grey hair, whilst the other was pretty much bald. They gave me their names, and showed me the relevant identity. The bald one was Smith, the grey one, Wright, although I had hoped he would have been Jones.

"Mr Hardacre?" they asked as I opened the stern doors to them, "Mr Zipoly Hardacre?"

"Yes," I answered, enjoying watching their faces as they came to terms with my first name, "and please, you can call me Zip. It's a long story."

"Thanks," Wright said, "can we come in and have a bit of a talk with you?"

"You can," I said, "but I'm a bit thin on chairs. Maybe we can nip across to a café instead?"

They agreed and we got ourselves comfortable around a small table overlooking my boat. There was a bit of small talk about what it was like to live on the canal and how long I'd done it for, then they got down to business.

"I presume you know why we want to talk with you." Wright took the lead.

"Slater?" I asked knowingly.

"Yes, Sir," Smith spoke for the first time, "We'd like to ask you a few questions if we may. But first, why did you think we were here about Slater?"

"Come on," I laughed as I replied, "what happened to him has been all over the papers and you guys don't know where to go with it. So, naturally, you are looking at the revenge element and who might have a motive. Yes, I do have a motive, and yes, seeing what happened to him did bring me a perverse satisfaction. But that's very different from my being guilty of carrying out the action."

"Where were you last Friday?" Smith asked.

"On the boat all day, as usual," I answered, "If I remember rightly I was just finishing off around the Walsall Canal before heading here. I'm usually out at a pub for a while but I think on that night I listened to the Radio. Radio 4 Extra had a two-hour dramatization of Moby Dick. I got caught up in that."

"Can anyone collaborate that story?" Wright asked.

"I doubt it," I said, "you might find witnesses who went past the boat, but it's not the busiest canal. I could summarise the plot of Moby Dick if that helps."

"Sir, this is not a laughing matter," Smith interrupted, "this is a serious incident and we have to consider you as a suspect. As you said yourself, you had the motive."

"And the means and the opportunity?" I asked, "What do you think I am? I've read what they did to him. Do you think I'm capable of that?"

"Then there's Jean Carter," he said, "we know that she had an issue with Slater and that the two of you arranged to meet. Sounds a bit strange doesn't it."

"Yes," I smiled at him, "I met Jean Carter. We met at the Castle Arms in Leek. Go and ask the guys there what they heard. We met, we argued and I walked away, I wanted nothing more to do with Slater."

I was pleased that this had happened but forgot to tell them about our second meeting, after all there were no e-mail records to lead to it.

They looked at each other, clearly unsure which way to go with this. Then Wright stood up as if preparing to go.

"Okay Sir," he said, "I think that gives us all we need. But please don't trivialise this whole thing. His family suffered more than you can imagine and whoever did this is a sick and twisted individual."

"What do you mean?" I asked, "What happened to his family?"

"It wasn't in the papers," he replied, "but they were put through a certain ordeal that I'm not prepared to go into. His wife and his two children."

"I'm sorry to hear that," I said, "I didn't know."

They shook hands with me and advised that I should be available should they wish to see me again soon and that I should ring Stafford police station if I remembered anything in the meantime. And then they went.

Of course, I remembered quite a lot. But I didn't intend sharing it with them at any time in the near future. I remembered more than I wanted to. Every last detail.

I'd slipped away from the boat that Friday, when I knew that nobody was around, leaving the radio turned up higher than usual and a couple of windows open. I left some lights on and had the fire lit, with the stove top fan blowing a pillowcase that I'd hung up nearby. It was no great subterfuge but to anybody passing it would look like the boat was occupied with somebody moving about inside.

Getting to Slater's had been a challenge. I didn't want anyone to see me so had planned a route that took in the canal, a golf course, a woodland and finally the backs of his neighbour's gardens. The night I'd chosen had been one when the latest celebrity shenanigans were at their final stage on TV so I imagined most people would be preoccupied with this. Sidling up to Slater's patio doors, I was able to see that his family were so occupied, although he appeared to be working upstairs.

I slipped into his kitchen and carefully took aim at his family, firing three rapid shots into his wife, his son and his daughter who didn't have time to even cry out before they fell. Then it was fairly easy to climb the stairs and get Slater in the same way.

It was an hour before he came to. I'd positioned him in his office chair, tied him up nice and tightly and then pushed that chair into the master bedroom. As he opened his eyes I took some perverse pleasure in seeing him begin to register what he was looking at. His wife and children lay in front of him, still as death and with a certain amount of gore around their throats. Their faces were as pale as snow.

"Not nice is it?" I stood behind Slater and spoke to him through tissue paper to disguise my voice which I'd raised to the highest pitch that I could.

He couldn't answer me. His mouth was taped up. He just muttered and shook his head and tried to get loose.

"This," I continued, "is what we call a righteous correction. You have killed somebody's wife and children, you've killed a young cyclist and an elderly couple. And you would keep on killing if action wasn't taken."

He began to sob a little, looking up to the bed and seeing his own family laid out there. Of course, the shock and awe of it all would take much longer to register, but the effect was enough for now.

"The problem we have," I said, "is that you don't seem to regret anything.

Your victims may have let you go and left you alone, but somebody needs to act. Seeing this, will you change your ways? We're not sure. So, now we have your attention, we are going to make sure that you don't get into a car again. Sarah, please prepare the sedative."

I'd rehearsed a lot of the subterfuge that I'd wanted to lay down, but there was a degree to which I had to bite my lip and stop him knowing just who it was that was behind him. Yes, I wanted the world to know that justice was being done, but I didn't want to pay for it with my freedom. This was just a rebalancing. As I'd told Slater, a righteous correction.

"Of course," I whispered in his ear, "we are not sadistic lunatics. Take one last look now, and then we'll carry on with the operation. And when I say take a long look, I mean do just that. Take a good long look at what you see."

Sliding the needle into his arm, I watched him fall asleep again. There were just a couple of things left to do now. Firstly, I had to go ahead with the most difficult part of the whole thing. I'd practised on pigs, but this was different. I steeled myself then carefully popped each of his eyes out of their sockets. I cut them off with a scalpel and used a cigarette lighter to cauterise the small wound. He wouldn't be driving again.

I then made his family as comfortable as possible, cleaning off the offal that I'd carefully placed on their sleeping bodies. They would wake in distress, especially if they woke before the ambulance arrived. But at least they were still alive. I might have made my mind up to balance the scales of justice, but that balancing act was not about taking lives to match what Slater had taken. This was preventative action and with Slater blinded, there would be no way he could get behind the wheel of a car again. It had been the only option open to me. Short of killing him, anything else I had done ran the risk that he would still be able to drive. This way, he lived and bore the scars to remind him of what he'd done. There was a perverse satisfaction in thinking that the last sight he had ever seen on Earth was an image of at least some of the harm that he had caused.

I called the emergency services from his bedside phone, then slipped back to the boat the way that I had come. As far as I could tell, I'd not been seen. This was a one-off, and my first attempt at a criminal act, but I know now that I was lucky to get away with it. I wasn't planning any other such escapades, but if I did choose to, I'd do a lot of things differently.

I was woken up the following day by Jean Carter, telling me what had happened, and trying desperately to get some idea of whether or not I'd been involved.

"Jean," I said sleepily, "I'm pleased that it's happened. It's what we talked about and now we can rest easy. But don't press me anymore on it."

"Okay," she said, "but there's just one thing. Slater told the police that the people who did this had used the phrase righteous correction."

"Did they," I whispered, "I wonder where they got that from."

Chapter Twelve

When I'd been at university, I'd had a part time job with a national chain of electrical retailers. It was a means to an end in terms of paying bills, but may have helped me with my selling career in later life. Whilst I wasn't as career-obsessed as the full time staff there, we all respected the Area Manager, who was a passionate and enthusiastic guy, always willing to talk to any member of the team. He was very keen on the notion of empowering the store team and instilled in everybody the belief that making a decision, whether it proved to be right or wrong, was better than always seeking help or worse still, sitting on the fence. It was better to make the wrong decision with the right intention than to never be confident enough to make any decisions.

I had made my decision about Slater and right, or wrong, I had to live with it. That wasn't easy. The weeks after my first foray into vigilantism saw me struggling to sleep, and worst still, battling nightmares when I did. Up until that point, my experience of blood and gore had been limited to the birth of my children, so to have done what I had done marked a new boundary for me. A boundary that I didn't want to cross again in the near future. As I've already said, there is an element to which I can be perceived as being cold-hearted and detached, but that is a learnt behaviour and not the natural me. It's not easy to look at things in black and white, when grey seems so tempting. After a month, I'd allowed myself to move on. I'd made my decision and, whatever the pros and cons, I had been able to move on from it, despite a little more interest from the police.

They came to visit me again a week after their initial visit. This time they had a search warrant for the boat. I don't think that this was a reflection on me not inviting them in when they first visited, but more of a last-ditch attempt on their part to try and find the perpetrator. I was comfortable with them searching for as long as they wanted. The scalpel that I'd used had been one of many that I kept for my woodworking, and had long ago been ditched in the water; even if they retrieved it, I could quite honestly argue with them that I often dropped them in the cut when I was working on the deck of the boat. As to the gun, well that was a different matter. In true boater's fashion, I had constructed what I called my gun out of various bits of general hardware and had fashioned it according to an 'it'll work' plan. The breakthrough for me had been in finding an obscure website that discussed mediaeval poisons, and so to the tranquiliser that I had distilled out of some very basic ingredients. I didn't want to get rid of the gun, perhaps because I'd put so much time into making it, or perhaps because I thought it may come in handy again. Knowing that the police would very likely want to search for this weapon though, I made sure that it was well hidden on the boat.

To the uninitiated, boats are little more than a metal shell with a wooden floor and lining. Because they tend to be bespoke and individual, they all look that bit different, therefore, an unusual hiding place could easily pass as being a part of the boats internal fittings. The gun in question was embedded in sheet rock insulation behind a tongue and groove section of panelling on the wall that looked like all the others. Short of taking every panel off the walls and essentially stripping the boat back to basics it would never be found.

Not surprisingly, it wasn't found on that search. There were also a couple of lucky breaks for me with regards to the alibi that kept the spotlight off my involvement. Although I'd researched what was on the radio on that Friday, and ensured that I'd used the internet to listen to it several days after broadcast, there had in fact been a couple of walkers who had passed my boat and confirmed that they could hear the radio and see movement inside. Similarly, the barman at the pub confirmed that Jean and I had met but that we had parted after angry words. They never did find out about the second meeting. Nor did I have any links to somebody called Sarah who appeared to be the perpetrator's accomplice. Not surprising really as she only existed in my head. In short, everything fell into place and the fear of my being caught became less and less. As did my concern about the justice of what I'd done.

So it was that I moved on and took the boat further afield and out into Shakespeare country, choosing to return back to Staffordshire after this rather than going too far away. My idea was to totally absorb myself in one area before moving on, rather than travelling for the sake of it and only seeing areas partially. Of course, I was also able to do a bit of casual work whilst in the West Midlands and used this to take my mind off things. Jean didn't contact me again. The police stayed away. I began to relax again.

Whether I was suffering from some hidden pangs of guilt, or whether I simply began to appreciate how well off I was, I used a lot of that Summer to seek out opportunities to help people out. This was less a Good Samaritan crusade than a simple opening of my eyes to the need that was about me, and that I was in a position to alleviate. Somewhere along the line, I got it into my head to try and do three good deeds every day, partly with a view to writing a book on this subject (although I think that's already been done), or at the least to create a daily diary demonstrating how easy it was to make a big difference by doing small things. Most days, I failed to do even one. It would start off well, with my heading off for a walk, open-minded about whatever opportunities might be there to be discovered, but it then became a trip to the pub, one too many beers and a stagger back home. There were some nice highlights though, and it's something that I still try and do to this day.

On the canals there are some very wealthy people and there are some very poor people. A lot of the wealthy are as unhappy in their wealth as the majority of the poor are happy in their poverty. There are also families and lone boaters, who likewise might be as happy as anybody with their own company, as I was, or dreadfully lonely even in their companionship. I never knew where people were until I started taking the time to talk to them.

My reason for revealing this is that I want people to understand that I am not a 'bad' person, despite some of the bad things that I've done. Am I trying to balance what some would called the Ying and Yang of my Karma, storing up good deeds against the atrocities that I have committed? I don't know, but there are reasons that I record these events as they have all shaped what I do, sometimes mentally and sometimes by leading to practical solutions.

My crusade for personal fitness was going ahead nicely and there were muscles building up on me in places where I'd never seen them before. As well as cycling, I was running a lot and lifting weights. It wasn't practical for me to join a gym, but I found that I could discipline myself to work-out every day. Okay, so the benefits of this were often negated by the several pints I enjoyed afterwards, but I definitely felt better in myself. I'm not a body worshipper, nor was I out to make myself presentable to the opposite sex. It just felt good to wake every morning and feel the purging surge that exercise gave me.

Because of this, I would often help fellow boaters by running errands to local shops, sometimes on foot but mainly on my bike which I adapted to hold a fair amount of luggage. The heavier the bike was, the harder the ride and the deeper the burn that I felt, proving the enduring truth that I discovered about helping other people out, that it also helped me as well.

Aside from practical help like this, I opened myself up to simply meeting people and listening to their stories. If anything, this was the biggest revelation of all as it took me out of myself and led me into a wider and richer world than I could ever have experienced in my own insularity. I guess that's a lot of the problem we have with our social media obsessed society, in that everyone is so wrapped up in themselves, they fail to empathise with others, despite being exposed to more knowledge of others than ever. In myself, I was one person, dipping into the outside world for practical reasons, whilst escaping into the fantasy worlds of the fiction I read for most of the time. Once I had committed to shutting my mouth and letting others talk to me, I became a part of real lives and a multitude of real lives beyond my own world.

There were three key benefits that I discovered in this approach to life. Firstly, I was able to view behind the social veil that hides so many lives and meet the best of people and the worst, some of whom had got their act together, but the majority of whom were missing something, despite often having everything. Secondly, I made practical contacts with people who had ideas and skills that I would tap into in the future. Finally, and most markedly, I began to hear more stories of injustice. Individually, these elements might have given me pleasure and helped me enjoy my life in peace. Together, they catalysed into a vision of my future that I tried hard to ignore, but which wouldn't go away.

Chapter Thirteen

It was nearly six months since I had taken action against Slater, and much of that night was nothing more than a distant memory to me. I had closed that chapter on my life and was moving on. Occasionally, I would think about what I'd done and consider how fortunate I'd been in not being caught. If I were to do it again, I would do some things differently. If it had been more challenging, I might also have had to think about alternative strategies. This got my mind thinking about crime in general, and I found that I could ponder solutions to problems for hours, revelling in the fantasy of a criminal life where my skills would outwit the most thorough investigators. I'm sure I'm not unique in thinking this way. Our prisons are full of people who thought they had cracked the conundrum of the perfect crime, whilst our living rooms are inhabited by the moral majority who would never consider criminal activity, for the most part, but who also believe that they could do it better. It doesn't help that so much television output is devoted to crime and murder. Mind you, I was as much a fan of crime thriller writers as anyone else.

I was moored up at Wolseley Bridge again, tucked away down the far end of the moorings and enjoying unusually warm Autumn evenings under trees that were refusing to yield their leaves. Yes, there was a main road not far away, but the view from my preferred barbeque spot on the expansive towpath took in trees that had grown in bizarre shapes, the river that ran behind the canal and the livestock in the fields. All of which reminded me of the imaginary distance that I was away from the real world. I wasn't going to go back to a house, I knew that now. There was simply too much here on the waterways to keep me going for the rest of my brief life.

With the onset of the Winter, my thoughts turned to what I would do to occupy myself whilst holed up in the boat on those cold days. By this stage, I had a decent little workspace in the boat, with a good, solid bench on which to do my carpentry. I also had a lot of off-cuts of timber that were destined to act as kindling until I started to notice the hidden beauty in even the humblest pieces of wood. So, with time on my hands and the materials close by, I began to work on more intricate articles of woodwork. The first of these was an ebony and oak duck, this being followed by a full range of wildlife, progressively more detailed each time, although they were abstract still to the extent that they remained in the natural colours of the chosen piece of timber. I could spend hours working on just the smallest of details and this I did, watching the canal freeze around me and the snow fall gently on the towpath. I didn't move the boat any more than I needed to comply with regulations and to keep myself stocked up with the essentials, and I continued my fitness regime even on the coldest of mornings.

This was a very simple life. Yes, I was fortunate that I didn't need to worry about money, but even still, my expenditure was very low. Once my supply of suitable timber on board diminished, I simply foraged for replacements and was never short of materials. My stock of carvings grew and my skills developed as I learnt how best to bring out the natural beauty of grain with varnish, polish and stains.

The contrast between the life I was now living and what had gone before was stark. Previously I had been a 'normal' family man, doing what 'normal' family men did, with a nice house, decent job and a mainstream life that I thought was giving me everything. And I have no regrets about that life. There is something wonderful about modern life that I would never criticise, and I still marvel that so many people, doing so many different things, all manage to work together in some sort of elaborate, progressive harmony. But now, my life was nothing like that. I was alone and happy to be so, I had no stress or strain to mar my days and I was free to experience whatever each day would bring. Would I have my old life back, with Fran and the children? Yes, like a shot, but it couldn't be, so I made the most of what I had.

Of all the months of the year, I probably like February the best: it's still cold and Wintry, but it is such a short month and promises the Spring at its end. February 2020 was as good as any I had known, and I began to plan the year's cruising, aiming to take in half of the nation's canals before the next Winter. It was time for me to travel further afield and with the work I was doing with wood, I felt that, despite not needing the money, I could justify my travelling life by selling my wares along the way. There would always be opportunities to earn money with my other boat maintenance skills as well, so I applied to have my boating status changed to licence me for this activity. My insurance went up slightly, from not very much to a little bit more, and the boat licence fee was a little extra, but nothing compared to the income I could generate. I certainly didn't want to be tied to making this my new life now that I had experienced such freedom, however, I could see from my work that I could make a difference and make beautiful things that would enhance people's lives.

The decision to start selling my carvings was very heavily influenced by a wonderful couple that I met on the Staffs and Worcester canal in Penkridge. Their boat was immaculately tidy but clearly a very old vessel, lovingly maintained but hinting that its owners were not the wealthiest of people. I met them first at The Cross Keys pub, where we struck up one of those casual conversations that led to a more involved discussion that revealed that we were neighbours along the towpath. Like many on the cut, a polite enquiry on my part revealed them to be of that breed of boater for whom boating has taken years off their lives and I was surprised to find out that they were both about to hit eighty years old. Their story was interesting. It was also an important turning point for me. The week I spent with them changed my future in two ways. Firstly, it encouraged me in my craft work and gave me an opportunity to work on new ideas. Secondly, it led to the resurrection of my alter-ego and to the life that I now lead.

Chapter Fourteen

Jack and Elaine had been married for fifty years. They'd met at school, courted for nearly a decade and married in their late twenties, sadly against their parent's wishes, but those same parents had recognised that they had got it wrong long before they passed on. Sometimes two people were just made for each other and destined to be together forever. Jack had been a teacher and looked the part with a moustache that would put Mr Chips to shame. Elaine had been a secretary, that is, when she wasn't bringing up children. They were happy together, that much was evident as soon as I met them, but there was a certain sadness about them that intrigued me. They had always enjoyed boating and had been active in numerous conservation groups through the seventies and eighties, having met each other on a cold and dreary dig in a long abandoned lock chamber. Although great supporters of canals, they hadn't intended living on board in their retirement, but circumstances had led them to where they were now. In all my time on the cut, their story remains the most poignant to me and, to this day, despite all it has led me to, I feel a certain rage at the way they have been treated. That said, they were stoical about their situation and it was evident that a love that had survived all the ups and downs of their many years together was the bond that would keep them at peace throughout the rest of their lives.

It was on the third day after I'd met them that they invited me onto their boat for dinner, asking me to bring some of my carvings with me. The weather had taken a turn for the worst and the nation was gripped in a big freeze, so I wasn't surprised that my first impression on entering their boat was the rich aroma of a stew simmering away on their stove.

"I'm sorry we can't offer you anything more exotic," Elaine said, "We need to watch the pennies these days."

"Not at all," I replied, "I can't think of anything I'd like more just now than a proper stew. I do a lot of them myself, especially when the weather's like this, it saves struggling to the shops."

"That's very kind of you," Jack said. "Now please, settle yourself down and try a drop of this."

He handed me a glass of wine.

"That," he said, "is the best drop of booze you'll taste on the cut. Don't ask me exactly what it is, because I'm not sure that I'll be able to tell you. Don't worry though, it's only made from the stuff we can get hold of on the towpath. I think this is probably nettle based, with a few flowery tones."

I tasted the wine. I coughed and tasted it again.

"Good grief," I laughed, "that's good stuff!"

"Glad you approve," Jack smiled and took a long draught of his own drink, "It's a passion of mine and it keeps me busy. Mind you, it does mean we have to fill up with water a little more often than usual. Everything has to be sterilised to start with."

He then gave me a ten-minute lecture on how to make a decent brew from free ingredients, offering to lend me some of his kit if it was something I wanted to have a stab at.

"Thanks," I said, "I'll think about it. I'd not really thought about home brew before, but if it tastes as good as this, maybe I should."

We moved across to the small dining table that had been neatly laid up in the front cabin where the stove-top fan seemed to deposit most of the boat's heat. Elaine came through with a huge pot of stew and placed it in the centre of the table, before returning with three bowls and a ladle.

"And this is my speciality," she beamed, "I hope you're okay with meat because there's a decent portion of rabbit in there. Everything else is just good old Winter veg with a few of my own herbs and spices to give it a little bit of a kick."

I tasted the stew. It was as good as the wine. This was proving to be a meal worthy of a Michelin starred restaurant. My type of food, simple, clean and quintessentially English. We ate in silence for the first five minutes, relishing the taste of the stew and feeling the wine get to work on our inhibitions.

"Now then," Jack broke the silence. "I'll be honest with you, there's a bit of an ulterior motive in our asking you over tonight."

I looked across at him and raised my eyebrows.

"You see," he continued, "we love what you've done with your carvings and you obviously know what how to make wood work for you. We were wondering if you'd do us the honour of making up some panels for the boat doors. We were thinking of some sort of carving, maybe inlaid with some veneers. Is that something you'd be able to do?"

I knew that I could do it and, to be honest, I was never going to refuse these two, but I wanted to make sure that I got a feel for what they wanted.

"What sort of carving?" I asked, "I've not done relief work before, but I can give it a go."

Elaine excused herself from the table and went across to the small writing bureau that sat in the corner of the lounge. She opened the top draw and pulled out some photographs, then re-joined us.

"We were wondering if you could carve this."

She showed me the photographs which were shots of a chocolate-box cottage during various seasons of the year. In one, it bloomed with the richness of Summer and every corner of the photograph was bursting with colours. In another, Autumn cast a beautiful gold glow over the place, and in another, the scene was transformed into a Dickensian snow scene. The house itself was pure Cotswolds, straight out of any BBC drama, with multiple mismatched annexes beneath a thatched roof.

"This is beautiful," I said, "I could do justice to this in wood. Two scenes maybe, one of the height of Winter and one of Summer?"

"That's what we were thinking of."

"But," I asked, "is this your house?"

There was a pause and the two of them looked at each other, clearly a little uncertain about how to discuss what was obviously a painful topic. Jack spoke first: "It was, son, it was," he paused and topped up our glasses, "We lost it though."

"Oh, I'm sorry," I said, "Please, you don't need to talk about it if you don't want to. I'd love to do the panels for you."

"That's kind of you," Elaine said, "it would mean a lot to us. And don't worry, we've come to terms with the situation now. We made some mistakes. And nothing we can do will change what's happened."

She turned to her husband. "Jack, love, you try and fill Zip in on what happened. He should know."

"Of course," he answered, reaching across to hold her hand.

He then told me the story of how circumstances had shifted them from being a happily retired couple in their dream home, to where they were now, living just above the breadline, but, blessedly, still as happy together as ever. It had started with their daughter's divorce in her mid-forties. They had two daughters and Rebecca was the older of the two. She'd married fairly young and gifted Jack and Elaine with three lovely grand-children, all girls, but her husband had been a little erratic in his behaviour, so, when the opportunity came up, Rebecca had divorced him. At first, she moved her family in with her parents, but then she found her own place and was all set for starting again. As a chemist, she made a good living and neither Jack nor Elaine were worried that she couldn't make the break. It was just after she moved into her new house that the problems started.

"I still can't put an exact date on the change," Jack said, "but it was somewhere in her second year of being single again. The divorce was all settled and the kids were in a new school and making new friends."

Around this time, Rebecca met Jeff. Or, to be more precise, the Rev. Jeffrey Rodgers of the New Sun Temple of Light. Quite how Rebecca had been drawn into this sect still baffled her parents, but drawn in she was, and drawn in hook, line and sinker.

"She changed," Elaine struggled to keep the tears back, "She had this sort of vacant look in her eyes and where they'd once sparkled with enthusiasm, now they seemed somehow dim. Dead almost."

"We were worried of course," Jack continued, "and we visited her as often as we could, but there was no reasoning with her. She said that, as a scientist, she was trained to weigh up the evidence before her, and that she'd done just that, coming to the conclusion that this Rodgers guy was the spiritual leader that he said he was."

They couldn't understand how their daughter had been so easily and so fully drawn in to this thing, but they didn't have the answers to turn her away. Rodgers offered what he called Spiritual Completeness, and somehow Rebecca thought that she'd found it with him.

"Had it been simply a 'religious experience' for her, we'd have lived with it," Jack said. "After all, if it made her happy, then what real harm could it do. But it became more than that."

I listened intently as they told me how Rebecca had moved herself and the children into the country house that was the home of the New Sun Temple of Light, and had given up her job to be a full time worker for the cause. She'd effectively cut herself off from the rest of the family and they had no contact with her for over five years, despite their repeatedly trying to visit.

Their other daughter, Jayne, was by this time living in the States, settled with a family of her own, but also trying to make contact with her sister as best she could. The ex-husband and other parent of their grandchildren had disappeared and was somewhere off the radar.

"This left us on our own," Jack explained. "Of course, we contacted the police, social services and anyone else we could think of, but each time the answer was the same. Their visits to the place had shown that the children were being well looked after and were being well schooled. Without any evidence of wrong-doing, there was nothing they could do."

Then they'd received a phone call out of the blue from the Revd. Rodgers himself. He was as soft and smooth in his manner as they'd expected and had invited them to come and visit Rebecca at their earliest convenience. They went the next day and after penetrating the various levels of security surrounding the temple, they were ushered through the house and into a vast and lavishly adorned office. Rodgers was dressed in a black cassock and seated behind a large mahogany desk.

"Thank you for coming," he said, making no effort to get up from his seat to meet them. "Please sit down."

Once seated, Rodgers cut straight to the chase.

"I've asked you here," he began, "to discuss the children."

"They're okay aren't they?" Elaine asked.

"Yes, yes, they're fine," he dismissed their concerns with a wave of his hand, then paused before adding, "Well, not quite, actually."

He then continued to tell Jack and Elaine that he was worried about the children now that they were getting older and starting to act a little more independently. The youngest was fourteen now, making her siblings fifteen and seventeen respectively. They had been fairly passive until just recently when they'd begun to question some of their mother's ideals.

"Not that we don't encourage this," Rodgers said defensively, "It's just that there has to be a degree of discipline in an order such as ours which must be maintained."

It was Jennifer, the youngest, who seemed to be the most troublesome. Although she remembered the least about what life was like out there in the real world, she had a fiery streak in her and was not only demanding answers from her mother, but was also doing her best to undermine the beliefs of the other two.

"Quite frankly," Rodgers continued, "we don't want her here anymore. And I think it best if her sisters left with her."

"What about their father?" Jack asked, realising as soon as he had said it that Rodgers had tried that route already.

"A waste of space," he said, "We tracked him down but he doesn't want to know. So, I'm afraid it's down to you two."

"What do you mean?" Elaine asked.

"Exactly what I say, you need to take the children."

"Just like that!" Jack's voice rose with his anger, "You drag them into this … this, so called religious order, then when they start asking questions you dump them? Are you serious? Because if you are you're going to be in serious trouble."

"I don't think so," Rodgers smiled as he spoke. "You see, we need to keep this situation very quiet. For all our sakes."

Without pulling any punches he laid out his thoughts to them. Rebecca wanted to stay, and incidentally, didn't want to see them today. Of the three children, it was felt that Sarah, the oldest, might want to stay on, but that both Jennifer and Sally had indicated that they were happy to leave. Unfortunately, the deal would have to be all of the children as leaving one behind was felt to be potentially disruptive to the order of the temple. It was then that Rodgers dropped the bombshell.

"Of course," he said, "we would expect a certain remuneration for our having been so involved in the children's development. I can assure you that they have had an education that surpasses even the best public schools, on top of which, the life experience that they have had here is beyond valuation. I've prepared the necessary documents here."

He passed a thick wad of papers across to Jack and Elaine, then rose from his seat.

"I'll leave you with those," he said, "I'll send somebody in with tea and biscuits while you read them through. When you're ready to see me again, just press that buzzer on the desk and I'll come straight away."

Back on the boat, Jack refilled all our glasses, took a long drink and composed himself:

"Those documents were indescribable," he said. "The most hideous and pernicious pieces of paper we had ever seen."

Although full of legal jargon and complicated appendices, the summary of what they had been given was that they were to 'buy-out' the children's membership of the temple and were to do so by donating their home to the Revd. Rodgers. In return for this, they would have full custody of the children and no further action would be taken over the allegations raised by Rebecca in a six-page dossier that they read with horror.

"We couldn't believe what we were reading," tears filled Elaine's eyes, "the things that Rebecca said that we had done to her were the most disgusting and depraved lies."

"We never so much as slapped that girl," Jack continued, "nor her sister. If anything, we were too soft. And as for the sexual side of things, well, I hope you don't need me to say any more."

Once they'd read the documents, ignoring the tea and sandwiches bought to them by one of Rodgers' followers, they sat in silence contemplating what to do. They really didn't have much choice, but the shock of it all was hard to bear. They knew that they had to rescue the children from this place, even if it cost them all they had. And their resolve was further hardened by what had been done to Rebecca to make her write those accusations. She was probably beyond hope now, but there were three lives that could still be rescued. So, they pressed the buzzer, signed the documents in front of Rodgers and waited for the children to be brought to them.

"And that was that," Jack said, "Those three beautiful kids that we'd known came into the room looking like they'd been drugged. They recognised us, but only Jennifer truly seemed to appreciate what our presence really meant to them. And then we bundled them into the car and headed back home."

I couldn't believe what I was hearing. I'd passed this so-called temple on my travels, set back as it was Staffs and Worcester canal just past Brewood. To think that what had seemed to me to be a monastery, was in fact the site of Satan's forces instead, was almost too much to bear. I felt sick at what had happened to Jack and Elaine.

"So," I asked, "where are they now? The kids?"

"Well," Elaine brightened up noticeably, "that's the happier part of the story. Jennifer went straight into school and did well for herself, she's now finishing a degree in some ology at Leeds University. Sally's gone into farming and settled down on a farm in Yorkshire with a young man. They both seem to have adjusted well. Sarah was harder to work with though. She reluctantly went for counselling and eventually her therapist seemed to break through and give her some sort of hope back for the future. She is still working out where she wants to go with her life, but works part-time running a charity shop in Edinburgh. It gives her something to focus on and they pay her accommodation. I think she'll get there in the end."

And the price of saving these youngsters and giving them the hope of an independent life had been every penny that Jack and Elaine had ever earned and saved. They had enough to live on, and they had the boat, but more than that, they had the satisfaction of knowing that when they'd been asked to give their all for others, they had done so without any hesitation. And of course, they still had each other.

Chapter Fifteen

I left Jack and Elaine at Penkridge the following morning and headed back towards Great Haywood. They'd given me the photographs of the house and I would start work soon on the panels that they wanted. Meantime, I had to get away. Words can't describe how I felt about what had happened to them. These were ordinary people, with an extraordinary tale to tell, but who was listening to them? Of course, I'd heard the stories on the radio of elderly couples being scammed into losing their life savings, but this was something different: The New Sun Temple of Light was a registered charity; Rodgers had been featured in numerous lifestyle magazines; the temple grounds had even been praised for their sustainable management. Who knew what was behind the scenes? And why was there no negative press?

With all these questions niggling at me and a nagging desire to know more, I decided that I'd follow the approximate route of the Four Counties Ring and take a look at the temple as I passed by. Whilst one of the most popular cruising rings, it was still out of season, so wouldn't be too busy, and it would be good for me to have a specific journey in mind. There was also a semi-sentimental reason behind this as it was the only long voyage that Fran and I had ever undertaken, although that voyage and that other boat seemed so much further in the past than they actually were.

I gave myself a month to follow this route that can be done in a week at a push, as this would give me time to properly explore the area whilst taking breaks to work on Jack and Elaine's commission. It would also mean that I would be back in time to escape the Easter madness, by retreating to one of the quieter arms of the network. In true canal fashion, that month was a very loosely defined time period, as I was keeping my options open and might divert across to Wales if the mood took me. For all I'd been through, I had a lot to be thankful for and, although I sometimes raged at the loss of my family, they were never coming back and I needed to acknowledge that I had a degree of freedom now in my life that many never experienced. There are positives to find in everything.

Leaving Penkridge behind, I filled up with water, stocked up with essentials at the nearest Co-Op, then made my way through the locks to Gailey where I moored for the night just beyond the beautiful round house that stands defiant against the modernity of the A5 which has almost destroyed the tranquillity of this spot. The following day, I cruised out to Cross Green, mooring up outside the pub and treating myself to a decent steak and a few too many pints of their guest ale. I'd like to report that there were incidents worth recording along the way, but it was all very quiet and uneventful. This suited me fine. There were times when I enjoyed meeting people and making new friends, but just now, I was in a content but insular mood, still brooding to some extent on what I'd heard in Penkridge.

For all my plans to take my time on this journey, the next day saw me passing through Hatherton Junction and up the Shropshire Union canal to Brewood, where I decided to moor up for a couple of days. They say that 'the Shroppie' is one of the most beautiful canals to cruise and that first leg does nothing to detract from this notion. The high banks and the close woodland surrounding them make that piece of waterway something unique in the way it is part of, but so distant from, the real world. Moorings aren't great though so it's not really a route that you can take over a long period, hence my enjoying the view but passing through relatively quickly.

At Brewood, I took out the photographs of Jack and Elaine's cottage and spent a couple of days creating panels of the right dimension and pencilling in the outline of the carving. I also took a few bike rides along the tow path to check out the temple that Rodgers had built. It was where I remembered it, and as non-descript from the towpath as it had been the first time that I saw it. Having searched the web for details of the place and seen it's exotic and luxurious interior, the view from the canal was somewhat disappointing. It looked like nothing more than a large farmhouse, with a couple of acres between it and the waterway which it was shielded from by an overgrowth of vegetation. They obviously weren't interested in their proximity to the canal. The details that I'd read in the magazines told me that if I were to approach from the road, the view would be a little more dramatic, with a large glass pyramid having been built as a gatehouse and the front of the house extended to make a long, formal, covered walkway to act as an entrance. Inside, I knew there were 'communal' areas that were palatial and had been built with no expense spared and to provide the members with every imaginable modern luxury. There were rumours that the individual living spaces for members were less well appointed, but no photographs existed to confirm or deny this.

On my third trip to the site, I took binoculars with me and slipped over the broken down boundary fence to have a closer look at the building. The going wasn't easy and the brambles scratched and tore at my coat but I was able to make it far enough through to get the view I wanted. There was livestock in the fields adjacent to the canal, what seemed to me to be a mix of semi-rare breeds. A member of the community was moving between these pens on a tractor, attached to which was a trailer filled with hay bales. The noise of the animals told me that this must be their feeding time. That helped me as, with the labourer's attention distracted, I was able to move closer to the main building undetected. To be honest though, there wasn't much to see. And I don't really know what I'd expected to come across. Did I really think that I would see some sort of ritual sacrifice going on? No, deep down I knew that whatever wrongs went on in that place, they were well hidden.

That evening, I sat in the pub with the local paper and tried to forget the temple and all I knew about it. Yes, Jack and Elaine appeared to have been victims of a side of Rodgers that was not publicised, but who appointed me to take action. I thought back to what I'd done to avenge Fran's death, but that was different. That was personal. This antipathy to Rodgers was based on one account from a third party and that was the extent of my involvement. Then, as the pub started to fill up, I was joined by a local.

"Mind if I sit here?" he said.

"No, feel free." I absentmindedly waved him to a seat.

"You on the boats then?" he asked, seeing the cork ball on the set of keys I moved towards me as he sat down.

"Yes, just here for a couple of days."

He was a ruddy-faced man of about sixty, dressed in country attire that had seen its fair share of use. We had the usual conversation about living on a boat. How long had I done it for? Where had I come from? Is it cold? Then he said something that sent a bitter chill through me.

"I'm still trying to make contact with my son," he said, "He's got himself mixed up with a weird bunch just outside the village. Says he wants to stay there, but he's got a wife and kids to look after."

"You mean the temple?" I asked.

"You know about it?" he was genuinely surprised, "I have to say, it's no type of temple that I'm used to. Bunch of nutters it seems to me."

Apparently, his son had hooked up with Rodgers a month or so back when he'd been called out to do some electrical work on the house. The work took him three days but on the last day he didn't come back, just rang his wife and said he was staying.

"Said he'd found his true spiritual home," he laughed, "whatever that means."

We talked for another hour or so, during which time he gave me a potted history of both his family and the impact that the temple had had locally. It had been welcomed at first, but then, once it was clear that it was generally a closed shop for trade, that welcoming mood had changed. They didn't really see the members, although Rodgers was often seen flashing along the roads in a Bentley convertible. Despite the secrecy there were occasional times in the year when the farm had a spurt of activity and lorry loads of produce were carted out of the place. On these trips, it was not unusual to catch a glimpse of some of his followers in their brown sack-cloth robes.

"I don't know what to make of it," he said, "Tony isn't like that at all. And I just can't get in to see him. You hear about these things don't you, brain-washing and all that, but I don't know, maybe he has found something there."

I tried to reassure him that it would be alright but with my prior knowledge my words seemed hollow.

"Have there been many locals joined up?" I asked.

"No," he said, "that's the funny thing. I just hope it's not the start of the whole village being taken over. There's something queer about that place, I just wish there was something that could be done."

And I wished the same. I wished that somebody would expose what was happening and that Rodgers, for all his publicity-tainted smiling face, would be seen for what he was. But what use are wishes? Something had to be done. Someone needed to do what the justice system was blind to. I walked back to the boat, deep in thought. Memories of events the prior year came back to me and that thought again of the justice system failing. Was now the time for another righteous correction?

Chapter Sixteen

Justice comes in many shapes and sizes. For every instance of injustice, the justice needed to correct the balance is unique to that one situation. The Bible used to put it as 'an eye for an eye and a tooth for a tooth', which makes sense, a like for like recompense. But in the real world, left and right, black and white, justice and injustice are not so easy to interpret.

This was my train of thought as I contemplated how, were I to go ahead with it, would I tackle Rodgers and his so-called temple.

Now, I don't mind admitting that, of the two of us, Fran was the one with the most get up and go, whereas I had a more laid-back attitude to the future. Since moving onto the boat, yes, I had taught myself new skills and done things that I never imagined I would be capable of, but my life still ran on 'canal time'. There was always tomorrow to do that extra bit. Not that this is necessarily wrong, it's just that there are times when things have to be done immediately. Granted though, not too many. I had the panels to make for Jack and Elaine they were progressing slowly but also needed me to be in the right mood to do them credit. Other than that, there were few pressing demands on my time but a raft of projects that I had sitting on the back-burner.

Since acting against Slater, though my conscience was clear about what I'd done, there were a lot of nagging thoughts about how I had done it and how I would have done it better with hindsight. The objective was to do the right thing and not to get caught. Although my logic on this is certainly up for debate, that approach wasn't about my own protection so much as ensuring that the balance of justice remained. A wrong corrected by a right had to be a closed circle and my facing trial and conviction would prevent that closure. Potentially another injustice skewed the balance. When I applied these thoughts to the Rodgers situation, it was clear that I would need to work a lot harder to remain invisible, whilst at the same time develop new tools to assist me. That was where the plans that I had put aside came in.

I retrieved the pile of notes that I'd secreted in one of the secret storage compartments on the boat's side panelling and laid them out on my workbench. The drawing for the gun that I'd used was there, and I looked at it with a certain amount of satisfaction, not least because this was a bizarre piece of equipment that I had actually made and made to work. The constraints of my working environment along with the cover that it provided, given my nominal employment status as a wood-worker, meant that that material had to be the principal medium that I worked with. Somehow I'd been able to cut, carve and create a working gun from that material, albeit with a fair number of metal components scraped together from the various boxes of assorted junk that I had accumulated at the boat-yard. As I flicked through the other pages, I drew out a couple of sheets, balled up and threw away as many more, then put the rest of them to one side.

My drawing skills had improved alongside my carpentry ones and I was quite pleased with the detail in the drawings before me. Pleased and vaguely amused as well, seeing what my mind had led me to, and thinking about how DaVinci must have felt when he doodled that helicopter of his. One of the plans was for a drone. They'd been popular a few years back, but restrictions on their use had slowed demand for them just as the technology had improved beyond measure. The one that I planned to create was a variation on the theme and not exactly of a standard spec. It might work, it more likely wouldn't, but it was worth a go. The other plan was equally left-field. It was something that I'd thought up on one of those Winter nights when it had been freezing outside but I couldn't sleep because the wood-burner has made the boat feel like an oven. To be fair, it was a plan that also didn't necessarily need to be secreted away as it was something that I'd toyed with making commercially. With a few adaptations, it might serve me now and answer the problem of my need to move about invisibly despite the fact that my only transport was twenty tons of steel that moved at a maximum of four miles per hour.

I made the decision to go after Rodgers. Normally, I would have gone at this like a bull at a gate, but this time I needed to check my impetuosity and take time to properly plan and prepare. With that in mind, I continued my cruise out and away from Brewood to give me some clear thinking time and to put some distance between myself and my target.

Three months later I returned. I'd had a thoroughly enjoyable time out and about, heading along the Llangollen Canal and returning via Chester, all the while working on my special projects and gathering together the materials that I needed. Post is a bit of a problem when you live on a boat, but with some careful planning and by tapping friendships that I made along the way, I was able to order anything that I needed on-line and have it delivered as I travelled. I knew that this left a trail behind me but I had no alternative to using my debit card. To cover my tracks a little I began a fake journal where I casually made note of all that I'd bought and a fictitious reason for that purchase. I wasn't too concerned about the postal aspect of things though as I reckoned it was very unlikely that any of the people who had acted as recipients for me would even remember helping me out. Even if they did, there was never any suspicion on their part and everything they took in for me was harmless in itself.

As I came back down the Shroppie, the final pieces of my plan fell in place. The boat looked pretty much the same as it always had, but there were unseen changes that nobody would ever have guessed by looking at her. I felt like a covert operative on a special mission, and let's be honest who has never fantasised about having a secret identity? I drew the line at putting together a special outfit though. Everything that I would carry was practical and necessarily both unexceptional to look at and of course, disposable. The only regret that I had about my preparations so far had been having to kill the owl. It was necessary, but nonetheless still something that I wished I hadn't had to do. Still, needs must.

The nights were longer now and there were more passing boats as we were in peak boating season. Both factors which I hoped would work in my favour as I moored up near the 'The Anchor' at High Offley, possibly the most interesting pub on the waterways, and fortunately, a bit of a tourist draw. I needed people to see me there and I needed them to see me having a few drinks. At about seven thirty, I entered the pub and was pleased to see that it was busy but not overly so. I recognised a couple from the boat that had moored beside me and, having had my pint pulled for me and poured from that famous plastic jug, I invited myself to join them as there were no other free tables. They were happy for me to do so and the evening passed very pleasantly. More boaters arrived and then an impromptu sing-a-long began which went on to closing time. I made sure that I joined in with gusto and that those around me saw me visiting the bar regularly and racking up the pints. We all got merrier and merrier, apparently, although what nobody noticed was that not a single pint of mine actually made it from mouth to stomach. This was one of those sleight of hand tricks that I pulled off the web and not something I can take credit for. It worked though. Every time I looked like I was downing the beer, it was siphoning into a bag ready to be emptied every time I went to the toilet. It meant that I had to keep more clothes on than seemed wholly appropriate for the season but fortunately there had been a few showers earlier in the day, so I didn't look too out of place.

I staggered back from the pub alongside my neighbours and we said a drunken farewell to each other and boarded our respective boats. I listened to make sure that there was no-one else around and heard the satisfying click of bolts being dropped that assured me I wouldn't be disturbed. I locked my own boat up for the night and changed my clothes, rinsing the various pipes and tubes that had served me so well before returning them to the innocuous home-brew kit from whence they had come. I changed into my working outfit.

After checking I had everything I needed, I took a few minutes to calm myself ready for what was probably the trickiest operation of the night. Now was the time to find out if my own Leonardo 'helicopter' would actually work. Not that it was a helicopter, in fact it was quite the opposite.

I worked the necessary catches and lifted the floorboards in the boat's bedroom. There was a little water in there, which wasn't unexpected, but I did make a mental note to seal the compartment more effectively at a later date. I could see this because I'd installed a few LED lights there as well, because what really mattered about that compartment was that it housed my strange invention. To look at, it could best be described as a torpedo shaped coffin, it's lid opening as the floorboards were lifted. Inside, it was lined with heavy material, the cut of which was broken by numerous switches and monitors. Putting it together had been a challenge but also a real joy. Installing it had been the main problem.

A month ago, I'd booked the boat in to a yard to be lifted out and blacked. Nothing unusual there. I'd chosen the yard well though, as it was unmanned at night and pretty much in the middle of nowhere. They had CCTV but when they'd pulled the boat from the water I'd made sure that she wasn't visible on any cameras. What's more, because I was living on board her while the work was done, they used me as an impromptu security guard and gave me a set of keys so that I could use the workshop if I wanted to. Because of this, I'd been able, over the period of a few nights, to use the yard's own cutting and welding equipment, to cut out a ten-foot-long section from the side of the boat and convert it into a waterproof hatch. When the guys at the yard came back in the morning, watching me hard at work applying the blacking, they saw nothing unusual and were no wiser about the changes I'd made. With the boat back in the water, I cruised away with the boat blacked and ever so slightly modified.

The contents of the waterproof compartment had been made as I cruised back from the yard. The construction was basic and functional, with its shell being formed using glass-fibre and resin over a thin ply shell. Aside from getting a little high at times on the fumes, I'd found the fibreglass easy to work with and was able to shape this baby vessel into a neat and streamlined form. It was strong enough to withstand a hefty blow, yet light enough to be manoeuvrable, plus, the interior fitting had been straightforward as I could form all the necessary cable channels, control boxes and battery compartment out of the same simple material.

Climbing into this boat within a boat, which I chose not to name but simply referred to as the pod, I lay down and let the lid close over me. Reaching out to the controls at my right hand side, controls that I had practised with until they had become an extension of my hand, I pressed the sequence of buttons that started the launch process. I felt the pod lift as the chamber it was housed in slowly filled with water, then I heard the soft buzz of the motors that moved the hatch from the side of the boat. The pod was pushed gently sideways and I looked up to the monitors above my head on which was displayed a black and white image of its progress into the main waterway. The hatch on the boat closed and I let the pod sink to the bottom of the water.

Allowing a few minutes to orientate myself, I checked all the video screens and was rewarded with a full three-sixty-degree view of the filth and debris that made up the bottom of the Shropshire Union Canal. A heavy duty battery, sealed to prevent gases building up, would provide more than enough power for me, whilst the oxygen tank that kept the air fresh I knew to be good for a fair few hours. Double and triple checking everything again, I threw caution to the wind and started the motors. The pod rose slowly in the water, settling itself just six inches above whatever surface it sensed was closest to its base, then I felt it move smoothly off down the canal in the direction of Brewood and my date with a certain Revd. Rodgers.

Chapter Seventeen

There were still a lot of uncertainties about how this thing was going to pan out. My objective was clear, my strategy to get there carefully planned, but I was relying on a fair amount of luck. It was also important to me that my reading of the Revd. Rodgers' vanity level was correct and that it was as high in reality as I believed it to be. It was this vanity that had led him to escort several of the Sunday magazines on tours around his private apartments and so give me a detailed description of, and crisp and clear colour photos of, the area I had to target. That vanity too, I hoped, would lead Rodgers into my hands.

It was twelve miles along the canal to the nearest place I could disembark for the temple. Whilst this would have taken me half a day on my boat, because the pod was streamlined and using electrically powered jets to drive itself through the water, it was able to travel much faster. The journey would take an hour each way, as there was only so much speed I could build up without risking grounding the pod or worse, trapping it in something that had been dumped in the water. This was one of two trips that I would make and was thus also a trial to some extent. My second trip had to be absolutely faultless, so taking my time this time made a lot of sense.

Had anyone been walking the towpath whilst I was making my journey, and had they taken a very good look down into the water, there was the slimmest of chances that they might see me. Given that it was night, there were clouds obscuring the moon and a lot of this towpath was also unsuitable for walking, the chance of me being seen was negligible. This meant that I could concentrate on the side and front cameras, as well as the GPS tracking system and the multiple anti-collision alerts that kept the pod free from harm. I'd tested it a couple of times, but this was the first time that I was totally dependent on all the systems working and working as they were intended to do. There was only one major obstacle that I had to overcome on the route and that was the lock at Wheaton Aston. For all my good intentions and despite racking my brains over this problem for days, there was just no way that I could get the pod through locks without coming out of the water. In time, I still believed that I could find a solution to this but on that first night I had no choice but to come up to the surface, lift the pod onto the bank and slide it to the top of the lock. This was achievable at this particular lock, as it is remote and has a good deal of space around it. The pod was heavy but, pumped up on adrenalin, I manoeuvred it past the lock and was soon back in the water.

Everything else went like clockwork, and I arrived at my destination without a hitch. I chose to wedge the pod into the bank just beyond a bridge on the opposite side of the canal then allow it to surface and let me out. This was never going to be easy and I ended up a lot wetter than I wanted to be, but that couldn't be helped. I took out two rucksacks from the foot of the pod, laid them on the bank and then closed the pod lid and allowed it to submerge itself again.

Crossing the bridge to the other side, I located the hole in the fence where I had first entered the temple grounds and eased myself forward as far as the edge of the first field. It was thornier than before. However, I was also better protected: my outfit was an adaptation of heavy duty Kevlar motorbike gear on the outside, with a wet suit inner lining. It was warm but it was also as black as the night and not a single thorn penetrated its outer layer. I settled into a natural dip at the edge of the brambles and opened up the first of the rucksacks. This is where the owl came in.

Carefully unpacking it, I stood the replica owl on the ground next to me and pressed a button on one of the two smart watches I was wearing. It made a barely perceptible whirring sound and then looked up at me. Though I say so myself, it was beautiful, even in the limited light of that night. Some of that beauty was natural and that had been why it had been so hard to sacrifice the actual owl that became the template for this electronic copy. It had probably taken me longer than necessary to craft the replica but looking at this beast now, I felt that I had done justice to its forerunner. The feathers were the only part of the original bird that remained. Everything else had been meticulously carved out of ebony, which created the structure that surrounded a bastardised high-end drone that had cost me a small fortune. In daylight or on close inspection it would never pass as natural when in flight, that had been too much to aim for, but stationery, or seen briefly moving across the night sky, it looked as it should. I played with the watch on my wrist and the bird hovered into the air, wings still firmly down. A few more movements of my controls and it was airborne with wings extended and flying out to a branch that I knew would give me a good view of the whole compound. The bird flew as well as it had when I'd practised with it over the past few weeks and it was a relatively straightforward matter to set it down in the tree and, using the very small monitor that I had bought with me, do a sweep of the grounds and identify the relevant CCTV cameras. It was a strange feeling using the bird's electronic eyes to stare at the cameras that, in turn, stared back, but I was confident that if anyone was monitoring these images they would only see an owl and not another camera looking back at them. Although there were cameras all over the complex, I could gain no intelligence about how often they were monitored, so I could only work on the assumption that they were being checked all the time. To target every camera wouldn't have been possible, but my idea was to pick the relevant ones and disable them. This was my next move.

Having been asked to keep an eye on security at one of the marinas that I'd stayed in, I was aware that as technology had advanced (so too had the least technological influences impeded those advances). Night vision cameras were great, but they had to be cleaned regularly as they offered a very useful place for spiders to make their nest. Withdrawing two smaller drones from my rucksack, I activated them and set them off towards the cameras. They were nothing like spiders but each had a small artificial web underneath it with a life-sized spider that moved back and fro. Landing them on the cameras, I zoomed in on them from the owl's eyes and was pleased that they were both in place; anyone monitoring them would see nothing but a bright light in the shape of a spider, moving around in a web, and would only curse and make a resolution to have them cleaned the following day. I moved forward along a carefully planned route and passed by the first camera that was pointed at the window to Rodger's office. All was still inside, so I flicked a knife through the side of the opening and disengaged the latch. Climbing in to the office I paused to listen for any sign that I'd been noticed. There was none and all remained silent. Sliding my rucksack to the floor I withdrew a small package wrapped in tissue paper. The desk that I had seen in the glossy magazines was, thankfully, the same one and, more importantly was in the same place. Vain as he was, Rodgers had little difficulty sharing with the world the craftsmanship of the furniture in the temple and we all knew that he sat at a Thomas Cheddleton (of Bond Street) desk. I'd researched the design and, using my own carpentry skills, had easily been able to replicate the style and colour of the gilded paper-stand that was integrated into this design. Although looking like the most advanced piece of bespoke carpentry, Cheddleton's designs actually cut a few corners when it came to embellishments. It was this weakness in their design that enabled me to unscrew the paper stand and replace it with my own. It looked the same. The only difference was that my replacement had a camera and microphone built in; the camera focused on the safe combination lock, the microphone tuned to pick up anything said near to the desk. I smiled when I switched the monitor on and saw everything working as it should.

Exiting the office, I dropped the window catch back in place as best as I could, then I skirted the building to where the other camera had been obscured. This time I faced a bigger challenge. Rodgers' bedroom was on the third floor of the building, but I was currently at ground level. Worse than this, it was a certainty that Rodgers would be in his bedroom just now. There was no easy way to penetrate that inner-sanctum but I had a plan and it was too late to back out now. Using the remote control on my wrist I flew the owl past me and up onto the window ledge that I was targeting. The cameras showed me into the room but not before they had shown me the gap under the open sash window. If it had been shut, I would have had to revert to a more complicated plan. Fortunately, on this night, plan A seemed to be able to continue. I scaled the drainpipe beside Rodgers' bedroom and joined the bird at the window ledge. The window moved up smoothly and I found myself in the bedroom with the man himself. Speed was of the essence here and despite my revulsion at seeing the half-naked form of Rodgers sprawled across the sheets, arms draped over one of his younger followers, I moved in close and jabbed both of them in the heel with one of my tranquiliser darts. They stirred momentarily, but were they to remember anything in the morning they would put it down to having been bitten by an insect. They now slept even more soundly than before and I knew they wouldn't wake up.

Cheddleton furnishings were predominant in the master bedroom as well. The top-of-the-range four poster bed that clearly got a lot of use by Rodgers was another of their better works, but again, had a small design fault. The bed was a true four-poster in name only as it was simply a large bed with four extended legs that rose up almost to ceiling height. Each of these legs was topped by a perfect cube that had a central circle of mirror to reflect light down onto the occupant of the bed. I unscrewed the bottom right one of these and replaced it with the replica that I had made. It was a little too easy and perhaps Cheddleton's should be more protective of their designs. Still, I wasn't complaining.

With cameras and microphones now installed in both rooms, I climbed back out of the room and headed back to the canal. Back again at the fence, a little earlier than I had anticipated, I sent the owl over most of the complex and used its built in hard disk to store the video. It would have been too time consuming to review what I saw on site, but I did keep it waiting when it found the security control room and was pleased to see that the guard on duty was diligently watching the cameras but had clearly not seen anything worth reporting. All in all, it had been a productive night. Now, all I had to do was make the return journey back to the boat without incident. Needless to say, although taking a little longer than I had hoped for due to my having to avoid an early morning boater who was enjoying the experience of cruising in the dark, I made it safely back to the boat and by five o'clock was climbing out of the pod and back into my boat's cabin. I was exhausted. Locking everything back down, I didn't have the energy to put the bed fully together but chose instead to crash out on the sofa. I slept like a baby.

Chapter Eighteen

Transcript of conversation recorded 02/07/2020, Revd. Rodgers and Anton Stern:
(Sound of Rodgers pressing office intercom)
Rodgers: Anton, can you come in please.
Stern (on intercom): On my way.
(Sound of door opening and Stern entering the room)
Rodgers: Sit down, I need to run a couple of things by you. (Pause). Right, first of all, last night. The one you sent to me, she was okay but she was perhaps a little too, hmm, shall I say, compliant. Have we not got any new blood in yet?
Stern: Sorry, she was the most suitable that I could find for you. The parents are one of my own preferences, but maybe you're right, they become so much a part of the temple so quickly. We've got a new family just in this week, I'll see where I can get with them.
Rodgers: Thank you. Now, from pleasure to business. We need more revenue. I've got a mountain of plans here for projects but the finances just aren't there. Top of the list, we need another temple. The properties our followers insist on giving us are only ever suitable for selling on or letting out. I want a big score.
Stern: Incomes good at the moment. You know the state of the finances. But …(pause)…I do have to say that expenditure seems to be a little excessive just now. Perhaps we could have a period when you maybe…(pause)… rein in a little of your own spending.
Rodgers: (Laughing) You've come a long way Anton. I appreciate your being so candid.
Stern: Thank you.

Rodgers: But, no. I spend what I need to spend and if there are to be savings, make them elsewhere. Don't ever forget that every penny that comes into this order is because of me. The worker deserves his wages. Give me another option.

Stern: Well … (long pause) … there is something we've discussed briefly before.

Rodgers: Go on.

Stern: Our own particular tastes in, shall I say, companionship, are shared by a number of prominent and dare I say wealthy people. Perhaps now is the time to start our very own 'gentleman's club' for the select few. We have the …(pause)…, the staff as it were. I think this may be the opportunity that we need. It also fits in with expansion as each new temple could have its own, what shall we call it, relaxation annexe?

(Long pause, Rodgers moving papers on desk, writing things down)

Rodgers: You think we can do it safely?

Stern: I think so. The only risk is bringing in the wrong people, but with the initial contacts that we both have, we should be able to avoid undesirables. And, of course, the risk is more with the consumer than with the supplier …(pause)… provided we ensure that we keep accurate records of what goes on. You never know, there may be a secondary stream of income from the need our clients have for keeping their tendencies secret.

Rodgers: Blackmail?

Stern: A little too strong a word maybe, but, yes. Of course, it is up to you and I am very conscious of your own position as the Pastor of this flock of ours. Does it fit with the moral vision of the temple?

Rodgers: Anton, please, you and I have had this discussion too many times. I take it you are playing devil's advocate here.

Stern: (Laughing) Who me?

Rodgers: (Laughing) Yes. I told you when I first took you on that this was a temple in name only. As indeed is my title, bought at great expense off the internet, merely a name only. This temple is not about a God who doesn't exist. It's about my own god, my own self. And you, my friend, are as committed to that cause as I am myself.

(Pause)

Rodgers: When I was ten years old and was first made to get down on my knees and perform unspeakable acts on my friendly, local priest, I knew that whoever God was, He was too absent for me to love Him. Then I came to the conclusion that He wasn't even there at all. As I was used and abused in ways that even I still find shocking, that passivity changed to revenge and now, you know, my passion is not only to live as if God doesn't exist, but also to do things that, just on the off-chance that He does, will tear at His loving heart every time I do them. I am my own god and not the same in any way as that God that saw me suffer so much. I killed because of God's servants. He is responsible for what I am and when I die, either it will all be nothing, or I will stand and face Him and challenge Him to blame me for the things I have done.

Stern: I didn't think it would be a problem. I'll start the ball rolling. Maybe Sir (name deleted) might be a good contact. They tell me most of the Cabinet these days are seeking a little discreet pleasure.

Rodgers: Go for it. Invite him as soon as possible. I need this second temple.

(Sound of Stern rising and leaving and door closing)

END OF TRANSCRIPT

I was in Pelsall when I recorded that one. It seemed like an age had passed since I had visited the temple, but in fact it was only a fortnight ago. The friend's I'd met at The Anchor had woken me at midday on the day after my adventure and I think it helped the illusion that I had been completely drunk because I looked a real mess. I'd forgotten that I'd promised to lend them a book. We exchanged pleasantries and swapped phone numbers in case we were ever near to each other again. From my side, this helped immensely to secure my alibi and I made a note to use the 'pretend drunk' routine again. Since then I'd been moving around and mooring up where I could get either free Wi-Fi from a pub or a decent signal on my mobile dongle. I'd heard about the website Anonymous Images from somebody at the marina a while back, and, having checked it out to make sure it was as secure as they claimed to be, I'd signed up to it in order to upload the feeds from my devices in the temple. Essentially, it stores a continuous feed of data, which the user can then access and refine at their own leisure. It could have been made for me. Of course, it meant that there was a lot of data that needed deleting, but the two units that I had installed in the temple both had sensors that meant they only switched themselves on when there was activity.

The information I was retrieving was pure dynamite. When I'd built the devices I'd over-engineered them to run for three months if necessary and had hoped that this would be long enough for me to gather enough data. As it was, I was a fortnight down the line and I had enough to not only hang Rodgers but also draw and quarter him at the same time. It was tempting to carry on collecting information, but that last conversation told me that now was the time to act. It was one thing for him and his followers to do what they did, but when they aimed to make it a commercial operation I couldn't justify waiting. The problem that I now had was how to get back to the temple without raising any suspicions and without taking the boat back the way I had come. If I was going to do this, I needed anonymity and I needed anything that I was alleged to have done to be deemed impossible from my situation.

As the pod only worked on straight canals without locks, it was perfect for the Curly Wyrley that I was now on, but there was no way that it would be able to negotiate the Wolverhampton flight or any other locks that got in the way. Wheaton Aston had been a one-off and I had to think of a solution, and quickly. So far, my 'creations' had been inspired by nature. There was something special about this to me, as I'd seen enough on my travels to know that for all of man's advances he couldn't improve on what was already here. However, by marrying technology with nature, the best of both worlds could be sought: the pod was no more than an electronic fish, and the owl was the majesty of natural flight harnessed to carry what I needed. Surely nature could inspire me to overcome my current obstacle? I packed my rucksack and headed off for a long walk to see what I could see.

Chapter Nineteen

Sadly, the lock problem remained. It would have to go on the back-burner for now and I would have to rely on a little good fortune to remain anonymous in the second stage of my current project. I abandoned any ideas to be clever and simply returned with the boat to Brewood. If Rodgers was to put two and two together and place me as being a boater, then that wasn't a problem as the plan that I had for dealing with him was such that even if he knew my full name and National Insurance number there would be little he could do. Just to be on the safe side though, I went to the local pub that evening and was fortunate enough to be seen by the same old guy that I'd met last time, although he was heads down in a game of dominoes. I made sure that I was seen to drink a few pints and that I left with my adopted stagger, seemingly incapable of doing anything else that night.

It was one in the morning when I emerged from the boat and made my way through to the temple. My surveillance had yielded a very useful piece of information that I was now able to exploit, in that Rodgers made a conference call every Wednesday in the early hours of the morning using the computer in his office. It seemed he had close contacts with some high-powered people in Japan and, as they were eight hours ahead, his calling them at half-past two in the morning made a lot of sense. I had to be in the office before that call.

Wanting to take no chances this time, I used the owl to keep me shielded as I passed through the grounds to where I knew that the single security officer would be stationed in front of his bank of monitors. The newest addition to my electronic menagerie was a small mouse that had a limited range but packed a very powerful punch. Flattening this and sliding it under the door of the surveillance room, I let it reform itself before guiding it to the guard and onto his shoe. It bit quickly and just as the guard looked down to see the source of the irritation, his eyes closed and he was deep in sleep. Job done. Now, to the main target of the night. Unplugging the hard-drive that recorded all the CCTV images was a two-minute job, after which I simply took the relevant keys and let myself into Rodger's office the easy way.

The safe opened without a sound, as I knew it would, and the combination remained the same one that I had seen him enter every day for the past fortnight. To be fair, the guy was as security conscious and diligent as could be expected, but complacency slips in when the enemy is unseen and as unimagined as my devices were. Sifting through an assortment of varied documents, I was tempted to investigate some in a little more detail and get a deeper understanding of the scope of Rodger's operation, but time was of the essence. The folder I was looking for was simply marked 'Property'. I withdrew the papers and copied them all on the large photocopier that sat in the corner of the room. If Rodgers had come in then, I was prepared, but as it happened I had the safe closed and the photocopier was silent again by the time I heard the door open and he came into the office.

There was a small bathroom on the side of the office and I slipped in there, hoping that Rodgers would keep to his normal routine of simply booting up his computer and making the connection to Japan. He did. Whilst I heard him rambling on about issues that really didn't bother me, I checked through all the documents I'd copied and made some mental notes. Then I heard the familiar goodbye from Rodgers and let him cut the connection before I emerged.

His face was a picture when I came out of the bathroom, especially as I had an extremely authentic copy of that most well-known firearm, the Walter PKK, in my hands. Before he could react I spoke.

"Revd. Rodgers, I presume." I said, listening as the words distorted themselves through the mouthpiece of the mask that I wore, "Please, don't do anything rash, and do, sit down and compose yourself. If you stay calm, you are in no danger. And we are alone, in case you were wondering. Your guard is having a little nap and the cameras are not recording anything."

"What do you want?" he asked.

"A predictable opening comment," I answered, "and not unexpected. Let's say first that I want a chat. After which I'll outline, in a little more detail, what I need you to do before I disappear into the night."

He capitulated and I poured him a large brandy from the decanter that sat above the safe.

"No ice, I'm afraid," I said, "but still, you may need this."

He mumbled a thank you and took a long drink.

"Here's the deal," I sat myself opposite him in the seat that Stern felt so comfortable in, "First off, I want you to enter the following web address into your computer."

I gave him the web address for an alternative Anonymous Images account I had set up, then asked him to enter the username and password.

"If you click on the file marked 'Righteous Correction,'" I told him, "then a few videos and audio files will load. I want you to watch and listen carefully."

He did as he was told and I sat calmly in the chair watching his countenance change as each new file loaded. A little earlier than I had expected he hit the keyboard and stared at me.

"Enough," he whispered, "I get the picture. What is it you want?"

This was the time for my prepared speech and I ticked off every point mentally as I explained the nature and content of the material I had on him, highlighting some of the finer points of his breaches of our country's moral, if not its legal, code.

"It would be easier," I concluded, "for me to simply go to the press or the police, but I can't control how things would pan out in that case, and besides, I have a very specific objective in my mind. I want the balance of justice to be restored. It's not for me to tackle the legal side of things, I'm no lone vigilante taking the law into my own hands. My involvement with you is through one of the many people that you have robbed of their homes and life savings. I want those monies restored."

"Okay," he said, "Who are we talking about?"

"Oh, please," I laughed, "wouldn't that be a little too easy. I identify the people, you restore their money, then the whole vengeance cycle starts again. There are fifteen that I have identified through your records. The only option I'm offering is that they all get back what they are owed."

He eyed me suspiciously and I could see he was trying to work the numbers in his head.

"Of course," I continued, "this may seriously impact your expansion plans, but you come out of it in one piece, albeit a little poorer."

"Okay," he said, giving me that same smile that had drawn in so many of his followers, "you've clearly done a comprehensive job here and I'm quite impressed. Suppose I do as you ask? What guarantees are there that that's the end?"

"None," I said, "I've told you clearly what I want you to do. You restore the money to these people and you go on public record saying that you have been misguided in your religious ideals and that the temple is no more. When you do that, and you specifically use the phrase 'righteous correction' to explain why you are giving that money back, then that's the end of my involvement. You'll still have money, I'm sure, and then you can take your chances. If the law catches up with you for your other transgressions, then you face that head on and take the hit. If not, you still have your freedom and probably more money than you'll need. Maybe a trip to Japan is in order?"

"You know what this is all about don't you?" he seemed resigned to the end that was coming, "You've heard the recordings and you know that I am as much a victim in this as anyone else. I don't know who you are and I don't get why you are doing this, but yes, it seems that I have no choice but to go with it. What sort of time-frame were you thinking of?"

I outlined my thoughts on this and reiterated again how important it was that he follow my instructions carefully. Then I rose to leave.

"I'm trusting you here," I said, "please don't betray that trust. Weigh it up and do what I am asking. There may be hope for you yet."

With that, I left the room, and headed out to the main road, before doubling back onto the canal. I had a week at most to wait. Something told me that Rodgers would consider his options carefully and yield. Of course, nothing was guaranteed, but by the time I was back on board New Hope Arising, I'd come to the conclusion that he would do the right thing. I'd wait in Brewood until the announcement, it would be interesting to gauge local reaction.

Chapter Twenty

Maybe it was because I was on a high after things had gone so smoothly with Rodgers, or maybe it was because I chose to apply Occam's Razor to the problem, but the day that Rodgers was to make his press announcement, exactly a week after my visit, was also the day that I solved the lock problem. The solution was that there was no solution. If I was to move and move anonymously, then I would have to use more conventional modes of transport, but there was no reason why, should I be seen, I couldn't disappear as easily as if I'd been hidden all the time. I get ahead of myself though. That was one for the future. The press conference was my priority.

Whether it was because Rodgers had made himself a minor celebrity, or whether it was more out of curiosity during a fairly quiet news period, I was pleased to see the depth of coverage that the news conference attracted from all the major papers and the satellite news channels. It wasn't important enough to be screened live, but, by the time it was concluded, it was important enough to be the lead for most channels. Although not present, for obvious reasons, I was updated on how it all panned out in detail by an old friend.

It began with Rodgers rambling on for a good ten minutes before leading into the part I needed to hear. Having outlined the growth of The New Sun Temple of Life and the difference that Spiritual Completeness had made to many of his follower's lives, he stunned the assembled journalists with the following:

"Despite all that the temple has achieved, however, I have had my own spiritual awakening of sorts and now believe that our goals and objectives may have been misguided. This feeling had developed after much soul searching and therefore it is my intention to liquidate my church with immediate effect. As part of this process, I am aware that a number of families have felt it their duty to make a substantial contribution to our cause. I believe that their gifts should be returned and have already instigated this action. In doing so I hope that this will be seen as a righteous correction, to use a phrase I heard recently, although my errors, if they can be called such, were only ever driven by the best intentions."

Even in defeat, Rodgers kept up the smile and you could see by the way he manipulated this conference just how he had got to where he was now. He would lose a lot by what he was doing here, but I was under no illusions that he would still have more money than most people would ever dream of having. There was also a nagging concern in my mind that he would try a different tack and pop up somewhere else as a source of harm. This became a less likely happening however as the press conference continued.

"I do not intend staying too long to elaborate on my decision," Rodgers said, "But I am open to answering a few questions."

A couple of the nationals raised some interesting points pertaining to how guilty Rodgers felt and trying to establish his personal plans for the future but he fielded these with the deftness of the best politician. Then came the headline-making question.

"Revd. Rodgers," a softly spoken female voice began, "Jean Carter, the West Midlands Sentinel. Would you be able to confirm that the pictures I have here are images of yourself engaged in sexual acts with minors?"

The room went silent as she made her way to the front of the press pack and placed three ten by eight photographs in front of Rodgers. He looked at them and then at Jean and then around the room, seeing for the first time the uniformed police officers walking towards him.

"I have nothing to say," he just about managed to murmur, before the police officers took his arm gently and led him away.

Jean Carter stepped up onto the podium.

"Ladies and gentlemen," she began, "I apologise for disrupting this conference but, as you can see, the Revd. Rodgers now has some more pressing concerns to address. The photographs that I have here are part of a comprehensive dossier that detail a number of illegal activities that appear to have taken place at the temple, but I would ask you please to refrain from asking for any further details. The police have all the files and will no doubt respond in due time."

"Meanwhile," she continued, "I would like to clarify the point that Rodgers made about his actions being a righteous correction. We have all become a little more familiar with this term of late, sometimes in its correct context, but too often as an excuse for vigilantism of the worst kind. That those who took the ill-advised decision to give substantial donations to the temple, sometimes amounting to all that they had, have now been recompensed is a true example of righteous correction. The person who encouraged Rodgers to make this move has asked me to clarify this. However, rebalancing the scales of moral justice is not an excuse for our taking the law into our own hands and so, we must wait for the due legal process to come to the right decision about any further allegations. Thank you for listening to me."

She walked down from the platform and was followed by the cameras as she calmly left the conference room and slipped into a taxi.

The effect of Jean's contribution to this event was felt across the nation. Although innocent until proven guilty, Rodgers' name instantly became a byword for evil. More importantly to me, the term 'Righteous Correction' was again on people's lips, more so than it had ever been after it entered the nation's consciousness as part of the Slater affair, and that the debate about the difference between harm and crime was in full flow.

For my own part, I had broken no contract with Rodgers and was comfortable that my actions had rebalanced the scales of justice in the way that I had wanted them to. In this new role that was becoming a part of me, I had done what I set out to do and Jack and Elaine, along with many others, would be reunited with their past wealth. In my role as a citizen however, I had a separate duty to ensure that I reported any illegal activity that I discovered. At first, it had been my intention to make Rodgers pay for his abuses and his criminal acts by punishing him in one of various ways that I had thought of. But the process of pursuing him had made me change my mind. I still had images of Slater's eyes in my mind and wondered if I had done the right thing in that first foray into justice. From now on, I would avoid the guts and gore of physical corrections as much as possible, and concentrate instead on perfecting the balance I achieved in bringing justice to situations of injustice.

With the potential for so many people to misinterpret righteous correction as a revenge thing, I had asked Jean to make her statement when I'd met with her to hand over the dossier of evidence that I had on Rodgers. I knew that I could trust her to be discreet and, as she already knew some of my past activities and had remained silent, I knew also that she was on my side. I didn't want anyone to know who I was, but with Jean there as my unofficial spokesman I had a chance to communicate with the outside world and try to explain what I felt compelled to do.

Jean was a good person and her passion for journalism was driven by the best motives. If I could help her progress her career, then so be it. As part of our planning ahead of the press conference, I had asked her to make contact with the relevant people in the big national papers and open a door for me to communicate. I'd also given her two credit card sized wafers of pure heart of oak, engraved with my calling card. On the back of the first was the name Slater, on the second, Rodgers. How many more names would be added to this list I couldn't tell. Something in me told me that this was only the start. With all the vigilantes coming out of the woodwork now though, I had to keep control of what was happening and these calling cards were my solution. Whenever a true 'Righteous Correction' had taken place, the scene would contain one of these cards with the victim's name, if indeed they were a victim in the true sense, carved on the back. It wasn't within my power to ordain what newspaper editors chose to report, however, it was my belief that they too were concerned about any Tom, Dick or Harry taking the law into their hands and would likely take note of the presence of a calling card as they decided on what stories to carry.

Meanwhile, I had plenty to keep me occupied. I had the canal network to explore and I had work to do in developing some of the tools of my trade. I also had a relationship to keep working on as Jean and I were, despite our both trying to resist it, becoming more than just close friends. This wasn't something that either of us had pursued and we were both conscious of the need to keep our contact off the radar, but there was a growing understanding between us that we shared a new goal for our lives and perhaps that included sharing ourselves with each other.

So much had changed for me over the past few years. Bathrooms and sanitaryware and family life had been replaced by boating and invention and a moral crusade. Had I taken time to think about where this was leading me, things might have been different but something was driving me that I simply couldn't stop. That's why the name that had been bugging me ever since I began recording Rodgers was at the centre of my mind as I planned the best approach to correct the injustices that the mysterious Sir (name deleted) might have been involved in.

Chapter Twenty-One

'The Sunday Voice', 16th August 2020:

'Shock at Peers' Suicide Pact'

Members on all sides of both houses of Parliament are reeling today from the apparent suicide pact that led to the death of four Peers yesterday. A team of Metropolitan Police officers are trying to piece together the chain of events leading up to this tragic incident in which the victims, yet to be formally identified, appear to have driven a ministerial car to a remote beach in Lancashire before setting it on fire with themselves inside.

Whilst speculation is rife about there being something more to this than a simple case of suicide, police sources have confirmed that they are not pursuing anyone else in relation to this incident. In a brief statement, the lead investigator, referred to certain documents that he was in possession of, which appeared to offer solid and substantial evidence to support the view that these individuals took their own lives.

One of the four victims is believed to be Lord Walker of Rotherham, the sixty-eight-year-old Peer who was recently linked to the scandal surrounding the New Sun Temple of Light. As a close friend and supporter of the now-defunct Temple's spiritual leader, Lord Walker had faced a great deal of public criticism about his involvement with this movement. Officials from the House of Lords have refused to confirm this information.

++++++

'The Salford Express', 10th September 2020
'Confessions of a Tax Evader'

Officials of HMRC in Manchester are trying to understand the motivation behind a local accountant's confession that he has helped numerous local businessmen to evade large sums of tax through the use of a number of creative accounting tools that he has developed. The unnamed accountant was previously thought to have been a model of best practice in his field, so there was a ripple of shock when he turned himself in and presented a dossier detailing every penny that he now felt that his clients owed. Some have speculated that the perpetrator of this fraud recently underwent a spiritual enlightenment of sorts, whilst others have argued that he was feeling the weight of possibly being caught and arrested.

HMRC are currently reviewing the files and contacting all those who have been named to allow them to give a defence or to pay back any monies owed. It is unsure whether the accountant will be prosecuted, although he has stated that he is fully prepared to serve time in prison if that is felt appropriate.

In a twist on the recent debate about the execution of justice in the UK, it is understood that the dossier presented to HMRC was headed with the title 'Righteous Correction'.

++++++

'The Leicestershire Herald', 24th October 2020
'Migrants tell of being held as slaves at burnt-out pig farm'

Fourteen Asian nationals who were rescued from the

burning wreckage of a local pig farm last week, have told police and social workers about the conditions they were forced to work under for little or no pay.

The piggery at Lower Meads Farm was destroyed by fire two days ago. Firefighters and police who attended the scene were unable to save any of the buildings but on their arrival they were surprised to find the workers huddled against a fenced off area that was being sprinkled with water from the farm's supply.

The search for the farmer, Todd Williams, has been scaled down now that the fire is fully under control and all the buildings have been searched thoroughly. With the stories coming to light of the conditions under which the workers were held, it is believed that Mr Williams has fled and is now in hiding.

Interpreters are still to question the immigrants in detail, but it is already apparent that they were smuggled into the UK a year ago and have since been kept in conditions of virtual slavery on Williams' farm.

++++++

'The News Review', Issue 56; December 2020

'Righteous Correction or a Revenge Culture?'

Mystery still surrounds the identity of the self-styled vigilante who leaves a calling card with the initials R.C. carved into a wafer of Oak with his victim's name engraved on the back.

Is this a 'righteous correction' of injustice, as this individual believes it is, or are we facing the threat of vengeance and lawlessness as people seek copycat corrections?

In this issue of the News Review we have an exclusive interview with one of the victims of the 'righteous corrector' who had his tongue cut out as recompense for his involvement in a telephone scam that defrauded vulnerable people of their savings.

In this interview Robin Johansson admits that he was one of the team leaders of this operation and that he is currently helping police with their enquiries into the dealings of the company he worked for. Communicating through a laptop computer, he outlines how the scam worked and the levels of commission that he was receiving, however, when asked if he felt that his 'punishment' fitted the crime, his response was vociferous:

"No matter what wrongs I may have done; did I justify this as the payment for my crime? I am not innocent but I don't believe that I deserve this disfigurement as any sort of correction of the balance of justice, however righteous or not some people may say that it is. I am a UK citizen and we have a justice system that has moved on from primitive revenge. There are factors behind what I did that a jury should be able to weigh up and a Judge should be able to make a balanced assessment of a fair sentence. We don't live in the dark ages anymore and I will not hide away in shame at my past errors nor will I be held up as some sort of example to others."

You can read the full interview from page 12 of this edition which precedes a short paper by one of this country's leading criminologists who considers where the boundary lies between true justice and revenge attacks.

++++++

Another year was coming to an end and there was a lot going on in my life. I kept any press clippings that I could safely get my hands on, more to remind myself of how I was developing in my role than to gloat on what I'd achieved. Truth was, I was under a huge amount of emotional pressure and needed to take stock of what I was doing and where it might be leading.

In general, I tried to avoid the crude surgery that had been the mark of my first outing with Slater's eyes, but it wasn't that easy. With the Right Honourable Members of the House of Lords, whose guilt I had ascertained from documents retrieved from Rodgers, I had given them the choice whether to flick the switch that would detonate the car they were strapped into, or whether they would leave the vehicle and make it to a hospital to have the wounds where their genitals had been, dressed and treated. Whether right or wrong, this was vigilante justice with a choice. Had they sought treatment, they knew that they would face prosecution and that the evidence supplied to the police was damning. I was guilty of mutilation and abduction but not of murder.

With Johansson, I just wasn't convinced of his remorse which meant that the removal of his tongue seemed fair and appropriate and prevented him from turning back and reoffending. For all his clever words in the press, there was a side to him that he did not reveal, but which I had seen as I had him pinned down in his office. It was his 'right' to seek to gain as much wealth as possible and not his fault that some people were so gullible. In his eyes, it was the system that was wrong, not him, and he was only following the much-vaunted public attitude of 'look after yourself'. That said, with hindsight, I should have been able to think of a more imaginative and yes, less cruel, approach.

With Williams, the punishment was to let him go and live his life in hiding but without any financial resources. He would live in fear, poverty and isolation, relying on handouts to survive, forgotten and ignored in his suffering. Just as his slave workers had been. As with all of my victims, Williams had been given a choice but there was no way he was going to free his workers and face any prosecution that might be forthcoming. Similarly, as undocumented migrants, there was an uncertainty as to what would happen to his workers. Taking the approach that I had, had meant that they were supported by public sympathy and that justice would be balanced by their being allowed to remain in the UK as a recompense for their time in bondage.

The accountant was easier prey altogether. Having watched him at work on his computer for a week or so through the eyes of one of my electronic friends, I simply accessed his accounts and transferred half of his money to HMRC with the threat that the rest would go if he didn't go and speak to them.

Jean and I were meeting a little more regularly now, although always in places where we knew our contact would be unseen. She was my main source of information on perceived injustices, providing me with the necessary details that she gleaned from scanning news reports. It was important that she be one step removed from all of this and I was careful only to draw this information from her within the natural flow of our casual conversations. Neither of us were sure about what we were doing, but Jean had to be as innocent as possible of any direct involvement.

Although she knew that I was the individual in question, she didn't concede that she knew it for certain and the option remained that I could simply have been an intermediary. The decisions had to be mine and she only provided me with an initial framework of reference by which to justify those decisions. Most of the time between events, aside from continuing my life on the water, was taken up in analysing, collating and cross-referencing the data I accumulated to ensure that my eventual actions were as correct as possible. If my response was personal, or purely a vengeance attack then it was a no-go. Similarly, at that time, I felt that my calling, if that's the right word, was to act against individuals rather than making judgement calls on big business. I wasn't out to change the world, only to make small corrections and protect a few individuals. I still believed in our justice system and my moral compass was set in a direction that I was comfortable with. Still, it was all stressing me out a little, so I took a break through the Winter to pursue another project that I had been considering.

Chapter Twenty-Two

Despite the very real hints of uncertainty that surrounded my self-appointed role as a corrector of injustice, everything else in my life seemed settled and promising. I loved everything about living on a boat and had no intentions of ever returning to bricks and mortar; I was stretching my abilities in all manner of technical areas and discovering new skills that were far removed from anything I had practiced before; and I was developing a very close relationship with a very special woman.

The 'blood-money' that was my compensation for losing Fran and the children was being worked through a little faster than I had anticipated, but this was offset by the times when I was able to find specialist work adding my own style of craftsmanship to some of the higher valued vessels on the cut. Working on the innovations that I needed to help me in my clandestine side-line, had the useful benefit of helping me to think about and design new ways of maximising the use of space on board canal boats. This in turn led to commissions and a steady stream of income.

But being a jobbing craftsman stole a degree of the freedom that I so enjoyed and was reluctant to give up. On the one hand, despite not necessarily needing the money, the work gave me the satisfaction of having felt like I'd paid my way, as I was still a little uncomfortable with being an early retiree at my relatively young age. I was also able to make a decent contribution to the lives of the people I worked for and had designed and created some unusual but very effective solutions to on-board problems. Yet, on the other hand, I didn't want to be bound by work or tied to being in any specific place for any length of time.

The solution to this came about quite naturally as I worked on the interior of my own boat to make it a little more hospitable and less starkly clinical. Aside from my workbench, I didn't have a table on board as such, eating all of my meals off my lap whilst I sat in the well-worn leather armchair that was my only comfortable seat. Feeling this to be a little too casual, I decided to put in a small sofa that I could stretch out on a little when lounging outside wasn't practical, and as part of this I designed an integrated table. The concept was simple. The sofa had two halves that faced each other, allowing me to choose the direction in which I sat. In between these two sections there was a centre section that looked to be part of the same sofa, but which converted to a table. Nothing radically innovative, I accept, but the way that the cushioned top of this centre console lifted and converted itself into a table was like nothing I had seen on boats before. The mechanism was simpler than it looked, although it took me many a night to perfect it so that it worked quickly and smoothly every time. I happened to mention this to a fellow boater and they were interested enough to ask if they could come and have a look. They ordered the same for their own boat and by the time I had completed theirs, I had orders for another half dozen.

Whilst I was happy with the success of this design, and was already working on several more, making them for a living was not my ambition. It wasn't just the time that was a factor, it was also the practicality of having to get together all the necessary bits and pieces without having either an address or any transport. This was similar to the problem I faced when working on other projects. Even the most discrete of friends that allowed me to have stuff posted to them, raised the odd eyebrow at some of the things I ordered, and it was only a matter of time before some incriminating link was established between my two personas.

I was moored in Beeston when the solution to all this presented itself. As was becoming the norm for me, I was in a local pub and had just met up with one of the boaters moored near me called Tony. His boat was an old Springer, like my own first craft, although his had obviously seen better days. To look at, he was the sort of person that most people who dealt in that world beyond the canal would have changed direction to avoid. That never bothered me. I'd met too many great people on the cut to ever consider judging anyone by their outside appearance. As we talked through a variety of subjects, he opened up to me and told me a familiar story.

"I got in with a bad crowd," he told me, "and I've been in the nick for the past couple of years. I'm out on parole now. It was stupid really, just drugs stuff. I wish I'd known how it would screw up my whole life."

I asked him what his plans were.

"Couldn't tell you," he replied with a shrug, "Prison didn't teach me anything I didn't know. Nothing legal anyway. And once you tell someone you're an ex-offender, they seem suddenly less reluctant to employ you. I had my own business before I went inside, renovating cars, vans, anything I could get my hands on really."

"Can't you go back to that?" I asked, a little naively.

"I could, but I've had to sell all my tools and equipment just to have enough money to live on and, with the boat, I haven't a penny left. What's worse is, I'm still liable for the rent on the premises and I'm having to keep that up because I can't afford the landlords taking me to court whilst I'm on parole."

We talked about what his skills were and I shared a little of my own story, then we returned back to the start because something he had said was nagging at me and was only just becoming a little clearer in my mind.

"Whereabouts is your workshop?" I asked.

He told me it was about half a mile up the towpath from where we were moored as he wanted to be near to it to make sure it didn't get damaged.

"I've told them it's insured but hell, where am I going to get that money from. No, I just need to make sure no low-life decides to torch the place. Then I'd be really stuffed."

We agreed to meet the following morning at the premises and I immediately knew that I had found an answer to my current problems. The workshop was about two thousand square foot inside and was set in a complex of similar buildings. It still had the last vestiges of equipment from its former life but was pretty much an empty shell. The rent, to anyone with a modest income, was not a great deal, although to Tony it was taking up most of any income he was currently getting. While we were still on site, I ran the numbers in my head and was happy with what came out.

"Look Tony," I said, "I know it's not really your field, but do you reckon you can work with furniture?"

"I don't see why not," he answered, "I used to do the upholstery on the vans and we did some work on motor-homes every now and then. Why? What are you thinking?"

I told him what I had in mind and we went back to my boat so I could show him the sofa-table and a few other items I was thinking of making. It all happened very quickly, but once he'd agreed that he could make these up, I set the ball rolling and within a month the first 'Boat Space' factory was up and running. I paid Tony per item produced and took over the rent of the place, investing some of my savings in the minimum of necessary equipment. I left him alone to do what was needed, and he didn't let me down. If I'd planned it all in detail, it would likely never have happened, but with very little to lose, I went for this project and it paid off. I was able to keep on playing with new designs on my own boat and in my own time, simply sending new ideas to Tony to build in the showroom. Orders kept coming and he managed the place easily on his own. My only involvement was being there to give any advice if he needed it and to work with the cash coming in and going out.

There were only three rules that I imposed on Tony. Firstly, that any deliveries to the site that I arranged were left to one side and not touched. And secondly, that when he needed to employ additional staff that they be ex-offenders like himself. Finally, I told him that when I needed the space to work on my own projects, I would do this overnight but that nobody was to see what I was working on. This left me with the space I might need at times to work on my specialist projects if they couldn't be completed on the boat. Other than these rules, I left him to run the business and he made a roaring success of it.

I hadn't planned on owning a bespoke furniture factory. Then again, a lot of what I was doing just then hadn't been anything I would have foreseen for my future. Life was throwing me opportunities and I was enjoying embracing them. I also hadn't planned on sharing my personal life with anyone else, but as with the other strange twists and turns my life was taking, that just seemed to happen as well.

Chapter Twenty-Three

Jean Carter's career as a journalist had taken off since she had exposed the detail of what was really happening with the Revd. Rodgers and the New Life Temple. It had seemed the right thing to do, to give her the opportunity to make the most of that scoop, and I felt that I had repaid her for helping me through the darker days of loss that I had endured. Using Jean had also allowed me to stay that one step detached from the wider world and remain anonymous in my justice campaign.

After the Rodgers affair and the inevitable fallout over the issue of vigilantism and certain copycat actions, Jean had also been my contact with the press and had, on several occasions, been able to have corrections printed on my behalf. I didn't want the world to know what I was doing, nor did I want to be held up as some sort of elusive masked avenger. My actions were purely for the benefit of the victims of injustice and were, I believed, a measured and directed response that targeted the perpetrator only. This was no moral crusade to change the justice system or begin a debate about whether the system currently in place could be improved. I remain a fan of the justice system. It works.

Both Jean and I were conscious that because we were linked in a tentative way, we needed to be very careful about our contact. It had been Jean's presence that had led the police to my door after the Slater affair, and we both wanted to avoid this happening again. We had pre-paid mobiles that were specifically for our own use and would make arrangements to meet in discrete locations. As I've already explained, it was important to me that Jean be more than one step removed from my activities and we never discussed what I was doing in explicit terms. The term 'Righteous Correction' was referred to between us only in the same way that any other individual might discuss it, and there was never an explicit confirmation on either of our parts that I was taking any action or that she was supplying information. When we met, we talked around subjects and she might drop into the conversation a situation that she had come across in her work, which I would later investigate in more detail. Alternatively, and as was more often the case, I would raise the subject of something that I had been made aware of and ask Jean to provide a little more information. We met only infrequently, maybe once a month at most but I looked forward to those meetings. I was becoming a more solitary person and was more than happy with this. When you live on a boat you meet a lot of people but they remain casual acquaintances for the most part as they are either passers-by, strangers in pubs, or other boaters who have also chosen that lifestyle to stay that one step detached from the complexities of the world out there.

There are some practical reasons behind this as well, since boats are small and it is unusual to invite anyone into your little domain. When you are in a house, you have the space to hide away those little things that you don't want others to see, but on a boat the scope for this is limited. Boating also has its own sanitary challenges and visitors are not always welcome to contribute anything to the contents of that toilet cartridge that you know you will have to empty quite soon. As a bloke, I am not ashamed to say that I peed in milk bottles and ditched it into the bushes when no-one was around. I know I'm not the only one to do this and actually, it's the ecological way to do things.

It was after the Leicester incident in October that I first invited Jean to meet me on the boat. We needed to have a catch up and couldn't find somewhere suitable locally and this was before I had the factory. She parked a good distance away, checking out, at my request, any CCTV cameras that may have been able to track her, and selecting a parking space on the streets outside a car boot sale that was well underway. I welcomed her on board and we settled down to a light lunch inside the boat, even though it was one of those surprisingly warm early Autumn days when the towpath was the place to be. It was warm in the boat but we wanted to avoid being seen outside together.

We talked about the usual stuff and confirmed the necessary information that we were both seeking. Jean was interested in the pig farm event and so I speculated on what I thought might have happened there and how it was nice to think that the migrant victims might have a chance of staying in the country after what had happened. There was a lot of talk about the threat to the UK from migrants around this time, but this group seemed to have gained a degree of public sympathy. I could tell that Jean was at ease with this situation and felt that justice had been done. Naturally, we discussed the legality of the whole thing. What Williams was doing was illegal and the correct approach should have been to inform the authorities and let the legal system do its bit, but we both knew in this case that by the time anyone arrived, there would be no migrants to find. As the invisible people, they could disappear without trace and this would do them no good. The world I had uncovered that surrounded these people traffickers was a very grey area. We both agreed that this might send out a message.

Having worked our way through a first bottle of red, I opened a second and Jean seemed happy enough to have another glass or two. The afternoon drifted on and that second bottle made way for a third. We were both relaxed and enjoying being together. We moved on to more personal issues.

"Don't you ever feel lonely?" Jean asked, "Here on your own with just your books and your woodwork to keep you company?"

I thought about it and replied that I was more than happy to be alone with myself, but that I was never lonely as there were always people about either on the cut or in the pubs. The situation I was in was perfect for me, free of the commitment of any relationships but also able to dip my toe into companionship when I wanted to. I also explained to her why this was important to me after what had happened with Fran and the children.

"If I get too involved with anyone, I'll only spend most of my time worrying about losing them," I told her, "I'm comfortable with my own company and I feel as safe as possible. Obviously some other aspects of my life make me vulnerable but even there, it's only me that will lose out. Do you see where I'm coming from?"

She understood completely, but the conversation didn't end there.

"Do you not miss the intimacy of a close relationship though," she chose her words carefully, "I mean, that feeling that you get when you can give yourself fully to somebody else."

"I can't do it Jean," I answered, "How can I give what I am to anyone else? It can only end in loss. I know it might sound a bit melodramatic but I see myself as being a cause for hurt. Better to keep a little distance and protect myself and others."

Now that the words had been spoken though, I knew exactly where she was coming from. Jean was the closest I had to an intimate friend but we had always been just a couple of people who worked together. Since losing Fran I had been fortunate to have been freed from most of the ties of lust and desire that had so marked my life beforehand, and I certainly didn't think that I missed sex in any way. Maybe I was wrong though and there was a deeper need inside me to fully share myself with somebody else.

Although she was a few years older than me, Jean had a classic and very simple beauty that I had never really thought about before. I don't think it was the red wine distorting my view but on that October afternoon I saw a little more of that beauty and something more besides which stirred in me, feelings of an unexpected desire. Relaxed by the alcohol as I was, it seemed that my inner feelings were able to penetrate the layers of protection that I had built over myself and I saw Jean in a different way.

"Anyway," I tried to steer the conversation to safer ground, "what about you? I don't hear you telling me about any special friends."

"Oh," she answered, "I get the odd offer for that sort of thing occasionally, usually from some drunken old editor who wants to play away from home, but I'm a bit like you in that respect. I haven't really said much about him but my ex-husband was less than the ideal partner. No, I don't want this to be a case for the avenger of justice, but he treated me very poorly. He was a high flyer in finance and I was the little lady who earned pin money. Over the years he crushed my self-belief and I'm only glad I walked away from him. That was five years ago and, I'll be honest, it's only now with the things I'm involved in with you that I'm starting to get my confidence back."

This candid confession told me that Jean's defences were down too. It seemed only natural to reach across to her and hold her hand. Because we were in the confined space of the boat I knelt in front of her and without really thinking about it we hugged. The minute we found ourselves touching, the bond between us changed. We kissed lightly, then more passionately, tasting the wine on each other's breath. I pulled away.

"Is this what you want?" I asked.

She didn't reply but instead she reached out and pulled me back to her. We kissed again and then, like frisky adolescents, we pulled each other's clothes off and dived into the bedroom. The release of that evening was what we both needed. We made love all night and woke late the following morning exhausted but sated. We both knew that this was not the start of a long term relationship that would see us marrying and living together in blissful happiness. That wasn't what either of us wanted. What we had found though was a level of intimacy that we both needed but which would never be a bond that would chain us to each other.

I still had reservations about sharing myself with another but that morning when we woke together, I let those reservations fall silent and simply enjoyed being one with another person again after so long. We would part shortly, and we would meet again in perhaps another month's time for a similar time of companionship. That was something to think of another time, for the moment we were content to have each other.

Chapter Twenty-Four

The factory was up and running without my involvement by February 2021. Although it still felt like only yesterday, it was over five years since I had lost my family. The images and memories remained as strong as ever, fading away more often though, now I had new people and new projects to keep me occupied. When I was on a roll, I felt like I couldn't stop with the new inventions and each week brought a hastily constructed prototype into the factory. At the same time, I was working on certain other 'tools of the trade' and had started to explore the details of electronics in a lot more depth. It was like being back at school in many respects as I had to start from scratch and work my way through any books I could get on the subject.

Due to the nature of what I was working on, I had to go this alone, but that just made it more interesting. Occasionally, things worked as they should, but more often I had to laugh at myself extinguishing small fires or trying to stop out-of-control mechanisms. Still, I made progress.

Jean and I enjoyed our time together and it was good for me to have somebody to share my ideas with and also to give me a reason for making changes to the boat. It had been my need to provide a sofa and table for our time together that had led to the first piece in the Boat Space range. A number of other designs had been to make our time together on the boat more comfortable. We'd settled into a mutually convenient relationship and we both felt a lot better for it.

Throughout this time, despite my planning ahead for other situations that might arise, I had not been out and about rebalancing the scales of justice as much because I had not been made aware of any specific incidents that I could get involved in as anything else. Yes, if I really looked for them, there would be situations enough to keep me active every day, but that wasn't what I wanted to do. I needed a break from it all to decide if this was still right for me and to let things come to me if necessary. That's how it had started, and that's how it needed to continue. Not that I believed that I was led to situations by the Hand of God or by any external forces. Maybe I was, but I still struggled to reconcile what I did with God's later revelations of forgiveness over judgement. No, this was a personal thing to me and I would wait and see what came my way.

By March, I had my next project planned. It was to be a departure from what I'd previously done in a number of ways. Firstly, it would be a long term mission and my estimate was that it would be at least six months in the planning and another six in the execution. Secondly, it was to be a project targeted on a wider source of injustice rather than an individual perpetrator, with a view to sending out a message to the people who pursued this way of life. Finally, it was a project driven not only by a sense of injustice but also by a desire to correct an anomaly in a legal system that was at fault in prosecuting the victims of this injustice more than the perpetrators.

The idea for 'The Mallory Project' as I now refer to it, was not an overnight revelation but developed instead as the sum of much of what I witnessed in my travels. There were numerous occasions when I was accosted on the streets of larger towns and cities by both male and female prostitutes offering me their wares. Despite retaining in my mind some vestiges of porn-fuelled fantasies about being with a whore, I was never tempted. As with so many things in life, the reality was far different from the sanitised and distorted images portrayed in fiction. The people I saw both revolted and fascinated me. The revolt was easy to overcome by taking as little time as possible to reject their propositions, but the fascination grew. How did somebody transition from being a care-free child full of hope for the future, into a broken and empty individual prepared to perform the most degrading sex acts for a pittance? As I explored this murky world in more depth, the answer I found so often was drug addiction. Ordinary souls like you and I had taken a series of wrong turns and had found themselves escaping into the momentary release that drugs offered, before becoming inescapably bound by addiction. I began to seek out these people and would pay them for their stories rather than their bodies. Those stories were remarkably similar: a fall into addiction followed by criminalisation in order to feed the habit which in turn closed more and more doors to legitimate means of keeping going. These were examples of the 'revolving door' prison system in the UK that I came across repeatedly in studying the literature. Something stirred in me. Yes, these people were criminals and, in that respect, the justice system that found them guilty and punished them was not at fault. But was this justice? In what sense could it be fair that in a society where people who overeat, who drink too much or who get their kicks out of dangerous sports are all supported with vast sums of government money through the excessively generous NHS, whilst those whose addiction of choice is arbitrarily made illegal have no safety net at all?

I resolved to take action. This was not to be a singular response to one person's evasion of justice but a class action suit against the people at the top of the tree. Too many people were already fighting to make changes to the legal system and to how drug addicts were treated. I'd leave them to tackle it as best they could from their side. For my part, I was going to go after the other big players in this field, the drug barons. Call me naïve but I felt increasingly convinced that by cutting off the suppliers then the powers that be would have to intervene to pick up the pieces, and in so doing some change might be effected. The problem I faced was that the people at the top were so far removed from their activities that they were invisible. If I was to reach them I would have to climb the ladder rung by rung. Which is what I did, and which is why the Mallory Project would take so long.

I began with the people on the streets. In every town I visited, I sought out the ragged and toothless debris of society and I watched what they did. When I felt the opportunity was right, I made my move and, like a mountaineer inching step by step up a rock face, I closed the gap to the summit a little each time.

Chapter Twenty-Five

I met Bridie on a wet and chilly evening in Chester. She stepped out of a doorway and whispered the usual come on.

"You looking for some company?" the accent was Southern Ireland, Dublin most likely, but the voice was distorted by the gaps in her mouth where well-kept teeth, if the others were anything to go by, had once had their place.

She could only have been in her early twenties, but she had the haggard and jaded look of a woman twice her age. Eyes that I felt sure had once sparked with lustful humour, now stared blankly at me. Her hair was lank and lifeless, betraying a natural red lustre just below the surface and her clothes were a third-hand attempt to look seductive.

I asked her if she had her own place and when she confirmed this I followed her down narrow streets to a semi-derelict block of flats, then on up into her home. My heart raced as it had done on a number of similar occasions but this was not with lust but instead with the fear that others might be hiding in wait for me. I was armed, discretely, in case this happened, but so far had been lucky. She led me into the bedroom and beckoned me to sit on the bed which was the only piece of furniture in the room and which was kept as clean as she could. A dirty mattress could put off even the toughest of clients.

As she began to undress I stopped her.

"No wait," I said, noting the look of alarm that sprang up in her eyes, "There's no need for that. Please sit down next to me."

As I unrolled a wad of ten pound notes and counted off enough to keep her off the streets for a few nights, I explained that I only wanted to talk to her. She was naturally wary, but when I handed her the money she seemed to relax.

"Will you be wanting a drink then?" she asked.

"Let's have a cup of tea," I replied, hoping that she had the necessary means of making one.

We went through to the small kitchenette and she put the kettle on.

"You sound just like my Da," she laughed, "It was always a cup of tea with him."

As she made the tea she was quiet and I could see that memories were stirring in her. Memories of a past life of normality that was a far distant world now, though still so close in time. She placed a mug in front of me, put three sugars in her own and then sat back and looked at me as she sipped her tea.

"Don't worry," I reassured her, "There's no weird hidden agenda here. I just want you to have a break. I'm interested in your story, how things went astray and yes, if I can do anything to help you, please ask. But I'm not here to patronise you, or judge you or try and convert you. I'm just an ordinary guy who has been blessed with a few quid and your need is greater than mine. You don't need to tell me anything and I'll go when you want me to."

"Although," I continued, "I wouldn't mind staying to finish this tea."

She smiled and visibly relaxed. Closing her eyes, I sensed that she was coming to understand that tonight and maybe tomorrow night as well she wouldn't have to do those things that she most hated.

"You're a good man," she whispered. She then proceeded to tell me her story. The average family in Dublin, the father who died suddenly and the stepfather who came onto the scene all too quickly. The abuse, the threats and the escape into drugs, starting with smoking the odd joint with her friends before seeking a higher high and discovering heroin. Leaving Ireland, she'd tried her luck in London before realising that the gold-paved streets were littered with corpses instead. Then she'd drifted from city to city, ending up in Chester a few months back. Here, she had met up with like-minded friends and she was looked after as long as she was paying her way.

After several failed attempts I realised that I'd finally stumbled on what I was looking for. The block of flats was owned by a man who called himself their protector and who kept them supplied with their fixes provided they paid for the privilege in cash or, if they were short, in any number of other ways. I let her talk and made a note of as much as I could, probing a little more deeply when the chance arose but always careful not to scare her into silence.

"I know you said you'd help if you could," she concluded, "but really, I don't think there's any way out of this. A few of the girls have tried to reach out and get help but they always come back, and with stories to tell that you wouldn't want me to share with you. I'm not happy with this way of life but there's a certain safety to it and, let's be honest, I'm not going to be around for long am I?"

I had to respect her choices. But that didn't mean that I agreed with them. A couple of different turns in life and I might have been sitting with Bridie on a comfortable leather sofa in a three bedroom detached house discussing politics and drinking wine. All because of the drugs, the need for the drugs and, most importantly, the need to slip off the radar into this murky world because heroin addiction wasn't a fashionable disease.

When I left Bridie, I walked slowly back to the boat and poured myself a large whisky as I sat in front of the fire. There were plans to be made and now, at last, I had the chance to move forward. Picking up a notepad I sketched some ideas and scribbled a few lists. I looked long and hard at them, committed them to memory then scrunched up the paper and threw it on the fire.

A few days later, I was back at the block of flats. According to Bridie, their protector came twice a week with their supplies and always at twelve noon. If they missed him, they went without. They made sure they kept these appointments. From my vantage point on the roof I saw a car pull up and two hefty guys clamber out of the front seats. They looked around, then one of them opened the passenger door to allow a much smaller and slightly-built man in a long black coat to get out, whilst the other went to the boot and retrieved a small black briefcase. I figured the pretence was good. They looked like rent collectors coming to receive their dues and so, despite their prosperity, they didn't look out of place in this derelict dump.

To avoid being seen, I settled back to my vantage point in front of a computer screen and activated the first of the rats that I would use to follow them. I had six of these beasties with me. They moved quickly, could scurry away in seconds and looked as natural as possible given the complex mechanism underneath their soiled brown fur. I'd chosen the rats because they wouldn't look out of place here and because I had enough of them to cover each floor of the block of flats. They were very sophisticated in their own way, but as yet, I couldn't get them to climb stairs.

The first rat moved off at my command and followed the protector and his team as they began their rounds. The computer I had was monitoring video and audio feeds coming in from the devices and I was pleased to be receiving a very good signal and images that were better than I could have hoped for. It would have been possible to skip this part of the plan but I was still looking for more detail and believed that more clues would be forthcoming from the conversations I'd overhear. I also wanted to get the evidence together to remind me of the righteousness of what I was doing. I thought I knew what their tactics would be, but having the record to remind me would reassure me if I ever had any doubts.

The things that I heard didn't disappoint me at all. At each door, the occupant would hand over their money and wait to find out what else would be required of them to receive their fix. Some were simply handed their goods and the team moved on. Others were less fortunate and had to beg for their supplies. It was on this expedition that I realised that the drugs took precedence over anything else, even the tiniest hint of humanity that might still burn in the hearts of one of the addicts. The protector, who I now knew went by the name of Carl, and his two sidekicks, Pete and, surprisingly, Jeremy, knew how powerful their position was. They were perfect examples of failed individuals who had found their own niche in life by bullying and abusing whilst under the protection of an unbeatable force. They could get away with anything and they did. When the first girl was asked to perform oral sex on Pete, I wasn't surprised. By the time they'd finished their rounds though, the depravity of what those girls had been forced to do was too shocking to bear. I felt sick. But I had to carry on.

Before the team got back into their car I had all the rats stashed away on their respective floors and was working to manoeuvre the last one up to the vehicle. This was a critical moment and one that had to work for me. As they started the engine, I drove the rat forward until it was under the car, then I hit the red button on the remote control and watched as the rat span upside down and clamped itself to the base of the exhaust. Not the ideal spot but magnets were unpredictable. All I could do now was put my stuff together and wait to see if the rat stayed in place.

Later that night, I picked up a clear signal and was able to locate what I hoped was Carl's car parked up at his home. It would either be that, or it would lead me to what was left of my little creation somewhere in the road. Irrespective, it wasn't me that would be going and looking. I sent the owl instead.

Chapter Twenty-Six

The owl landed smoothly on the roof of a small detached bungalow set in a modern development on the outskirts of Warrington. I received its images clearly and used its eyes to search the area. All was quiet. I let the bird fly down until I could see the car that I recognised parked in the drive. I was one step closer to my goal.

Everything now depended on factors that were somewhat out of my control but, since I had the address, I could always abort this mission and come back another time. If, on the other hand, the owl performed as I hoped, then that opened so many more doors for me and meant that I was no longer as bound by the geography of the canals as I had been.

In one sense it was probably best that I wasn't present to confront Carl in person since I would have had difficulty restraining myself after all that I knew he was capable of. That wasn't the plan though. People like Carl were two-a-penny and were nowhere near the top of the ladder. I only wanted information from him and had to be content with that.

The owl moved to the doorstep and I pressed a button on my computer causing it to drop a small mobile phone from beneath its wing. I then moved it to the door and caused it to peck loudly on the woodwork before moving it back to stand in the middle of the driveway.

As the door opened, I rang the mobile, watching as Carl looked around before realising that the call must be for him. He picked the phone up and before he could say anything I spoke.

"Listen carefully," I said, "and don't think about hanging up. I have you in my sights and can make this very painful. Understand?"

I saw him nod.

"Okay," I continued, "let's keep this short. That bird that you can see in front of you is not an illusion. It is armed with a lethal poison dart and will fire it at you if you get within six feet of it. I will allow it to release the dart if you make any attempt to move back into the house. It's your call whether you believe me or not, but please don't take the gamble."

"What do you want," he whispered, clearly conscious of the neighbours overhearing this conversation.

"Names," I said, "All I want is names. You answer my questions and you get left alone. You withhold information and you die. And please, no flannel and no heroics when we're finished. I won't link you to the source of my information and nobody need know that you told me."

"Who are you?"

"It doesn't matter who I am," I replied, "but I will tell you this. I want a piece of the action and I want to go to the top. You help me now and we can work together when things change. You lie to me and your activities at the flats appear on the internet."

I could see the look of fear on his face which changed to horror when I hinted at the crimes I'd caught him committing. It didn't take him long to comply. He told me all the names that he knew and what they all did in his particular organisation. He told me the immediate structure of command and then he gave me what I really needed, the name of the person who he believed to head up the team.

"Look," he said as he finished, "I don't need to tell you that if Mallory finds out I've talked, then I'm dead. Please, don't let him know it was me. I'll work for you, no problem."

"When you visit those flats," I said, "you put the fear of God into those girls. I can see that fear on your face just now and I don't think you like it. If this comes off, I'll be back in touch, but meanwhile you need to know that I am as ruthless as anyone you've ever met and I fully intend to take over Mallory's operation. But even I draw the line at degrading vulnerable girls. Until you hear from me, do your job but tone it down. I'm watching."

I hit another button on the keyboard and watched as the mobile burst into flames in Carl's hand. He dropped it as the owl flew off and I heard the front door slam shut. All in all, a good night's work.

***

Tom Mallory lived in luxury. That much was evident when I walked along the tree-lined avenue on the outskirts of Sandbach in Cheshire. The house was a one-off, single-story building, carefully faced with all the right details to ensure that it had passed through all the relevant stages of planning. I didn't look too out of place along this wealthy street as it was an acknowledged route from the town centre to the canal so the sight of a scruffy boater didn't raise any eyebrows. I didn't need to see the place close up as I had enough surveillance footage of it to fill several hard drives. As I was in the area though, there was seemed some sort of sense in my fitting the property into its surroundings. They say that sometimes the best place to hide is right out in the open and, if Mallory was the person that I suspected him to be, then I had to give him some credit for pulling this one off. To his neighbours, he was a successful businessman, working in the export and import business and a pillar of the local community. His wife was active in the Women's Institute and his children attended the local Roman Catholic academy.

I was now three months or more into this project and was progressing steadily and constantly refining my plans for the next stages. I was still actively following up on the other names that Carl had given me, but so far each one had continued to point to Mallory as the top of the tree. The challenge that I now had to overcome was getting the proof I needed. Hearsay, rumours and an assortment of random facts were not enough for me to base my actions on. Mallory had to be who I thought he was and if I couldn't prove this then the mission would be aborted. Which meant that, for now, I had to play the waiting game.

I was moving the boat steadily down the Trent and Mersey at this point, not going any particular distance each day and making the most of longer term moorings as I was also moving a van around with me. I'd hired the van as an expense against Boat Space and was using it to visit the factory most nights to work on some prototypes that I'd designed. Some of these were commercial designs whilst others were for my own personal use. Since Tony was doing a faultless job in running the business I was pretty much leaving him alone and had told him that I didn't want him getting distracted with my work, and that I would therefore work when the factory was shut. He was savvy enough not to question this too much and I was careful not to stay totally focused on my own pet products as I needed to show him something coming out of my work. Aside from building up my fleet of workmates, including a couple more owls, another half dozen rats and my latest development which was a cruder fleet of adapted drones that didn't seek to hide as any form of creature, I was also working on another scheme that crossed over from my personal to my business life. The concept was essentially an electric vehicle that could travel both on water and land and which was small enough it could be stowed on a boat.

Of course, that was the commercial application, but before we progressed with that, I wanted it for my own work. The constraints of being on a boat and tied to the canal network had been less of a challenge for me in my work since I'd been able to use the birds to help me out. I was also a lot less wary now about being seen out and about and thought it would actually look a lot more suspicious if I was never seen at a train station or walking along the towpath. In my night work though, I wanted to be able to be that bit more mobile and not rely on the pod and the need to be on lock-free stretches of the canals. The first prototype that I'd built had everything in place and worked very well but only for a too brief period. That was why I was using the workshop to develop the concept some more. It was coming together nicely and I was confident it would be ready when I needed it.

Meanwhile, I was using the battery technology that this vehicle required to develop a number of other items that fitted well with the Boat Space portfolio. I didn't know how long I would have to wait to move forward on the Mallory project but I had the van for three months and even if I still had to wait, that would give me time to get the necessary equipment together. There were also a number of items that I'd asked Jean to obtain for me. They weren't the sort of things that I wanted linked to my name nor did I want Tony to stumble across them. She had some useful contacts in the criminal fraternity and had the credibility with them that meant she could pull in some favours. I kept my requests limited as Jean's protection was more important than my own, but she was happy to help me as best she could. We'd meet to exchange gifts at the factory and we had some nice evenings there. I could tell that she wanted to know more about what I was planning but she never pursued the matter too hard. We trusted each other and enjoyed the overt side of our relationship without allowing it to be impaired by the hidden side of our lives.

Time sped rapidly by and I found myself doing the full circuit of the Four Counties Ring again, revisiting old haunts whilst all the time waiting for news from Mallory. Six months after identifying him, I was beginning to get impatient and was concerned that the various tracking devices that kept me informed of his movements would begin to run out of power. I had to give the guy credit, he was very discrete. I didn't doubt though that his hands-off approach to his illegal activities was something that could only go so far. There had to come a point when he would have to break cover.

Then I got wind of the meeting. Various feeds of information that I had set up came together with matches of a particular date and location which pointed to a meeting of the big players. The small fry like Carl were being asked to gather old debts, whilst the middle-ranking players were starting to stockpile cash rather than feed it out into the laundering network. This all happened against a backdrop of Mallory changing his usual transport from the Bentley to what was obviously a heavily armoured Range Rover, whilst at the same time arranging for his wife and kids to go to their lodge in France for an extended vacation.

I pieced together the final parts of the jigsaw and wondered why the police couldn't do the same. Of course, I realised that they could have if they had so desired, but on what evidence did they suspect Mallory? This reassured me that my pursuit of justice was more than a personal mission. I could go places and do things that the official system couldn't countenance. I didn't think of myself as being above the law but I could console myself that I might be working in parallel with it.

There was to be a meeting. More than that, there was to be a meeting to exchange goods for cash. This made sense. Mallory may have left the dirty work to his minions but there would be times when large shipments requiring large payments would mean that he would need to attend. I had two weeks to prepare to gate-crash the party.

Chapter Twenty-Seven

Despite the months of preparation and planning that had been leading up to the main event, I still found myself working around the clock to finalise my approach and get the necessary equipment ready. I could have done most of it by remote, but there was one aspect of the project that meant that I needed to be there in person. Sabotaging the meeting was only part of the plan. I had to leave with Mallory if I was to be successful.

It was a crisp October evening when they met. The location was, as per any cheap television detective production, a disused warehouse on a little used industrial park just outside Stoke. This was helpful to me as it meant that I had less distance to travel from the boat and, more importantly, less distance to transport my cargo, both what I was taking with me and what I intended to return back with. I sent the owls ahead and positioned them on the roofs of nearby buildings. Then I waited for it to get dark. Once I was comfortable that I couldn't be seen I moved an assortment of switches on the boats electrical control board into a unique combination and watched as the bow of the boat seemed to split apart and give birth to a tangle of metal and rubber. A small arm attached to this apparatus raised it over the gunnels and onto the towpath. As it released its hold the arm retracted and the boat came back together. Meanwhile, there was a faint hissing from the package that it had deposited before it began to expand and form itself into its working form. Two large rubber balls inflated at either side, attached to a super structure that slowly unfolded before locking itself into position. This was the boat bicycle that I had been working on for so long. The product I would sell would only be a poor relation of this one, but I had the finished product. The round wheels were Kevlar reinforced rubber balls attached to a carbon fibre frame that surrounded a lithium ion battery that had cost me more than the boat itself. Not only was this an electric bike that could cope with all terrains, it was also capable of riding along the surface of the canal. That latter aspect was the part that I wanted to keep out of the commercial version. I didn't want people cycling down the canal as it was bad enough that they raced along the towpath. It worked for me though and I was happy that it had worked faultlessly so far.

The seat of the bike inflated and I climbed aboard after stowing everything that I needed for that night in the waterproof trunk over the rear wheel. I keyed in the ignition code and started it up, heading off first along the towpath before crossing the canal and riding out along the route I'd so laboriously planned in the weeks before. The journey would take twice as long as it needed to but it would cross over territory that nobody would conceive a bike capable of traversing and would do so without, I hoped, my meeting anyone on the way. I had tried to convert a helmet to keep me in touch with other events whilst travelling, but I couldn't get used to the restricted feeling that this gave me so had abandoned it for a small monitor that I hooked to the front handlebars instead. The picture quality was poor and it was difficult to concentrate on steering the bike, maintaining my course and keeping an eye on the screen. Of the little I could see, there was nothing I saw to concern me and I was comfortable that I would be in position before anyone else turned up.

I only just made it. The bike had a few hiccups along the way and some elements of the terrain had changed even in the little time between my walking them and that night. As I stowed the bike and climbed up next to one of the owls on an adjacent building I heard the rumble of tyres and saw headlights in the distance coming nearer. Rushing to get everything set up I opened two laptops and booted them up whilst simultaneously opening up the box of drones and laying them out side by side. I didn't have the luxury of time but I did allow myself a moment to give these an admiring glance. They may not have had the advantages of being artificial creatures but they certainly had a beauty of their own. And I knew what they were capable of.

The Range Rover was the first vehicle to arrive, out of which four armed bodyguards stepped swiftly and took up their places surrounding the vehicle. Mallory remained inside. Five minutes later a battered old Transit van joined them. The contrast between the vehicles couldn't have been greater. Nor could the contrast between the two teams. Mallory's men were all dressed in the same sharp black suits, whilst the new arrivals were wearing overalls smattered with paint. Not that I imagined for one second that they were here to discuss a painting and decorating assignment.

Mallory climbed out of the Range Rover just as the side door of the Transit opened to allow a squat, oriental gentleman to clamber out. They shook hands and each nodded to their own teams who swapped places and checked out the contents of each vehicle. After a few minutes, during which Mallory and the other person seemed to chat amiably, the teams reassembled and nodded to their respective bosses. Another handshake followed, then packages were transferred from one vehicle to another. I was recording the events but that was more habit than anything and I couldn't think that I would need the recordings. Tonight was about action instead, and I had to make sure my timing was perfect.

I waited until the exchange had been completed and the teams were at their most vulnerable, having felt that the meeting had gone according to plan. They were gathered as close as they ever would be and so I let the first owl swoop down and release its cargo over the gangs. It was back out of sight by the time they had their weapons drawn and were preparing to fire, although they held off on the shots as they were trying to wipe fluid from their eyes.

"What the hell!" Mallory shouted, fixed on the spot and trying to work out what had happened.

"Wait," one of the Oriental guys said, "it was only an owl. I think it pooped all over us."

They paused then they both started to laugh. Who uses the term 'pooped'? They soon stopped though when the second owl swooped and sprayed a black soup over both vehicles. The guards ran to wipe it off but it had set hard on impact with the glass and they only succeeded in removing a few stray patches.

"This better not be your doing," Mallory whispered to his counterpart whose reply couldn't have been any more emphatic.

"This is nothing to do with me," he shouted, "is it one of your tricks?"

The two men stared at each other then decided that the balance probably pointed to a third solution and that they might be better sticking together.

The third owl swooped and dropped a mobile phone at their feet before climbing swiftly beyond pistol range. I rang the phone and waited for one of them to answer. It was Mallory who took the initiative. I didn't let him say a word.

"First of all," I said, "put this onto speakerphone. You'll see the icon on the screen next to the end call button."

He looked and fiddled with the phone, then he placed it on the bonnet of the Range Rover whilst the others gathered around.

"Okay," I began, "let me explain something to you. The dye on the cars is for obvious reasons, you aren't going anywhere just now, but you need to know about the first spray. That was a marker and you are all nicely covered in it. If you cooperate you won't need to worry about it, it will wash off after a few days. If, on the other hand, you choose to cause problems then I will show you what will happen. Look across to your left and you will see a small canister of lighter fluid. That has a different marker on, you will be pleased to know as this is what happens when my buddies target a marked object."

I pressed a button on the keyboard and the first drone rose silently into the air, swooped down behind the buildings and came at them from the other side. It hovered, then moved towards the canister and send out a bolt of fire. The canister exploded.

I released the rest of the drones and let them circle the two teams.

"I can arm them instantly," I told them, "so consider them your guardians just now. Are we clear so far?"

Mallory nodded but I wasn't going to fall for that trick.

"Are we clear?" I asked again.

"Yes," he said, "perfectly."

I told them to gather all their weapons together and then to strip naked. Not because I had some perverse desire to see them like that but because I needed to know that they had nothing concealed. I then told them to choose one person to go to where the canister had been and open up a small holdall that we stowed there. It contained light jumpsuits that they were told to put on.

"Now," I told them, "this is where we have to work closely together. I want the merchandise and I want the money and I want us all to get away from here in one piece. So, here's what we're going to do. I want both of the bosses to tie up their teams and I want the goods and the cash into the Range Rover."

Mallory looked like he was ready to comply, but there was something about the other guy that concerned me. He moved slowly towards his team with his back to me then he made a dash for the Transit. The drone fired and his head exploded. Nobody else tried to do anything stupid.

With the Range Rover packed and everyone tied up apart from Mallory, I packed up my belongings and clambered down from the roof. I only had a crude balaclava on but that was disguise enough. I told Mallory to get into the driving seat and positioned a drone behind his head as I ordered him to keep looking forward. The three owls came down from the roof and joined me, although one of them peeled off briefly to spray the windscreen with the necessary reagent to disperse the black mess. I loaded the boot with everything and climbed in after Mallory.

"I'm guessing," I said, "that your friends will find a way out of their predicament. That's fine by me. Maybe they'll tell their story to some others. But as for you, I'm afraid we are going to spend some time together. Now, put the following in your satellite navigation and let's go."

He programmed the GPS and we set off, ostensibly heading for somewhere near Manchester Airport. We wouldn't get that far though. I'd set my own GPS and already chosen the spot where the car would stop and we would carry on using alternative transport. We hit that point after only ten minutes at which point I told Mallory to stop, to pull up a small farm track and get out of the vehicle. He did as he was told and as I climbed out I stabbed him with a needle and he went down, out for the count.

I reactivated the bike and loaded it up with everything that I had bought with me or accumulated that night. It strained a little under the load, particularly when I climbed on board with Mallory strapped to me, but it moved off okay and we headed for our next stop. I wasn't planning on having Mallory on the boat but had chosen a much more suitable place for him. We arrived there after a difficult half hour journey and I deposited him behind the locked doorway that had long ago sealed off this old mine working. Injecting him again, I checked he was breathing okay and then went back home looking forward to relaxing over a nice glass of wine and thinking about how smoothly everything had gone so far. Tomorrow would be the start of a tough month, but tonight I could allow myself a little satisfaction, albeit tempered by the knowledge that I now had to add murderer to my list of crimes. I wouldn't lose too much sleep over it though.

Chapter Twenty-Eight

In absolutely no way whatsoever would I ever claim to be proud of what I did during my month with Mallory. There were times when I felt so sick about myself that I even contemplated cutting the project short. This was new territory for me and, although I saw where I wanted to be, getting there was a struggle. The practical side of it was easy enough. Mallory was incarcerated in a small cavern that was all that was left of a larger mine, long forgotten about, along a disused arm of the waterways. I'd noticed the spot on my travels and it was perfect for me as I could continue to cruise the boat whilst using the pod at nights to visit my captive. If I was moored near to people, I used remote controlled audio visual equipment to make it look like I was on board, or I reverted back to the drunken idiot routine. If I was moored alone, there was less need for these types of diversions but I made sure that I was seen on the boat whenever possible.

The real challenge was in keeping the images of Bridie and her ilk at the forefront of my mind whilst switching off from the false image that Mallory's sheer normality portrayed. He may have been far distant from his crimes, but they had their roots in him and only by targeting him could I get my message across. I kept a diary of Mallory's decline, partly for my own remembrance but also as a reminder to him if he ever recovered.

Day one was a day of introduction. Mallory was just coming around from the tranquiliser that I had dosed him with twenty-four hours previously and I was there to welcome him back to the land of the living. The jumpsuit that he wore was wet with sweat and urine. His face was a little swollen as a side effect of the tranquiliser, but other than that he looked every bit the part of the prosperous businessman. He groaned as he woke.

"Good evening, Mallory," I said to him, "I trust that you had a good sleep."

He looked around and tried to take in his surroundings and I watched as the events of the previous night came back to him. He tried to lift himself but his hands were tied so I eased him into a sitting position. Telling him that we needed to take care of some basic housekeeping first, I explained that I would untie him, allow him to have a wash and use the rudimentary toilet facilities that I had prepared for him. After that, he could put on the clean clothes that I had bought for him and have a bite to eat. He nodded to acknowledge that he understood.

"Please don't try and be clever," I said, "you remember what happened to your friend last night."

Once he was dressed and tidied up, I retied his hands and feet and sat him on a camping chair that I'd left there previously. It wasn't the most secure of anchors but it had been portable and I had been able to chain it tightly to some of the old mining machinery that had been abandoned underground.

"Now," I explained, "this is what is going to happen. You are my prisoner here and will be for a little while. During your stay with me, you will be fed and watered and allowed clean clothes. Other than that though, you will sit in the darkness and be forced to think about your way of life. When I consider your sentence to be finished then you will be returned back to your family and I will disappear. Is that clear?"

He nodded.

"Good, then let's begin." I opened a small pouch on my belt and first removed a pair of latex gloves, sliding these tightly onto my hands in front of his face. The fear in his eyes was tangible. Next, I removed the apparatus that I had acquired on one of my visits to the less fortunate, and laid it out in front of me.

"Of course," I said, "it might have made more sense to have used new gear, but then again, how many of your clients have that choice to make? I hope for both our sakes that these bits and pieces are at least free of the deadlier diseases."

He watched as I mixed a powder he obviously recognised and heated it over a candle. Then I approached him with the hypodermic and gave him a shrug that said, struggle and it'll only hurt the more. He understood and I was able to hold his arm down and draw out the required amount of blood. I drew up the heroine into the syringe and returned to Mallory, giving him the first dose of what would prove to be quite a few. As the drug took hold his eyes rolled back in his head and he groaned with a pleasure that he tried very hard to contain. He slumped forward in the chair and I laid him out on the floor.

"Goodnight," I whispered as I left him.

After a week of visiting Mallory twice a day, he was beginning to crack. I decided to ease up a little on his suffering and bought him a battery powered radio that I sat in the corner of his cell tuned to Radio Four. It might bring him some relief. It might also give him the opportunity to hear the first news reports about his disappearance. The family were very worried, naturally, and the police were actively seeking any leads, having spotted his car only once before it had disappeared. This had been the first of the favours Jean had done for me in alerting some people she knew about an abandoned Range Rover with the keys left in the ignition. I knew I didn't have to worry about it being found in one piece.

We talked more than usual during that second week. Or at least I spoke to Mallory more. Each night, before giving him his medicine, I described some of the people who I had met on my travels and how his business had messed them up. They had been remarkably frank with me a lot of the time and I, in turn, held nothing back from Mallory.

"This is the story of Macca," I told him, "I met him in Manchester although he was a Scouser, judging by his accent. He could remember quite a bit about the days before, which was a surprise. He had been a grade A student and was waiting to take up a place at one of the top universities when he'd first met up with some of your people. He might have been book smart but he was a little naïve about the wider world and had had little contact with the darker side of life. He'd been excited to be picked up at a night club and taken back to the flat of a girl he met. He'd lost his virginity to her and was thinking all sorts of starry eyed things about love and marriage when she'd first produced the needles. He'd been terrified of course, but she was doe-eyed and he trusted her and he had his first taste of a high that he could not believe existed."

I paused and handed Mallory a bottle of water with a straw in, opening one for myself as I watched him gulp the liquid down as fast as he could.

"Then," I continued, "It was the old familiar story. She kept him coming back for the sex, and he shared her other passions because he didn't want to lose her. Then he found that the sex took second place and he was coming to visit her for a hit. It all happened very quickly. He stole all he could from his parents but they noticed and he walked out on them. He felt his morals disintegrate and before long he was sucking off strangers to get the money he needed for his fix. Imagine that, that could have been one of your kids. Still, it's only business isn't it?"

The stories were graphic and Macca's was one of the less disturbing. I felt like I might be getting through to Mallory. I'd researched him a little online and found an amusing nugget of information that I shared with him.

"I understand that you are something of a homophobe, Mr Mallory."

I explained about the article I'd seen with his name on it and tucked away inside a monthly newsletter from one of the more radical churches. It had railed against the depravity of those who indulge in promiscuous sex and most notably the queers who couldn't seem to get enough.

I let that one permeate into his sub-conscious and dosed him up for the night before returning to the boat.

By the end of week three, he was hooked. I visited twice daily and before I even had a chance to untie him to wash and use the toilet he was begging me for his fix. He was a pitiful sight and I wondered how much longer he would be in touch with his old self and understand why this was all happening. At the beginning of the fourth week I made him wait.

"I have a visitor for you," I said, smiling.

I escorted a blind-folded middle-aged man into the room, and removed the blindfold. He looked at Mallory and smiled.

"Your sort of thing?" I asked the stranger.

"Oh yes," he whispered, "I'm impressed. One hundred we said?"

I took the money and watched as the man went up to Mallory and licked his face. Mallory turned in disgust but the visitor only slapped him hard and pulled his head back around. He licked Mallory's lips and slipped a tongue cautiously into his mouth. Then he stood up in front of Mallory and undid his trousers.

"Hey, boyfriend," I said to Mallory, careful to avoid using his name, "you'd better comply or you never get a fix again. Understand? Oh, and make like you're loving it, after all, our friend is paying you well."

I turned away at that point but could hear what was happening. It was over fairly quickly and the visitor grunted in satisfaction. I injected Mallory and left with the stranger having put his blindfold on again. Just as I left, I threw the hundred pounds at Mallory.

"Your tip," I laughed.

It never ceases to amaze me the people who exist out there and the particular peccadilloes that they enjoy. It was easy to find the right person if you knew where to look and I'd even made money off the deal.

Chapter Twenty-Nine

I had the 1st November set as the date that I would return Mallory to his family. It had been tempting to stretch the experiment for a little longer and send him back as a Christmas present, but the den was starting to stink and I wasn't sure how much longer he would last out. Before returning him though, I had to complete what I had started. That final day with him still gives me the occasional sleepless night when I recall how I delivered the Coup De Gras.

An early frost made the going difficult on the way to the mine so I didn't arrive until a good half hour after I usually would have done. By that time Mallory was sweating profusely and shaking fit to break the chair he was in. He heard me arriving and I immediately noticed how he calmed down, looking at me with expectant eyes. Was this a day of simple relief or was there a hidden horror for him to face?

"Good news," I said to him, "this will probably be your last day here. I'm sure you're relieved, especially as you'll have heard that the police are scaling back their enquiries in the search for you."

I took out his fix and began to prepare it. Looking at him as I performed this ritual I struggled to see any semblance of the man who had sat there just one month ago. How much of his past life he still remembered, I couldn't be sure about? I'd made him into an addict and he had only one thing on his mind at that moment in time. I explained to him how things were going to be.

"I'm not sure how much of this you comprehend, but today I am going to ask you to pay for your accommodation and for this," I held up the teaspoon of heroine.

"Fact is," I continued, "that you would give me pretty much all your worldly goods to get this just now. But I don't want money. No. I want your remorse instead and I really can't gauge how remorseful you really feel and what the chances are of you going on the straight and narrow and paying back some of your dues."

I put the kit aside and took off my backpack, opening it to reveal an assortment of tools. He looked at them with horror.

"In the old days, they used to hang people for stealing just a loaf of bread. Then they eased back on the punishment a little and decided only to cut off the perpetrators hand. They still do this in Saudi I think. Now, when I think of what you've stolen, all those wasted lives that could have been so different, I wonder just where the correct punishment lies. So, here's the deal. I can leave you here for a week, with enough food and water to survive and then tell the police where you are. They come and get you, end of ordeal. Only, that means a week without your medicine."

He nodded, waiting for me to continue.

"Or, we do a swap. You give me your hands, that way you have a permanent reminder of what you were and what you stole, and I give you all of the medicine that you want and return you back home with a stash to last you a lifetime."

I let him think about my offer. It didn't take him long. Heaven only knows the depths of despair and agony that you have to plumb to make the decision that he made, but within ten minutes he said simply.

"Hands."

"Okay," I said, "but just to be sure, you're going to do the work yourself. It shouldn't hurt too much and I'll stop the bleeding after I've given you your fix."

I set up the circular saw and explained to him how he would get the job done most efficiently. It was battery powered so not as fast as he might have liked but I had fitted it with a very fine and very sharp blade.

"The first one will be the easy one," I told him, "then you will have to move quickly and use your arm to do the second one, like this."

I demonstrated the moves and checked that he understood. Tears streamed down his cheeks and he begged me for mercy through the filthy rag that was stuffed in his mouth, still stained with the semen of his mysterious visitor.

"There is no mercy," I told him, "this isn't about me. I want you to think about all those people I told you about and what they would want from you if they were in my position. This is an easy option so be grateful."

I looked away as he fell to his knees in front of the fast moving blade. For a second I thought he was going to cheat me and try and kill himself on it but then he placed his wrist on the flat metal bed and with a scream pushed the blade down. Having done the one, I was impressed with the speed with which he used his maimed arm to do the other. Clearly he was desperate to be free and knew that speed was his best release.

I stuck the needle in his arm and injected him with a slightly higher dose than normal. To my horror and lasting shame, he looked at me and, before drifting into unconsciousness, whispered "Thank you."

I sealed the wounds with a blowtorch that cauterised them and then applied a field dressing I'd come across somewhere that essentially glued everything together. The two hands lay by the power saw on the floor. I decided that I probably didn't need that piece of equipment again and so I left it where it was.

The following morning, I rang his wife. I kept the call short and gave her clear directions as to where he could be found. I knew that the police would be monitoring the call and trying to find me so I made the call very brief. Along with Mallory, whoever arrived to collect him would find a detailed manuscript of my diary and that would say more than I ever could to his family. How much she knew about where his money came from I couldn't say. Maybe she was an innocent party in the whole thing, or maybe she had an inkling but didn't want to pursue it. Either way, the document I left with Mallory and posted to their home as well to ensure that she saw it, would tell her everything that her husband was and how they might be able to atone a little for what they'd done.

Before I'd left Mallory, I'd put the largest calling card I'd made to date around his neck and photographed it twice; once, with the Righteous Correction legend showing, and once with the hundred or so names that I'd carved on the back. They were the names of every addict I had met. I sent the photos to the press via Jean, with the simple request that if they printed them they did so with the comment that I was after every top drug dealer in the country. I wasn't, but hopefully the message made some people think twice.

By the following New Year, I was astonished by Mallory's response to his ordeal. He had come clean to his family and the police after a painful period of detox, and had plea bargained a non-custodial sentence in return for more names and addresses than were already being pursued by the combined drugs forces across the country. As supplies ran dry, he campaigned for a more sympathetic approach to drug addicts and was in the process of starting a parliamentary campaign to allow addictive drugs to be supplied on the NHS to any who needed them. This would be more cost effective as the sources of the drugs were running out of outlets and the NHS could pay a reasonable sum for any supplies. Sometimes the people I worked with changed in a positive way. It wasn't always like that though.

I'd allowed myself a little celebration that Christmas and although the weather was crisp and snowy I'd been able to cruise around a little and go back to where it had all started and pass by that house on the canal side where things had been so promising. I don't think that heading back to my old home was my mistake. At the time, there was something nagging me though and I just couldn't shake the feeling that somewhere along the line, I had messed up. What it was, I simply couldn't put my finger on, but it had kept me awake certain nights and had been the only negative that had lingered with me through that Winter. If I could have seen it and understood it, I might possibly have been able to address it and maybe even correct it.

But whatever it was, it didn't come to me. The feeling remained and hung like a hazy shadow over me. That's why the knock on the door wasn't unexpected.

PART TWO

Chapter Thirty

It was just after midnight that they came. The knock on the door was firm but respectful, that's why I knew it wasn't a bunch of drunks messing about. When I opened the door, I looked out to see three uniformed police officers waiting on the towpath. My overnight bag was at my feet and I was as confident as I could be that there was nothing incriminating in sight.

"Zipoly Hardacre?" one of the officers asked.

"Yes."

"We'd like you to come with us please, we need you to answer some questions," he waved a warrant card in my face to which I gave the briefest of glances, "And can you make it as quick as you can because we're freezing our nuts off out here."

At that time of night and with a clear sky above that had bought with it a deep frost that had locked the boat into a field of ice, I understood why they were keen to get moving. Perhaps I should have asked for more information, and maybe my willingness to follow them might be taken as a sign of guilt later, but I wasn't going to argue. Leaning down, I picked up the bag and took the boat keys off their hook, then I climbed on deck and locked the place up. It was only secured with a padlock which I knew they could easily break off if they wanted to check inside. Not being overly familiar with police procedure, there was something a little unusual about their approach. Maybe they weren't so sure of their facts or maybe this was a completely unrelated matter. Wishful thinking on my part.

The boat was moored just below the bottom lock at Stone as I'd been to get water earlier. Adjacent to these moorings, beside the run-down but still standing scout hut, I could see three police cars parked in a line with their lights flashing, and in the distance another flurry of blue flashing lights. They led me to the middle car and I climbed in, resting my bag on my lap. The officer who followed me in and sat next to me looked at the bag.

"Nothing dangerous in there I trust, Sir," he asked.

I told him that they were just a few essentials that I might need, proper coffee, smoking gear, vape sticks and the like and I offered to show him the contents. He declined and the cars set off in convoy. At the edge of the car park the road narrowed to one lane and we slowed again as the second wave of police vehicles headed towards us. The drivers of our cars didn't stop, but instead mounted the grass verge and drove up and over a recreational field to emerge behind the other vehicles. Again, I was surprised. Then again, what did I know about the police other than the stuff I'd seen on television?

As we headed towards the motorway, the guy in the front passenger seat turned around to speak to me.

"Mr Hardacre, I need you to listen carefully to what I have to say."

I nodded my agreement.

"I know that some of this may seem a little unconventional," he continued, "but, if you have some inkling of why we are taking you in for questioning, I'm sure you will appreciate that this whole situation is somewhat unconventional."

I wasn't going to give anything away at that point, but I nodded again and listened.

"The place we're going to," he told me, "is a very high security facility. Because of that we can't risk you knowing its whereabouts. Now, I'm authorised to blindfold you, Taser you, inject you, or do whatever is necessary to ensure that you are unaware of your surroundings."

Was I really hearing this?

"But," he continued, "between you and I, there is a certain degree of respect that a lot of us feel for you, so I would like to offer you the easy option. I have a couple of tranquilisers here and a flask of whisky. If you want to go along that route, trust me, it will be easiest all round."

He handed me the pills and the flask and I hesitated only momentarily before deciding that I had nothing to lose and swallowed the pills. The whisky tasted good so I afforded myself an extra sip. Within minutes I was fast asleep.

I woke up in a starkly furnished room that reminded of me of my first halls at University. The lights were dim but as I swung around in the bed they obviously sensed my movement and, by the time I had stood up, the room was brightly lit by hidden fluorescent lights. The toilet was behind a screen in the far corner. Stumbling up and feeling the last of the effects of the whisky and tranquiliser, I relieved myself and tried to get my thoughts together. Clearly, this was a police cell, and I had arrived here asleep and been put to bed. I was wearing a comfortable but nondescript outfit of plain black jogging bottoms and t-shirt, so they must have undressed me as well. I was relieved that they hadn't removed the cord tie that held the trousers up. At least they trusted me to a degree.

As I went back to the bed, I saw a few of my essential possessions laid out in the bedside table, but the bag was nowhere to be seen and they had obviously cherry picked what they would let me have. There was an ashtray, so I presumed I was alright to have a smoke.

As I rolled and lit the cigarette, a key turned in the door and a policeman entered the room with a heavily laden breakfast tray. I raised my eyes at the sight.

"Morning Sir," he said, "Governor thought you might like this. Wish my missus could do a spread like this. Best breakfast I've seen in a long while."

And he was right. It was a full English with all the trimmings, toast and coffee and an assortment of spreads. What is it they say about the condemned man enjoying a hearty meal? I tucked in and polished the lot off a little quicker than I should have done. It was good, but I wasn't going to kid myself that this was to be expected every day. I relit the cigarette that I'd stubbed out when breakfast arrived and then lay on the bed to think about what was going on here. This was a prison cell and I was in some form of custody, but as yet, I didn't know the charges. I had no idea where in the country I was and there were some strange occurrences related to my capture that still needed clarifying. Still, I was alive and comfortable and the breakfast had been a pleasant bonus.

I heard noises outside and then another officer appeared, putting his head around the corner of the door and asking me to follow him. I did as I was told, pocketing a vape stick as I left.

He took me to an interview room and escorted me in, asking me to sit on a vinyl-padded utilitarian chair that he placed on one side of the central table. On the table was a familiar looking recording machine and a jug of coffee on a tray. Without asking, I poured myself a cup. Part of me was reassured by this scenario, as this was exactly how a police interview room seemed like it should be. The door had even had a standard government style sign with 'Interview Room 1' etched into it. It was comfortingly normal.

I sipped my coffee and watched the door. After about five minutes it opened and two men dressed in jeans and casual shirts entered the room. They shook my hand then sat down opposite me. Showing me their warrant cards they gave me their names, too nondescript for me to remember now, and then the older of the two spoke.

"First of all," he said, "I need to ask you if you want to be represented?"

I thought about it. What was the point? For now, I was happy on my own. I told them so.

"Okay," the second officer flicked the recording device on, muttering the mundane details of date, time, names and my refusal of representation, before looking across to his colleague who was obviously the senior of the two.

"Mr Hardacre," he began, "we need to talk to you about Righteous Correction. Does that term mean anything to you?"

I replied that it had a meaning to a lot of people and that it was something that had been bandied about in the media for a number of years. I explained what I interpreted it to be then waited.

"Thank you," he said, "Now do you want to be a little more specific about what it means to you personally?"

I sensed the tone in his voice and was desperate to know how much they knew. I didn't want to play their games though, so I sat back, drew on the vape stick and thought.

"I'll tell you what," I said confidently, "why don't we act like grownups here and save ourselves some time? Tell me what you have that puts me in the frame as being more than just a passing observer of this Righteous Correction phenomenon, then we can move forward. This isn't some second-rate cop show we're making and I hope that you know enough about me to know that I prefer to say things as they are. What have you got?"

They conferred with each other, left the room for a minute or two, then returned. the older of the two answered my question.

"If that's how you want to do it, that's fine by us."

He then detailed the list of crimes that had been attributed to Righteous Correction, explaining that up until now the perpetrator had been elusive. However, in the recent case of Mallory, there were two sources of evidence that pointed to a particular individual. The first, was a pattern of internet searches around Mallory that had been monitored for its peculiarity.

"You see," he said, "these days, internet traffic is monitored by various agencies and anomalies are flagged up. Most of the time they turn out to be dead ends, but sometimes they form the basis of a bigger picture. In this case, Mallory, as no more than a fairly successful business man, as he was once thought to be, would have yielded few hits and not really gained much attention. Over the months before his incarceration, we tracked an individual looking into some strange aspects of his life. That person even returned to a church newsletter website and doubled its hit rate in one week."

"Go on," I said.

"Well, that same individual seems to have used different throw-away sim cards and internet hotspots to gain web access, a suspicious pattern in itself, but also one that caused us a lot of trouble in locating him. However, we were able to track the general locations from which these cards were purchased and used. We married these against patterns of movement on the ANPR records but couldn't get a match. Then some bright spark suggested that they might not be in a car. That led us to overlaying a grid of our references over various maps, expecting to find a pattern of train use, but to our surprise it was a different network that matched. Any idea what that might be?"

"The canals?" I laughed, replying with a genuine respect in my tone for the work they'd done.

"Indeed," he couldn't resist a hint of smugness as he replied, "the canals. Our perpetrator was using the canal system. Therefore, they were licensed. Therefore, we could check boat movements against Canal and River Trust records and against points where CCTV covered the waterways. Only one boat seemed to fit our profile. New Hope Arising. Your boat, Mr Hardacre."

There was nothing I could say. It seemed feasible and I was more embarrassed with myself for being so naïve as I was angry with them for figuring it out.

"You said there was a second source of evidence?" I asked.

"Yes," he answered, "not quite as solid or reliable a source as the first, but useful anyway. Probably inadmissible in court as well but still very damning. We were contacted anonymously by an individual who was concerned that he might be involved in a situation that might be personally embarrassing. He had made contact with somebody over the internet and arranged some sort of S&M meeting where he would take a dominant role. He had thought it was all consensual, if a little bizarre. But then he had seen the picture of Mallory."

"Yes," I whispered, "I had reservations about that whole thing from the start."

"Are you making some sort of confession, Mr Hardacre?" he asked.

And that was that. They asked their questions and I answered as plainly as I could. I only volunteered responses to their enquiries and was pleased that a few incidents had been overlooked. Still, the evidence was damning enough. I was confessing to multiple crimes, each of which carried a hefty prison sentence. I couldn't lie. The truth was important to me and all I could do was to fall into the arms of that justice system that I still believed in and hope that it was lenient.

We finished the interviews at the end of the day and I returned to my cell. They'd left the book that I had packed in my bag and I wasn't going anywhere, so I made myself a cup of tea and settled down to a few hours of escape in the arms of Mr Pickwick.

Chapter Thirty-One

The following morning, I was surprised to receive another decent breakfast. I made the most of it this time, fully expecting that I would be transferred later that day to a more mainstream detention facility. I'd slept quite well, but now, as I was facing the reality of the morning, even the breakfast failed to bring me much joy. More than six years had passed since the injustice of the death of my family had started me on this journey. It was now coming to an end. I had done what I'd felt led to do and had tried in every way possible to avoid being caught. But that had been a fool's hope I now realised. All I could do now was wait on the outcome of events. I would have my fifteen minutes of fame and my day in court, but then I would have the years of incarceration to follow. Had it been worth it? I couldn't say.

By lunchtime, I still hadn't been collected but a tray of sandwiches had appeared, after which, I showered, changed my clothes and tried to lose myself in the rambling adventures of Pickwick and his pals. But even Dickens couldn't ease the growing sense of restlessness that hung over me. The door finally opened at half-past-two, when an extraordinarily well-dressed man walked into the room.

"I've already told them, I don't want a brief," I said to him.

"Oh, come now, Mr Hardacre," he replied jovially, "stylish clothes do not a lawyer make."

He introduced himself as Anthony Chow. Sir Anthony Chow to be precise. I looked a little more closely at his features and could just about see the oriental ancestry around his eyes. It must have been a number of generations back.

"Please, gather your things and come with me," he said, "we need to move out."

I grabbed my belongings, followed him along the corridor, past the interview room towards what looked like a conventional reception desk. He nodded to the desk sergeant who raised the gate in the desktop to let us through. We went into the first suite of offices then we stopped and

Chow withdrew a key card from his pocket, inserting it into a box beside a bookcase containing multiple old and battered lever arch files. The bookcase slid to one side and we entered a brightly lit passage. Now I was intrigued.

"Everything you see now," Chow explained as we started the long walk down this narrow walkway, "is, needless to say, highly restricted. Don't even think about taking mental notes or planning how this will help your defence. Some people walk through that door and leave shortly after. Some never get that chance."

"Which sort am I?" I asked.

"I'm afraid that I must leave that question dangling," he said with a smile, "but please, try to relax. All will be made clear soon."

We turned off the main run and into another passage that had a number of closed doors along its length and which terminated in a lift. He pressed the call button and the doors opened. He beckoned me into the lift, followed me in, then typed in a sequence of numbers on a small keypad situated where floor numbers would normally be found. The doors closed and the lift began to descend.

When we stopped and the doors opened I looked out into what could have been any modern, open plan office space anywhere in the country. Workspaces with monitors atop and keen employees hard at work making the only noise in the otherwise silent environment. A few of the staff looked up and nodded at Sir Anthony but most remained fixed on what they were doing.

"I hope you don't mind me saying," I whispered to Chow, "but this all seems a little bit unreal, a little bit too James Bond, if you know what I mean."

He smiled at me, obviously having heard the same before.

"What you need to remember," he said, "is that quite often fact and fiction can be hard to distinguish one from the other. Fleming got his inspiration from somewhere I'm sure."

"And you're for real?" I asked, "I mean, you could have come straight off the page of a Le Carre. You don't mind me being so blunt?"

"Absolutely not,. he smiled as he answered, "Indeed, I should thank you for the compliment. I acknowledge the fact that we occupy very different realms up there in the wider world. What you see with me is, whatever you may think, exactly what you get. But don't let your preconceptions twist your thinking. We are all parts of one great nation and each of us plays our part. I enjoy certain privileges I know, but with them come some restrictions."

"Enough of the chit-chat", he said as we halted beside a heavy oak door which opened for us, "please, come into my parlour."

Chow's office was sumptuous in a classic English style. We walked across the thick carpet and stopped at a long bar where Chow poured us each a large measure of whisky from a decanter, clinking ice cubes into the crystal glasses.

"One of our great levellers," he said as he passed me a glass and raised his own, "good old alcohol. I like to think it's one of the things that puts the Great into Great Britain, although I appreciate you may be more of a pint man than a single malt person."

"Now, who's being prejudiced," I asked as I swirled the brown liquid, sniffed it and announced to his surprise, "Fitzpatrick 'Monarch of the Glen', 1946. A very rare tipple and believed to be down to just a handful of crates across the globe."

"Touché," he said, "Now, please, sit down, we have a lot to talk about."

I sat opposite him as he settled in his own chair, bending forward and putting on reading glasses before opening a thickly packed, buff file that lay before him.

"We can dispense with all the personal details," he began, "as we seem to have all that we need and you already know the stuff yourself. Although we are all a little intrigued by the name. Tell me, where does Zipoly come from."

I explained about my parents and the derivation of my name from a drunken dunking into a Scrabble bag.

"Aha!", he exclaimed, "I shall look forward to telling the others. How interesting. I was a little concerned myself that it may have been one of those attention seeking attempts by pop stars or benefit claimants that have given us the hideous Pixies and Chantelles of this world, but Scrabble. How very interesting."

"Now to business," he continued, "You are currently sitting in a secret bunker in a secret location somewhere in England. It is the headquarters of an organisation called ORB. The name is a recent development as we were originally the New Franciscans, but we had to change that when the initials NF took on an alternative meaning. Saint Francis as you may or may not know is the patron saint of justice. That should explain a little about what we do here."

"And ORB?" I asked.

"The Order for Restoring Balance," he replied, "Not quite as subtle, nor indeed as stylish, as the Franciscan reference but better than some of those crazy utility names one has nowadays."

He explained to me that the order had been in existence for many centuries and that it was an officially unofficial part of the British state and existed in a protected no-man's land. It had a singular duty, which was to correct imbalances in justice.

"Which is why I'm here," I said.

"Exactly. We've been watching you from your early days. We've even given you a little help along the way. But more of that later. Unfortunately, the police have also been trying to track you down. And were almost successful."

"Almost?" I asked.

"Yes, almost," he answered, pausing to work out where best to begin the explanation, "you see, those gentlemen who arrived to bring you into custody were not conventional police officers. I won't bore you with the details, suffice it to say that they work at our bidding. We'd caught wind of the regular force wanting to take you in. The truth of the matter is that all of the evidence that you were presented with in our interview is what the mainstream police actually have. And those two officers who interviewed you are genuine police officers who work between our departments. However, we couldn't allow you to simply disappear into the criminal justice system, so we pre-empted their move and we took you into custody instead."

That explained why the procedures had felt a bit unusual and why we had raced away from the oncoming cars in Stone.

"We wanted to be able to get to know you a little better and to see if we could be of mutual assistance. We can't do that once they start to process you in the system, too many questions start to get asked. Especially in the more unusual cases like yours."

"Your work is extremely interesting," he continued, "inspired and creative, yet also incredibly discrete. The carved 'Righteous Correction' plaques are a little crude and perhaps too vain, I feel, but the tools you've developed and the justice that you have designed is quite impressive. It's a lot like what we do in ORB, although on a much smaller scale. I, in particular, like the notion of you being a boater. In this age of technology and high-speed everything, the canals remain a natural and majestic part of our heritage. And when seeking a new generation vigilante, very much the least likely place anyone would expect to find one. Although, we must remember, that was a contributor to your downfall too."

I agreed and he proceeded to tell me what he proposed.

"We have a number of paths we can take from here. Firstly, you can leave now and enter the official system and let the criminal justice process do its thing. It's your choice. We estimate that you will receive a sentence of between fifteen and twenty years, although you are likely to be a free man in ten. That is, if you are found guilty. Juries can be a tad fickle when it comes to emotive cases like yours."

I concurred with his estimate of the likely sentence facing me, but I had to ask, "Or?"

"Or, you can come and work with us. But you may feel that that bears a higher price than the ten years in prison."

"That's if I go to prison," I countered, "You yourself are aware of the possibility of my acquittal at the hands of a jury of my peers. I could take the risk."

"That's very true," he replied, "and, truth be told, I think you have a higher likelihood than many of such an outcome, but there is a problem with that third way."

"Which is?" I asked.

"Us," he leant closer to me as he answered, "Unfortunately, we would not be able to permit such an outcome. In our very different ways, we both operate to plug the gap where justice fails. Were you to be acquitted of crimes that you yourself have confessed to carrying out, all because the general public wanted to make a hero of you, we would have to act against you. Not only does such a situation make a mockery of the legal framework of the nation, but it would also set an unacceptable precedent. The floodgates would be opened to anyone who wanted a crack at being a vigilante. We've come too far from that to return. You couldn't be allowed to walk free."

He explained that, should I decide to join ORB, that decision would be irrevocable, as it would mean the death of Zipoly Hardacre. Were any information to leak out about his connection with 'Righteous Correction', as it very likely might, it would only ever remain rumour and speculation. They couldn't prevent that happening and, there were some benefits to such an outcome as it would bring about an acceptable closure for all concerned.

Having been killed off, I would be reborn with several new identities, as well as a very different physical appearance, and so would become a clandestine operative working on The Order's own brand of righteous correction but with the back-up of their potentially infinite resources.

Should I choose to take this route, the RC plaques, and any other form of calling card, would have to go as I would become an anonymous part of a complex machine.

"Before you decide," Chow concluded, "we want you to take a few days to relax, get a better feel for The Order and enjoy some free time before the momentous changes ahead. I have assigned you a companion to look after you while you are here. Bit of a complex character but he should help you to unwind."

He picked up a phone on his desk and spoke quietly to somebody on the other end of the line. A few minutes later, there was a knock at his office door and a young guy with ginger hair, a loose fitting, short-sleeved, nylon shirt and sandals came bumbling into the room.

"James," Sir Anthony said, "this is Mr Hardacre. He'll be with us for a few days so can you please show him around. He'll be staying in the King Henry suite. Any luggage has already been sent there."

"Think carefully about our offer," he turned back to me and we shook hands, "and believe me when I say that we would very much like you to be a part of our team."

I was escorted out of the room and away into the bowels of the complex by a very excited James who said that it was an honour to meet me and that he felt like he already knew me quite well as he had worked to support some of my missions. It transpired that despite his youthful looks and generally nerdy demeanour, James had a lot of hidden talents and was a lot more than what he appeared to be on the surface. He certainly helped me to have a good time whilst I was having my couple of day's rest in this bizarre subterranean world.

The complex was a self-contained town in its own right, fully equipped with everything that its inhabitants could need. Aside from traditionally cobbled streets of terraced houses for accommodation, there were also several restaurants, numerous office units and a fully functioning high street complete with the usual familiar names. The centre of the town seemed to radiate out from a market square, off which were several paths leading deeper into the complex. The only giveaway that this was anything other than a normal town, was the absence of traffic. People walked everywhere.

James informed me that I had a free pass to all the facilities that were available, which included a spa and leisure centre, complete with Olympic-sized swimming pool, a bowling alley and a cinema. Of course, there was also a perfectly recreated pub at the centre of the square and, on seeing this, I instinctively knew that, whatever was going to happen in the future I'd be able to have a good time here at ORB's expense.

On that first night, I had my fill of rib-eye steak at the pub, washed down with several pints of a very special Porter that I had only come across once before on draught. James was good company and his excitement was infectious, although as the hours passed, I craved a little more solitude and a bit of a break from his rabbiting. He escorted me to the cinema, arranged for someone to guide me back to my accommodation after the show, then he left me for the night.

Settling down in the luxurious seats of this movie theatre, I had to chuckle at what I was about to watch and wondered whether any planning had gone into the fact that they were showing Batman.

Chapter Thirty-Two

When James and I met over breakfast the following morning, he told me a little bit more about himself and how he had come to be where he now was. He was still only in his early twenties but had been with ORB for five years, joining them when he was only sixteen.

"I'm the youngest person they've ever recruited," he told me, obviously proud of the fact, "but then again, I'm probably not their usual fare."

He explained how he been orphaned as an infant and been brought up in a number of children's homes, where he had escaped the constant threat of bullying by burying himself in study.

"I think they all thought I had some special talents from the moment that I first started playing with electronics. I could just about cope with the other things they taught me at school, but when it came to electronics and the physics that surrounded it I was ahead of my teachers before I could properly do joined-up writing. I just love the subject and can't get enough. It's the same with maths and chemistry to a degree, it's like I can see the worlds that the numbers and theories represent, and I understand it better than I understand how to get along at a party."

He told me how he had been identified as some sort of science prodigy and given the opportunity to fast-track through the education system, gaining a double-first from Oxford in electronics and physics just after his fourteenth birthday.

"I stayed at the University for another couple of years doing research and trying to develop a few broader life skills, then on my sixteenth birthday, Sir Anthony paid me a visit and offered me the chance to work here."

He paused and slurped noisily at the milkshake he'd insisted his breakfast must be accompanied by.

"As soon as I saw the place, I knew it was for me," he continued, oblivious to the quantity of drink spilled down his shirt, "I didn't quite grasp the ethos surrounding ORB, and still struggle a little with it today, but that didn't really matter. They gave me free reign to explore my own projects and to come up with solutions to problems that I'd never really thought about before. That's why I'm still here. Every day is a dream to me. And it's great now that I'm starting to be a little bit more social as well. What isn't there not to love about the place?"

The more he spoke about ORB, the more his enthusiasm rubbed off on me, but I wasn't so gullible as to accept everything he said on face value. They'd clearly chosen him to show me the operation for a reason, but nonetheless, he did a good job of selling the deal.

"When we were in the office," I asked, "Sir Anthony said something about you knowing me well and being my minder. What did he mean by that?"

"Yes, that's right," he replied, "I've been assigned to you for the past few years. Ever since the Rodgers affair. That's when ORB first tracked you down and started to support you."

"Support me?" I asked.

"Oh yeah, I've been helping you out a bit," he smiled as he realised the enormity of what he was telling me, "I'm a big fan of yours. Some of the things you've done are so cool and the things you've made to help you along are really interesting. A bit primitive in the execution but right up there when it comes to imagination. We've learnt some tricks from you, particularly in using remote units based on nature. You'll see some of the stuff we've come up with if you join us."

He went on to tell me that ORB had first picked me up when I'd started getting the surveillance feeds from Rodgers' temple, and since then had intervened a few times to cover up some of my errors. When he told me how they'd done this, I realised how much I still had to learn about avoiding detection and I felt a bit stupid. He wasn't patronising about it though. If anything, he seemed to look up to me and be impressed by my invisibility.

"The police had no idea," he told me, "and we didn't need to do anything too drastic to keep you undercover. That was until the last case. They told you, I guess, how the official forces had identified you? Easy mistake to make. You get so bogged down in the details of shifting ISP providers, changing computers, ditching mobiles etc., that you forget to think about the bigger picture and what can be deduced from what's happening around the person you're tracking. Still, we managed to stay one step ahead, but it was a close call. I think you saw the others coming just as we got you away didn't you?"

I related the events of that night and confirmed what he had heard. As far as the official channels were concerned, I was currently in detention, even if there was a little confusion and a degree of frustration in some police departments concerning just who was holding me.

We finished breakfast and James led me out to continue our tour of the complex. Like most of the people we passed, we'd chosen to walk everywhere, although the option of a personal, electric vehicle was available to celebrity visitors like myself.

"You don't really see many people use the vehicles," James explained, "partly, because the distances aren't that great, but mainly because the Council prefer to see people on foot. It's a sort of unwritten rule. Same as the food we eat. It's all monitored and they might have a quiet word if you're spending too much time at the fast-food places. I don't mind. I'd be like a whale if I had it my own way!"

Walking was perfect for me. It meant that I could properly take in what I was seeing. And it meant that I could stop every so often to gaze up at the artificial sky and see if I could find some chink in its too-perfect construction. Needless to say, I couldn't, nor could I find fault with the houses, the streets and the tree-lined avenues that were a faultless facsimile of a small English town. Of course, everyone knew it was an illusion, but it was easy to forget at times that we were hundreds of feet below ground.

We had lunch at a well-known burger restaurant, the franchise of which had been negotiated long before that same chain had arrived on most of the UK's high streets, then we stopped off at the library where I was able to acquire something a little easier to read than my current fair, along with a town map.

To James, this all seemed perfectly normal.

"In Summer," he told me, obviously aware of my fascination with the sky, "they set it so that we get the best of the sunshine and of course, it never rains. We can do rain if we have to, and snow even, but funnily enough, nobody has ever asked for either of them."

The artificial sky began to darken a little and I realised that the best part of the day was now over. Exhausted, I asked James to lead me back to my suite where I parted company with him and flopped down on the sofa. Resisting the temptation to close my eyes and drift off to sleep, I forced myself to make the most of the free hospitality that ORB were offering me and opened the food menu on the television screen. The choice was faux-normality, with multiple takeaway restaurants offering very comprehensive menus. I knew, because James had told me, that the reality was that this food came from one source, but that didn't really bother me. How many times in the past had I ordered 'authentic Italian pizzas' that had been delivered to me from a nearby industrial estate?

The choice was a little overwhelming, but in the end I opted for a Chinese which I ordered with a few clicks of the remote, adding some beers to the order and making a note of the expected delivery time. It arrived within thirty seconds of that time and was delivered to me by the Concierge along with the necessary crockery and cutlery. I'm sure that if I'd asked him to serve it to me as well, he would have obliged.

After eating and finishing off the beers, followed by a few brandies, I tried to start on the new book I'd got, but just couldn't get into it. Turning the television on instead, I watched the news and fell asleep to the sound of all that was happening out there in a world that I currently felt so far detached from.

By the time that James arrived the following day, I had showered and shaved, picked out a very comfortable outfit from the well-stocked wardrobes and worked my way through a very pleasant and healthy breakfast that had been placed outside my door at exactly the time I'd specified. I'd also had time to sit down and start writing down some of the questions I still had to ask him. How many he could answer, I wasn't sure. How many he would answer truthfully, I was even less sure of.

"Do you ever get away from here?" I asked as we headed off to his workplace, which was our chosen destination for the day.

"Sometimes," he answered, "although I don't really like to be away too much. Most of the people here have the usual five week's holiday that you'd get on the surface, but there are restrictions about where they can go."

He explained that there were a few people who were outside operatives, which is what I would be if I joined, and they spent most of their time in the real world and lived a pretty much normal life up there. Aside from this elite group, there were the people who were permanently stationed down here, like himself, who fully understood that they had broken contact with the outside world.

"There's a guy though," he continued, "who you've probably heard of. Jason King, the internet billionaire."

I knew of Jason King. The man who had been in the right place at the right time when social media technology took off and who was amongst the richest men on the planet. He was also the man who had changed his name when he had taken over one of the smallest nations in the UN and become the constitutional monarch of a country in the South Pacific. He'd done it all amicably and he was no colonialist. The country had never been richer and he had developed the tourist trade to fund one of the best educational and healthcare systems in the world. He'd explained at the time that he had always had a hankering to be a king, but he had no intention of abusing that power in any way.

"Well, King's domain is made up of a few islands, one of which he lives on and keeps a bit private," James explained, "Anyone who works for ORB has exclusive access to that island. It's a proper holiday out there in the fresh air and the levels of luxury are incredible, but it's the only place we're allowed to go. It's not really my cup of tea but I've been a few times."

"And what about people that you're close to?" I asked, "Is there any way to stay in touch with family and friends who maybe don't know about ORB?"

He thought for a while about this one and what to tell me, then he just shrugged and said, "We don't have outside contacts."

I understood from his point of view that this wasn't a major problem, but I pushed the point, asking about those people, like myself who'd joined after a more involved life in the outside world.

"You need to realise," he answered, choosing his words very carefully, "it's as Sir Anthony said. When you join ORB, you don't just part from your old life, you completely separate. I guess that's the biggest part of the decision that you have to make, but it is a total and irreversible separation."

It was as I thought and this, I knew, was going to be the hardest part for me. I didn't have many people out there who were what I would call close. Fran's family had drifted away and our contact was sporadic. The friends and people I met in my work and in my travelling were no more than passing acquaintances. But Jean had become something special to me. I was beginning to understand that the choice would need to come down to either Jean or ORB and that the deadline for that choice was looming.

Chapter Thirty-Three

Security was tighter and more visible at the entrance to the laboratory complex than I'd experienced anywhere else in that strange underground town. Armed guards stood either side of a narrow entrance gate that also doubled up as a metal detector. James passed swiftly through but I was subject to a number of detailed and, at times, embarrassing checks before I was allowed to follow. We joined up at the end of the entrance passageway and walked together into what looked like a large warehouse. On either side of a central walkway, several rows of converted shipping containers were stacked three high. Each had a separate stairway leading to a locked door behind which was a laboratory.

"We each have our own space," James explained, "where we work on our own projects. We all do different things, although we occasionally join forces and work together on anything that might crop up as an emergency or on one of the bigger experiments."

We entered his laboratory, which was the sort of chaotic space I'd imagined it to be. The entire surface of his desk was scattered with papers and there were numerous additional stacks of documents randomly dotted around the floor. At the far end there was a long bench. He beckoned me to follow him to it, his eyes lighting up with the excitement at being able to share with me some of the things he was working on.

"My field of research", he told me, "is mainly based on physics, but I've had to teach myself a lot of chemistry as well. I've got two real special areas of interest, but they're both sort of linked. Take a look at this."

He picked up a small, black sphere off the bench and blew away a few specks of dust that he saw on the surface. Without warning he threw it towards me.

"Catch," he shouted.

I wasn't expecting it and before I'd had a chance to react I saw the ball move out of my reach. As my hand swept past it, I watched and waited for it to clatter to the floor, but it didn't make it that far. It stopped several inches short of the floor and just hovered there.

"Good, isn't it?" James beamed with pride.

I watched as he played with a band around his wrist and the black ball rose up again and made its way back to the desk, where it settled itself into a cradle that had obviously been made to hold it.

"That's one of my latest gadgets," James told me, "I know it's only small but it demonstrates the principals of what I'm working on with ion technology. It's a bit like your drones but you notice it has no visible means of elevation. It's all inside."

He tried to outline a little more of the technology to me, but I had to admit that it was over my head. It was something about manipulating the ions that surrounded any moving object to cause them to work with it to allow it to move, rather than working against it as nature intended.

"My other work is similar," he continued, "but nowhere near fruition yet. If I can crack it, the world will never be the same again. So far, I've only been able to make it work theoretically and I guess I'm a long way from home with it, but essentially I'm looking at being able to create anti-gravity. Can you imagine what that would be like ?!"

He revealed to me that one of the reasons he'd been assigned as my mentor was because of the work that I had done with flying objects and in improving means of storing electrical power. But he also made it clear to me that I was a long way behind anything they had going on down here.

"Don't feel bad about it," he said, "it's like I told you before. You have the imagination and can see the bigger picture, whereas the geeks, like me, have the knowledge to make things happen. I hope you decide to stay with ORB, because we could do some amazing things together."

I don't know whether I felt flattered or humiliated, but James was such a thoroughly innocent and nice guy that it was hard to take any sort of offence. And to be fair, he did have a valid point. He spent the next half hour showing me some more of his work and a few other quirky prototypes that he'd built. Then his watch bleeped and he looked down to read the message that scrolled across its screen.

"They want to see you straightaway," he informed me, "It looks like that's it for you and me for now. I hope we meet again soon."

He settled himself at his desk, opened a folder of papers that were covered with complex equations and began to study them. I took the hint and headed to the laboratory door. As I let myself out, I thought I heard James say something to me but, looking back, I realised that he had slipped into his parallel universe and was muttering away to himself. I closed the door quietly.

On leaving the lab area, I was escorted by one of the guards back through the complex and into another anonymous office decorated in the same classic manner as Chow's had been.

"Help yourself to a drink," the guard told me, indicating a bar area full of every imaginable type of liquid refreshment a man could ever desire, "They will be along shortly, they're just tied up for a few minutes with a minor problem."

Deciding that it would be wise to keep my wits about me, I spurned the temptation of the alcohol and played around with the complicated hot drinks machine at the far end of the bar, somehow managing to make myself a simple coffee. As I drank this I looked around the room, certain that I was being monitored but nonetheless fascinated by everything I could see. Like Chow's office, there was a gilt-framed portrait of the Queen and another of the current Prime Minister, both of which dominated the walls. The other pictures seemed more personal to this room and I went to check them out. There were numerous photographs or reproductions of portraits, depicting the great and good through the ages, starting with the Saints. There were also a number of prints of classic paintings, the largest of which was undeniably a Lowry complete with eponymous matchstick men. My eyes had just caught site of a canal scene when the door opened and two men entered the room. One of them was a good six and a half foot tall and as slim as a rake, whilst the other was a short, barrel of man.

"Sorry to have kept you," the taller one said in an accent that was pure home counties, "some blighter's gone and taken a pot-shot at the PM. It's chaos up there."

He introduced himself simply as Batchcliffe. I took this to mean that he was Lord Batchcliffe and replied appropriately.

"Oh, don't let's stand on ceremony," he said amiably, "you can leave the deference for another time. We're all equal down here."

"And I'm Anderson," the other man spoke up in a broad Lancashire accent, "Tom Anderson. And just that, none of your Sir or My Lord to me if you please. Mister if it's a formal do, but for now, Tom will be fine."

Although the Lord was a new face to me, I knew a little about Tom Anderson and had seen his face many times on the television or in the papers. He had a business empire that spanned retail, manufacturing and various other sectors and was currently one of wealthiest men in Britain. Whilst Batchcliffe was clearly top drawer, old money, Anderson I knew was somebody who had grown up on a council estate. Two different characters one could hardly imagine in the same room together.

"I trust that you've been well looked after over the past few days:" Batchcliffe beckoned me to sit down, "You've been with James haven't you? Brilliant lad. So pleased we took him under our wing."

I replied that yes, I had been with James and that he had made sure that I had a good time and that I'd seen all I needed to of the place.

"Well, what do you think then lad?" Anderson asked as he stood behind me and placed his hand on my shoulder, "Not what you'd expect to see in a damned great rabbit warren is it?"

"You're right there," I answered, "The whole thing still seems a bit unreal, but I'm sort of coming around to it. I just can't believe that this place exists under the normality of the world up there. Talking of which, is the Prime Minister okay?"

"He's fine," Batchcliffe answered, smiling, "incompetent fool that had a go at him couldn't have hit a tree if he was standing next to it. We think he was working on his own but you can never be too careful can you."

The two men poured themselves drinks and added a whisky that they gave to me without my asking, then they sat opposite me and I knew that the introductions were over.

"So," Anderson took the lead in the conversation, "have you been able to make a decision? We really do need to know now, but we have a little time if you still have any further questions."

I took a long drink of the whisky and relaxed as it burned its way down my throat.

"I think I'm there," I said, "but I just have a couple of final questions if that's okay. The first of which is, I guess, the big one. If I join ORB then how does the new identity thing work, or more precisely, what happens to what is now me?"

"That's the thing uppermost with all our recruits," Batchcliffe answered, "and understandably so. We spend so much of our lives building our identity and becoming the people we are and then somebody asks us to give it all up."

He paused and looked across to Anderson to check he was okay to carry on and field this question alone. Anderson nodded.

"This then," he continued, "is pretty much how it works. Zipoly

Hardacre will die. We think that a boat fire will be best cover, as that's the most plausible and the easiest for us to manage. He'll be buried, cremated, whatever, and all his worldly affairs will be tidied up. That's part one. We can do a few extra bits and pieces at your request but generally we manage the whole thing as you need to move on. Whilst all that is happening up there, we work with you down here on your new identity. I have to tell you though that the process is more than just new papers. You will have a new physical appearance. Our surgeons will work with you to minimise the changes needed, and will focus on key points of identity. When they're finished, nobody will recognise the new you. Once you are over that hurdle, you will spend three months down here getting to know your three new identities, losing all traces of the old person and, most importantly, training with us."

"Three identities?" I asked.

"Yes," he answered, "three new identities. Two male and one female. Don't worry though, we don't go that far with the surgery. You'll have a primary male identity with an alter ego that you can move to if there are problems. We can also keep supplying you with new identities as you require. The female ID may never need to be used, but we find it's a useful diversion and it can generate a lot of misinformation for the very minimal expense of a decent wig and some simple prosthetics."

"There is one extra thing that you need to be made aware of," Anderson took over the conversation now, "and that is that your DNA will be tweaked a little bit. It won't change anything about you, but we've found this way of putting a little marker on it so that the current tests don't work. All of our operatives have had it done and none of them have grown two heads yet. It just means that if things go wrong and a body turns up it can never be identified as somebody who has already been long dead and buried."

"And while we're on this subject," he continued, "I know your next question is going to be about family and friends. The blunt answer to which is, no, they can't even get a hint that you are still about. In your case, I think the concern will be Ms Carter, if I'm not mistaken. Well, even if your paths cross accidently, you cannot let her know you are still alive. Please, don't underestimate this side of things. Zipoly will be dead and we will do everything necessary to ensure that nobody knows otherwise. Okay?"

I appreciated Anderson's candid intervention. Yes, Jean was the fly in the ointment, but at least I now knew where I stood with that.

"What about the boat?" I asked, "Can I still live on the canals?"

Batchcliffe was straight in with his answer: "My dear boy, of course you can. That's part of the reason you're here. We want you there on the water and we want to have an operative who lives that lifestyle. Who'd suspect a boater of being able to do what you've already done? Think of how long you evaded the police. And with our help, we can keep you totally anonymous. No, the boat is a condition from our side. But we will help modify your current vessel I'm sure."

They explained that they had already moved the boat away from Stone using an operative who was taking on the role of one of my friends helping me out while I was forced to be away. They'd done this to keep it protected and to stop the police delving too deeply into its secrets.

"For the fire," Anderson continued, "we have a dummy shell of a matching craft that we will use. Seems pointless to get rid of your actual boat. Meanwhile we'll bring that here and work on modifying it whilst you have your own remodelling done."

We bandied about a few other minor points but after another couple of whiskies I could tell that I needed to give them a decision and couldn't keep prevaricating. Losing Jean would be the hardest part. Losing my old identity wasn't so much of a problem, but I did regret the end of the Righteous Correction tags. The ethics didn't concern me as it seemed they were only doing what I had set out to do alone but in an infinitely more professional way. As to being off the radar, I had no issue with that and especially as I would still be out there as a bloke living on a boat. I think it was that that made my mind up for me. Love never lasted and only caused heartache in the end. The waterways however had given me a lot of peace over the years.

"I'll do it," I told them, "Zipoly was a stupid name anyway!"

Chapter Thirty-Four

When I woke up after the surgery it took me a few moments to understand where I was. The antiseptic smell that filled the room reminded me that I was in a hospital, but when I tried to open my eyes they just wouldn't comply. I let out a small waking moan and felt a hand close over mine.

"Welcome back, Sir," a soft female voice whispered in my ear, "everything went just fine, but you need to take a few minutes to wake up properly. Have a sip of this."

I felt a straw placed against my lips and sucked thirstily at the sugary fluid. Whatever was in that drink went to work straight away and I felt the cobwebs in my mind clear immediately. After a few minutes, I relaxed, knowing that I had come through the first stage of my transition to becoming an ORB operative.

"The doctor will be along shortly," the voice beside me said, "meanwhile, don't panic about not seeing anything. Your eyes are bandaged. Doctor will fix this when he comes. Do you have any other discomfort?"

Surprisingly, I felt no pain whatsoever. I thought this might be due to the effect of drugs but when I started to stretch and feel my body I realised that it felt as it should. I was tired and I had the usual waking pangs of unused muscles, but nothing that hurt specifically.

"I'm fine," I told her, "I presume that the surgery was successful."

"Oh yes," she whispered, "very successful if you ask me. You're looking good."

It seemed a bit inappropriate at this stage that my carer wanted to flirt with me but I was encouraged by it nonetheless, as it meant that I must at least look fairly reasonable. She left me after making a few adjustments to the machine I heard whirring at my side. Whilst I waited for the Doctor, I came to terms with what this all meant. Zipoly Hardacre was no more. Presumably the death scene had been acted out and I was now awaiting a post-mortem in some fictitious mortuary, after which my sham funeral would go ahead. I thought of how Jean would be taking it all. She was tough enough to cope, I knew that much about her, but it was never going to be easy for either of us. I'd asked if there was any way that she could be included in what was happening but had let the subject drop when the ORB guys started to get a bit aggressive about the whole thing. Nevertheless, they sorted out my will and arranged to shift the money that I had stashed on the boat from Mallory, plus all the assets in my bank, straight over to Jean. The only proviso of this was that the Mallory money be used to support drugs rehabilitation charities.

The Boat Space business was bequeathed to Tony, along with the gift of a few redundant designs that ORB had on hold. Much of their work was massively advanced but was deliberately held back from the outside world as it might make their existence known. They also had certain vested interests who they had to pander to and so were restricted in what they were allowed to leak out. Despite this, they provided Boat Space, via assets 'retrieved' from my boat, with a number of useful designs that would help Tony keep the business growing. The most useful of these was a new form of solar panel that delivered a twelve-volt output at least ten times as powerful as current units. I was pleased that Zip might be remembered for this small contribution to boating and ORB didn't have an issue with this as it simply pre-empted the Chinese and stole a march on them that benefited UK manufacturing.

The door opened and a broad Scottish accent snapped me back to the moment.

"Good morning, Sir," it boomed, "glad to have you back with us and congratulations on making such swift progress. As the nurse has no doubt told you, everything is fixed and healed and you are a different person altogether. Just need to sort out the last part now. Let's have this blindfold off."

I felt his hands reach around the back of my head and fiddle with the tapes that held the bandage over my eyes. Fresh air washed over my eyelids as he removed it but I had a moments panic when I realised I still couldn't see.

"Nothing to worry about," the Doctor reassured me, "we had to stitch your eyelids together a wee bit. Give me a minute and I'll free them up for you. Be sure and open them slowly though."

I felt a fine scalpel brush across my eyelids which help me resist the urge to open my eyes until I was sure the Doctor was finished. When I felt safe,

I let my eyelids rise slowly and saw his hand shielding them from the light. Gradually he moved his hand away and I could see again.

"Okay?" the Doctor asked.

"Yes," I answered, "it all seems fine. Everything looks a little different though, clearer than it used to and vaguely more colourful."

"Aye," he said, "your old eyes were going a little short-sighted and we detected a hint of colour blindness there too. These little beauties are top notch."

"You mean you changed my eyes?" I asked incredulously.

"Aye, didn't they tell you?" he seemed surprised, "Easiest way to change appearance and a damn sight less painful or troublesome than simply playing with the existing pair. Don't worry, it's perfectly safe. We've been doing it for years."

I asked for a mirror and sat myself up in the bed while they got it. When it arrived I took a deep breath and then forced myself to look. It was incredible. Though I'm not a vain man who spends a lot of time in front of the glass, I know what I look like. Or at least, I knew what I had looked like. The person that stared back at me that morning was not somebody I recognised. The old blue eyes were now hazel, the too-short nose I'd inherited from my mother was now classically Roman and my chin was just that little bit bigger and thinner than I expected.

"You pleased?" the Doctor asked.

"I suppose so," I answered, "it's just a bit shocking at first."

He explained to me all that they had done to my face which amounted to a series of minor tweaks that produced a major change in my appearance in the least invasive way. They had offered me some choices in what they were to do, but I'd felt happier just letting them do what they needed to. After all, the new me was their creation, it may as well look the ways they wanted it to as well.

"Behind the scenes," the Doctor explained, "we do a lot of profiling on witness testimonies and offender appearances. What we've done with you is take away as many recognisable points and create a normal looking, but overall unremarkable appearance. If you ever get seen anywhere, the likelihood is that any description of you being circulated will be at best vague and at worst misleading."

He continued to tell me that they had tweaked my DNA as I'd been advised that it would be and that while I was under the knife they'd also fixed a couple of potential future problems that I might have and had replaced the cartilages in both my knees ahead of the training schedule I would be facing.

I thanked the Doctor for his help and let him ease me out of the bed and into the armchair that sat by the window. He poured me a glass of water and wished me well, then he was gone.

I drank the water and looked out of the window to the small park that was laid out behind the hospital. I could have been in any city in the country, but I knew I was still deep underground. Whatever the future had in store for me it was too late now to turn back. The deciding factor for me had been the desire to make a difference in some positive way and this was the best way for me to do it. ORB was straight out of a sci-fi novel but they seemed to know what they were doing and the people I'd met believed in the cause. Given the speed of my recovery, I was reassured that they had the resources that they claimed to have and looked forward to seeing more of what they had for me. This was only the start, but I felt confident about where I was headed.

On the table beside me I saw an open padded envelope that seemed to be full of papers. As it had no name on it, and as it was there in my room, I assumed it was for me. I took out the bundle of papers and started to read them. The top sheet explained the rest:

'Dear Operative,

Please find enclosed a selection of personal profiles for you to select from. We ask that you please take your time over this process as it is a one-off exercise that will define your identities for many years.

Please select one primary male profile, a secondary male profile and a female profile. When you have done this, place the chosen profiles back in the envelope and destroy the others. The envelope should be left in the tray outside your door.

Regards

The ORB Team

Underneath this letter were page after page of individual profiles of people who had never existed. One of them was to be the new me. The task ahead seemed daunting and it was tempting to simply pick out three at random, but I stuck with it and after a few hours had made my selection.

Chapter Thirty-Five

New recruit, Stephen Barratt, arrived at the Training Centre half an hour before his appointed time. He didn't want to be late for his first session and had been up for several hours already, anticipating the start of this intensive next stage in his development. Or should I say, that I arrived half an hour early for my first session. I was now Stephen Barratt. Zip no more.

I'd always wanted to be a Stephen, if only because I'd grown up obsessed with watching re-runs of 'The Six Million Dollar Man' and he was a Steve and he was cool. The choice of Barratt was no choice at all as the Stephen was contingent on taking this second name. Still, it was nondescript enough. I'd chosen my other two identities as well, but these were parked in the back of my mind and I hoped I'd never need to use them. It was challenging enough taking on one new persona, especially as I had, for the past few days, been snared, tricked, harassed, enticed and bullied to admit my true identity but in each case I'd been able to stick with the new script of my life. I knew Stephen Barratt better than I knew Zipoly Hardacre and I seemed to have passed this test.

At precisely nine o'clock my instructor opened the door of his office and called me in. He asked me to sit and then informed me that I was in for possibly the hardest three months of my life. They had tested me and found me to be fit, but fit wasn't fit enough for ORB. I would be pushed to new heights of endurance during my training and made to do things that I would now think to be impossible. When he'd finished detailing all this he smiled at me and said:

"Should we get started then?"

The programme began with what I would describe as run-of-the-mill stamina exercises. But they were only conventional in the sense that they involved running, lifting, climbing and swimming. Beyond this, they took training to a new and almost cruel level. If I threw up with the effort, I had to clean it up and carry on with the exercise. If I collapsed, they left me where I was and waited until I dragged myself back up and completed the task. If I failed to hit the required mark, I did the exercise again, and again and again. It didn't take me long to come to the realisation that there was no failing to make the grade in this training.

Every night I fell into bed exhausted and aching, only to wake again all too soon and have to drag myself back to the programme. There were times when I was running on less than empty, but somehow I kept going. There were also times when I could do nothing but stop and accept that I couldn't do what they were asking me to do. But this was not a choice that I was allowed to make. Somehow, I always got there, and usually in one piece.

They patched up my scratches and the odd broken bone. They injected me with painkillers then pushed me back into the training field. They cursed me, they laughed at me, they taunted me. But still I kept going. It eased off a little after the first month although I didn't kid myself that there wasn't worse to come.

Stage two of the programme saw my physical training ease back a bit as I spent most of my time with various teachers and professors who sought to develop me mentally. I was made to stand perfectly still for hours on end whilst multiple distractions surrounded me. I was given exercises in morality and philosophy and made to choose who died and who lived in a thousand different scenarios. I was humbled to think of myself as nothing. I was taught how to make myself believe I could do anything.

Then I returned to the physical exercises.

That third month of training was nothing short of a nightmare. However, I realised that the psychological tools they had equipped me with had been given me for a reason. I deployed them as best I could and as well as I could remember how to. They saw me through those darkest times, but only just. I nearly lost it completely when they submerged me in a narrow tunnel that was blacker than night and which I was informed had only one way out. Holding my breath, I inched forward in the water, setting aside any thoughts of drowning and thinking to myself that behind it all there were people who would come to the rescue if I got into trouble. Then I hit the sealed end of the tunnel and I realised that they had put me in facing the wrong way. It was my mistake of course, had I thought carefully about the situation I should have realised that this was what they would do. Nevertheless, I still had to get out and now I had to travel twice the distance with half the oxygen left and swimming backwards. I panicked and in that panic released a bubble of precious air that I could ill afford to waste. They weren't going to beat me. I channelled the panic into anger and drove myself harder than ever whilst keeping my heartbeat to its lowest possible rate. I resigned myself to death and was just on the point of blacking out when I felt my feet move upwards and I realised I was nearly out. With one push I made it through and surfaced in a darkened cavern full of beautiful clean air. I gulped it in and waited for what I knew would be the second stage of this session.

It began with a dim light flickering on briefly above a ladder on the wall. I started to move towards it, then stopped myself. They wouldn't make it that easy. Again, the ladder was illuminated but just as the light faded I caught a glimpse of something else. Just to the side of the ladder were a series of rocks that offered me an alternative route out. I swam across and grabbed for the first of these rocks, pulling myself up and reaching out for the next one. They weren't set out in a straight route upwards but every time that I thought I had run out of options, I was able to reach out and, after much fumbling, find another. By the time I was at the top and ready to pull myself over onto dry land, I was on the opposite side of the cavern and could see clearly the fraying on the ropes that held the top of the ladder. I would have been almost at the top when they gave way and sent me back to square one. With a victorious smile I heaved myself over the lip and lay exhausted on the welcoming dusty ground.

"Congratulations Barratt," my instructor stood over me, "not everyone gets out of that one."

I was too exhausted to say anything. I picked up my gear and followed him back.

That was the last I saw of him. He obviously passed me as fit to operate as the next day I arrived at the centre only to be escorted back to the office complex. Sir Anthony Chow was waiting for me there.

"Good to meet you, Mr Barratt," he greeted me, either completely failing to recognise me or, as I suspected, choosing to act up to my new identity.

"Pleased to meet you, Sir," I answered, maintaining the pretence.

I wasn't sure how far to take the play-acting, so I erred on the side of caution and we exchanged the usual pleasantries as he asked how I had got on with the training and I answered that it had been tough but very satisfying.

"We're very pleased with your progress," he told me, "and you should know that you are up there amongst the top of those who survive the course. The reason that we're meeting today is that I wanted to personally tell you that. And I also want to share with you a little bit of detail about the Order for Restoring Balance, or ORB as you know it, before we part company. After today, we may meet occasionally but this is the last time we have an official discussion."

"The first thing you need to know," he continued, "now that you are one of us, is how all this pans out in practice. It's really very simple actually. At the head of the Order, if I might use that term, there is a Council of twelve good men and true. Of course, nowadays, that includes women, good and true. This Council has a President who is elected annually and who is the nominal head of the Order. As you will have guessed, myself, Batchcliffe and Anderson are all Members of the Council. The role of the Council is to agree the actions that need to be taken, as a broad sweep only though, how those actions are executed is left to our operatives. We will provide you with the necessary means of communication and will contact you with brief details of the tasks that you are being requested to fulfil. Each of those actions, objectives, missions even, will be graded on a scale of one to four."

He paused and sat back in his chair, clearly trying to gather his thoughts.

"Grade one is the highest priority with four being the lowest. Of course, this scoring is not for you to concern yourself with and there will be times when you will see a four and wonder why it's not a one. Let me explain. A category four would be pretty much akin to the things that were done previously under Zipoly Hardacre's righteous correction banner. I understand you are familiar with those."

I smiled and nodded.

"Good," he continued, "so let me give you an example that might surprise you. Jack the Ripper. Mass murderer, brutal son of a bitch all told, but we dealt with that as a four. By the time we were involved, the killings had stopped. You may have heard rumours about his being a well-connected gent and that was in fact the truth of the matter. We intervened because justice had to be done. However, his identity remained secret. Not our choice as the New Franciscans, as we were then, but still we corrected the balance. On the other hand, a grade one would be a matter of national security. We had quite a few of those during the Second World War and we're starting to get a few more just now. So, at a grade one level we, for example, can arrange for a King to abdicate but save a little face. If you get my gist?"

I nodded understanding and let him continue.

"Of course, our work is secret. We don't leave little plaques behind.

We just do the job and go. Aside from those two examples that I've given you, you will never be able to tell for certain what we've done. This is an important point and especially so for you. You are anonymous from now on. You do not exist nor does ORB. Any hint of our participation and we start to have to go along the cover-up line and we don't like that. And don't let yourself be distracted by trying to think whether we've been involved in something. If there's a doubt about something that's happened, chances are we weren't involved. Take the Diana situation. All those conspiracy theories but because those theories raise their heads you can be assured that we weren't part of that scenario. If we had been, we'd have done a much better job and it's unlikely we'd have been so ruthless. Fact is, it was a car accident."

He stopped and looked at his watch.

"Look," he said, "I'll have to dash soon but please, join me in a last drink."

He poured two generous whiskies and topped them up with ice, passing me mine before sitting back down but this time directly in front of me on the corner of the desk.

"Just a couple of final points then," he said, "starting with your codename. Yes, I know it sounds cheesy but get used to it. From now on, you are The Kingfisher. The canals helped us come up with that one but also the fact that you are elusive, flit about and disappear when you're seen, and you have a certain elegance in your work. An elegance that I am confident will continue to develop."

"Finally then," he continued, "this is the plan for the next few weeks. We want you to work with James and help him as he puts together some new kit for you. When you go and see him, he'll have a nice surprise for you. We'll be in touch when the time is right and your work will start. Please don't forget that you are in a very special, but very lonely position now. We all know the downsides of the work we do here. It is a sacrifice and whoever you currently are means nothing, you are an invisible part of a bigger machine. But we do value you."

He stood up, shook my hand then excused himself as he left the room. I finished the whisky and was just about to help myself to another when the door opened.

"Hi," a familiar voice said, "I'm James. You're to come with me."

He reached out his hand to shake mine and held the grip as he looked me up and down.

"Good to see you again," he laughed, "but don't let them know I know."

I asked him how he knew.

"You seem to forget," he said as we headed out of the office, "I'm one of those socially inadequate savants who sees the world in a slanted way. I look at hands. I struggle to look people in the eye. And they haven't touched your hands, they never do. Don't worry though, your secret's safe with me. You just wait till you see what I've got to show you."

Chapter Thirty-Six

I spent just over a fortnight with James before they called me for my first assignment. In that brief time, we achieved a huge amount and would often work late into the night on various projects that were fascinating to me even if the science left me standing. He was a genius but humble with it. I learnt a lot from James.

Our working together began with our arriving at the laboratory complex and his pointing to a new structure that had been built behind the existing units. It was about twice the length of the other units and was clearly only temporary, as it was curtained off rather than having permanent sides.

"Here's your surprise," he told me as we approached it, "I hope you like it."

He peered behind the curtains and I heard him saying something to the people inside who emerged a moment or two later wearing paint stained overalls and wiping their hands with rags. When they saw me they smiled and nodded. James then played around with a small console at the side of the far curtain before joining us just as the curtains started to move.

As they slowly opened to reveal what they were covering I looked on in surprise as my boat began to appear. At least, I thought it was my boat. The hull was identical, although it now shone with a mirror-perfect finish, and the superstructure had been painted in a different colour scheme. As the curtains stopped moving, allowing me a full view of the bow and stern of the boat, I knew that it was my old home. The stern was tidier and had been built up a little with new seating and cupboards, but the bow still sported its bridge-bars and swept up majestically into what I had always thought of as a smile.

"We've tidied her up a bit," James said as he came to stand beside me, "and, of course, she's had a paint job, but it's your boat alright."

"But I thought mine had been burnt out," I replied

"Oh, that was a bit of sleight of hand," he said, "we found another boat just like yours and swapped the licence plates and any other identifying features. They wanted to use your old one and give you a brand new boat, but I wanted to check out what you'd done in this one, with the pod and all. To be honest, I also thought you'd prefer it this way."

I thanked him for making the right call and walked over to the boat, checking out the new paint job and looking for anything I might recognise on the exterior. James explained that whilst the whole boat had been stripped back, sealed with super tough epoxy and painted with a new non-stick paint that they had developed, they hadn't wanted her to attract undue attention.

"I know you're not a traditionalist," he explained, "but the best way to keep you off the radar is for you to fit into the surroundings. She's got the new name of 'Kingfisher', which is the most popular boat name, and that paint scheme is devised from our studying the most anonymous boats on the canals."

"But," he continued with a wry smile, "don't let the outside fool you. I'm sure that once you've seen her inside, you'll forgive the less than exciting exterior."

He led the way towards the aircraft steps that were placed at the stern of the boat and I followed him up them. We stood on the deck and he showed me what was behind the various new seating and storage units, revealing a new engine control panel, the standard paraphernalia of electrical hook up cables, batteries and gas bottles, as well as two lockers that were currently empty. He lifted the deck boards and I looked in amazement to see that the old diesel engine had been replaced by a new, fully-electric unit that was half the size of any I'd ever seen. There was no propeller shaft either and when I questioned him on this he explained that the boat still had a standard prop but that it was operated by electro-magnets to allow for the hull to be fully sealed.

"You need to keep the engine under your hat while you're out and about," he said, "as it's a little beyond current technology. To help you with that we've had a bit of a play around and think you'll like this bit."

He turned the engine on and I heard a slight buzz as it came to life before the familiar sound of my old diesel engine filled my ears.

"We've put in speakers and an audio programme that simulates an old engine sound," James told me, "It means you can have the best of both worlds. You've got the coolest engine on the cut but it sounds like your battling with an old Lister. And yes, it will be smoky as well but again, that's just a ruse."

He killed the engine and entered a four-digit code into the panel on the door which swung inwards with a hydraulic hiss.

"After you," James beckoned me to enter.

The moment I stepped into the boat, LED lights flickered and flooded the place with a pure, white light. I looked at what had been my home. They'd certainly been hard at work on her as she was not the boat I'd left behind.

"Wow," I said, "this is beautiful."

"Come on," James followed me in, "let me show you around."

We stood in the galley area at the stern of the boat and I played around with the new kitchen units, opening up cupboards to find a microwave, entertainment centre and, to my delight, a full set of new crockery, cutlery and utensils. Other than that it was a traditional galley, smaller perhaps than most, but certainly the most luxurious I'd ever seen. We stepped through into what looked like the dining area where new seats and a new table had been fitted neatly into the space.

"This is where it gets fun," James said, reaching down and pressing a series of buttons hidden away behind a panel under the central bench seat in the dining area.

The table retracted and the seat lifted out of the way to be replaced by a single captain's chair and a bank of computer monitors.

"This is your control centre," James explained, "everything on the boat can be accessed from here, although you also have remote access from this tablet."

He detached one of the smaller screens that turned out to be a small tablet computer and on which were various readouts and images of buttons.

"Don't worry about getting used to it all just now," he continued, fitting the tablet back in place, "you've got a couple of weeks for that. Today is just an overview, so, let's have a look at the rest."

He pressed a few more buttons and the dining area reverted to its former state, then he led me past a lavishly appointed wet-room which he told me was state-of-the-art but had no other secret functions. It was simply my toilet and shower area. We moved into the lounge and I was pleasantly surprised to see that they'd kept it fairly uncluttered. New leather sofas had been built in a continuous curve that was broken only by a table in the centre. The opposite wall matched the sofa's curve but with bookcases sat either side of a log burner.

"Like the wet-room," James told me, "this is pretty much as it appears. The only extra thing you need to know here is that, as with the rest of the boat, there are storage units above your head that are hidden."

He reached up and pressed his finger gently onto the surround of one of the lights and a panel of the ceiling slid down slowly on hydraulic arms.

"It's fingerprint activated," he explained, "and all of the storage is hidden from the outside under what appear to be roof-boxes. They don't open from the top, but nobody would know that."

He retracted the storage box and we continued through to the bow of the boat where there was fixed double bed and a wardrobe. He showed me that the bed was as per any other narrowboat bed, with a retractable end piece to allow access to the bow doors. The wardrobe too was conventional, although it was full with new clothes wrapped in white plastic shrouds.

"We'll look at your uniform later," James laughed, "but I'm sure you'll love it. Meanwhile, this place looks pretty normal doesn't it?"

I agreed and immediately wished that I hadn't as he reached behind me to another control panel and started to play with buttons again. The floor started to retract and I saw a familiar site underneath.

"We've modified your pod a little, but the principal is the same. The big difference is that you can now get out either side of the boat. You can also exit through the front as well."

Finally, he took me through to the bow deck and showed me the new version of my bike that appeared at the touch of a button from a hidden panel in the raised front section. He then pressed a few more buttons and showed me how the sides of the boat now dropped down on invisible hinges to allow me direct access to the bank at any time. I wondered what else lay in store for me as I got used to this vessel but if what I'd seen so far was a taster, I was sure the main course would be even more of a delight.

We stayed on the boat for another half-hour or so whilst James programmed everything to my fingerprint, then we left and went back to the lab. He asked me what I thought and I had no difficulty in telling him that I was impressed. My admiration for him would continue to grow as I explored the boat over the next couple of weeks and discovered just how many secrets it held.

We called out for pizza for lunch, using the time that we were waiting for its delivery to plan out a schedule of what we would do whilst we were together. I was happy for James to take the lead as he had a bit more experience with all this than I did, but we worked well together and were able to set some clear goals for what we wanted to achieve. Primarily, we wanted to perfect some of the creatures that I had started to work with and to integrate James's work on ion drives into the same. We sat down and wrote a list of what we thought might be the most suitable of animals to try and create, then we set to work to, almost literally, put flesh on the bones of our ideas.

Throughout the time that I had been pushing myself to the limits on the training field, James too had been pushing himself to new heights in developing the ion drives that would form the heart of my support equipment. On the bench in front of us we now had an assortment of different sized spheres, all of which incorporated an ion drive and a small transceiver that, when placed into the various creatures that we developed, would provide both mobility and communication. They would all be charged by induction whilst they awaited deployment, James having incorporated this system into one of the ceiling storage compartments.

"What you need to understand," he told me as we began to work on the exoskeletons to surround the spheres, "is that I see the world at an atomic level. I know that sounds a bit odd, but you know the difficulty I have with people. Well, I'm never happier than when I'm lost in the world of the invisible. I want to harness that power and bring it to life. Not that it isn't the heart of life anyway. Think about it, we get so excited about the things that we can see, the stars, the universe, the deep sea, but we don't realise that the real miracles are happening in the places we can't see them. There's a biologist bloke in one of the other labs and he's as excited about the trillions of bacteria that keep us healthy. Well, it's the same with me but with atoms. Everything I'm working on, I'm trying to make smaller and smaller and you'll see some of the results of this soon. Meanwhile, I need you to help me design the outsides of these little beasties and then we can get you out into the field."

His passion was infectious and I was happy to add what he needed to his creations by working on the animal designs that would hide what was inside. We used a complicated three-dimensional printer that scanned my models and allowed me to build enough superstructure for our purposes which it then forged into being using the appropriate materials. Whilst I was familiar with this type of printing, I had only ever seen it work on plastics, but James had been able to develop a system that could break any material down at the atomic level and rebuild it as required. So it was that the wooden models that I had used were refined into aluminium, titanium and an assortment of other rare and exotic metals. We kept the specification down to the minimum that we needed, which meant that the birds and animals only had to look the part and which kept their build time down. It also meant that we were able to keep the physical structures as uncomplicated as possible. So it was that my old, bulky owl who took up so much space on the boat, was converted to a compact, amorphous bundle that only came to life when placed over an ion sphere.

When it came to more conventional weapons, I was allowed to keep using the toxin that I had started with, although I now had a supply of a more refined product that could be delivered at various doses ranging from soporific to fatal. Again, each of the creatures that we developed had incorporated into it the ability to deliver a dose of this chemical.

"As I work on miniaturising everything," James told me, "I've got some really exciting plans for other buddies to help you out. We want to get to the stage where we can use virtually invisible weapons and I believe we can do that. I can see where it needs to be, but it may still take a bit of time."

We finished in the lab two weeks later and spent a couple of days with the boat. I had been staying on it whilst working with James and had familiarised myself with most of the new enhancements and control systems, but there were still some things that I needed explaining. In particular, I had been banned from accessing the wardrobe. Apparently, this was to be my final surprise.

What I had worked out so far was that the drive system operated from some sort of high powered batteries that recharged at a phenomenal rate from the solar array on the roof which covered the fake roof-boxes. According to James, I would never need to plug in anywhere nor refuel. The idea was that I would run the boat with the engine noise playing whenever there were people about, but that I could also operate in a stealth mode whereby the boat was silent. This would allow me to move at night. Whilst on a normal boat night-cruising was challenging at the best of times, the control centre that they had installed meant that the boat steered itself. I could switch from manual control using the traditional tiller and rudder, to a system of compressed air propulsion controlled by auto-pilot. In that mode, the boat continually sensed for obstructions and other craft whilst maintaining cruising speed.

Aside from the usual GPS and other navigational aids, the boat was fitted with highly encrypted internet access and a fully secure communications system. It was the sort of vessel I had dreamt off and tried to work towards but it was infinitely more impressive than I imagined. Most impressive was that they had worked out how to get around the lock problem that had me stumped. James explained.

"Okay, so you launch the pod as usual, but now it steers itself and moves twice as fast as the one you made. But, here's the difference, and remember, this only works at night. As you approach a lock the pod slows and sends up a drone to scan for any people who may be about. If the coast is clear the pod engages its ion drive and comes out of the water and over the lock. It keeps doing this until your clear."

"But what if someone sees me?" I asked. "Are the drones that accurate?"

"The simple answer," he said, "is that yes, they are. If they detect even the slightest hint of human activity they will abort. Trust me, it's fool proof. While you were doing your press-ups, I was having prototypes of these flying all over the canal network and we never had a single problem."

Perhaps I needed a little more convincing, but nevertheless, it was an elegant and practical solution to a problem that I had never cracked. Besides, I think that by this stage, I was comfortable that if James said something had been tested, it had been tested beyond any conventional limits.

"Now then," James said as we were finishing our time together, "let's reveal the mysteries of your uniform."

He pressed his finger against the door of the wardrobe and, after it had fully opened, he took out the wrapped clothes that hung there.

"I'll put your fingerprint into that later," he said, "but normally these items will be out of view like this."

He pressed a button in the wardrobe and the inside rotated to reveal a set of normal, everyday clothes. He put the wardrobe back to where it was and started to take the wrapping off the items he'd taken out. They were three identical suits that had a fancy-dress look about them but which unfolded into a more conventional shape, rather like bike leathers.

"Three outfits," he explained, "all essentially looking the same but each a little bit different. Here, try this one on."

He handed me one of the suits and, with a little help from James, I squeezed into it and looked in the mirror.

"Not bad," I said, "The Kingfisher is revealed."

The outfits fitted snugly and were made of a material that felt comfortable but strong. Overall, the first impression was that they were fully black, but on closer inspection and as the light shifted, there were flashes of iridescent green and blue all over the surface.

"This is your main outfit," James advised, "reinforced Kevlar and a number of new materials that you don't need to know about. It's stab-proof, reasonably bullet-proof and, most importantly, like the others, it's pretty much waterproof. You'll see on both arms a covered panel that has all the controls you need for anything you are working with, alongside which you have a helmet that completes the set and also incorporates all the technology you'll need."

He placed the helmet on my head and pressed a button at the side. A full replica of the boat's control systems lit up in front of me and a voice whispered in my ear that I was now in standby mode.

I took the helmet off and asked about the other outfits.

"Essentially the same look," he said, "but one is super lightweight which makes it suitable for times when you need to be that bit more agile. Unfortunately, the compromise with that is the level of protection. Not suitable if you expect to get into trouble but it has another feature I'll tell you about in a minute. The second outfit is the opposite. It's heavy duty for serious combat but again there's a compromise as it only has minimal electronic controls and it's damned heavy to move about in."

"Now," he continued, "one last thing. Three pairs of boots, all the same to avoid confusion and all waterproof etc., but when you are wearing the lightweight suit you should be able to use the ion drives incorporated in the soles to allow you to elevate. I'll keep working on this side of it as I'm hoping to get you to the stage where you can fly, but meanwhile, don't put any weight on and don't use it unless you must. It doesn't have a huge amount of power or battery capacity yet."

"You seem to have thought of everything," I told him.

"Well," he smiled, "you know how we tech geeks like our comic book heroes don't you? I just used them as a model and tried to cover every aspect. Of course, we'll keep working on everything and when you next come back you can update me on what works and I can soup you up a bit."

We put the gear away and locked up the boat, then headed off intending to have a meal together. We didn't get that far though. As we left the laboratory area, a uniformed officer approached, saluted and informed us that Steve Barratt was called to active duty and was to accompany him immediately.

"Here's goes," I said to James, shaking his hand, "wish me luck."

"I will," he smiled, "but with all that gear we've given you, and your own special skills, I don't think you'll need much luck. Just be careful out there won't you."

I followed the officer to the central reception area where he directed me to a side-room. Inside, there was nothing but a chair and a monitor on the wall.

"Take a seat," the officer told me before leaving the room and locking the door.

The monitor flickered to life and I was given the instructions for my first mission. The broadcast ended by asking me to sit quietly and allow the gas that would be introduced into the room to render me unconscious. I heard the slow hiss and let myself fall asleep.

Chapter Thirty-Seven

When I woke up on the boat it took me a few minutes to recall the circumstances that had put me there. The gas they'd used had no lasting side-effects and I felt like I had simply had a good night's sleep. The reality was that I'd been out of it for three days, during which time the boat and I had been moved back onto the canal network, although at that point I wasn't quite sure where. I got myself up, showered and dressed before deciding to find out where I was. It might have been easier to have simply turned the navigation computers on but instead I decided on the old fashioned method of looking out of the boat's doors. The towpath at Fradley Junction was immediately recognisable as I'd spent many an hour or two there with the barbecue blazing away. At least I was on familiar ground.

Returning back to the main cabin, having set the kettle to boil in the galley, I reminded myself of the mission I had been given. Or at least, I reminded myself of the very sparse message that remained on my monitor and which simply said:

'Justice Peter O'Rourke, Lenient sentencing. Grade four.'

I'd expected to have been given more than this, with a clear objective and anticipated response, but that had been all the information I received. Thinking about this I was pleased on the one hand that those above me felt confident enough to give me such a free rein. On the other hand, I thought that this might be my first test of judgement and therefore my first chance to fall at the first hurdle. I could understand why they were so vague. This was all off the record and it kept them a step away from whatever I did. Still, I had to think carefully about where to go with it.

As I settled with my coffee, I started a search on the web for Justice Peter O'Rourke and established that he was a senior judge, in his late fifties, divorced, two adult children and one grandchild. He had an exemplary record and there were few negative press reports about him other than the standard fare that seemed to want to trash any member of the judiciary at every opportunity. With this basic search yielding nothing, I used the dedicated ORB secure database that I had been given access to, and searched a more comprehensive database of court journals, trolling painfully through these to garner more information. It was slow work and by lunchtime I was little further ahead. I decided that a trip to the pub for some lunch and a pint might help me along. That was a mistake. The pub at Fradley, the 'mucky duck' as it was known, could always be relied upon to have a number of guest ales which usually changed before you'd worked your way through half of them. I got chatting to some fellow boaters and the afternoon passed into the evening. I wasn't too concerned. The mission didn't seem to be an urgent priority so I had time on my hands and, after all, I hadn't had a proper blow-out like that for a long time. When I staggered back to the boat it was late in the evening and I was only fit for bed. As I lay down I was disturbed by a flashing light in the dining area that I hadn't seen before. I dragged myself up and saw that it seemed to be coming from some sort of answering machine. I pressed the button.

"Let that be the last time," a male voice that I didn't recognise said in a stern tone, "You have work to do. Make sure you make progress tomorrow. Goodnight."

It seemed I'd upset them already. Still, I'd needed the break and the return to normality that it gave me. Did they not realise that my visit to the pub was the perfect chance for me to explore and test out my new identity? No, they probably didn't. Besides which, I couldn't even convince myself that this had been my motivation. I resolved to get onto O'Rourke first thing tomorrow and make sure that I moved forward with it, then I stumbled to the bedroom, fell onto the bed and slept like a baby.

The following morning, I woke early and, remembering the message, started work straight away. If O'Rourke wasn't obviously a problem, then I had to look a bit deeper and take a closer look at the sentencing that I was being told was too lenient. As a novice when it comes to the legal process, I was at a disadvantage, but just when I was beginning to give up hope, something jumped out at me from one of the press reports related to O'Rourke. It was an article that described the jailing for ten years of an ex public schoolboy for the rape of a female friend. Ten years seemed reasonable to me, then I noticed that this same person had committed the offence whilst serving a six month suspended sentence for a similar offence. Now I was getting somewhere, but exactly where I wasn't sure. I had no way of following this up, since the perpetrator was now in prison, nor did I exactly know what I was following up. Perhaps the parents of the offender might be the safest bet. I didn't really want to hassle a defendant who had clearly had a traumatic enough time.

The guilty party was a Mr Roy Stanfield, son of a Major Charles and Mrs Olivia Stanfield. It wasn't difficult to find their address, although it was a little bit further afield than I had hoped. Then again, maybe this would be the opportunity I needed to take the boat on a trial voyage. It had been too long since I'd last cruised the waterways. A trip to Milton Keynes was just what I needed.

Prior to leaving I checked out more information around O'Rourke and was fortunate enough to come across a posting on a blog that named him as the judge who, it was alleged, had covered up for a fellow judge in a domestic abuse case. There were no other details that I could find on the mainstream web about this, so I posted an anonymous message asking for more information about this allegation and awaited the reply. Meanwhile, I planned my route to Milton Keynes and set off on a fresh and sunny Summer morning.

The journey from Fradley to Milton Keynes would normally be a week's cruise. I allowed myself a little longer as this gave me the opportunity to play with the boat and check out some of her new features, whilst at the same time it gave me time to formulate my plan of action. At this stage, I knew that whatever O'Rourke was guilty of, it was not massively time sensitive and I was putting nobody at risk by stalling: He was currently in the middle of a long-winded libel case that had little prospect of ending this side of Christmas.

With the limited information that I had been given, my first objective was to establish whether there was an imbalance of justice that needed correcting. This was probably not in my remit as an ORB operative, since they had already established that action needed to be taken. However, I remained the same person that I had always been inside and this was, and would always remain, a core part of my morality. Besides which, establishing that action needed to be taken would also help me to understand what that appropriate action should be.

Since my only solid lead was the Major, I built the first stage of my strategy on using him to deliver the evidence I needed. During the second week of my voyage therefore, I sent out an ambassador ahead of me in the form of pigeon, figuring that whatever the circumstances of the Major's home situation, these were creatures that seemed to be at home in any environment and would go unnoticed. It was a straightforward job to send it overnight and put it to rest on the roof of his home. The following day, taking advantage of the Summer heat, I flew the bird into an open window and allowed it to release several listening devices that I manoeuvred into hidden positions close to a number of telephone points in the property. I was less interested in what they picked up in terms of information, than in them simply providing me with a constant feed of the Major's voice that I allowed to build up on one of my computer's hard drives.

When I arrived at Milton Keynes, I moored up in a small marina, making sure that I picked a spot where the boat was visible to passers-by and to any surveillance cameras on the piers. It would have been fine to have stayed out on the cut, but doing it this way would enable me to check out how the new boat performed in keeping me invisible whilst I was in a very visible location.

On the day after I moored here, I received a reply to my blog post, with a little more detail on O'Rourke's apparent support for a High Court colleague. Apparently, this fellow judge had been accused of keeping several maids in a state of slavery in his London apartment, although the case collapsed after O'Rourke successfully argued that, as the women were illegal immigrants and, as the case relied on their testimony which they couldn't even give in English, it was nothing more than a malicious attempt by organised criminals to discredit the defendant. The women were placed in a detention centre for six months and had recently been deported. This at least gave me a little food for thought and some more flesh on the bones of my mission, but I still wanted more information so I sent a request to ORB to track down the person who'd posted the original message and supply me with a name and address. Such messages were never acknowledged or replied to, but I was confident I would hear something on this fairly soon.

Meanwhile, I had the voice file established for the Major, and could begin work on using this to explore O'Rourke's culpability in more depth. The plan was fairly simple and utilised one of James's boxes of tricks that he had left me with, which was a compact voice synthesiser. I left the boat and took the train to London making no attempt to disguise myself as, to any observer, I was simply off on a day trip to take in a few tourist attractions and see a West End show. One of these attractions was the Dickens museum which was conveniently situated very near to O'Rourke's London home. As

I passed his house, I surreptitiously dropped a couple of items in the small hedge that shielded the house from the main road, before continuing with my day out. The museum was superb but the show was even better. I got the late train back and still had the catchy tunes from the musical running around my head when I went to sleep that night.

Chapter Thirty-Eight

If you found a big spider in a privet hedge, depending on your feelings towards arachnids, you'd either recoil in horror or take a closer look at it. What you wouldn't do however, is suspect it of being anything more than a large spider. That had been my hope at least when I left the two of them at the judge's house. These were a combined effort by James and I and were limited in their capacity but nonetheless beautiful in their execution not least because we had been able to make them in such a way that they didn't have to rely on their ion drive to float to their destination, but could walk there instead.

So it was that I spent the following morning manoeuvring the two spiders up the wall of the house to park one on the window ledge outside O'Rourke's study and the other by his bedroom. They gave me a visual of what was happening in the house and, with a little bit of tweaking, I could see into both rooms. The judge was at home, seated at his office desk. Now was the time to start building my case against him. I dialled his phone and watched as he answered, then I switched my own microphone on and spoke to him.

"O'Rourke, it's Stanfield," I began, the computer making my voice a perfect match to that which it had been recording for weeks, "need a few moments to talk if possible."

Not only was the voice a perfect match, but the script that the computer had helped me put together based on the Major's linguistic style meant that this was exactly what he would have said had he been making the call.

"Charles?" O'Rourke seemed a little wary, "I thought we said that we would only talk face to face at the club. Is your line secure?"

"Of course," I replied, "and yes, I know our agreement but I just need to run something by you. This will be the last time."

"Go ahead then," O'Rourke resigned himself to the conversation, "but make it quick. I'm in the middle of a very complicated case just now and could do without the interruption."

"I need you to help the boy again," I said, "he's not coping well in prison and he won't last the length of the sentence."

There was a long pause at the end of the line and I could see on my monitor that the judge had been caught off guard by this request and needed to think about his response. I watched as he removed his reading glasses, leant back in his chair and ran a hand over his face.

"I'm sorry," he told me, "not again. You know I put my career on the line in the first case and I've suffered a lot already for what we did. I don't care too much about the response from the fillies who seem to think that I'm some sort of monster, but I do care about the reputation I have in the Party and amongst some of my most valued colleagues and clients. You know his last victim was pregnant don't you? She lost the child."

"But he's cracking up in prison," I pleaded in the Major's voice, "I need you to help. I can keep him out of trouble if you'll just intervene and help with his appeal. Please. I'm begging."

"Sorry," O'Rourke replied, "it's not going to happen. Firstly, we both know that my influencing the first case and giving a non-custodial sentence, means that we both have blood on our hands. Secondly, you and I also know that he will reoffend. Your son's a devil and I'm glad he's safely behind bars. I'm sorry, end of conversation. Goodbye."

I watched as he dropped the phone back in its cradle and tracked him as he helped himself to an early morning drink. I was almost tempted to join him but it was still a little early even for me. Whilst he may have needed the liquor to calm his nerves, mine would have been a celebration. I had the first piece of evidence I needed. Now, I needed more.

I checked the secure e-mail account that I'd used to contact the blogger and was pleased to see a reply. They gave me a phone number but refused to meet me which I figured made sense and probably added to the weight of what they knew. The number was for a pay phone and they requested I only dial it at precisely seven in the evening as they would be waiting. They gave me a week to call, but I determined to deal with this one promptly. While I waited for seven to come, I kept myself busy adding flesh to the detail of Stanfield minor's crime. As it was a rape case, the evidence was not public, but there were ways around this and I was able to cross-reference police and hospital files to establish the details. Roy Stanfield had been under a suspended sentence for sexual assault when he had met, befriended and eventually raped Clara Jones, a nineteen-year-old student who was three months pregnant. On their first proper date alone, he had subjected her to a frenzied attack, having tied her to her bed and gagged her. I didn't need to know any more of the details, but the result of this assault was that Clara was now in a psychiatric ward having tried several times to commit suicide, whilst the foetus of her miscarried son was buried in an anonymous grave.

Just that information would have been enough, but I made the call that evening anyway. I was glad that I did.

"Hello," the voice that answered the pay phone was firm but cautious.

"Hello," I replied, "I think we need to talk about judges, am I correct?"

"Yes, perhaps," I could sense the caution in the other person's voice.

"Okay, first off, please listen to me before you put the phone down," I had a pre-prepared script in front of me as I wanted to get my side of the story across straightaway, "there is no way either of us wants to be identified, and I can assure you that this line has been checked and it's clean, and also that I am not with any authority that can take action against you. I will avenge O'Rourke if what you tell me is relevant. Justice will be done."

She seemed happy with this and proceeded to talk to me.

"Judge O'Rourke has hurt a lot of us," I detected a hint of Eastern European in her accent as she continued, "we have tried to go to police but we are not legal so they will not listen. You need to help us."

"Go on," I reassured her, "I'll help if I can."

"We all come over together in one shipment," she explained, "we pay much money but get a flat to share and we each have job. My sister, she works as a cleaner in house of judge called Walters. He beat her. His wife beat her. She tried to escape but her handlers took her straight back and she was beaten again. She was beautiful girl, but they burn her face with iron. Now she scarred and ugly. She went to police and they came to see Walters and his wife. Then nothing happened."

"What do you mean, nothing happened?" I asked.

"I have other friend who works for police in offices," the girl told me, "she looked at the file and there was page attached to it saying that there was no case to answer and that this a malicious complaint by an illegal immigrant. It was signed by judge O'Rourke. Then they pick up my sister and deport her."

The speaker's voice broke and all I could hear was her crying before she put the phone down. I would have liked to have heard more, but I had enough. I logged into the ORB site and made the request for information on this case and the alleged deportation. It didn't take long for the reply to come back. There was already a file on Walters at ORB centre and he had been flagged as a potential grade four target for the future. Of course, in the strictest sense of the law he was both innocent and a victim of a malicious slur, but I knew that in this instance the law and justice had taken different paths. The Order's providing me with this information was in response to its relevance to my current case, but had they wanted me to pick up a little more? Was it within my remit to take additional action on my own initiative? I chose to run with it anyway. What's the worst that could happen?

Alongside the information relating to the alleged beating, there was also a file that detailed the deportation of a Tanya Volosky who had been forcibly removed from the country three months ago and returned to her home country. The picture that accompanied this report, clearly a mug shot from her time at a detention centre, showed me a face that was repulsively scarred with burn tissue surrounding a pair of what were obviously once beautiful eyes, but that now seemed to have no sparkle of life left in them. There was nothing practical I could do for her or her sister, but I could avenge their treatment and try to prevent it happening again to somebody else.

I now had enough information to act and a supplementary file of data that would help me pursue other activities when this assignment ended. I still had a burning desire to do what I did and hoped that ORB would be supportive in my additional goals. Meanwhile, I had to put an end to the O'Rourke problem and so I planned the journey down the Grand Union from Milton Keynes to London. This would be a proper test of my ability to stay anonymous, although from what I knew of London, despite the technology that surveilled every human within its boundaries, people rarely took the time to acknowledge each other's existence.

I moored the boat in Little Venice, having asked a few other boaters to shimmy along a little to provide me with the room for me to squeeze into a forty-eight-hour spot. Despite this inconvenience, it was reassuring that the towpath was full and that there were plenty of people and boats around. There was a huge degree of safety for me in being so close to so many and in such a restrictive environment. I would be able to get out and about unnoticed, but I knew that I could do little on the streets of that city that wouldn't be monitored. This was going to require a lot of planning and no small amount of luck on my part.

Having got to know the neighbours on my first day at the mooring, I made sure that they saw me drinking a couple of bottles of wine on the deck of the boat before retiring for the night, giving it the drunken stagger and making a bit of a racket as I locked myself in. Once safely out of view, I set up a program on the computer that randomly switched television channels and turned lights on and off as well as using the boat's speaker system to simulate movement on board. If, as was the worst case scenario, somebody knocked on the boat, I could also communicate with them via a headset in my helmet. This left me free to leave the boat via the pod which I duly did, having put on the medium weight suit that transformed me into The Kingfisher. I still had reservations about this whole action-figure idea, but it felt good nonetheless.

As I set the auto-pilot to steer the pod to my chosen disembarkation spot, I allowed myself to relax and review the plan I had in my mind. It had taken me another fortnight to get here from Milton Keynes during which time I had been able to send out the required assistance that I needed and which was all now in place, safely secreted on the roof of O'Rourke's house. I could have moved much quicker, and would have done so if prompted by my bosses in ORB, but the rest of my plan depended to some extent on being able to co-ordinate the judges' movements now that there were two in my sights. I had managed to engineer a visit to O'Rourke from Walters who would be bringing his wife for an impromptu get-together. At least that's what they thought they were there for.

The only way that I could get close enough to the house was by leaving the pod and navigating my way through the capital's underground water system. It wasn't the most pleasant route but fortunately I was only underground for a short while before I emerged in a side street to the rear of O'Rourke's. I slipped into his garden, hid to the side of the property and used the various monitors in the helmet to check that the boat, the pod and my helpers were all as they should be. My heart was racing, but I was focused on the task ahead.

On hearing a taxi pull up outside, I used the spiders to observe Walters and his wife arriving. They rang the bell and waited. Via a speaker that I had hidden by the door, I heard the exchange as the door was opened.

"Good evening, Peter," Walters said, "I hope we're not early."

"Joshua," O'Rourke replied, "Erm, no, at least, I'm sorry but did Margaret arrange this? I'm awfully embarrassed but I wasn't expecting you. Oh, good evening, Helen."

"Good evening, Peter," Walters' wife answered, "I thought we'd arranged this evening with you both. I hope we've not made a blunder?"

"Well, never mind, never mind," O'Rourke said, "come in anyway. Seems one of us is in the naughty corner but we're not doing anything tonight and it is good to see you."

I watched as he led them into the sitting room and switched my mode of surveillance to enable me to see and hear their confused greeting as each thought the other had arranged the night's entertainment. This was my cue to start work. I flew the owl off the roof and into an open skylight window before manoeuvring it down into the house and onto the television set that sat in the corner of the sitting room. The occupants expressed the degree of shock and confusion I expected them to, but before they could do anything to act, I calmed them each with a shot from the bird's beak that saw them crumple one after the other.

When they came to, they were seated together on the floor in front of the settee and I was sat opposite them with the visor of my suit reflecting their mystified looks back to them, set as it was to one-way mirror mode.

"Please relax," the synthesised voice I was using whispered gently to them, "we need to talk."

"Now look here," O'Rourke tried to stand and come towards me but the effect of the drug and the cable ties that held him down prevented much movement, "this just isn't on. Do you know who we are?"

"I know exactly who you are, Justice O'Rourke," I answered, "in fact, that's why I'm here. Now please, let's all settle down and I'll explain."

I didn't need a lot of time to detail to them what I was doing there. First of all, I outlined the charges that I was raising against them and backed these up with the facts that I knew. Then I showed them the picture of Tanya's disfigured face, followed by one of Clara that I had been able to capture as one of my creatures circled the grounds of the secure hospital where she was detained. I concluded by telling them that there was no need for us to have a big debate about the situation, and that guilt had been proven on all counts. All they need do now was cooperate as justice was rebalanced and then I would be on my way.

"But what do you want from us?" Margaret O'Rourke, as the innocent of the bunch was the most fearful and also the most vocal, "I mean you can't just come in here and raise these sort of allegations."

"Please Mrs O'Rourke," I tried to be as calm as possible, "let's not talk about allegations. Your husband is guilty as I've detailed. Look at him, he won't deny it to you. And your friends are the same."

Nobody offered any defence and this seemed to silence her as she realised the culpability of her husband and friends. Maybe she also began to think about some of her own hidden transgressions that had not been referred to.

"Let's begin then," I said, "Firstly, you will both retire immediately from any form of public life. Let's take that as a given shall we?"

Nobody said anything.

"But now we also have to rebalance the scales of justice a little. So we'll start with the Carla situation. Your daughter is twenty-five, O'Rourke, correct?"

He nodded.

"Then let's see how she likes the treatment Stanfield inflicted on his victim."

They looked at me in shock as the owl picked up the sound of their daughter being tortured and raped over an agonising twenty-minute ordeal. I made them listen and warned them that if they weren't silent then I would provide a video feed. Needless to say, they said nothing.

When that was over, the four of them were sobbing and broken. But I still hadn't finished.

"Vanity is more of a female trait, I feel," I told them, "So, unfortunately this will have to affect you, Mrs Walters. I will however allow the gentlemen to choose who pours the acid. Before we go along that route however, I will be leaving you soon and you need not bother making any calls as the police and an ambulance will be along shortly. I'll leave you to decide the story that you tell them. Perhaps a strange sexual activity that went awry?"

The stench in the room was beginning to get to me, since both judges had long since evacuated their bowels, but I was nearly through.

"Before I go though, I expect compensation to be filtered to both Tanya and Carla. You are judges, you should know the correct amounts."

I then had to watch as I put the vial of acid on the floor in front of them, activating a couple of mice who ran into the room and put the two ladies to sleep. They didn't need to know who had done the deed, and for all my cold-hearted ruthlessness in this, I still had a modicum of compassion. I stayed to make sure it was done though.

Chapter Thirty-Nine

I'm not sure whether the delay in feedback from the guys at ORB was normal practice or whether they were waiting to see how it all fell out. Either way and whatever the cause, it was a week later that I received a message from Chow. The e-mail caught me early in the morning just as I was about to go out for a ten-mile run having found myself getting out of shape, despite my working the locks and manhandling the boat back up from London towards the Midlands. It came through on a dedicated server that had lain silent until that point but which now beeped incessantly and demanded my immediate attention. Nonetheless, I allowed myself time to make a cup of tea before settling down in front of the screen and logging on:

Project: O'Rourke
Operative: Kingfisher
Status: Completed
Notes: A successful resolution. O'Rourke tendered resignation after accident involving friend's wife at his home. Friend also resigned. Simulated rape of O'Rourke's daughter caused severe psychological trauma to all who heard. Bank transfers identified to several victims.
Rating: 72%
Feedback: Involvement of additional party a success in this case but should be cleared prior in future. Imaginative use of voice simulation programme to be communicated to other operatives. Some areas of concern regarding visibility: note, underground locations often monitored and presence in garden a weakness. Rebalancing actions in line with ORB thinking and appropriate.
Next Project: Lillian Starlet Model Agency – Anorexia; Grade three.

I read the report with mixed feelings. More so because I had another project that I wanted to pursue before being given this new assignment. It was a sensible precaution that the heads of ORB communicated in this detached and clinical way, but it did little to boost my confidence. Still, a 72% didn't seem too bad for my first go and there were enough positives there to encourage me. Of course, I knew some of the details already and the impact that my actions had had on O'Rourke and Walters. It had been three days before they were able to contact their daughter, who I knew to be at a retreat in Scotland where mobiles were not allowed and contact with the outside world was frowned upon. I had thought about taking that a step further but there had to be an end to the cycle and I was pleased that ORB agreed that for O'Rourke and his wife to believe their daughter had been raped was enough to bring about justice.

The brief message I got from Tanya's friend confirmed a payment to her that would set her up in her home country, whilst a slightly deceptive call to the clinic where Clara was being treated informed me that she was soon to be moving to a private hospital. All in all, a good result but with one loose end that I couldn't leave. Hence my journey back up to the Midlands and to an industrial estate in Banbury. If ORB didn't like this, I could be in trouble. Fortunately, the Lillian Starlet Agency was based in Manchester, so my diversion was on the route.

+++

'The Oxfordshire Press' 23rd July, 2022
'Occupants of Sealed Container under Investigation'

Oxfordshire Police remain tight-lipped about the circumstances surrounding the discovery of six men and two women in a sealed shipping container on a remote farm near Banbury. It is understood that all of those found were currently under investigation for people trafficking offences and initial lines of enquiry are seeking to establish whether this was an experiment that went wrong. The occupants had no food or water and the container was said by them to be infested with rats, although there was no evidence of this when they were freed.

Following their discovery, local police searched a number of properties and have retrieved information that they describe as being 'significant'. Those found in the container, now released from medical care, have been transferred to secure locations where they are said to be helping police with their enquiries.

An anonymous tip off received by this newspaper led to the recovery of the victims but, at present, no further information is available. Anybody with information that might help clear up this mystery is invited to come forward.

+++

'Fashion Monthly', September, 2022

'Surprise Resignation of Model Agency Directors'

Three members of the board of the Lillian Starlet Model Agency have resigned with immediate effect citing 'medical issues' as their reasons. Whilst the agency is refusing to release any further details, it has confirmed that the three board members, Chief Executive, Marie Star, Operations Director, Jennifer Pershaw and Events Director, Katia Von Ess are all currently undergoing treatment after contracting food poisoning at a private party they attended a month ago. Our reporters have been in contact with the private clinic where the three are being treated and have been led to understand that they are suffering from an infection caused by an antibiotic resistant strain of the c-diff bacteria.

The three directors were last seen in public at the launch of their new 'Zero Plus', initiative where they were met with a great deal of public outrage at their proposal to take catwalk sizes below what many agree are healthy levels.

The c-diff bacterium is a virulent strain that can take a long time to recover from and which, in some cases, can lead to fatalities. Victims are unable to retain any nutrients and it is this severe and uncontrollable weight loss that is the most dangerous aspect of the disease.

+++

'The Bolton Advertiser', 19th September, 2022
'Mourners Pay Tribute to Game Show Host'

Mourners in their hundreds gathered at Bolton Town Hall last night to pay tribute to the popular game show host, Billy Bray, whose sudden death shocked many fans earlier this month. It is understood that the fifty-five-year old star of 'Your Place or Mine', suffered a heart attack at his home from which he never regained consciousness. His family have said that he had been under immense pressure following a recent court case where he was acquitted of all the charges of under-age sexual activity that had been raised against him, and that this may have been a contributing factor in his passing away.

In a new twist however, it is understood that, prior to his death, Bray contacted police and offered new information about the case which they continue to pursue. The nature of this information is, as yet, undisclosed, but it is rumoured to name several other prominent celebrities and their relationship to Bray who famously left the court in Chester by making a tearful appeal for the prosecution of those who had smeared his name.

+++

'The Midland Herald' 2nd October, 2022
'Local Employer Admits Breaches of Health and Safety'

Roger Palmer, Managing Director of Palmer's Parts, the automotive supplier who returned to work recently after losing a leg in an accident at home, made a surprise confession last week when he admitted that his company had failed to provide adequate Health and Safety training and equipment to its workforce. Rejecting calls for his resignation, he has apologised for his past failures and has pledged to stay with the company until its practices are the best in the industry.

Palmer, who was found not guilty on charges of negligence in March of this year, has reportedly reached an agreement with unions and government officials to pay compensation from his own personal fortune to those employees who pursued claims in that unsuccessful legal action.

"Having an accident myself," he commented, "has focused my mind on the importance of following procedures that I may have inadvertently failed to adhere to in the past. I hope that this action of mine gives us all the opportunity to move forward and establish a new industry standard that respects every employee as a human being."

A separate investigation by the CPS in relation to this case remains ongoing as there were concerns that much of the evidence presented by prosecutors was found to be inadmissible.

+++

My average score remained around the mid seventy percent mark, although I now understood that anything more than this would represent what ORB would acknowledge to be a phenomenal success. They seemed to have either not linked me to the Banbury case, or had chosen to let that one pass, as the assignments kept coming and I cut my teeth on them. Each one presented new challenges. In the case of the model agency, I had had to secure stocks of resistant bacteria that were kept in very secure conditions in only a few laboratories in the country. Administering this treatment was easier, although the hours spent with Star, Pershaw and Van Ess had been an unpleasant and trying time as I explained to them the effects that the bacteria would have on them. They were fighters and I hoped that they would come through, but it was important that they endure the skeletal suffering their illness would produce. They knew a little about what they were in for after being shown numerous photographs of models from their own agency and others who had literally starved themselves to reach the parameters of the catwalk. Some hadn't survived and I think that they were most shocked by those post-mortem pictures.

Billy Bray was a different matter. No matter how hard I pushed him to confess he still denied everything, even after I'd shown him the files I'd retrieved from his computer and his safe. It wasn't a heart attack, although nobody would ever know any different. What would come out in the next few weeks however is the truth about this paedophile predator who may have escaped justice down here but who was surely suffering elsewhere. Palmer on the other hand was both repentant and apologetic. I was pleased how quickly he'd changed his tune as taking one leg off was difficult enough. If he followed through on his promises, then my work would not have been in vain.

When the report on Palmer came through, I was pleased to see that no further project had been assigned to me in the near future and this meant that I could have a few weeks to rest and recover. Things had been moving at a frantic rate and it would be nice to chill out for a short while and get myself back onto canal time. I moored up the boat along the Caldon canal and let the last of the Autumn sunshine refresh me as I sat on the towpath spending all day reading the Sunday papers.

Chapter Forty

It was near to Froghall that I first saw Jean again. I'd taken the boat through the tunnel to explore this canal terminus and had seen her sitting at the pub I passed on my return. She had a glass of wine and was looking out over the water. She gave the boat a half glance, recognising it as a similar design to New Hope Arising and gave me a wave, but neither were more than customary gestures. My old boat was a burnt out wreck and I no longer existed. Pulling into the moorings and with the boat securely tied up, I decided that a trip to the pub was just what I needed. With a pint in hand, I sat at the table next to Jean and followed her gaze as she stared out over the water.

Though I generally didn't smoke much anymore, I still carried a small amount of tobacco and papers with me as a reminder of its grip over me and for those rare occasions when a cigarette served as a useful social prop. I rolled the cigarette and lit it, enjoying the taste after such a long period of abstinence. It was obvious that I was going to approach Jean. I wouldn't be able to resist. But how I made that approach was the challenge and I was lost in thought when I heard her speak first.

"Penny for them?" she said, "You looked miles away."

"Sorry," I turned to her, "was just thinking about something. Beautiful day isn't it?"

We exchanged the usual canal side pleasantries and I edged along the seat to be nearer to her, making sure that I kept my hands out of her vision. James had tipped me off to that and I rarely let anyone look closely at them.

"I like your boat," Jean said, "reminds me of one that a friend of mine had."

"It might be the same one," I offered, "what was theirs called?"

"Oh no, it won't be the same," she sighed as she told me what I already knew, "his was burnt out a while back. With him on it."

"I'm sorry," my reply seemed inadequate, "That must be tough."

"Not your fault," she said looking closely at me, "but yes, it's still raw. We get by though. You may have known him, guy called Zipoly?"

I pretended to think hard about it before agreeing that yes, I had come across him in my travels and had even ordered from his company, and now that she mentioned it I remember it being in the news about the boat fire. Then the headache started. I felt it first as a tingle just above the bridge of my nose but it grew quickly to be an intense pain that stabbed behind my eyes.

"You alright?" Jean asked.

"Yes, sorry," I struggled to speak, "just got a blinding headache come on. Must be the cigarette. I'm trying to quit."

By this point the pain was just shy of making me sick and I had to excuse myself. I took the pint back into the bar and was going to leave it there when I realised that the pain was receding. I sat inside and sipped it slowly, feeling the intense thumping in my head ease off with every drop. Something wasn't right here. Finishing the pint, I put the glass on the bar and walked back to the boat, glancing into the beer garden as I did and seeing Jean still sat there and still staring out over the water. She caught my eye and I waved before clambering back onto the boat.

"Now that was weird," I said to myself as I sat in the lounge of the boat and opened another can of beer. Had it been the cigarette that caused the headache, or was it the stress of seeing Jean again? It shouldn't have been either but there had to be an explanation. I went for the emotions, rather than the tobacco. After all, I'd been out of the loop as far as proper relationships went for a while now and Jean was a blast from the past. Not just as my friend and lover, but also as a tangible link to the regular world that I no longer inhabited. When I'd agreed to become what I now was, I knew what I was giving up and, in general, I'd managed to keep my emotions switched off and stay focused on the clinical tasks in hand.

It was a good number of years since I'd lost Fran and the children and nearly a year since I'd lost Jean. The former experience helped with the latter as it had taught me how to move on from the chains of emotions and live without being beholden to those who were gone. There is a time and a place for grieving, but it has to end. There is a time and a place for commitment, but that can never be bondage. I was a new man now, one who had chosen to forsake the past for a future of solitude. I was never lonely, as life on the canals remained a life of passing friendships and shared joys, but those meetings had to be only fleeting. I had no desire nor any scope to cement any firmer ties.

My head was clear now, both from pain and from the pangs of the past.

Today was the moment in which I lived and yesterday was gone. I had a purpose in life now and the support of a large organisation who ensured that I lacked for nothing. Money was never an issue now that I was part of ORB and I could even have waved a black card and driven away in a Ferrari if I'd wanted to. They knew I never would though. It was this line of credit and the cash that was always around that meant that I didn't have to work. It would have been impractical to be fixed to a day job and try and do what I was doing, and generally the planning and execution of missions was more than enough to keep me occupied. I still read a lot, but in a more structured way now, for example working my way through the complete works of Shakespeare alongside study notes and reference books. If it wasn't literature, then I'd be teaching myself something else instead. Having tried a few languages but not being able to get to grips with them, that objective was a no-go. Similarly, I tried to play a musical instrument but again, couldn't make it work. Patience had always been a struggle for me and it failed to win through in either of those areas. Despite this, I was more successful with electronics, a bit of general science and also, for variety, some history. The history in fact was my current passion and it was fascinating to read over events from the past and consider how often justice and injustice have shaped the way that mankind has developed. I also had to keep an open mind as to how much ORB, either in its current form or in its past incarnation had influenced the course of history.

I was deep in the First World War when the secure server summoned me.

Subject: Meeting
Priority: Urgent
Message: Prepare for visit to HQ. Courier will be with you at 14.30.
Confirm activation code 3815
END

You had to give it to ORB, they didn't use an excess of words. Knowing the drill, I put together all that I needed for a visit, which wasn't a great deal. The courier arrived exactly on time and gave me the code I needed to hand him control of the boat for as long as ORB wanted him to have it. Wherever I ended up next, it was a certainty that she wouldn't be at on the Caldon when I returned. As I programmed the pod and took a last glance out of the boat window I could see that Jean had left the pub. I climbed into the pod and let the gas take me away as I put myself into the safe hands of my masters.

The next thing I remember is waking up in a soft leather armchair and hearing a familiar voice asking if I wanted a drink. I turned and smiled at James, telling him that a black coffee would be about right.

"Was I out long?" I asked.

"You know I can't tell you that," he chided me, but nonetheless shook his head as he said it, telling me that my journey had been fairly short.

"They want to see you at eight this evening," he told me, "and it's a full Council meeting so make sure that you look the part and that you get there at precisely eight o'clock."

"Am I in trouble?" I asked, racking my brains to think about anything I might have done.

"No," he said, "well, at least I don't think so. Come on, they don't exactly confide in me do they. I just do my job and when they say they want Steve Barratt in for an eight o'clock then I do what I have to do to get Steve Barratt in on time."

I was pleased that James was still James. It must be quite liberating to be free of the complexities of so many social norms. He was robotic in his work but there was a humour and a humanity that was enviable below the surface, still retaining the innocence of childhood even in the very adult world in which he lived.

"You can change in the lab," he told me, "you've still got a couple of hours and I thought you might like to see some of the things I've been working on."

We went through to the lab and as we entered, with a sweep of his hands, he showed me the workbench.

"Tada!" he laughed.

I couldn't see anything and told him so.

"That's the point," he said, "I've made everything smaller. Much smaller. Go and have a closer look but please, don't touch anything."

I made my way over to the bench and saw that it wasn't quite as empty as it looked. There were several trays laid out, each with a dozen or so tiny insects on them, the largest of which was a miniature version of the spider we'd created together.

"This is a joke?" I asked

"No," he beamed at me in triumph, "they all work and the spider does exactly the same as the old one. I've cracked the first bit of the anti-gravity problem, so they don't need as much power. There's still a way to go, but it's progress."

"The smaller ones," he continued, "don't do much but ORB asked me to put them together for you. We've christened them nanobots. It's a bit cheesy but it describes them well. They work at the atomic level and they can't be detected."

He continued to explain the thinking behind these new devices. They had limited functionality but were programmed to target a specific DNA profile only. Once they locked onto this target, they entered the bloodstream and worked their way through the host to perform their duty. Having completed their job, they disintegrated and joined the millions of other cells in the victim's body.

"So far," he told me, "we can only get them to stop the heart, or trigger a limited brain death in the victim. In future, we hope to be able to do more."

I was amazed and told him so. With a weapon like this, so many more possibilities opened up, although I did note they were limited to death only. I didn't join ORB just to be an assassin, but these things would have their uses.

"They'll be installed on the boat by the time you're finished here," James advised me, "meanwhile, let me show you something else. But keep this one quiet please as no-one is supposed to know about it."

He opened the wall safe and drew out a black box. As he lifted the lid he turned it to me and I saw inside a brightly glowing ball resting on a glass plate.

"What is it?" I asked.

"Remember what I said about my other interests?" he whispered as he spoke, "Well one of them is nuclear fusion. Limitless power for all. Imagine it. And this is the beginning. But you haven't seen it."

He snapped the case shut and told me to get ready for my meeting.

Chapter Forty-One

This was the first time that I had seen the whole Council assembled. These were the twelve self-appointed, good men and true, who directed everything that happened in ORB and who I now saw represented a wide span of the British society they were so keen to protect. Anderson, Batchcliffe and Chow, I recognised. The other faces were familiar to me but I couldn't name them all. They made no attempt to hide their identity as they knew that their secret was safe with me. Of the faces I did recognise, one was a prominent government Minister, one was a pop star turned campaigner and one was an Asian businesswoman who was a regular on TV quiz shows. The split was seventy-percent male to female, a similar percentage Caucasian to other ethnicity and their ages spanned from early middle to quite late old. An interesting mix all round.

The twelve were sat around an oval conference table bedecked with the usual paraphernalia of notepads, pens, coffee cups and water bottles, and I was beckoned to take a seat at the bottom end of the oval. Directly opposite me, one of the people I couldn't quite name, but who I deduced to be the current President, stood and addressed his colleagues and myself: "Thank you all for attending this meeting," he began, "and thank you too, Mr Barratt, for joining us. Needless to say this is not one of our regularly scheduled meetings and we appreciate the efforts that everybody has had to go to in order to be here. Before we proceed with the main topic of the meeting, Sir Anthony has asked if we might first of all take a few minutes to discuss with Mr Barratt his progress so far. If there are no objections to this then please, Sir Anthony, go ahead."

"Thank you," Chow began, "this shouldn't take too much of your valuable time gentlemen, but I feel that the time is perhaps apposite for us to share some of our thoughts with Mr Barratt, particularly in light of recent events."

My mouth went dry as I waited to hear what he had to say.

"I understand that you met recently with, shall we say, an old flame," he looked at me with piercing eyes, "and we would like to know the circumstances of this please."

I explained to them how I had bumped into Jean on my travels and what had occurred at the pub, finishing by advising them that I had cut the encounter short due to a headache.

"Thank you for your honesty," Chow said, "I think that gives us some idea of the accidental nature of that meeting. However, your behaviour was inappropriate and, whilst the full council is here, you need to understand that they all share this view. I believe I am correct in saying this?"

He looked around the room to his colleagues and waited as they all acknowledged their agreement with his assertion.

"Good," he continued, "Mr Barratt, you are not the person that you once were and you made, what I remind you, was a voluntary choice to cut all ties with the past when you joined our organisation. The Order is bigger, more important and more resilient than any of its members. It is particularly more so than a new recruit like yourself. If this sort of thing happens again we will drop you faster than you can blink. Do you understand?"

I nodded shamefully.

"Next time, you will have more than a headache I can assure you," he looked at me with a glint of victory in his eyes, "yes, the headache goes with the territory I'm afraid. You have been fitted with an implant that recognises certain scent patterns from your old circle of friends. Just so you are aware, that implant also recognises any DNA that we feel it necessary to respond to. It responds to either a threat to your anonymity, as in this case, or, and this you need to know, any threat to a Member of the ORB Council. It is a safety mechanism that we have had to introduce following certain incidents in the past. At the same time that the implant is building your headache to levels beyond those any of us could bear, which incidentally continues to termination, it transmits a signal to headquarters to advise of the nature of the meeting. You were very fortunate that your meeting coincided with our call to you as we do not like to deal with these things as special cases. We have better things to do with our time. Understood?

I said that it was crystal clear.

"Good," he continued, "now to your progress to date. Firstly, let me explain to you how our council works. We operate only on unanimous decisions, and I must inform you that your retention was not unanimously agreed at first. However, I have persuaded my friends that the case we need to discuss was an error of over-enthusiasm rather than one of outright rebellion. I am pleased to tell you that they have agreed to give you another chance."

He paused to take a drink of water and, I'm sure, to let his words register with me as I sat there wondering just what he was talking about. Surely, this was nothing to do with Jean.

"The issue is not your capability," he explained, "which you have proven beyond doubt, nor is it your understanding of our values, which again, you have shown imagination and commitment to deliver. The challenge we face with you, is in stopping you doing your own thing. The people traffickers. Great work, but not authorised. Our work is too sensitive for us to support lone vigilantes using the Order for their own personal objectives. Heaven knows, we all see multiple injustices around us every day, but the Order requires that we take a collective decision on those whom we intend to act on. Yes, that means that you will have to turn a blind eye at times. Welcome to our world. We can only do so much and we must stay focused on those things we agree to do. I have supported you once on this, and, as I have said, the Council has bowed to my wishes, but I must tell you that another lone initiative will be the end of our partnership. Is that agreed?"

I confirmed it was and apologised for my actions.

"That's all I have to say," Chow prepared to sit, "other than to commend Barratt to the Council for the excellent work that he has done despite his foolish transgressions."

"Thank you, Sir Anthony," the President stood to take over the reins of the meeting again, "and thank you Mr Barratt for your sterling work. Please don't let us down on the loose cannon bit. Now to business. We have an urgent grade one crisis on our hands. If I might now hand you over to my colleague, Alastair Humphrey, he will give you the details, some of which you will no doubt be familiar with. Alastair."

Alastair Humphrey was the government Minister I had previously identified. He spoke with a surprisingly gentle, almost feminine voice as he explained the nature of the crisis.

"As you are all aware," he looked briefly at some notes scribbled in front of him, "the Prime Minister's wife passed away yesterday after a fairly brief battle with cancer. Our thoughts and prayers are obviously with him and his family, however, we believe that there will be further implications surrounding this tragedy."

"Every predictive tool that we have run this through," he continued, "despite being models that we must recognise as inherently imperfect, concur on one thing. They all seem to indicate a very high likelihood that the Prime Minister will resign and hand over to his Deputy. Parliament still has three years to run and, speaking as a member of the party in power, I can safely say that we would not risk another general election, given our fairly fragile majority. Loyal as I am to my party, from the point of view of the Order, we cannot allow the Deputy Prime Minister to take over. The party has no reason to veto the succession, however, we here are a little more aware of his activities and the threat to justice that his appointment would bring about. There is a possibility that the Prime Minister may stay in office, in which case, it's business as usual. Sadly, I do not feel this is particularly likely."

He continued to give an overview of the problem to those present. John Harmason, the Deputy Prime Minister, had been investigated on several occasions within the current somewhat closed confines of parliamentary enforcement, the outcome of which had been unofficial reprimands. His transgressions ranged from creative use of the expenses system through to inappropriate lobbying in return for certain favours. There was a degree of protection from prosecution afforded to him by the House of Commons' managing its own affairs and by the party not wishing to air its dirty laundry, but his main defence remained the lack of concrete evidence that could be secured.

"Within the party," Humphrey concluded, "there is a high degree of respect for Harmason and I do not believe for one second that he will be opposed. At our level, within ORB, however, we feel that we do have enough evidence to act. Granted, our own findings would be classed as inadmissible evidence, but we have enough to agree that, in the office of Prime Minister, Harmason would cause a lot of damage in the limited time he has available. Not least, there will be the disestablishment of the Church of England, new laws to separate religious legal systems and, as far as we know, a return to capital punishment. Harmason would be a Prime Minister for hire. Added to which, I think we would all agree that his rewards to date have been more than sufficient and we would not feel that justice had been done were he to be promoted again. We cannot be too specific about the problem with Harmason, but have confidence that the issues will reveal themselves as his method of operating is more closely observed by our operative. I propose therefore that we charge Mr Barratt with the task of preventing this succession. All in favour?"

Twelve hands were raised around the table and, as Humphrey sat down, the President rose again to conclude the meeting.

"Given the nature of this proposal," he began, "I am pleased that we are all in agreement. This is somewhat of an unusual objective for us to pursue, and is perhaps the most game-changing that any of us have been involved in."

"The Order," he continued, "is not, and never has been, a political entity. It is a cross-party, cross-community, historic, national institution that remains dedicated to the balance of justice. In this case however, justice and politics have become inseparably intertwined around the person of Harmason. Our objective is simple, the prevention of his taking office as Prime Minister, but how that happens remains a mystery to me and most likely to yourselves."

"Barratt has been chosen," he looked at me as he spoke, "because he delivers and delivers effectively and perhaps, most importantly, he delivers imaginatively. We cannot prescribe the course of action he must take, but I feel that we can trust him to endeavour at all times to deliver the result we require without resorting to termination. Of course, if that is the only alternative, we will not interfere."

All the faces in the room were on me and I kept my features as expressionless as possible as the President went on to explain that were this mission to fail I could no longer be a part of the Order. This was the closest that ORB had come in recent times to an intervention in the workings of the duly and democratically elected Government of the country. As such, they were very close to compromising their role. Their agent therefore would have to be a lone rider. He wished me luck and hoped that we would meet again after a successful resolution, but tempered this by commenting that in the event of failure he would like to thank me on behalf of ORB for the work that I had done for them to date.

The meeting was closed and I took that as my cue to leave. I was escorted back to the laboratories but, on finding that James had finished for the day, I booked myself into the nearest unoccupied apartment. As with all the rooms down here, it was well presented and everything was free for me to use. I cracked open a beer from the mini-bar, ordered a room service steak and settled in to relax for the evening and begin to plan my next moves. I'd been put through the mill at that meeting. From the onset, I had been criticised and chastised and made to feel a failure. The mood had then changed and suddenly I was their chosen operative for this most unusual mission. Perhaps I was as good as they had said, or maybe I was just their most expendable operative. I wasn't sure. Either way, this was a make or break project that demanded a more sophisticated approach than the most obvious and simple one of killing Harmason off.

When the steak had been delivered and polished off, and another couple of beers taken to wash it down, I prepared everything I needed before settling down to sleep, wondering where I would wake up in the morning. I hadn't had a chance to say goodbye to James and I still had a lot to ask him, however, the choice of whether I was here tomorrow or back on the boat was out of my hands.

Chapter Forty-Two

As it happened, I was able to spend the following day at the ORB facility and catch up with James to discuss his new projects in a little more detail. He outlined for me, in lay-man's terms, how the nanobots worked and talked me through how to programme them on the boat's computers. They had supplied me with a number of different sized units and a variety of substances that they could administer. It was the DNA targeting that most interested me though.

"All you have to do," James explained, "is to get hold of the smallest sample of the target's DNA and the computer will interface with the nanobot once it has sequenced it. This can usually be done in a matter of hours, however, it depends on the type of sample obtained. Saliva and blood are the best, but you should be able to get a sequence from even just a fragment of hair. The nanobots can scent DNA from quite a distance, but they can only process the most dominant elements in this way. They need to get closer to confirm the exact match and they have a failsafe built in that means they cannot activate their objective until they confirm that they have the right host."

He gave me a live demonstration and I watched in wonder as he set one of the smaller nanobots in motion. It paused briefly, then set off towards a rank of small-animal cages on the other side of the lab. We lost sight of it but he asked me to keep an eye on the rat in the yellow cage. I watched as it sniffed the air, lifted its head in a mystified way, then fell fast asleep.

"Tranquilised," James reassured me, "and with a specific dose that is timed for six minutes exactly."

Sure enough, the six minutes passed and the rat opened its eyes.

Finishing with James, I walked through the town, stopping only to treat myself to a burger for lunch, before I volunteered my presence at the imaginatively named, Transit Dock. They settled me in, made sure I was comfortable, then the next I knew I was waking up on the boat. It had been an interesting but challenging week so far which is why I had few doubts about the decision I made to give myself a 'me day' to get my head around all that had gone on and to explore my new surroundings. They'd moved me to the Lancaster Canal, overlooking Morecombe Bay. This was a new location for me and in that part of the country, where beer is a little too reasonably priced and chip shops know how to cook proper food, I made sure that I made the most of both of these advantages.

The Prime Minister resigned a couple of days later, citing personal circumstances and proposing a swift hand-over to Harmason, the current Deputy Prime Minister and MP for North Preston. That explained why they had moved me here. I felt the clock start ticking and began my research into Harmason and the possible routes I could use to scupper his promotion. There was a lot of information but most of it was, for my purposes, anaemic and of limited value. This wasn't really a surprise as, despite what ORB's feelings were about this man, he was generally seen as a strong leader and had a loyal following, both in the party and in the country at large. If I was to crack the challenge ahead I knew that I needed to look deeper into his past whilst getting to know him a little better.

The latter part of this process would be fairly straightforward. My alternate identity as Jason Gould was a card-carrying member of Harmason's party which meant that I could visit his local haunts without attracting too much suspicion. This would be the first time that the second male identity ORB had given me would be used, so, as I continued the rest of my research I adopted this persona in order to get it off pat. The team at ORB had done a brilliant job in providing me with the three identities that I held. Although most of the time I was anonymous in my work, they clearly understood that certain allegiances could come in handy and had therefore loaded up each character with useful and contrasting facets: Steve Barratt was an active supporter of the opposition party, whilst Jason Gould was a contributing member to the party in power; Barratt was Chelsea, Gould was Manchester United; Barratt was straight, Gould was gay; Barratt had a crew cut, Gould had shoulder length hair. And so on. The information was all out there on the web for me to discover and it was in this way that I had taught myself about myself. It was difficult enough to try and become a different person, therefore I had figured that all I needed to know was what anyone else would be able to discover in the public domain. Alongside all of this, Jackie McCann waited in the wings as a third option for me, but the challenge of a gender change was a little too much for me just now so I saved her for some time in the future.

The biggest problem I faced was in trying to pinpoint what it was about Harmason that had so shaken the people at ORB and necessitated my mission. Members of Parliament, despite the amount they were pilloried in the press, were generally good people. I believed that then and I still believe it, despite the bending of the rules by my current prey being less than exceptional in the behaviour of this particular and peculiar breed of citizen. My only hope was to get to know Harmason as well as he knew himself and allow my instincts to guide me to that part of him that was the major concern. It had to be visible somewhere in his past but exactly where, I had no idea. For that reason, lengthening the span of my research was the logical approach and the one which I adopted, beginning at the beginning with the child Harmason, in the hope that this might lead me to discover what had led to the creation of the man he was now.

Born in 1960, John Wesley Harmason grew up in a number of towns and cities across the UK, moving with his family at roughly five year intervals. This nomadic existence, was due to the fact that his father was a Methodist preacher, happy to move as called and keen to share his message across as much of the country as possible. In this, he was ably assisted by a wife who could make friends with the highest and the lowest at the drop of a hat. Harmason was the youngest of three boys, but became an only child at the age of twelve when an outbreak of meningitis felled the whole family. He survived along with his parents but was given the news of the death of his siblings when he was in the latter stages of recovery. From that point on, it appears that Harmason began to divert away from the family tradition of Christian service into politics, which resulted in his leaving home to study at his choice of University rather than take up the place reserved by his father at a Bible College.

It was whilst at University that he began to leave more of a publicly accessible trail, writing often in the various publications produced by the students and speaking at conferences towards the end of his undergraduate days. On graduation, he stayed to complete a Masters, after which he went straight into the central headquarters of his chosen party and began the long, slow climb to his position as Deputy Prime Minister which he had held since his party came to power six years ago. Newspaper reports of that dramatic election, and Harmason's role in it, praised him as one of the driving forces of the victory, whilst noting that the office he succeeded to was the safest place for the party to reward him but keep him reined in.

He was not a politician who pretended to be anything other than what he was, and his outspokenness had been a source of controversy throughout his career.

Most notably, he was an unapologetic misogynist, a strict disciplinarian calling for the return of national service, a ruthless advocate of stiffer prison sentences and an outspoken atheist who rejected all that his, now retired, parents had stood for. Despite all of these traits, or maybe in some cases because of them, he regularly topped opinion polls as the most respected of all politicians, and this barely changed when he was tarnished with some dubious claims made on his expenses. It was generally agreed that, because of his popularity, he was almost untouchable and at every party conference he appeared on stage and spoke with such conviction and charisma that his transgressions almost disappeared from sight. Any of these minor character flaws might open the door to my discovering the real problem that ORB had with Harmason, but nothing jumped out at me as I researched each aspect, only to find it leading to a murky end that only seemed to show him up as being a little more honest in his recognition of his failings and flaws than most of us have the courage to be.

He was on his third marriage and had numerous children from these, as well as one or two from mistresses. None of this he had ever tried to conceal and, in fact, he seemed to enjoy goading his denigrators about his masculinity whenever this topic came up. None of his ex-wives, lovers or female supporters had ever hinted at his being violent, cruel or in any other way threatening, although they all agreed that he was, as one of his lovers admitted in a magazine interview, "an acquired taste.".

Having dismissed this side of my enquiries, I looked at his support for discipline and the use of the armed forces to nurture strength and order into a youth that he believed was being mollycoddled to death. There was nothing especially worrying here, indeed, a lot of what he wrote and said made good sense. What was particularly impressive about his passion for this topic was that he was able to back everything up with sound academic research and solid empirical examples. He might be obsessive in his opinions but he was no ill-informed bigot. This same attention to detail could also be seen in his approach to criminal justice. He was clearly frustrated at lenient sentencing and overly luxurious prisons and had been nicknamed 'Hammerson' by the tabloids on more than one occasion. Behind this public persona however, there was a less well publicised string to his bow and he had written a surprising number of articles in favour of sound restorative justice principals particularly when applied to offenders who had been abused. In the same article in which the press had picked up on and reported his demand that child abusers and pornographers should, "have their balls cut off and be made to eat them," he had also called for better facilities for survivors of abuse and commented that love and support for these victims was the only way to break the cycle.

Despite all that was written about Harmason, I found myself not hating him as I thought I would but in fact building up a level of respect for his views. There was very little of what he stood for that I wholeheartedly agreed with, but I admired his unwavering principles and his sound grasp of both sides of the arguments. None of which drew me any closer to finding that chink in his armour that I needed to discover and discover quickly. I was already more than a week into my research and nothing was standing out for me.

Taking a welcome break from scanning over the monitors and getting nowhere, I went for a stroll along the towpath and, as usually happened, found myself exploring one or two of the local hostelries on a circuitous route back to the boat. It was in the third of these that I noticed a hastily printed flyer that had been pinned to the wall in the toilets. It advertised a meeting of Harmason's local constituency team to be held that weekend at one of the party-subsidised clubs just outside Preston. It explained that Harmason would be in the area prior to taking up his new role as Prime Minister and that he wanted to meet and greet his local supporters to thank them for helping him achieve his lifetime ambition. There was a number to call to book a place. I rang, explained who I was, received a very positive welcome to the area and was told that, of course, they would be honoured to have such a dedicated and supportive party member at the event. I was to pick up my ticket on the door.

I continued my research on Harmason right up to the event, still yielding nothing of substance and hoping that meeting the guy face to face would help me in my pursuit of the elusive skeleton in his cupboard. There were a couple of lines of enquiry that I wanted to pursue and these would best be broached in an informal conversation, especially after a few drinks had been consumed. The clock was ticking away and I needed a break. That night I was fortunate enough to get it.

Chapter Forty-Three

I had no difficulty getting in to the ticket-only event at the club and in fact was given something of a VIP status by the locals who had been advised that Jason Gould was an important contributor to the party. I spent most of the evening chatting to all and sundry about a wide variety of topics and explaining that I was visiting the area on business and had happened across this meeting. At nine o'clock a buzz went about the room and I saw a crowd flocking around Harmason as he made his grand entrance to the event. He took his place on the small stage at the front of the room that was usually the haunt of the up and coming ranks of stand-up comedians and folk singers, but which now had the soon to be Prime Minister of the country at its centre. I half expected him to launch into a long and tedious speech but he simply thanked all his supporters and apologised that his new duties would keep him away so much from his home crowd. He assured them that he would never forget his local constituency and that he would make it a priority to do what he could in office to support the region's economy.

Leaving the stage, he took his time to mingle with the crowd and catch up with old acquaintances before eventually making his way over to the table where I sat with the regional party chairman. We were introduced and he made small talk with us, thanking me for my continued support and offering to meet with me once he had settled in at No.10. As he handed me a card with his personal contact numbers on, I realised just how good a job ORB had done in creating Gould as an influential political mover and shaker.

The conversation then moved on to the subject of local politics and a number of things that needed to be settled before Harmason returned to London, which he confirmed he would be able to attend to as he was staying at his constituency home for a few days before heading back to Parliament. I skirted around as many topics as I could, but failed to get any traction, so I casually dropped his parents into the conversation and mentioned how proud they must be.

"Perhaps," he muttered, "we're not that close anymore. They're still one tambourine too many for me most of the time and I don't want them trying to divert the party from its natural course."

Clearly feeling a bit less comfortable on this topic, he excused himself and moved on to another table. One of the locals who remained seated next to me turned to his neighbour, who was wearing a clerical collar and joked:

"You need to watch out Vicar. You may be out of a job soon."

The vicar didn't say anything in reply and the conversation moved onto other topics.

I stayed a little longer but didn't want to miss the last train, so I left while the party was still in full swing. The regional rail service was basic but reliable and I was one of only a couple of people using the service that night with a carriage pretty much to myself. We rumbled along and I thought about Harmason and the little that he'd said. Like any politician, his public comments were measured and insipid. There just wasn't anything that I could see that ORB had an issue with.

As we pulled into the station, I disembarked and was walking back to the boat when the bells of the local church chimed the hour, snapping me out of the trance I seemed to be walking in. I looked up and watched as the clouds drifted away from the full moon and caused the steeple to be lit up before me. That was when I realised that I'd missed the obvious. I ran back to the boat and began a new search on the web.

Approaching things from a different angle I began to discover Harmason in places that I hadn't found him before: In the audience at obscure lectures that somebody had felt the need to post on social media; in library references where his testimony adorned several marginal publications; and on the odd posting on certain specific forums on the web, albeit under a loosely veiled identity.

Atheism was the link. Not that the media had any problems with this, since the new atheism of the twenty-first century was not only accepted but also deemed to be a positive step forward for the nation. But there is atheism and there is atheism. The most telling evidence was in the videos I was able to track down of two of the more controversial speakers on this topic, a Doctor Fellows and a Professor Callaghan. Fellows was an evolutionary scientist, whereas Callaghan was a social historian. Although an unlikely pairing, they had joined forces having reached the same conclusion from their own respective disciplines that if God was non-existent then morality had to be rethought. I watched the videos and could see just where they were coming from. Although I vehemently disagreed with what they were saying, they didn't mince their words and there was a certain logic in their arguments. My interest in the subject however was more to do with the audience. At three of their lectures, there on the front row, making notes and nodding vigorously, Harmason could clearly be seen.

I put two and two together and got to four. This was the concern that ORB had. I knew that the Order had started life with some religious overtones, having been named after the Franciscans, but I also knew that they were not driven by religious motivations, albeit there would always be some element of this in their work. They had picked up on Harmason's taking atheism to that new level and I could see straight away that if he were to be given the power then he would exploit the death of God to the full. It was all very well for an academic to postulate on the social change that could be achieved without the constrictions of any outdated morality, but to give this sort of notion the power of the Prime Minister's office was a step too far.

The following day I collated my data, refined my perspective and assured myself that I was on the right track. Then I made the necessary plans and waited for nightfall, at which point I put on the lightest Kingfisher outfit, slipped into the pod and travelled towards Harmason's house. It was a twenty-mile journey to his home just off the canal at bridge sixty but the new pod ate up the miles without any trouble, settling itself into the bank from which I was able to exit and walk to the mock Tudor mansion that he had built for himself. There were armed police on each of the entrances, a fact that I was able to determine by using a couple of my flying friends to reconnoitre the area before I emerged. This didn't surprise me, given that the inhabitant would soon be in the highest office in the land, but I had seen the blueprints to the house and knew that I could bypass the security. I needed the lightweight suit though and was glad that James had upgraded it on my last visit to his laboratory.

The walls that were topped with glass and razor sharp barbed wire, disappeared under my feet as I rose on the ion-drive boots which could now lift me higher and for longer than ever before. I assumed that the police guards would be unlikely to look up and see me, but sent out a couple of bats in the opposite direction to distract them anyway. Landing gently on the roof of the property, I eased myself down a hidden gulley and into the house through a skylight.

Harmason was on his own in his office. I waited in the hallway while he finished a telephone conversation then I quietly unzipped a pocket in my suit's belt and withdrew a slim wooden case. I opened the case and watched as the tiny nanobot scurried away and under the office door. I'd extracted the DNA from the card that Harmason had given me and the nanobot went straight for him. Allowing a minute or two for the creatures work to take effect, I followed it into the office and was happy to see Harmason snoozing in his big leather chair behind the desk. I closed and locked the door then waited until he started to come around, the drug only being programmed for a very light dosage.

"Who are you?" he managed to whisper as he came around, "And what do you want?"

"Good evening, Sir," I answered, using the helmet of the suit to deliver a gentle voice that had no similarity to my own, "Please don't be alarmed. I am here as a friend and I just need a few minutes of your time."

"Do you know who I am?" he said, "I could call out and have armed police here in a second."

"Of course I know who you are," I answered, "that's why I'm here. Go ahead and call out. Try it anyway."

As he began to speak the nanobot delivered a dose of anaesthetic to his throat and all that came out was a slight croak. It had been programmed to respond to his voice whenever it rose beyond a whisper.

"Please, Mr Harmason," I assured him, "I won't be here long, and I apologise for my unconventional approach. Believe me, when we are finished here you will be glad I came. Can I just tell you my story and we'll go from there?"

"Why not," he murmured, "doesn't seem like I have much of a choice, but it better be good."

I made sure that it was. I told him that I was the new righteous corrector and explained that I had killed the previous person doing that role as they were too moral and were letting too many people off the hook. I gave him the name of the old vigilante, confirming a rumour that circulated across the internet, and I told him how I had stripped Hardacre of all his tools before setting fire to his boat with him on it. I almost convinced myself in the telling. I then proceeded to offer my services in the new regime that I knew he was planning to implement.

"We were both there," I said, "at the last presentation made by Fellows and Callaghan. I watched you as much as I watched them and I knew that we would be partners in this. Let me just explain."

I continued to tell him that I understood what he wanted to achieve in his time as Prime Minister but I emphasised how short his time was if he was to make the progress he hoped. I could help him with this, as I had the tools and the equipment to crush any opposition. I was offering to build him his army of storm-troopers, fit for the new age that he would usher in.

This was the critical point now, and I waited when I'd finished my side to see how he would respond.

"You're taking a big risk," he said looking intensely into the visor of my helmet, "why should I believe you?"

"Oh, please," I replied, "I've managed to get to you at your home and I've demonstrated the kit I have, whilst at the same time I've told you bluntly that I killed Zip Hardacre. I had this one chance to get to you because once they make you Prime Minister I won't be able to get near you. But I can help you. I want to help you. If you're not interested, I'll go and you won't see me again. But you can't do it without me."

"You believe in what Fellows and Callaghan say?" he asked and I nodded in reply.

"Well, so do I," he said, "In fact, I don't just believe what they say, I'm determined to make their work my primary purpose in life. I have one shot at doing this and I can't blow it. Seems you have me over a barrel but then again, you do seem to have rid us of that do-gooder, Hardacre. Do you have any real proof of that?"

I unzipped a side pocket and flicked across a carved token with RC engraved on it. On the back was the name Zipoly Hardacre. He caught it and looked it over.

"Nice," he permitted himself a brief smile, "Okay, maybe we can work together. Let me share my vision with you. If you're in, we can sort it when I'm instated as PM. If not, we separate and that's that. You're hiding behind a mask and I will deny this conversation, so neither of us has a hold over each other. But first, can you get this throat thing off me?"

I withdrew the nanobot that came back to me and settled in its box. He looked amazed but then stood, poured himself a drink and told me of his plans.

"I decided God was dead, if in fact He'd ever been alive, when my brothers died," he began, "After all, if there was a God, that didn't seem like a nice thing to do to His devoted servants. My parents still believe it all. Their loss."

He took a long drink before continuing:

"Once I'd reached that point, it was easy to extrapolate. No God, therefore no consequences after death. And the evolutionists have helped lay the foundations for a new way of life. Over the past few years, everything has been about the death of God and the certainty of us all being simply an accidental product of millions of years of changes from a little speck in the primordial soup to what we are now. The majority view has shifted from believing we were created, to accepting that we are products of billions of years of evolution. It's taught in schools, it's accepted across the media and, more importantly, we are now at the stage where the Creationists are ridiculed as flat-earthers."

"We therefore have the opportunity," he continued, "to take this to the next step. Imagine, if we really chose to follow what the death of God leads us to. Imagine the world we could create? But yes, you are right, I can't do it on my own. There are others, loosely forming themselves into a group they call The Alliance, but they're not ready for action yet. With that in mind, I have to say that I am interested in what you can do."

We talked some more and he listened as I explained the tools that I had available and the plans I had for a new army that could implement the change he envisaged. Then I asked him to share more of his vision with me. This was what I was here for.

"I dream of a world," he said, "where we enjoy total freedom. Not just the freedom of equality that everybody seems so set on these days. But true freedom of the mind. The freedom to do what is best for the majority and to make decisions without being bound by foolish notions of divine retribution or idiotic religious morality. If we truly believe that we are simply a randomly evolved bag of assorted chemicals, that happens here by accident and then disappears to nothing, then we have to start living like that. How much waste is there in keeping the disabled alive? How much waste is there in keeping the demented in care-homes? Without God and with a new morality we can choose the sensible route and kill them off. That's freedom and that's the right decision. Why pump resources into maintaining a spastic or empty body when those same resources can be used to make life more enjoyable and fulfilling for a complete person who can repay the contribution? That's what survival of the fittest is about and now it's time that we walked the walk and stood up for this belief. This is a new justice where the law supports the majority and acts without all the foolish wrangling that goes on now. Look at our courts, we ask non-believers to swear on the Bible and then accept they tell us the truth! We lock up the ones who've blown their chances and more resources are diverted to keeping them going, when in reality we should terminate them. We need to cut through the chatter and cut out the cancers. That's freedom."

He paused to take a breath and have a drink.

"True freedom," he continued, "is the freedom to be gay and the freedom to beat up the gays. It's the freedom to love and to hate; the freedom to have faith or to crush religion; the freedom to care for the helpless or destroy them. This is a new morality of common sense unconstrained by false doctrines. I want to implement this new morality and, you are right, my time is limited. Yes, you can help me do it. When I take office, come and see me. Announce yourself as Zipoly to anybody at Number Ten, I can't imagine there's anyone else with such a stupid name, and I'll make sure they let you in."

We shook hands and I left, climbing back onto the roof and disappearing into the night. I couldn't wait to get back to the boat and review the material I'd collected. For a future Prime Minister, Harmason had proven himself to be somewhat gullible and surprisingly indiscrete.

Chapter Forty-Four

Harmason was sworn into office on the afternoon of the 4th of November, 2022. So began the shortest recorded incumbency of a British Prime Minister. It happened like this.

I worked away on the boat whilst Harmason tidied up his constituency affairs before returning back to London to take up his new position. Two things happened on the day of his inauguration: firstly, he became Prime Minister of the UK; secondly, I received a terse message from the ORB committee, asking me to attend an emergency meeting the following day. Regarding the former, everything went smoothly, with as little pomp and ceremony as possible in respect of the previous incumbent's late wife. With regard to the latter, I politely declined the invitation from ORB, asking them instead to keep their eyes open and perhaps contact me after the weekend.

Harmason was humble and respectful during the official ceremony, concealing his personal triumph against the backdrop of the tragedy that had opened up the door for him. He dropped that façade the next day and was guest of honour at a rally that he himself had organised to celebrate his promotion and to give his first speech to his followers. By some stroke of good fortune, the Albert Hall had been available to host this rally and Harmason had decided to grab the chance to bring in his new era from a traditional British venue. The party rallied around and tickets were sold out within hours of the event being announced, whilst the national television channels were happy to rearrange their schedules as the show would include live performances from some top musicians, acts that they would never have been able to afford themselves but who were supporters of 'Team Harmason'.

At precisely nine o'clock, as the last chord of an electric guitar faded away, he walked solemnly towards the centre of the stage just as a stage hand fixed a podium in place.

"Good evening, London," he said, "and to viewers at home, good evening Great Britain."

He paused as the crowd cheered.

"Tonight," he continued, "is a night that you will remember for the rest of your lives. It is a night when Britain begins its emergence from the shadows and once again becomes a truly global player again.".

More applause filled the theatre until he held his hand up for silence.

"Firstly," he looked down with sad eyes, "let me say that I would trade anything not to be here and for my friend and colleague to have remained in place alongside his wonderful wife. But, that was not to be. I take on the reins of power with a heavy heart but also with a new vision for a new Great Britain. Let me share that vision with you."

Monitors around the stage zoomed in on his face and televisions across the nation saw him smile as he began.

"I have a vision…", the monitors crackled and the television feed was interrupted. After a momentary pause, the images came back, but nobody was listening to Harmason on stage. They now enjoyed the feed that I had cut into the system.

"I dream of a world," he said, "where we enjoy total freedom. Not just the freedom of equality that everybody seems so set on these days. But true freedom of the mind. The freedom to do what is best for the majority and to make decisions without being bound by foolish notions of divine retribution or idiotic religious morality. If we truly believe that we are simply a randomly evolved bag of assorted chemicals, that happens here by accident and then disappears to nothing, then we have to start living like that. How much waste is there in keeping the disabled alive? How much waste is there in keeping the demented in care-homes? Without God and with a new morality we can choose the sensible route and kill them off…."

The rest you already know.

Without any need to edit the material, I had exposed Harmason for what he was and the world now watched agape as he floundered around the stage, shouting to the electricians and the technicians in the wings who held up their hands as if to tell him that there was nothing they could do.

He resigned the following morning, making his tenure exactly forty hours long. I, along with the majority in the country, believed that this was a record that would take some breaking.

The message I received from ORB was conciliatory and congratulatory. They understood that I couldn't just let him avoid taking office this time, but that I needed to ensure that he never took office again and that his worldview was rejected outright by the British public with little chance of a new pretender taking his place. As a way of thanking me they offered me a month's break away from it all and encouraged me to treat myself. I took them up on the offer and told them that I would spend the month traversing the Leeds Liverpool Canal and that they were welcome to send me any low grade issues they needed tidying up whilst I was on that particular route.

As the dust settled around the aborted event at the Albert Hall I used the confusion to have the army of mice that I'd used to feed into the circuitry return to their hosts. I then landed the three owls that had carried this cargo onto the roof of a train that was headed back towards me, flying them by remote from Preston back to the boat. With everything stowed neatly away, I took the opportunity of the lock free Lancaster to cruise overnight down towards Glasson Dock where my passage was booked for the following day to take me to Liverpool and that most wonderful of early canals.

Harmason was having less of an enjoyable time. The party dropped him both as Deputy Prime Minister and as a plain Member of Parliament, distancing itself immediately from his policies and installing a new top team to manage the country. It was inevitable that a general election would follow but would have to be scheduled for January at the earliest since nobody would dare to let politics disrupt Christmas celebrations. Ironic really.

With his tail between his legs, Harmason retreated to his home where, even to this day, he lives out a solitary life of retirement, making only occasional public appearances and usually to meetings where attendees can be counted on the fingers of a pair of hands at most.

+++

'Lancashire Echo', 12th November, 2022
'Puppy Farm Closed as Owner Disappears'

```
Police were called late last night to an alleged puppy
farm on the outskirts of Chorley after locals raised
concerns about hearing the sounds of distressed dogs. On
arrival at Park View Farm, officers discovered nearly one
```

hundred dogs and puppies who seemed to have been left abandoned without food in filthy and dangerous conditions. The whereabouts of the farm's owners, Jake and Kathleen Norris, have not been established and family members contacted by this newspaper have said that they have heard nothing from then since the night before the police attended.

The local RSPCA have removed all the animals from the site and are actively in the process of rehoming as many of them as they can. A spokesperson for the organisation said that whilst paperwork had been retrieved from the site to indicate that some of these dogs were premium, pedigree puppies, it would be unlikely, given the conditions on the farm, that these will ever be returned to the Norris's.

Police have confirmed that there were no signs of a forced entry to the Farm, nor of there having been any sort of struggle with the owners. They are speculating that the Norris's may have fled before routine inspections which were due to be carried out next month. No cash or valuable were found on site, adding to the validity of this speculation.

+++

'Lancashire Echo', 27th November, 2022
'Kennels Owners Return Home after Unexplained Absence'

Jake and Kathleen Norris who went missing from their home at Park View Farm earlier this month, have been detained by police for questioning following their surprise return to the farm last night. Looking gaunt and dishevelled, the couple were spotted by a neighbouring farmer who contacted the police before approaching the Norris's who were clearly disoriented but who were unwilling to say where they had been. After being checked over at the local hospital, the Norris's were moved to local police cells and are being held there for questioning into the disappearance of several thousands of pound's worth of customer deposits. They have also indicated that a prosecution is likely for animal cruelty. No further information has yet been released.

+++

'Leeds City News', 19th November, 2022

'Pardoned After Eight Years of Life Sentence'

Peter O'Malley, the traveller convicted of multiple sexual assaults at the beginning of this decade, has been released from custody and given a full pardon by Her Majesty the Queen. It is understood that Mr O'Malley, 54, will be offered a substantial settlement in compensation for having been wrongly convicted on six counts of rape.

The conviction was overturned last week following the criminal prosecution service's receipt of new evidence in the form of a deathbed confession. This document was written by two teachers from a local public school who had been questioned but later released at the time of the attacks. It is understood that they targeted O'Malley as a 'substitute suspect' having identified the now disgraced Detective Constable in charge, Ian Finch, as being open to influence due to extreme prejudices against the traveller community. Finch is currently in custody awaiting trial.

The two as yet unnamed teachers who committed suicide several weeks ago also left behind a video confession and certain items that they had retained from each of the assaults. Details surrounding these suicides remain sketchy but the police have advised that they are not seeking any other suspects in relation to either the original offences or the two suicides.

+++

'Yorkshire Herald', 24th November, 2019
'Compensation for All Charlesworth Victims'

Charlesworth Holdings has announced that it will repay, in full, any monies deposited by investors in the failed Yorkshire wind farm scheme that a BBC documentary recently revealed to be a scam.

Investors will also receive substantial compensation from the Directors of the company who had, controversially, been found innocent of all charges against them at a recent High Court hearing. It is not yet understood why the three Directors have chosen to make this offer which will leave them all bankrupt, however a comment by one of them, Mr Derek Halewood indicated that they had all suffered from 'troubled consciences' since the company collapsed.

Local widow Marjorie Tailor, who invested all her savings in the failed scheme and who is set to receive a substantial additional sum, said that things seemed to change after she had met an unnamed individual who was shocked by her story.

(See also: A New Vigilante Hero? Editorial, page 13)

+++

'BBC Radio Liverpool' 2nd December 2019
'Shipping Magnate Admitted to Local Secure Hospital'

The long running saga of whether local shipping billionaire Lord Bootle is mentally and physically fit to be prosecuted on corruption and money laundering charges took a new and unusual twist last night when the 62-year- old was detained indefinitely at a local secure hospital.

Bootle, formerly Terence Garnett, was first investigated over a decade ago but shortly after the CPS began proceedings he was diagnosed as having severe mental and physical health issues that would prevent him having a fair trial. Repeated attempts to discredit this line of defence have failed and it was only last month that a judge ruled that further attempts to pursue this case would breach Lord Bootle's human rights.

It is understood that the Peer was found wandering naked near his mansion just outside Formby. Police seeking to question him were eluded for several hours as he fled from them. It would appear that the Multiple Sclerosis diagnosed in Bootle has been miraculously cured since it took over a dozen officers to finally catch up with him and apprehend him.

Whilst he remains sedated and awaiting further psychological tests, a source close to the nursing team that is attending him has indicated that the Lord believes that he is being chased by a talking owl.

+++

Of the four missions I completed whilst on my mini-break, all but one was from the Order. I took it on myself to raise concerns about the mistreatment of the animals at Park View Farm, having heard stories about the place from locals, and was pleased that the Order sanctioned my request.

I visited as a potential customer first but saw nothing to concern me. That same night, I'd returned unseen and discovered the true living conditions of the dogs on the farm. My response wasn't overly sophisticated, but then again, I was on holiday and wasn't in the mood for being subtle with the Norris's. The farm was in a fairly remote location and not too far from a patch of moorland that seemed to be visited only rarely by the most stalwart of walkers. Towards the middle of the moorland, there was a natural cave which I was able to adapt quickly as a temporary 'kennel' for my guests. I picked them up on the bike, having sedated them, and waited whilst they came round. They were tethered to iron rings that I had drilled into the walls, wrapped in enough clothing to keep the worst of the night chill off and with just enough food and water to survive. My rats kept them company. I don't think they ever realised that these were automatons but they must have had a few questions over the period of their incarceration as to how they could have been trained so well. The rats ensured they were alive, fed and watered and, most importantly terrified throughout the whole of their ordeal. I released them on the way back and hoped that they'd learnt their lesson. Even if they hadn't, they were certainly not in any position to start up in business again as they were unlikely to get a licence and besides which they had generously donated most of their wealth to animal charities. Well, someone had on their behalf. To be honest, the right thing to have done would probably have been to make sure everyone got their deposits back, but I chose the route I did as I have an issue with people buying designer puppies.

Securing the evidence to see Peter O'Malley released was the first mission that ORB sent me out on. It was all straightforward really although I would have preferred the two guilty parties to have suffered more. Their confession was drawn out using a combination of fear and various innovative truth serums, after which I had left the scene and continued with my holiday. They were guilty. They could choose to face the music or run away. It was their choice to do what they did. My satisfaction was in seeing O'Malley and his family on the television news whilst I was enjoying an evening drink.

Charlesworth was a trickier proposition. The guys at ORB gave me a slap on the wrists for coming out into the open with Marjorie Tailor, but I managed to appease them and they seemed satisfied that my talks with her had been necessary. The truth of the matter was that I had approached Marjorie casually over the Charlesworth affair but that I had so enjoyed spending time listening to her that we had met on several occasions. I guess that after everything blew up, she realised that I was no longer about and that I had given her very little information about myself. It was understandable that ORB wanted the notion of vigilantism to stay off the public radar as much as possible, but I had never claimed to be perfect and they needed to understand that I was working in an imperfect environment.

That said, I was extremely cautious with Lord Bootle and kept the whole thing to myself, operating only at night and in ways that I could not be tracked. I used the owls because they were so versatile. They were able, on the one hand, to capture images of Bootle working in his garden and moving about in ways that a genuine MS suffer never could. On the other hand, they were great for delivering hallucinogens and for backing this up with conversation. When he finally cracked I believe that it was the first time that he had ever suffered a genuine mental collapse. Even putting aside the physical ailment he had claimed, the way that he had eluded justice by claiming mental health issues was the main reason that ORB wanted action. The members of ORB pretty much all moved in circles where they knew that they could use the same sort of influence to evade justice, which I think is one of the main reasons they so despised Bootle for what he had done. They were members of a privileged elite and that membership was not something to be abused. What didn't hit the papers, and I'm not even sure if ORB were aware of this, but I did follow up on Bootle behind the scenes and take the necessary action against both the doctor and the judge who had helped him in his deception. There are very few closed circles in what I do, but I couldn't leave this side of it untouched. I was gentle with them though and left them both with a feeling of confidence that they would think twice about perverting the course of justice again.

Chapter Forty-Five

Aside from the few Kingfisher diversions, I had a fantastic time cruising the Leeds Liverpool and could quite happily have repeated the journey immediately after, had I not had to return to my duties. Christmas meant that my month's break could be extended into the New Year which was helpful as there were a few icy mornings when cruising was out of the question. That said, it had been a while since we'd had what anyone might describe as a harsh Winter.

As with all the canals I travelled along, the Leeds Liverpool has its mix of beautiful, remote locations and slightly less attractive town and city moorings. Still, even in the most built-up of places I passed through, I didn't have any trouble at all. There were the usual hotspots of over-exuberant youths who liked to act brave from the towpath as well as the litter-strewn patches around sink estates that tangled up so many traditional boats. It may have been cheating a bit but I let the various boxes of tricks that my own boat was equipped with deal with any of these fiddly matters. I was on holiday and didn't want to be messing about with fouled up propellers and chewed up mattresses.

Their history, their scenery and their remoteness from the outside world all add up to make the canals of Britain a place where, whatever the weather, anybody travelling along them can feel a very special type of peace that can be found in few other places. Of course, I appreciate as much as anyone else, the wonders of modern technology and the giddy heights of man's achievements in the twenty-first century, but it's nice to escape all that from time to time and live in a hand-cut, four-foot-deep, channel of water. It's nice also to be reminded that this so simple of transport routes was one of the drivers behind the progress that we see today. And it was built to last, by hand. I'll never cease to be a fan of the canals.

Beyond all of the material aspects however, it remains the case that it's people who make canal life so interesting. It was what really hooked me at first when, paradoxically, I chose to escape from the rat-race and live a solitary life. When you are in your boat, you can choose to stay in your boat and, apart from the odd bump or request for assistance, you are generally left on your own. But come Summer, when the sun-kissed towpath cries out to welcome you with a book and a beer in hand, you can't help but want to be a part of the transient community around you: a community that is for that moment only, as most of its members will have moved on by the following day, to be replaced by new faces. It's this side of canal life that really does it for me. The canals are a great leveller and the last bastion of true community in this country, where the rich and poor, the young and old, the strong and the weak, and the successes and failures can all share time together and all be welcomed.

I tried to divide my time during that November and into December roughly half and half between places of isolation and places where there was something to do and see (usually a decent local pub scene). It worked well for me, although the stack of books that I had accrued to work through over this rest-period hardly got touched. Aside from the time taken to cruise and work through locks, there was also that wonderfully unique exhaustion every evening that any cruiser knows. It's the feeling of a physically tiring day topped by the satisfaction of reaching your destination, but it's also a feeling that is best enjoyed over a drink. If I tried to read after a strenuous day I simply scanned the words for a few minutes before nodding off. Still, I had the Summer ahead of me to catch up on reading. Why waste all those cosy chilled nights of Winter spent snoozing in front of the log-burner?

Now, I'm not one of those people who can maintain the discipline of keeping a daily log of travel, so a lot of the places I've visited and many of the things I've seen have blurred into one. The record of my journeys and my travelling hours and the rest of the detail of logs that would be held by more astute helmsmen, remains for the most part, accessible in the numerous hard-drives and data logs that follow me around on the boat's computers, but I rarely access them. People, however, I remember with a little more clarity. So many different people and so many enjoyable times just listening to their stories and helping out wherever possible. And these weren't just people on boats either. As the canals have changed from being an industrial transport network into a place for recreation and leisure, so too have the people who frequent them changed. Whilst the cyclists and canoeists seem to want only the use of the facilities, the walkers, the boaters and the fishermen are happy to become a part of a gentler subculture, even if only for a short time.

My first proper stop after Liverpool was in Maghull, where I met Chantelle. With a name like that you can't help but wonder that she didn't have the best start in life and it was true, she had been one of a large, Irish Catholic family and had grown up around the area surrounded by a benefits culture. Further to that, she'd followed the predicted route for her by becoming pregnant at fifteen with one of the three children that she now took walking along the towpath. I stereotyped her from the moment I saw her, but by the end of our time together I had learnt a valuable lesson in humility.

My plan was simply to stop overnight in Maghull, doing a supermarket shop and a fast-food breakfast the following morning before heading away from the area. That was until I stopped Chantelle on her return from taking the kids to school and, after asking her where the nearest store was, we began to converse. In my mind I was talking to a young mother who I thought would be on her way back to her state-sponsored accommodation to watch television all day until it was time to pick the kids up. The person I discovered I was talking to in reality was indeed headed back to a council house, but to continue her studying for the PH.D. in Psychology she was due to complete in a few months' time.

One thing led to another and after a, not unusual, conversation about the lack of luxury bathing facilities on-board a boat, she invited me to her house for lunch and a bath if I wanted it. I took her up on the offer and by early that afternoon we were enjoying a bowl of home-made soup with home-made bread and a glass of home-brewed wine. I'd spent the last hour or so relaxing in a hot bath and I felt so much better for it. We chatted over lunch and I had the usual male debate going on in my head about where this would lead to and how I would turn Chantelle down if she wanted to take things further. Again, I got a rude awakening when I asked her why she had opened her house up to me so readily and was there anything I could do to repay her.

"Truth is," she said, reaching out to hold my hand, "I felt a bit sorry for you. You've got this look in your eyes that seems to distance you from the world around you, as though you have a dark secret to hide. I just thought you might appreciate a taste of the real world for a few hours. Am I close to the mark?"

I didn't know what to say. Stupid Steve had it in his head that this no-hoper who had turned out to be nearly a doctor fancied him rotten and wanted to bed him, when in truth she was simply reaching out as one human to another. Once I'd grasped that, I felt a weight lift off me because I simply had no physical urges anymore and hadn't wanted to disappoint her, but at the same time I felt a new burden land itself on me. She was right. I had done things that I had never imagined that I would do and seen things that I couldn't describe but, throughout all the past years of being a vigilante, I had had nobody to turn to. I couldn't tell her how close she was to the truth, but I could open up a little to her. It might be just what I needed to clear the decks ready for my holiday.

"Is this part of your Psychology doctorate?" I joked, trying to avoid the inevitable.

"Yes and no," she replied, still holding my hand, "because I think I may be right and, as I told you earlier, my studies are all about helping people with issues."

"I've got issues, have I?" I smiled but saw the compassion in her eyes, "Well, you may be right. Let's just say that I've had my challenges in life."

I explained about my wife and the children and how I'd left it all behind to carry on life on the canal. I didn't name my family, after all they belonged to Zipoly Hardacre, but I gave her the rest of the details.

"In my head," I told her, "I'm pretty much over it, I think. It's been over seven years' now. I've kept busy and I've kept moving over most of that time and there's no other life I would choose. But you may be right. It can be lonely at times, and as much as you switch your mind off the facts of the tragedy, I'm not sure you ever can switch your heart off."

"What about relationships?" she said, "Don't get me wrong, I'm not dropping any hints, it's just that my study is very much focused on human relationships and I wonder whether you don't miss having someone to love."

I thought long and hard about this before choosing to answer honestly.

"There was somebody," I said, "but we couldn't make it work out. Neither of us wanted the commitment and then circumstances changed and I had to get out of her life. Since then, I've told myself I'm happier on my own. I don't think that's just fighting talk, it's probably true, but yes, there are times when it would be nice to share things with someone else. I still carry a lot that I can't share. You are right, it is something I need to think about. This is so good though, opening up just a little to you."

We took another glass of wine through to the lounge and settled down to talk the afternoon away. I steered the conversation towards her studies and her thoughts as a psychologist to the work of vigilantes.

"Do you remember that self-styled guy, the one who did the righteous correction thing?" she asked, "Must be a few years ago now, but he was the sort of person you mean, yeah?"

I agreed and said that I vaguely remembered him.

"Well," she said, "I looked into his case a little for my Masters, making a point about altruism I think, that there was a need to help in all of us but that need sometimes became an obsession. A validation of worth if you like. As though that guy wanted to do good, but needed to do more than the usual good that you and I try and do on a daily basis. Are you with me?"

"Go on," I said.

"Well," she continued, "if you look at the average person, whatever that means, they are generally good at heart and happy to help out. Society does a bit too much to promote selfishness but that core morality seems to stay in most people. But with this guy, it's like he wanted to do good but didn't have the chance to do nice things on a daily basis, so he had to create opportunities for big events. I speculated that he was an outsider of sorts, not working, with little human contact, but still needing to prove himself. I even concluded that this all pointed to there being some truth in the rumour and speculation about him being a boater, like yourself, who had died in a fire. You must have heard that speculation?"

I agreed that I had, and laughed at the suggestion that somebody on a boat could do what that guy had done.

"Still," I said, "you might have something there. Things stopped happening after he died. Maybe it was him. But where does that leave me though? Are you saying I should follow him and take on his mantle to free my spirit?"

"Of course not," she laughed, "I'm just saying that the sadness that I see in you might reflect that disconnect with the wider world and it might be worth looking at ways you can reach out. Not sure how that pans out on a boat but you must get opportunities."

Her phone alarm went off and she excused herself, telling me she had to go and collect the kids. We walked back to the boat and thanked each other for a lovely time together and I promised to look in on her on my way back. Then she was headed away and I decided to make the most of the last remaining daylight and move on myself with a few hours cruising. I had a lot to think about on that cruise. My prejudices, my weaknesses, my vulnerability and my vanity in thinking that only I was the defender of righteousness and justice. This holiday couldn't have come at a better time for me.

I know it can be tempting to overegg the pudding sometimes when considering the impact that a brief encounter can have on your life, but meeting Chantelle seemed to open up something in me that needed to be worked on whilst I was having my break along the winding stretches of the Leeds and Liverpool canal. This tale is as much about my own journey as it is the actual details of my travel, and so I lay out now how that starting point in Maghull came to help define the person I am now.

With Chantelle having noticed something in my eyes, which were, you will recall, not my eyes at all, I had to consider that the inner me was reaching out to the world in a new way. And I'm not ashamed to say that she made me think about what I was and where I was going. It was wonderfully liberating as well to interact with her in a close way that was not warped by the sexual desires that the old me would have introduced to mar the situation. Celibacy is no personal crusade for me but, having carried with me for many years the usual male desires that seek to see women as flesh rather than for what they are, it was lovely to understand that I now seemed to have been freed from some of the burden of this.

Once out and away from Merseyside and into the industrial heartlands of Lancashire my next precious, non-Kingfisher, memory is of a spontaneous barbecue afternoon with the inhabitants of a couple of other boats that I found myself moored next to. On one of the boats a very well-heeled executive and his family were enjoying getting back to nature and slumming it for a fortnight on a hire-boat. Granted, they had chosen a very nice hire boat but even the best of them is nothing more than a glorified caravan on water. The other boat had a couple my age aboard, who had chosen to give everything up to provide an alternative lifestyle to their one-year-old daughter. Had these two families met out there in the world beyond the waterways, they would have passed each other by and would likely have done so with a cursory dismissal of their respective lifestyles: one would have judged the other to be a part of the imaginary ruling classes, whilst the other would have turned away from new age, hippy scroungers.

Over that barbecue we all got to know each other and the playing field was well and truly levelled. I've always been wary of slipping into that arrogance that can sometimes pervade the canals when the liveaboard, experienced people like myself seem to be welcoming strangers into their special world, but, as with Chantelle, I myself was able to learn as much from my new friends as they might take from me.

Jeff was the Managing Director of a clothing company that supplied to the top names on the high street and had recently branched out into retail concessions. His wife, Annette, top-drawer, immaculate and beautiful, worked with a few charities but generally kept house for the family, whilst their two daughters, Katy and Claire, were both at University. See what I mean about the potential for stereotyping?

Sam and Sam, with their daughter Fifi, had savings from a house they had sold but otherwise clawed in income where and when they could on their travels doing whatever work they could find. Yes, they wore the new-age clothes and yes, they had the look of hippies, but again, the stereotypes just didn't apply.

In the middle was Steve Barratt, trying his hardest to be just an ordinary guy. Albeit one with an extraordinary alter-ego.

Chapter Forty-Six

In all the years that I had lived in houses, I can only recall one occasion when we got together as a neighbourhood to share an event. It was one of the Queen's Jubilees and one of the residents of our street had started the ball rolling and we'd ended up enjoying a huge street party. The event had gone off well and given us the opportunity to meet so many of our local neighbours and break down some barriers for a while. Once over, it hadn't been long before we'd all retreated back into our own lives, the memory of the street party having little more effect than us greeting each other a little more often when passing. It always amused me that in an age where the word community is so quickly evoked to describe sundry, random, human ties, those ties are in fact looser than ever. True neighbourliness had been one of the most pleasant surprises about joining the liveaboard boater community.

The barbecue began with my sitting outside the boat enjoying a cold beer, a new book and the heat of an unseasonably warm late November day. I heard the hire boat coming, looked up and watched as the crew made the last minute decision to moor here for the night. The engine was pushed into reverse and the noise itself was enough to tell me that the mini cabaret was just about to begin. The boat slowed as a shower of water and debris flew out from its stern, then it began the steady and unstoppable process of reversing whilst thrusting its bow into exactly the place where the helmsman didn't want it to be. There's a very special look that settles on the face of someone new to the waterways when they are faced with the choice of tapping another boat or taking evasive action into the opposite bank. I watched as the hire boat did both, bumping the stern of my boat whilst getting itself firmly stuck in a tree as it straddled the waterway.

"Need a hand?" I called, lifting myself up and heading to the canal side.

"Please," the driver said, "and sorry about the bump."

"Don't worry," I smiled, "it's a contact sport!"

They threw me a rope and I began to pull the boat back, trying as politely as possible to tell the driver that he might be better to stop reversing so hard and just leave the boat in neutral. As it slowed a little, I asked one of his crew to throw me a centre line and within minutes the boat was neatly tucked in behind me and pegged in.

The boat that was to moor in front of me had been sitting patiently in the centre of the water whilst all this was going on. In the process, a gust of wind had sent them into the bank at the rear. I clambered across the stern of the hire boat and caught the rope they threw, pulling them out of the mud before settling back down in my chair as they drifted effortlessly to the edge and secured their boat.

There can be a lot of hurt pride on the canal, but neither of the crews of these two boats seemed unduly concerned that they had benefited from a little help. For my part, it was just another day on the cut. Needless to say, very soon after the boats moored, chairs and tables were quickly put up and damp, dirty boating clothes exchanged for comfortable gear for relaxing in. A chat about the weather and the locality was enough to break the ice between us and introductions were soon made.

"Look, we've been planning a bit of al-fresco eating," Annette announced, "what with all this unusual weather and when I saw this spot I knew it would be absolutely perfect. That's why we made a sudden decision to pull in. But Jeff has way overdone the amount of food we've got. How about we all get together to eat?"

I agreed straightaway, glad for the company and not having to feed myself. The two Sams took a moment to decide but then also agreed, telling us that they couldn't make it a late one as Fifi would need to be in bed early.

Jeff and I sat together as Annette and her daughters prepared the feast. We talked around a few subjects but I was getting increasingly wound up by something that Jeff just didn't seem to be able to stop doing.

"Jeff," I said, "can I just borrow your phone for a second, I'll show you one of its features you may not be aware of."

He handed me the phone and I pressed the button to switch it off.

"But I need to be in touch with the business!" he protested as I refused to give him the handset back.

"Look mate," I said, "you are on holiday. Now, you've already told me that you are the Managing Director of your business, but you must have a deputy to cover for you."

He nodded confirmation.

"Okay," I continued, "so why do you keep employing them if they're that bad at their job?"

"No," he said, "Pete's really good, I can trust him completely."

"Well do it then." I said, "Trust him and let him do what you pay him to do whilst you enjoy a well-earned holiday."

"Point taken," he muttered, putting the handset in his pocket and cracking open another beer.

We resumed where we'd left off, but Jeff took a couple more beers until he started to properly relax. The handset he'd pocketed was the third upgrade of that particular phone that he had had over several years and he confessed to me that this was the first time any of them had been switched off other than for flights.

I told him a little of my own story and how life on the canal had changed my way of thinking about things, but it was when we talked about his family that he really began to grasp how little time he'd spent with them even in the close confines of a narrowboat. By the time they emerged from the craft armed with all sorts of culinary delights Jeff and I had lit the barbecue and it was well into its flaming stage. While it settled down and reached temperature, Annette and the girls joined us, as did Sam and Sam with Fifi in a pushchair. Sam had bought a couple of bottles of homemade wine, whilst Katy and Claire had spent the last ten minutes constructing a replica middle class bar on the back deck of the boat. I offered to bring some drink but everyone there looked across at the quantities already prepared and didn't even need to decline my offer verbally. Instead, I offered the music for the evening and went aboard to boot up the speakers and retrieve the mini I-pad that carried my whole collection. The speakers were standalone units that operated wirelessly so, as I placed them behind our impromptu seating area, I gave the computer to the girls to choose whatever they wanted to play.

"Is everything okay?" Annette looked worryingly at Jeff.

"Fine," he said, "why?"

"Your phone," she replied, "I don't see it anywhere."

"It's off," he smiled triumphantly, "they can do without me. Now, Katy and Claire, you two can do the same with yours please."

The girls hesitated, checking one last time for any urgent social media missives before complying with the request turning them off.

"We call it face to face conversation," I explained to them, "you never know, you might like it."

They gave me a bit of a dirty look, but as the gin and tonics they'd chosen began to soften them they soon relaxed and joined in with the rest of us.

Sam and Sam had been fairly quiet up until this point, but they too seemed to settle as Fifi dropped off to sleep and their first glass of wine worked through them.

"It's one thing I don't miss," male Sam said, "and I don't think we've suffered for not using ours since we've lived aboard. Of course, we've got a phone and we've even got the internet, but they don't get much use. And anyway, there are so many places the things don't work on the cut. I can still remember when we had our holiday boat and I would turn to jelly if I lost reception. We once had to cruise through the night to get a signal, I was that panicky, but when we finally got one, there were no messages. Funny how dispensable we indispensables really are."

I concurred and Annette said that she too had stopped herself being so tied to the phone and had dropped all of her social media profiles after finding herself spending more time on her avatar than on her real self.

"I got to the stage where it was just becoming one long drama, with my playing a role. I needed to stop myself and it's been really liberating. I now know that if someone gets in touch with me on the landline then they really are interested in communicating with me, not in sharing some celebrity drivel that I am then supposed to share with others."

We chewed the fat about social media, the pros and cons of technology and the special feeling that the canals was giving us all of relaxation, truly away from the madding crowd. Sam and Sam had given up a combined income that, when revealed, made Jeff choke on his Elderberry wine. But, they explained, they weren't some sort breed of new age hippy trying to change the world, they had simply stopped enjoying the mountains of stuff that had filled their lives.

"I got to the stage," Mrs Sam said, "where I was spending nights on the computer ordering more and more stuff and stressing myself about what I was going to do with the stuff that I needed to get rid of to make space for my new purchases. And then, I'd turn the telly on and all I'd hear about is austerity and the current financial climate and it drove me round the bend. Okay, if we're going to drown in stuff, then at least let's celebrate our ability to do it!"

"It's true," Mr Sam took over, "we'd get our pay at the end of the month and within days another new toy would arrive. But then we decided that the next toy we would try was a boat. That's when everything changed. We bought 'Maisie' over there one drunken night playing around on e-bay, but then we went to take her out and within the first few days of being aboard we were different people. The boat was really basic, still is to be honest, and it made us realise that we'd lost touch with each other because of all the stuff that we'd piled up into the house and because of the workload we had to maintain to look after it all. Within three months I'd packed in work and a couple of months later Sam followed me and we sold or gave away the lot. Never been happier."

And you could tell by the look of love that they exchanged that what they said was true. This was a couple in love, blessed with a baby and happy to tootle around the country picking up casual labour to pay for their very limited needs.

"Maybe one day," Jeff murmured from behind the barbecue where he was beavering away as chef for the afternoon, "but I still like my mod cons. Can't imagine what I'd do if I didn't have the business. I'm not criticising, just saying that as a business leader, I think I make my own contribution and not everyone can live on the edges. I'm proud of what I've achieved and I still enjoy the luxuries we can treat ourselves with."

"Please don't be offended," he said, passing a couple of burgers to the Sams, "I admire what you've done and I can see how the little one will get a special start in life with you, but it's not for me. That said, I can't remember any golf club or Rotary get together I've enjoyed as much as I'm enjoying this afternoon."

The conversation skirted around politics and religion, swooped into the mysteries of life and what the purpose of it all was, then soared into realms of multiple shared experiences of different towns and cities across the UK. Katy and Claire didn't miss their electronic chats and joined in with enthusiasm before leaving we, very merry, adults to more drunken chatter and offering to put little Fifi to bed and watch over her whilst we continued. The Sams were fine with this, but they left an hour or so later, leaving us under the temporary lights I'd rigged up and huddled around a blazing fire just as the local church bell struck nine.

Jeff, Annette and I stayed up until midnight. The barbecue cooled but the fire blazed merrily on, doing a wonderful job of scaring away any threat from the evening chill. When we found ourselves drifting into sleep, we decided to call it a day and parted with handshakes and hugs all round. I staggered into the boat and fell into a very satisfied sleep.

The following morning, we all parted company. The two Sams had to be in Leeds in a few days for the baby's check-up, whilst Jeff and Annette were tied to the timetable of their hire boat. As they departed, I noticed that Jeff was busy on his phone, whilst the girls untied and pushed the boat off.

For my own part, I needed a lazy day. I would set off again tomorrow, but the wine from the previous night was still making me feel a little delicate. I couldn't concentrate on my book so I listened to music and let myself drift in and out of sleep until I started to feel human again.

Chapter Forty-Seven

A week later, I met Sam and Sam again, just as I was approaching Leeds and they were departing to head to pastures new. We exchanged a brief greeting and then went our separate ways. My plan was to stop in Leeds, experience the buzz of this rejuvenated city a little, then begin a long and leisurely trek back the way I'd come. There were no definite plans but I felt that I wanted to drift back down towards the Midlands for the main part of the Spring and Summer.

I moored just outside the city and walked a few miles along the towpath, amazed at the transformation that had taken place along the waterway from the last time I had been here many years back when it was overgrown and semi-derelict. Leeds was now a vibrant and thriving city. It made a change to be back in the thick of it and I booked myself into one of the swankier hotels for a night of rest and relaxation and a long lazy soak in a bath.

Steve Barratt had an extremely strong line of credit so, having decided to have a few days away from life on the boat, I spared no expense in treating myself. ORB owed me after the Harmason affair and anyway, I was still working on-call for them even on this month or so of sabbatical. Besides which, I lived a frugal life for the most part so overall, I reckon I was still pretty good value for money. Over a full and hearty breakfast at the hotel I read through the local paper and browsed various leaflets that I had picked up from reception. Having listed the things that I wanted to do I finished off a third or fourth cup of coffee, left the necessary requests with the concierge and made my way out onto the city streets.

Being used to the relative calm of the towpath, it took a while to feel comfortable in the hustle and bustle of a city centre where every square foot of space seemed to have been built on or built up and where everyone passed by as strangers. Spying a large bookshop on the main street, I decided to make the most of the opportunity to stock up on the many volumes that remained in my 'books to read one day' file. Charity shops were always the best option for books, seeing as I could leave as many behind as I acquired, but they didn't always have the choice. I found myself an hour or so later, leaving the shop with multiple carrier bags which led me on an unscheduled trip back to the hotel to deposit this heavy load. Free of the burden and returning back to the high street, I found a coffee shop that had tables outside and relaxed over a long, tall cappuccino as I watched the world go by. I'd forgotten just how many people there were up here in the real world. It sometimes felt a little busy on the cut, mainly at the hot-spots and during the peak holiday season, but it was never anything to compare to this. I'd changed a lot over the years, that much I knew, but it was only then that I truly realised how much that change had left me seeking isolation rather than the comfort of crowds. It's not for everybody and, truth be told, I think the people rushing about those city streets were as content with busyness as I was with solitude. Then, of course, there were all the cars. Did I really used to spend hours a day on the roads, encased in a little metal box that was my own world-within-a-world? Those days seemed so long ago.

After the coffee I went clothes shopping. Not something that I was wont to do very often but this was a useful opportunity for me to obtain replacements for the very standard and non-fashionable gear that I liked. So conservative am I in my dress that I was able to find pretty much the same items in the same shops, although they seemed a little pricier than before. Once more, this left me with arms full of merchandise, so once again I returned to the hotel to sort out my purchases and spend a relaxed afternoon with a room service platter, my books and a very nice bottle of Chardonnay.

Reception rang me at seven that evening to advise me that the taxi they had booked to take me to the theatre had arrived. As I was already dressed and ready to go, it was only a matter of minutes for me to pick up the tickets skilfully procured for me by the concierge, leave the hotel and clamber into the taxi. The journey was short and I arrived at the theatre with time enough to have a quick drink at the bar, then I took my place in my box and thus began a wonderful evening watching a superb performance of Don Giovanni.

The music was still swirling around my head the following morning as I went through all the various treatments in the hotel's spa, following which it was another afternoon of laziness and relaxation, sitting on the balcony and listening to a combination of the sound of Mozart and its counter in the sound of the modern madness of the streets below. Another theatre event was booked for that evening and I seriously considered finding a 'companion' to join me. It was tempting. The money side of it wasn't an issue and I was a free agent. Thankfully, I managed to stop myself just before I dialled the number. It would have been great to have somebody to share 'Death of a Salesman' with and possibly a meal after, but then there would be the inevitable question of sex afterwards. Not that I wasn't tempted. In my book, there was no problem with the professional arm of prostitution and for the sort of money I would be paying, I would be a customer of a very willing and very well rewarded supplier. No, my problem was that I worried about breaking the seal, as it were, and opening up a need in me that I had kept the lid on for so long. Despite my being on my own, it was a very enjoyable evening nonetheless and a very powerful production of a play I remembered from high school.

Leaving the theatre, I found myself in one of my favourite chains of restaurants, seated in a private booth but with a good view of the rest of the place. It was busy and loud and the waiters and waitresses were as in your face as usual, but I always enjoyed the food they offered and worked my way through a sizzling starter of prawns followed by a beautifully undercooked rib-eye steak. This was a place to drink beer, which I was happy to do with great relish. In the past, whenever I'd been in one of these places whilst staying away from home with work, I had always made sure that I had a book to hide behind. All I had now was the programme from the theatre which I read in detail, after which I was forced to simply relax and do some people watching.

What struck me most, as I shifted my eyes from table to table, was how very normal everything seemed. There was a family of four celebrating a sixteenth birthday, a long table of work colleagues on a night out, a couple of lone diners like myself and multiple variations of couples and foursomes out on the town. The build up to Christmas was well and truly underway and, despite the extra workload this delivered and all the stress that people complained about, I could see a light of joyful expectation on every face around me. Christmas was that start-again time and that time when you could revel in excess. It was the simple time of family and friends and a feeling of unifying happiness that spanned the globe.

For all the fear induced by the press and all the doom and gloom that the media threw about, these people had each other, they had their own sources of passion and joy and they had a place, comfortably settled in a big old world that they were happy to be a part of. This was all plain to see.

What there wasn't, was any sign of violence, of corruption or of the numerous manifestations of injustice that my world said this world was rife with. It was a salutary reminder that I was on the periphery and that the mainstream of goodness and justice and equality in the modern world worked pretty well. I had got it into my head that, despite my anonymity, I was some sort of saviour to the nation and that without me there would be social breakdown. Here, alone in that restaurant, I realised how far from the truth that was. I was nothing more than a glorified janitor, mopping up the bloody spills that occasionally appeared or tweaking a nut or a bolt or a hinge to correct a tiny fault. I wasn't the person who had determined who this nation would have as a Prime Minister, I was simply an instrument that had been used to help others determine that process.

Had it been worth the sacrifice? This current foray into the world, Chantelle's sighting of the loneliness that I had deep down and which not even another person's eyes could hide, and the normality of the contrasting lives of Jeff and the Sams, all told me that I had chosen to be an outcast. Yes, I felt a sense of purpose in what I did and yes, there was a thrill in the planning and execution of my missions, but was my role necessary? I'd bought into the ethos of ORB, seen it as an extension of the personal drive that had put me in their hands, and yet, when considered in the cold light of day, who appointed them as the ultimate guardians of justice? I had never questioned what I was doing in this way and it disturbed me to think that I might have been misled in choosing to pursue this type of life. Jean had had to be forgotten. Love was not on the agenda. I had to live expecting denial or death any day and, for all the freedoms I was afforded, I was still captive to a wider power, having sought a life where I, like Sam and Sam, could live every day with just enough.

I paid the bill and headed back to the hotel room, the same thoughts bugging me all the way and frustrating me that they had come along to interfere in my little holiday. I put them aside as best as I could, determined to enjoy myself and celebrate the good things around me, but they still came back to haunt me. In fact, they didn't leave me until the beginning of January and my return towards Liverpool. My break away from it all was relaxing, a delight, productive and every other positive adjective. But it was also a period of hard and deep soul searching that didn't quite reach a clear ending. I had made my choice, I knew that, and on balance, I felt that what I was doing was right, was worthwhile and was necessary. I had no need to doubt what ORB was about and they were supportive of me and happy with the work I did. I would have been more comfortable with everything if I had moored the boat on that final day having achieved a clarity of purpose one way or the other, but you can't have it all I suppose.

It had been a good holiday and I had done some good things, met some great people and witnessed some grand sights. The weather had been unseasonably warm and supportive to me as I avoided too many days of being iced in. I was fit and healthy, free of the cobwebs and toned up with jogging and the working locks. That would have to be enough.

As for harbouring any doubts or reservations, they had to go. You can't live your life in two different worlds and being torn between various options was causing me unnecessary stress. With this holiday period ended, I had to choose to commit to what I now was and stop seeking to cherry-pick the parts of life that I wanted. Many were a lot worse off than me and few were given the resources that I enjoyed. No, I was still on the side of The Kingfisher. It was what I was and as such, it would have to be all of me and no less. For the time being, my decision was made, whether right or wrong.

Chapter Forty-Eight

ORB got back in touch with me properly in the second week of January, summoning me back to base with the request that I leave the boat at the Albert Dock and rendezvous with their representative at Liverpool One shopping centre. Alfa Romeo, bay 326, doors would be unlocked, drink on the seat to ease my journey.

The following day, I woke up in my old room at the ORB centre. It may have been the first knock on the door that woke me but I was fully alert in time to invite whoever was knocking to come in on the second knock. A porter bought me a full English breakfast with coffee and toast, greeting me cheerily and advising me that I had an appointment with the Order's President in exactly one hour's time.

Some people can't face a full fry up as soon as they wake up. I'm not one of those people and I tucked into the offering straightaway. The guys at ORB knew what was meant by a full English and they knew how to make it and what to make it with. I savoured every mouthful, washing it all down with cup after cup of coffee, whilst all the time thinking what the President might want with me. I wasn't exactly sure who held that title just now. ORB was an equitable body but they understood the need for a figurehead and hence, a President, who they rotated every twelve months. Of more interest to me however was the why of the meeting, whoever it was with. I'd never been asked to meet directly with the President so I was naturally a little curious and somewhat apprehensive.

Having tidied myself up and made my way to the President's office, I found that I was a few minutes early. This gave me a little time to relax and compose myself in preparation. A secretary watched me as I closed my eyes and regulated my breathing, looking to all the world like I was falling asleep but in fact allowing my heart to slow down to a comfortable beat. After five minutes of this I heard a buzzing on the secretary's desk and opened my eyes.

"Please go through, Sir," he said.

I knocked on the door, as much out of habit as anything, but opened it and entered the room before I had heard a reply. Behind a large mahogany desk sat a familiar face but one that I could not put a name to. She had been at the full Council meeting when we'd discussed Harmason, but had not been formally introduced. As I moved to the desk and extended my hand, I looked down at the name plate on the desk, hoping to steal a march on my host, but it simply identified her as 'President'.

"Thank you for coming, Mr Barratt," she said, grasping my hand firmly with two of her own, "it's a pleasure to see you again. Please, take a seat."

I sat down as I offered my own greeting, but I was still distracted by wanting to put a name to the face.

"We've not spoken before," she said, "and really, there is no need for you to know my name or indeed anything else about me. You can call me Madame President for now. Maybe not the way that the Order has done things in the past, but I am a bit of a stickler for formality and hope to breathe a little new life into our old Order."

"Madame President it is then," I replied as formally as possible.

"As the newly elected President," she continued, "I think there's some value in meeting up on a regular basis with our operatives, but our meeting today is at the request of the Council as we need to discuss a most urgent matter."

We had a brief exchange of pleasantries whilst waiting for the refreshments that the President ordered, agreeing that freshly ground coffee trumped even the best Earl Grey at any time of the day, then we resumed our main conversation.

"Firstly," the President settled back in her chair, "can I pass on the Order's most grateful thanks for your support over the last month or so, especially as we knew you were having a bit of a holiday. I trust you were still able to have a good break. You deserved it after the Harmason affair. Brilliant work if I might say."

I thanked her for the compliment in my humblest, just doing my job way, confirmed that yes, I had had a very nice holiday and that the few missions I'd performed hadn't been a problem at all.

"Good," she said, "so, let's get down to business. I'm afraid we have another Grade One problem for you. Actually, it might be fairer to say that we two problems. Before I detail them, I need to tell you where we go from this meeting. We need you out there as soon as possible but your support technician, James, has some upgrades and new equipment that he needs to sort you out with. When we've finished here, I need you to go to him, get everything you need and then prepare to leave this evening. Is that clear?"

I nodded.

"Okay, so here's the challenge. We have a rogue operative and a leak of very sensitive data. The two are linked because that same rogue operative is the source of the data leak. Her full codename is Angel of Mercy. She's been with us a couple of years longer than you and has proved to be very efficient in her work, particularly in situations where a sensitive approach is required, or where medical expertise is called for. I can't tell you how disappointed we all are. Amy, as we usually refer to her, is the last of our operatives that we would think would turn, but turn she has. We've only got the faintest trace on her just now but that trace indicates that she is firmly out there offering highly confidential ORB secrets to the highest bidders."

She paused and poured us both another coffee from the pot on her desk, looking over her reading glasses at me as she did so.

"Which leads on," she continued, "to our second problem. The data leak. Now, as you are well aware, we communicate with you and our other operatives along very secure data lines. Like a lot of the tools and equipment that we supply you with, I'm sure that you understand as poorly as I do exactly how these things work, but work they do. Some of our discoveries and inventions we share with the world, either as a free gift to humanity or as a source of income to pay for our work. But some things we hold back. There are certain technologies that the world is not yet ready for, and there are some that we do not believe can be scaled up safely in the wider world. Amy seems to have been able to acquire the details of our remote communications system and we can't let that out just yet."

She went on to explain as best as she could how the ORB system worked, freely admitting that the detail was probably beyond both our understanding, but conveying clearly enough the danger that it might create. The system worked by reducing communications to the sub-atomic level and used the Earth's ionosphere to send a signal that made the latest 5G mobile network look like little more than two tin cans and a string.

"The difficulty with this technology," she told me, "is twofold. Firstly, our models show that when it's scaled up to the levels that would be required to make it a worldwide standard, it seems very likely that it will create dramatic and unsustainable changes to the Earth's atmosphere. I think, or at least I hope, that if Amy knew that, then she may have been a tad more reluctant to steal it. However, she has it and is selling it to a conglomerate of three or four multinational telecoms companies. This is the second part of the problem. If they get hold of the technology, they will have a monopoly of all telecoms and data networks across the globe and that's something we can't allow to happen. Aside from the moral issue of the theft of the data, we know that these companies will hold nations to ransom and those who resist will sink into economic oblivion. We know there are power brokers out there just now, we're not that naive, but they are riding a natural wave of discovery and technological evolution that has built-in correctors. Our technology is a true category killer. Do you now see the problems?"

"Very clearly," I replied, pausing to think about my next words, "I'll do what I can to help, but I have a few questions, concerns if you like, and hope you don't mind me raising them."

"Please, go ahead," she said, leaning forward on the desk and making a temple of her fingers as she looked me in the eye.

"For one thing, why me?"

"Oh that's easy," she answered, "and don't take this the wrong way. I could tell you it was because you are the best, but the truth of it is that, yes, we know you'll get the job done as well as anyone, but more importantly, Amy doesn't know of your existence. You are our newest operative. There are currently six of you in the field, but the others were all trained and encouraged to support each other and therefore know each other. We felt that this was the right approach at the time, however, we had a few difficulties and so, when you came along, we trained you separately and only the Order and your technical support team know who you are."

"That makes sense," I said, "so now my concerns."

I paused to make sure that the words came out as I intended them to.

"I don't want to offend you, Madame President," I continued, "nor do I want you to think that I'm not up for this very privileged secret life anymore, but I am concerned about a couple of things, both of which are evident in this mission."

"Go on," her stare grew more intense and even showed a few signs of hostility,

"First of all," I met her stare head on, "this isn't what I signed up for. I became a part of this to further the cause of justice, not to mop up your problems. The work I do for ORB, in my mind, is to correct imbalances in the wider justice system and make restitution. I believe in that work. What you are asking me here has nothing to do with justice or rebalancing. You are asking me to become a defender of ORB rather than a defender of justice."

She started to say something but I surprised both of us by raising my hand to silence her.

"Let me finish," I said, "because the second problem I have with this is as fundamental, if not more so. You see, the perpetrator of the injustice in this case comes back to ORB, which I have a real difficulty with. How many more of the technologies that you are working on here could destroy the planet? And how the hell did you allow that data to be stolen? If I am to believe in the work that the Order does I have to have confidence in the Order itself. I've had a few concerns of late and, being completely frank with you, this situation doesn't help alleviate them. One of those concerns is the power of ORB. Is it the self-appointed corrector of an otherwise sound justice system, or is it working to a wider agenda? The smaller stuff I fully understand but you have had me out there preventing the succession of the lawfully elected individual who, by rights, should have taken over the role of Prime Minister. Don't you think that maybe oversteps the mark?"

The atmosphere in the room was tense. I'm not sure how many people have ever challenged the ORB hierarchy in this way but the current President seemed caught off guard by what I'd said. It was a full five minutes before she answered, having bought herself time to think by calling through to her secretary to ask him to hold all calls, and by taking an inordinate time in the bathroom.

"Okay," she said as she resumed her seat, "it seems that you are comfortable with honesty as the best policy, so let's lay our cards on the table. In truth, I don't disagree with some of the points that you raise. Believe me, as the new President, this is the last thing I want, but as to answers, I'm afraid that the only answer I can give you is that I don't know. This is new territory for ORB. We've never had an operative go rogue and we've never operated in an age with so many new and complex challenges. You may be right, but I think I should tell you that I don't see my role as President as being one of just a caretaker. I recognise that the Order needs to change a little and I'm up for that change. I think we can work together to deliver that change."

I was relieved that she hadn't flown off the handle as I thought she might.

"But," she continued, "now may not be the right time for us to have that discussion. The issue that has arisen out there is time critical. Yes, I accept that it's a problem that has originated with us. I'll grant you that. But surely then, the solution must come from us as well, don't you think? How about we park your concerns for the time being and then once this is all resolved we can convene a full Council meeting and discuss your points? Perhaps you and I could also meet prior to that as the vanguard of the new direction? I am the first female President of the Order and I want to make my mark so, as there is some substance in what you say, it would be prudent for me to have you on my side rather than against me. Meanwhile, we do have a critical situation to resolve and I believe that you are the person to bring that resolution about."

A little reluctantly, I agreed to go with this. I understood the nature of the current problem and although I was glad to have got some things off my chest, I agreed with the President that perhaps saving the world was the best short-term objective.

"If it's any consolation," she said as she rose from the chair hinting that it was my time to leave, "the Order are very pleased with your work and I for one, see in you a new generation of operatives. Please bear with us and know that you have our every confidence that this current crisis will be resolved. Do what you have to do and please don't pull any punches with Amy. She is very good at what she does but her time with ORB is over. If the opportunity comes to terminate her, don't hold back. If you don't manage it, trust me, we will. Good luck."

We shook hands and I left to see James. I was focused on the mission ahead but I needed a distraction. Yes, I knew what I had to do, but a premeditated death as one of the necessary outcomes was something I still struggled with. Still, it was what I had signed up for and, whoever and whatever Amy turned out to be, she had made that choice and I need be under no illusions that she herself would take any measures necessary to prevent being stopped in what she was doing. It would come down to being her or me.

After such a stressful morning it was a pleasure to see James's smiling face again as I entered his lab. He usually treated me with an uncomfortable deference which I was unable to persuade him to stop doing, but today he was so excited about what he had to show me and his welcome was a bit more relaxed.

"Kingfisher!", he shouted grabbing my hand, "Great to see you. Oh, boy, you wanna see what I've got for you today."

"Hi James," I replied, "don't overdo it mate. You'll have to make it quick though as I'm away again soon."

"I know all about it," he told me as he smiled proudly, "they've put me in the loop on this one so that I can give you some specific help. Can't believe you're going after Amy. She's brilliant. Not that you aren't …erm, you're both brilliant actually."

"Don't worry about it," I assured him, "I'm under no illusions about her ability. What can you tell me about her?"

He gave me a brief run down on the Angel of Mercy and how she tended to operate. In her previous life, she had been a nurse who had gone on to qualify as a medical doctor and had been extracted after she'd been identified righting wrongs in the various hospitals and institutions she'd worked in. Since then, she'd been out and about working for ORB on those projects that could tap into her medical knowledge and, more importantly, her caring skills.

"Rumour is," he continued, "that her known personalities are all nurses, and she even works for agencies at times. Not skiving like you! Oh, and her weapons of choice are medical too. If she isn't using syringes, it's scalpels, or at least, our take on scalpels. Which is why I've come up with a new suit for you."

He opened a wall locker and withdrew a suit that looked pretty much the same as the ones I already had. The only difference I could see was that the arms had a thicker run of padding down the side.

"Try this on," he said, turning away as I removed my street clothes and put on the Kingfisher uniform, "then add this and these to the combo."

He handed me a new helmet and a larger pair of boots than I was used to, these going halfway up my calves.

"Feel alright?" he asked.

"Fine thanks," I answered, "so what's new with it."

He showed me how this new suit was the best I had ever been provided with. The thicker arms were due to what he called 'wings' but which were in fact reinforced Kevlar drapes that unfurled and allowed me to wrap myself in their protection. These had been tested against even the closest contact with the weapons that Amy preferred and had withstood the test. The second improvement was the boots. These now had bigger ion-drives and the latest anti-gravity equipment powered by new high powered batteries that were the closest they had got to nuclear fusion yet.

"To all intent and purposes," he said, "this means that you can now fly. There was no point in us trying to emulate a real Kingfisher, but with those boots you can rise to a height of about two hundred feet, then you can use the stabilisers and boosters to move horizontally if you want. To be honest, whenever we tested it, we all preferred staying in an upright or crouched position."

The final new feature that he showed me was in both the suit and the helmet. They had created an outfit that now sealed itself which meant that I could use it underwater for long periods, or to protect myself against either a contaminated atmosphere or one that I didn't want to contaminate myself.

"It's great," I told him, "particularly the flying thing. Or should I say floating? Not sure which it is yet. What else have you got?"

"New weapons," he said, giving me a glass jar that seems to be filled with a clear liquid.

"Don't tell me, magic water!", I laughed.

"Hey, don't joke," he seemed hurt, "that stuff is deadly in the wrong hands. Pour a little out onto this slide and look at it under the microscope."

I did as he asked and was amazed to see that the clear water was in fact alive with millions of tiny organisms.

"It's stage two of the nanobot project," he explained, "Nanovirus."

"Virus?"

"Yes, artificial viruses, working on the same principal as normal viruses but made by us and with specific functions. You infect someone with that and there ain't a doctor in the world would be able to identify the source of the illness. You see, they don't replicate like normal viruses, they just get in there and target what they're programmed for. When they're finished they disintegrate, which they also do if they are removed from the host body before they're done."

"The perfect weapon." I said.

"Nearly," he nodded, "still work to be done on the type of effect that we can make them induce but yeah, the most perfect weapon to date."

He tried to explain to me in a little more detail how a single artificial virus worked to infect a whole body and that it was all to do with ensuring that the Nanovirus targeted the specific part of the brain that worked to repel invaders and convince it that there was a host of infection. The sickness induced therefore was not actually a plague of virus but the bodies response to what it believed to be a virus. I let him stop at that point, happy to know that he trusted the thing to work and not really wanting to fry my brain by understanding too much of how it all worked.

"And it's all been tested?" I asked, "I mean, well, viruses, these are serious weapons. I'm not going to be unleashing a deadly plague out there am I?"

"Of course they've been tested," he assured me, "and somewhere here I've got the reports from the guys who did the tests. The medical side's not my field but I trust the ones who've been doing the tests even if I can't read everything they write."

"What you really need to know," he continued, "is how to administer them safely. Your suit will be loaded up with millions of these little babies and when you need them, you just need to program them for how you want them to operate and then you fire them out through this tiny hole in the little finger of each glove. Don't worry, they can't get to you or any other ORB operative. They disintegrate when they meet your implant, that also means they can't attack Amy. You'll need some other way to tackle her."

We spent another couple of hours training with the suit and running through the workings of the Nanovirus application on my suit's computer. Then I heard the tannoy announce that my transport was ready and I bid James a fond farewell. I wasn't sure I'd ever see him again.

Chapter Forty-Nine

They'd moved the boat to a mooring alongside Birmingham University which is where I woke up after leaving the ORB base. It was an off-side mooring, so I guessed that somebody knew somebody and had asked for this spot as a favour. Given the time of year it made sense as all the official mooring spaces from here to the city centre seemed full. There was a nearby bridge across to the towpath so I wasn't stranded here and could easily walk to Gas Street and Birmingham proper. It became obvious to me why they had put me here when I found a printed flyer in my galley that was advertising various events around the 'Third International Global Telecoms Expo'. At first, this title seemed a little over the top until I realised that without the 'Global' it would be the 'TIT' expo. It was nice to know I still had my boyish sense of humour.

A quick search on the internet about this event provided me with the information that I needed and I started planning my next steps.

Nothing was certain in the work that I did, but this particular project had a lot of factors that required multiple hunches and assumptions to pay off. Given that it was a potential world-destroying situation however, I just had to hope and pray that my instincts were right. I agreed with the consensus of opinion among the heads of ORB which was that Amy could not be tracked down on her own. A technician at the centre had already confessed to having been duped into removing the tracking device that Amy had complained had been giving her headaches. A technician I knew to have since passed away.

Add to this the fact that we, as operatives, thrived on the challenges of stealth and the idea of direct pursuit became untenable. Hence my being deposited near to, and pointed towards, the telecoms conference where the heads of the biggest players in the field would all be found for a brief period in one time and place. If we tracked them to a point of confluence, Amy would almost certainly be at the centre. Yet, there were six of them and the intelligence was that she would pitch only to three. I reviewed the profiles of each of these CEO's to look for a hint of who would be in and who would be out, but this became a pointless exercise. Amy could be targeting geography, company size, personality or even gender. She could pick any three of six and still be guaranteed to be onto a winner. Of course, there may be more than three in the pot so that needed to be accounted for as well.

I began by securing a new identity as a member of the press. Neither Barratt, Gould nor Jackie McCann had the necessary credos, and time was against us, security was impenetrable and access to senior executives restricted. It was too late in the day to try to create a high-flying journalist's profile, so the option was simply to hijack the identity of one such individual and ask the ORB team to ensure that he was out of circulation. My theory was that, despite the intense security, commercial and personal reasons would leave the door open for limited press briefings. However, I knew that such briefings would have had to be booked months in advance. Short of removing a large contingent of journalists and reporters, I didn't stand a chance of meeting my targets.

This meant that a trip to 'The Feathers' was in order. It was one of the few remaining traditional spit-and-sawdust pubs left in Birmingham city centre, whose survival was due only to the fact that it was tucked away in an area that had escaped the developer's eye as yet. This, I discovered, was where the press pack had chosen to convene during the conference. The hotel being used by the delegates was way over the budget of even the largest news organisation and its drinks prices matched its premium splendour. The Feathers had therefore become an unofficial press centre and was enjoying the busiest period the landlord could ever remember. Old Tom even thought that this might be the end of the bad times and an opportunity for him to get the bank off his back and keep the place open against all the odds.

The virus put a stop to that. It hit everybody who had visited the pub on the day that I had my first pint there. Ambulances ferried the sick to a hastily constructed isolation unit in a nearby hospital, whilst the local authorities put an immediate end to Tom's dreams by shutting the pub down pending investigation. As one of the few remaining journalists still in good health, I was able to register with the exhibition organisers immediately. They congratulated me on my flying in so promptly to help out in the crisis, and all this was done with the deference due to a senior reporter for one of the world's largest press agencies. They even put me up in a complementary suite, so keen were they that their delegates had a chance to share their wisdom with the world.

All press interviews were halted on the day following the discovery of the virus, that is, all except mine. My boarding card and entry visa both showed me to have arrived after the outbreak, rendering me physically clean. The ORB guys had done good work in a short time and had even been able to intercept and detain the legitimate holder of my identity. I had a busy day that day. Interviews were kept short and oftentimes I found myself asking the same questions and struggling to show any interest in the dire projects my interviewees seemed so passionate about, but it paid off. As the evening closed I had shaken hands with each of the six most senior executives in the telecoms industry and in the process had been able to extract a DNA sample and insert a tracking device into their bloodstream. The marvels of James' miniaturisation schemes never ceased to amaze me.

Whether Amy wondered about the timing of the outbreak of an unknown disease so close to the Expo, I can't say. We'd made it look as close to a food poisoning epidemic as we could, making it seem a likely situation given the sanitary conditions in The Feathers. Even if she did have reservations, her options were limited and I was comfortable that she wouldn't change her plans. When ORB were out to catch you, you moved quickly. And Amy was a smart operative.

Janice Peterson, AKA The Angel of Mercy, AKA Amy had been intercepted bringing pharmaceutical companies, private clinics and corrupt medical practitioners to justice. This had all followed the death of her younger brother from what was deemed to be medical negligence. As a senior medical practitioner herself, she pursued the cover-up, avenged his death, then proceeded much as I had to follow up similar cases. Everything I read about her and the photographs that I had been supplied with oozed with a determination and resolution that belied what I had been told about her caring side. She was fairly short at just over five feet, had the physique of a downsized Amazon and had not skimped on the stunning beauty when they had reconstructed her features. I wished the circumstances of our meeting might have been different, but then again, it was difficult enough thinking about a relationship when one of you had a dark and secret side. It would be impossible for two operatives to make it work.

The breakthrough came on the last day of the conference. I had been monitoring the movements of my targets without success and was beginning to lose hope when a series of bleeps from the tracking computer woke me at five in the morning. Three of the CEOs were together and were moving through the hotel towards an annexe that, according to the plans I had, was no longer in use. Needless to say, this was something that needed my urgent attention and, with heart racing, I suited up and armed myself with as much as I could sensibly carry. If this was the anticipated showdown with Amy, then I had to prepare for anything. I also had to prepare for this being my last mission as only one of us could survive the confrontation. Locking the boat down, I sent a message to ORB advising them of my intentions, slid into the new and improved pod and followed the canal to the moorings at the top of the Farmer's Bridge lock flight. The hotel annexe adjoined the canal here although it was boarded up and awaiting redevelopment as a luxury extension once the last of the boats had been removed.

The portable tracker on my wrist showed the three dots converging into one in a former restaurant on the upper floors of the annexe. They stopped together, then moved a few yards forward as a group. Logic told me that this translated into a knock on a door, a wait and then entry into a meeting. Because I was still underwater, my sensors couldn't pick up another presence but I was confident that Amy would be found in the same location. With some trepidation I surfaced and, after checking out the locality for any unwanted witnesses, used the new suit to raise me up the side of the building and deposit me quietly onto the roof. Having found a suitable place to wait, I summoned an army of helpers who exited the pod and settled beside me awaiting orders.

Whether it was nostalgia or merely a carefully considered decision based on the operating environment, either way, I sent my original owl out on the first observation. It was getting a bit old now and despite James's attempts to revamp and repair it on numerous occasions, its capacity would always remain limited. But we'd been through a lot together and, if this was going to be my exit, then we may as well go out together. I watched as it circled the building, then as I lost sight of it, I switched to the view from inside my helmet. Thermal imaging sensors picked up movement on the far side of the building. I pulled up the blueprints I had and was able to identify the most likely location of my targets as a private dining room that adjoined the main restaurant. I set the bird down nearby and programmed it to alert me if the group moved away from where they were. I couldn't get a visual from outside anyway since the windows were all boarded over.

A steel door to the roof would lead me down into the main building, but it was locked from the inside. Short work for one of my spiders to slide under the door and pick the padlock, an action which I followed by sending in one of the smaller spheres I carried to manipulate and raise the rusty bolt that was now all that held the door. With the locks open, I knew I had access, but I also knew that this door would be unlikely to yield without alerting those inside to my presence. A distraction was called for.

One of the latest additions to my menagerie was a humming bird. Not very practical due to its small size but useful nonetheless. I flew it down to the nearest serviceable boat and checked the vessel over carefully. Timing my opening of the door to coincide, I worked the bird's beak into the ignition lock of the boat and made a noisy attempt to start it. As the old diesel fired into life, it filled the air with a solid and unmistakeable sound that perfectly covered the squeak of rusty hinges. The engine throbbed quietly in the early morning light as I made my way down the stairs and into the building.

Chapter Fifty

Once inside the building, the boots I wore carried me silently down the stairs, along corridors and to the room where Amy and her partners were meeting. Setting myself down at the door, I slipped a thin microphone threw the keyhole and began recording their conversation. The route I took and the justice dealt out had to be fair and reasonable and based on facts rather than ORB's speculation. The conversation was beamed directly back to the boat and an instant transcript sent through to headquarters:

Instant Data Transmission
To: ORB HQ
From: Kingfisher
Subject: Amy
Attendees: Bernhardt Kohl, CEO Europhone; Roger Balfry, CEO International Data Carriers; Gurvinder Singh, CEO Asia Tel.
(Transcript begins five minutes into meeting)
Amy: This is a very special opportunity gentlemen and we need to reach a prompt agreement on what we are offering on each side. For my part, I think you know that the technology works and that this is a scale-able and category-killing proposition. My terms are detailed in the documents that I have set before you. A fixed upfront fee of five billion sterling, plus a one percent annual payment based on revenues. Any comments?
(Pause)
Kohl: From my company's point of view, we have tested the equipment provided and are impressed. As instructed this was done using the minimum of staff and under a 'hypothetical' scenario so you can be assured that nobody else is aware. Quite honestly, given the implications of this technology for our companies, we have no hesitation in agreeing to your proposals. However, I need to know that my colleagues here will honour the spirit of this agreement and that we are all one hundred

per cent committed to a three-sided oligarchy with very clearly defined geographic borders. I have taken the liberty of bringing with me a proposal for this with the world divided by population in a fairly equal three way split.

Amy: How you decide to sort that side of it is up to you. Thank you for your agreement. Anybody else.

Singh: We are in agreement as well. We want to move quickly and need the detailed technical plans immediately we transfer your funds. I have production facilities geared up ready for manufacture and can also offer these services to my colleagues here. As you will be aware, the Asian market is on fire just now, so we are keen to get started immediately.

Balfry: We at International are also happy to proceed. I think we all know how this technology changes the whole telecoms playing field and we are sure that we can sell it in an environmentally and politically correct way. Perhaps, Mr Singh, we might pool our resources on this? I have the best of the PR teams I believe, but I defer to you with regards to manufacture. Might I suggest that Mr Kohl use his own influence in Brussels to smooth any European issues?

Singh: A sensible plan I think.

Kohl: Yes, that makes sense. I presume you have the people to ensure the Senate has no objections.

Balfry: As always, we have the funds and the connections to make sure there are no obstacles.

Amy: Well then, if you are all in agreement, may I congratulate you on the futures that you have. You will be the new colonialists, and the power of worldwide telecommunications, data transfer and even web access will be in your hands. Makes my fee seem rather paltry I feel. I have given you the Swiss accounts to place the funds into and I also require a safe haven which I believe, Mr Singh, you are able to offer me. I shall travel with you as a secretary if you can ensure my papers are in order.

Singh: Everything is set.

Balfry: Gentlemen, let's sign.

(Pause)

Kohl: I have taken the liberty of bringing a little something along, my friends. Please, let us toast our partnership.

(Clink of glasses)

Balfry: To a new era in telecommunications and to the combined forces of the three victors in a battle that has raged for over a century. My friends, after today, we control the information flow around the world; we are the new Emperors of data; in short, we own the world.

End of Transmission

I slipped the microphone from the slot and sent out a dozen nanobots into the room. As I opened the unlocked door, I saw the three CEO's slumped in their seats, and a mystified Amy standing at the foot of the table.

"Good morning, Amy," I said, "sorry to rain on your parade."

"Who the hell are you?" she stared at my suit, "No, wait, let me guess. You're one of my ORB buddies aren't you. Might have known they'd catch up with me. So, what are you then, The Birdman?"

"You can call me Kingfisher," I replied, "and yes, I'm with ORB. Can we be sensible about this or do you want to get straight into the fight?"

She sat down and beckoned me to sit with her. I declined and remained standing. She took a shot out of the bottle of Schnapps that remained on the table, then leaned back in the chair and looked hard at me.

"Where do we go from here then?" she asked.

"Well," I said, "I'd like to say that you come quietly, give yourself up to ORB and try to reach an agreement with them. Truth is, you and I both know it's not that easy."

She nodded and sighed.

"Of course," I continued, "you will also be savvy enough to understand that their teams will be making a beeline for this spot so time is very much of the essence. Your colleagues here will be out for another fifteen minutes at least, and I estimate that ORB will take an hour or so to be here. Guess it's your move now."

She took another long swig at the bottle.

"I'm not going back. I've had enough," her voice was soft and seemed resigned to her fate, "This wasn't just about the money. I wanted out, sure, and I needed the funds to escape, but I wanted to hurt ORB as well. You may still believe in them, but I've seen too much killing. I joined them for justice and I enjoyed what I did, but I feel like I've crossed over a line from being a corrector of injustice to, I don't know, almost a deliverer of vengeance. You ever feel like that?"

"This isn't about me," I avoided the question, "it's about you. How do we play this one out? Will you come quietly or do I need to apprehend you?"

She answered with a load laugh that was accompanied by the bottle flying with full force and smashing into my helmet.

"Come on then, Birdman," she shouted, "let's see what you're made of."

As the liquor dripped off my visor I saw her removing her jacket to reveal the top half of a light blue leather cat suit covered with the same sort of utility pockets that my own suit contained. Her left arm grasped her side and then a hail of sharp scalpel blades flew at my chest. The suit held but I wasn't confident it would withstand another attack. I unleashed a barrage of nanobots, enough to fell a herd of elephants, but she only looked at them with derision as they swarmed towards her. I couldn't understand it. They went straight past her and stopped at the window.

"Aren't you forgetting something," she laughed, "I'm ORB aren't I. Those little beasts can't attack their own. Remember? Maybe I should call you Birdbrain instead."

I felt like an amateur. She was right. This left me at a serious disadvantage but it also gave me a little time to think. Another hail of scalpel blades flew at me but this time I was prepared. I raised my arm and the curtain fell about me rendering that volley as innocuous as a stream of pollen. As the scalpels dropped I moved closer and caught Amy a bone-crunching smack across the jaw with my elbow. Fighting women was not my preferred way of operating, but she'd started it and I didn't really think I had much of a choice. I grabbed her around the throat and tried to wrestle her to the ground. That was when the shock threw me across the room where I lay dazed and, to my dismay, still sparking and smoking. They'd given her a form of Taser but had neglected to tell me.

We looked across at each other weighing up our opponents.

"Don't feel bad," she said, "I've taken out bigger and better men than you. I've told you, I'm not going back. Only one us leaves here alive today."

She ran at me with a syringe in each hand but before she could get close enough to penetrate the suit I shot away from her using the ion-drive boots which proceeded to lift me up towards the ceiling.

"Nice," she whispered, reaching around behind her for more conventional weapons.

"Too slow," I shouted as the first of the bullets hit the ceiling. "Need to try harder."

I pushed the suit to its maximum and evaded bullet after bullet until the last one hit the table top and I emerged from underneath it and hovered in front of Amy's face.

"Come!", I shouted, and Amy screamed as the door behind her exploded into a thousand pieces and my army of helpers emerged. The rats scurried all over her, piercing her skin repeatedly with bites that would have killed anyone else due to the toxic venom they injected. Despite her immunity to the poison they did a lot of damage and blood streaked their jaws. Then the owls and the eagles came in, flying low around her and stabbing at her with their talons and beaks.

She fired shot after shot from the Taser and felled a couple of the birds, but she was never going to win this one and eventually it ran out of power. She weakened and slumped to the floor and I approached her for a quick and merciful coup de grace. But she wasn't finished yet. She leapt at me screaming and her hand shot out at my chest now wearing a glove that was more knife than gauntlet. Lashing out at my chest I watched as she pierced the suit and took chunks of my skin away with every stroke.

"Enough," I shouted and with one last push supported by the boots I drove her towards the boarded up window and heard her cry as she fell out through the open space towards the canal below. I took a moment to catch my breath, then I went to the window. The helmet's enhanced vision capability meant that I could see into the water, but I could make out no shape to encourage me. Then a hand reached up and grabbed my helmet, throwing me off balance, over the window ledge and into the water below. As I fell I looked up and saw Amy attached to the wall of the building, fixed with the gloves she held. One hand removed itself and she spun round and waved at me as I hit the water.

The landing stunned me and I sank into the muddy scum that formed the base of the waterway. The suit sealed itself around me and the helmet activated a thermal imaging camera that saw beyond the water. Fresh air hissed into the helmet and I breathed deeply.

"Thank you James," I whispered, watching the dark red spot of Amy climbing down the wall. I waited until she was on the thin rail at the bottom of the building that had once been the edge of a wharf, then I reached up and grabbed her ankle. She joined me in the water and I held her as she struggled for breath. I wasn't going to bottle this one so I watched and I held her as tightly as I could until the last bubble of air left her lungs and she started to choke on the filthy water of the canal. This was death. This was an unpleasant death. This was a death that had to be though as, for all her moralising, Amy was the person who had been prepared to enslave and ultimately destroy billions of people either for a misguided motive of revenge, or simply for the cash.

She died in my arms but I waited another five minutes to make sure that there were no signs of life. I slipped the body over and into the pod, locking it down and setting it to return on auto-pilot to the boat. Part one was over, now I had other fish to fry.

Chapter Fifty-One

As I lifted myself out of the water, the morning sun was bright all around me but there was still nobody about. I drifted up to the meeting room and settled myself in one of the chairs. The cuts in my chest screamed to be attended to and were probably not helped by the filthy canal water that they had been washed in. The suit had sealed itself over them when I was in the water so I couldn't get access to them but at least I knew that this would also stop the bleeding. I allowed myself the single shot of Schnapps that remained in an untouched glass on the table. It burnt as it went down but it gave me a new energy.

Kohl was the first to stir. He sat up and wondered at the owl that sat before him on the table. I told him to relax and wait for the others. He didn't argue. They woke up shortly afterwards, at which point I explained to them the situation that they were in. I told them a little about Amy, apologised that she would not be able to deliver on her promise, and explained that she was now dead.

"Of course," I told them, "it would have been an easy option to have terminated you as well, but justice is a funny thing and I'm not sure that would have been the best route. I have an alternative."

I explained to them that their dreams of world domination were now no longer viable and that if they chose to pursue them in any way whatsoever, the viruses that had been implanted in their bodies would be activated and they would become what the doctors like to refer to as the living dead.

"I don't think I need explain," I said, "what it must feel like to be fully aware of your surroundings but unable to move in any way. You would spend every hour praying for death but the virus won't allow that. This would be a new persistent vegetative state where no doctor would feel morally bound to end your lives as all your bodily functions will be intact. You will, in short, have a long life, though not a particularly pleasant one."

I then laid out my plans for each of them.

"You all have a secret," I began, "in fact, you all have more than one I'm sure. So what we are going to do is to buy each other a little insurance. Now, this could take us a few minutes or a few days. I would prefer it to be swift, but I have no other pressing engagements so if you want to stall then so be it. Will you cooperate?"

They nodded reluctantly.

"Good, then let's begin. Mr Kohl, I want you to tell the other two the dark secret that you have kept from everybody else and which makes your position in your role a little precarious. Please, go ahead, and don't worry, the others will be having their say soon."

I'd chosen Kohl to start with because his darker side was something that he couldn't fail to recall.

"Gentlemen," he struggled to speak, "I am not proud to say this, but I have been embezzling funds from my company for many years. The sum is quite substantial and I have things set up that all the money we report as going to good causes is actually directed to my own bank accounts. I apologise."

"Good," I said, "see how easy that was. Now, while the others think please write that down and sign the document then pass it across to Mr Balfry. Mr Singh, your turn."

"I'm sorry," tears welled up in his eyes as he spoke, "I don't think I can do this."

"Was I not clear enough?" I raised my voice and moved closer to him so that he could see his own terrified reflection in the helmet's visor, "You don't have a choice. Now get on with it."

"I have an addiction," he whispered, "to young boys and girls. I have always been this way. I am so sorry but I can't stop myself and I always look after them and their families."

"You don't need to justify yourself here," I said, "all we are doing is getting the facts together. Now, please write that down and hand it to Mr Kohl."

I waited for Balfry to pluck up the courage. His was the worst of the confessions I was certain although Singh's foibles made me feel sick. I watched as he weighed up how to admit what he was capable of, then I looked him in the eye and nodded to him to begin.

"I don't know what to say," he whispered, "I only wish it were different. I am a murderer. In fact, I am a mass murderer. I don't know how much detail you need but for the past twenty years I have eliminated any of my professional enemies by using paid assassins. They all look accidental. I guess I just see it as business. Is that wrong of me?"

He wrote this down, signed it and passed it as instructed to Mr Singh.

"So," I said, "you all have power over each other. By rights, I should be taking the necessary action against you, but in this case I have decided that you should all have a second chance. Needless to say, you remain in your high powered positions but the transgressions stop. We can identify any breaches of that agreement and will activate the virus if we become aware of your failing to do your part. I might suggest that you also seek to atone for your actions in some ways but that is up to you."

They nodded and seemed almost thankful to me.

"Just to make you aware," I continued, "the technology you were intending to buy into would cause global meltdown if delivered on a large scale. If we overcome the problems with it, then your companies will all benefit, but for now you must destroy everything that you have that related to what Amy was trying to sell. It is for this reason that you are not being terminated. You are bent and corrupt and, in my view, the scum of the Earth, but this time you've been given a reprieve. Don't let me down."

I stood and looked out of the window. They got the hint and I heard chairs slide back and three of the most powerful men in the world leave the room in a silent shuffle. I was still at the window when I heard the helicopter land and the sound of feet coming towards me. ORB had got here at last. Shame there wasn't much left for them to do.

+++

'The Birmingham City Bugle' 2nd February, 2023
'Mystery Virus Claims First Victim'

The unidentified virus that caused the hospitalisation of nearly seventy journalists during the recent global telecoms expo in the city has claimed its first fatality with the death of the popular and well-respected presenter of the BBC's flagship current affairs programme, Clive Griffiths.

Doctors treating Mr Griffiths confirmed that he passed away in the early hours of this morning having never regained consciousness. His family have issued a statement asking for their privacy to be respected and thanking well-wishers for their show of support during his short illness.

Medical professionals across the country are baffled by this virus which has left more than sixty further victims in what is described as a comatose state. Efforts to identify the virus have been unsuccessful despite samples of the victim's blood being sent to numerous specialists. Aside from the journalists affected, who seemed to have contracted the illness after a night at The Feathers public house in the city centre, there are no other reported cases. The landlord of the pub and two of his bar staff displayed minor symptoms of the virus but have since recovered.

+++

On my return to the boat I popped some high strength painkillers, washing them down with a large whisky before settling down in my armchair while I waited for them to kick in. I woke in the same chair many hours later, wincing as I turned to look at what time it was. The morning was half over. With a great effort I forced myself up and tried to ease the suit off me. It was stuck fast which gave me no alternative but to struggle to the shower and try to wash out the blood stains that were fixing it to my body. I let the water run super-hot and after a couple of minutes was able to pry the fabric away. It fell to the floor of the cubicle where it stayed whilst I let the cleansing flood wash over me. The wounds on my chest and side opened up under the hot water and a stream of diluted blood trickled away out of the drain. When I began to feel at least a little more human I switched off the shower and towelled myself dry. The cuts were long but not as deep as I had feared. I wrapped the towel tightly around myself and searched through the first aid kit for a suitable treatment. ORB had supplied me with enough medicines to treat an army. This included special field dressings that formed a kind of synthetic skin across flesh wounds. It took me ten minutes and two packets of these to cover every mark that Amy had left but the dressings did their job and as I headed into the galley I left no trail of blood.

With a welcome cup of coffee in my hand, I dressed and opened the window blinds to look out across the water. Everything was as it was when I had last looked; cyclists and walkers ambled along the towpath in the mid-morning sun, swans circled looking for food, and boats put-putted by. There was no sign of any of last night's disturbance. As I took a long draught of the hot black liquid, I heard the familiar bleep that snapped me back to reality. What did ORB have to say this morning I wondered?

Project: Amy
Operative: Kingfisher
Status: Completed
Notes: A successful resolution. Amy body recovered overnight. Confirmed DOA at HQ. Cause of death, drowning. No indication that sensitive data in public domain. CEO's identified to be monitored closely over next few months.
Rating: 100%
Feedback: Excellent work. ORB secure. Collateral damage acceptable. President would like to extend personal thanks to Kingfisher - one-week R&R - enjoy!

I smiled at the 100% rating. If only they could see the state of me now. Still, a few days to recover would be a welcome change but that could start tomorrow. I wasn't in a fit state to work my way through a big lock flight just now, which meant a proper canal day was in order with plenty of beer, a decent pub meal and some catching up on my reading.

That day became two as I worked my way through some Steinbeck. I did cruise a little however, moving the boat into Gas Street for the second night, allowing me an evening in the city followed by a night watching the sun go down over a couple of pints. Everywhere was illuminated and since it was a dry and clear night, there were a lot of people wandering the towpath. I watched as they passed the moored boats, stopping occasionally to admire an old working vessel or the brightest of the shiniest, modern ones. Nobody gave my boat a second glance. If only they could see inside and know her secrets. Still, this was how it had to be. I was just another boater, enjoying the freedom of the waterways and tootling along anonymously on my travels. A couple of nights ago I had killed a secret operative of a secret organisation in this very canal, in the process of which I had saved the world from a global meltdown. Nobody knew that. Nobody would ever know that. I raised a glass to my dull and boring boat.

Chapter Fifty-Two

The days were beginning to draw in a little so I started through Farmers Locks before sunrise, planning a couple of days cruising to get me out onto the Curly Wyrley again which I knew would be quiet at this time of the year. It was a canal that I liked because its reputation kept many boaters away but this wouldn't be the case for much longer as the towpath became more and more gentrified and this lock-free length of water became more popular. It had suffered badly over the years and most of the interesting canal side details, including the pubs, had been allowed to fall into disuse. If I ever got to the stage of retirement, I'd reinstate at least one along this stretch and I'd make sure to write up in the title that it was never to become a false and faceless part of a major chain. For now, I had to moor up and walk if I fancied a drink which at least got me moving again and helped ensure that my injuries healed without too much residual stiffness.

A couple of days at Chasewater Reservoir, or more precisely at a quiet spot about half a mile back along the towpath, gave me a better opportunity to bring myself back to full fitness. The last few days of the Winter continued in the same vain and there was plenty of warm sunshine about. This was an extra blessing and allowed me to catch up on my running and swimming as well as give the boat's portable transports a much needed blow out. Most of my activity had to be at night, since the sight of a pod flying out of the water and up the side of the reservoir might have drawn a bit too much attention. Similarly, the bike was so good at what it did, moving from towpath to hill to water that if anyone had seen it they would have wanted one. As far as I was aware this was a very limited edition of just the one.

Moving on from Chasewater, I passed the still redundant arm that would one day complete the link to Lichfield, then moored the boat for the night at Silver Street where, the following morning, I filled up with water, disposed of a few weeks of rubbish and emptied the portable toilet cartridges. This was the less glamorous side of my life but I still loved it. Being moored up next to a supermarket also gave me the opportunity to stock up the cupboards and the fridge, something that I had long neglected to do. Too much eating out or being away from the boat had rendered most of my supplies out of date. Nice for one night, but a bit too close to that big old world I'd tried to escape for my liking.

After Silver Street, another short cruise took me to Pelsall Common. Moored at the end of the Cannock Extension, I had a fantastic view out over the dereliction of the old iron works that had now been reclaimed spectacularly by nature. A couple of centuries ago, the nails that built America were produced here. Now, all that remained was wasteland where paths gave away their history by revealing the melted remains of residue from the old furnaces. I loved it here. I also loved the Chinese takeaway that Fran and I had discovered many years ago and which, if truth be known, was the real reason for my staying there that night. As always, the food was superb. They didn't recognise me anymore, although there was a strange look on the proprietor's face when I ordered what I'd used to have as Zipoly. Or was that just my imagination?

The following morning was Sunday and it was the last day of my break away from it all. To be fair to ORB, they'd kept their part of the deal and hadn't contacted me. I almost began to forget that I had another side to my personality. Getting back into the roaming lifestyle of a continuous cruiser had done what it needed to and helped me forget the challenges of Birmingham. I still had the odd flashback to that night with Amy and had woken up more than once with the image of her taking her final breath etched before my eyes. I wouldn't give her the pleasure of making me doubt what I'd done though and I dismissed this all as nothing more than my mind assimilating facts which would soon be processed and stored far away in my long term memory. It hadn't been murder. Not in my mind anyway. This was simply an execution for the public good and I was no more a monster than Pierrepoint and the other executioners who did a thankless job that had to be done.

As I walked to the pub for lunch I spotted a boat that was one of the same family as my own. It was a touch shorter and in a less tidy condition, but the sweeping bow and pure nineteen seventies look of her marked her out as a sister to Kingfisher. Nobody was on board when I knocked, but after I'd finished my lunch and was staring at the canal over my third or fourth pint from the raised terrace at the rear of the pub, I saw a couple of guys approach her. I thought I recognised one of them. Sure enough, when

I looked back to the car park I noticed the 'Boat Space' logo on the new van that had been parked there.

"Tony?" I asked myself.

It was worth checking out, so I finished my drink and went over to them. I recognised Tony straight away. He hadn't changed a great deal although he seemed to have filled out a little. He was manoeuvring a large solar panel onto the roof of the boat, helped by a younger guy in jeans and a t-shirt and with a lumberjack's hat on his head.

"Alright Matey," the younger said to me as I approached.

"Fine thanks," I said, "this your boat?"

"Yep, just picked her up last week. Got her for a steal of a price."

He told me how much and I was impressed.

"That's mine over there," I said to him, "same make as yours. Do you know what date yours is? Mine's seventy-six I think."

"Don't know," he replied, "I'm new to all this. The girlfriend said we should wait but I saw this and had to have it. You smoke?"

"I'm okay," I replied, showing him the vape stick I was using.

"No," he laughed, "do you *smoke*? Y'know, bit of the weed? Go on, have a little bit."

I declined the offer, never having been able to get to grips with cannabis and always ending up with a headache after using it. I let him roll his joint as I approached Tony.

"You work with Zipoly?" I asked, getting his immediate attention.

"Hey?" he looked confused.

"Boat Space," I said, "isn't that Zipoly. The carpenter guy. I had some work done by him a couple of years back. He still around?"

"You haven't heard then?" Tony stopped what he was doing and turned to give me his full attention.

"Heard what?" I answered.

"Zipoly died. Boat fire," even after the gap of time I could see this hurt him to talk about, "He left me the business and some plans about solar panels which is pretty much what we do now. I kept the name in his memory."

"I'm sorry," I said, "I liked the guy. You must be Tony, his apprentice? He had a lot of time for you. I'm glad you're doing alright."

"Thanks," he replied before going back to the installation.

We might have talked some more but at that point the owner decided to collar me about various aspects of boat life that he wanted answers on.

Normally I'm happy to help whenever I can but this guy was getting just a bit too friendly. Then he shifted the conversation to the main reason that he was moving onto a boat.

"They can't track you so easily on the water," he told me.

"Who?" I asked.

"The Government," he lowered his voice to a whisper, "You know that they track each one of us don't you? They sell us at birth to the highest bidder and make sure that we pay back our value. They're everywhere. You've seen them spraying crops where there aren't any crops haven't you. Well, that's them. They spy all the time. That's why I'm having the solar fitted. I reckon it'll deflect their rays and protect me."

"Okay," I said, choosing to end the conversation at that point, "well, good luck with that. Look, I need to go now, got to take a leak. Nice meeting you."

"Cheers mate," he called after me, "and don't forget, they are watching you."

How he would have been able to handle even just a fraction of the truths that I could have shared with him I didn't know, but if there was any advert for the perils of cannabis use he was a great one. Still, that's what so much fun about life on the cut. You meet lots of interesting people.

Back on the boat, I finished the last of the Steinbeck's and poured myself a glass of wine. I avoided sitting out in my deckchair on the common in case I had an unwelcome visitor wanting to warn me about another aspect of his conspiracy theory. Instead, I turned the radio on, just in time to catch the two o'clock news:

'BBC Radio News' 14.00 Sunday, 13th February 2023

In a tragic end to the Birmingham Virus Crisis, doctors have confirmed that the last of the sixty-seven journalists who contracted this unknown disease, died peacefully in his sleep earlier this morning.

Doctors have remained baffled by this mysterious illness which has yet to be identified but which also shows no signs of having been transmitted to anyone other than the original victims.

The Prime Minister has ordered an urgent investigation into the cause of this virus and has promised as much support as is necessary to each of the families of the victims.

An hour long BBC News Special after this programme, which replaces the scheduled Sunday Play, will explore events surrounding the outbreak of this virus and ask if it was a cruel, natural phenomenon or whether human forces might have been at work."

***

Now I understood why ORB had been quiet. The wine glass fell from my hand as I realised that the sixty-seven journalists, all now dead, who I had administered the virus to, were the 'collateral damage' referred to in their last message. I listened to the rest of the news and then the programme that followed. Tears streamed down my cheeks as I heard about the lives and histories of my victims. Once that programme ended, I moved to the internet and saw faces to match up to the names that I couldn't forget. Needless to say, I didn't sleep that night but waited until the first opportunity presented itself for me to contact ORB without it seeming like a knee-jerk reaction. I sent the first message to James at just after ten. I was steeling myself for a wait but the reply came almost instantly. I can remember the precise wording to this day, 'James O'Reilly is no longer employed as a technician within this corporation. Please use an alternative contact or message our switchboard.'

I thought carefully about my response. Next time, I made a call.

"How may I help you?" the sterile voice answered.

"James O'Reilly please," I asked

There was a pause.

"I'm sorry," the automated voice chirped, "we have no listing for that name. Please specify your identity and serial number."

"Kingfisher, 53012." I replied coldly.

I waited as the connection was made.

"Kingfisher?" a voice said.

"Yes, who's this?"

"It's Adam. I'm your new technician. Sorry, man, James had to move on. What's the problem?"

Move on or be moved on I thought. I needed to play this one cool.

"Okay, Adam," I said as calmly as possible, "No real problem, just that I need some bits and pieces replenished after my last mission."

"The Angel you mean?" he interrupted, "Man, that was so cool. You're the man!"

"Thanks," I answered, "now, about my needs. I think you need the Nanovirus back and I need my own stocks building back up. Also got a couple of my pets need a bit of fixing up. That okay?"

"No problemo," he said, "I've got you at Pelsall, right. We'll arrange a pick up tomorrow. There's a boat yard at the end of the Extension Canal there. Get the boat to them and we'll take it from there. Hey, looking forward to meeting you."

"You too," I answered, cutting the connection.

The faces of the Birmingham Victims were there on my computer screen throughout my conversation. I still struggled to reconcile their deaths to my actions. What had I turned into?

PART THREE

Chapter Fifty-Three

A very different Steve Barratt opened the door to the porter who carried in the breakfast tray that morning. This Steve Barratt relished the prospect of a typically stupendous ORB breakfast as much as the old one, however, this one demanded more.

"Before you go," I told the porter, "can you please pass on to the relevant people that this room is not acceptable. My bags will be packed shortly and I expect them to be transferred to a suite more becoming of my status. Make sure it happens."

As the porter backed out of the room, the new Steve Barratt smiled before laying the fried-eggs over the bacon and slicing them in half to let the two flavours mingle. Gone was the uncertain, questioning, guilt-ridden Steve. Come now instead to claim his crown was Steve Barratt, The Kingfisher: the newest operative, but the best; the deliverer of success; the future of The Order for Restoring Balance.

I'd made my decision before being collected. For too long now I was clinging on to a semi-morality that was tearing me apart. Zipoly could no longer influence this new creation, nor could I try and walk the line between a fantasy life of relaxation on the cut and a working life that killed in cold blood. Having watched and held as Amy died in my arms, and having hardened myself to the images of the journalists killed by my action, I now bore no weakening emotions of regret. This was what I did and I did it for the right reasons. The war against injustice was timeless and universal, and in war there were casualties. I remembered meeting a man walking a dog along the towpath in Banbury once and the conversation turning to events of the Second World War. He told me how his Grandfather had died with a guilty conscience having wiped out an orphanage and the nuns who lived there, simply because he had been given the wrong target building. In a farmhouse next door to the one he destroyed, a troop of German soldiers watched on, not quite believing their luck. So it was with me. Amy had to die. The journalists were to be indisposed but the weapon I was given was faulty. Not my fault. So, unlike the dog walker's relative, I would not carry a weight of guilt that was not mine to carry.

Besides which, now I had my feet under the table, I had proven myself to be damned good at what I did. Old Zipoly was a cog in the wheels of a huge sanitary wares manufacturer, replaced as soon as he left. Old Zipoly enjoyed the wealth and trappings of a prosperous life because his wife was dedicated to a well-paid profession. Old Zipoly was just that, the old, the yesterday man. Now I was Steve Barratt, The Kingfisher, it was my time to shine. Harking back to the past could only bring conflict between the memory of the man I was then and the reality of the man I was now. There would be no more dithering and no more searching of the soul. Today was the start of the future for me and it was a future that I planned to run full pelt into, never stopping to look back.

Breakfast over, I telephoned through to the Administration Block. Identifying myself, I repeated my request for a change of rooms, asking also for some new clothes to be delivered, as I was planning to stay a few days. I then informed them that I would be visiting the labs if anybody needed me. It was to be a bad day for the poor soul who had answered the call.

"I'll see what I can do, Sir," she said, "I'm not sure that we have any suites available and the clothes will need to be ordered. This may take...."

"Listen," I interrupted her, "this is not up for debate. Do you know who I am? I am one of the Order's senior operatives and I don't do maybe. A suite, new clothes and, while I think about it, you can arrange a decent buffet to be delivered to the labs at one o'clock. Thank you."

Putting the phone down, I smiled. This was my time and I was going to make the most of it. The role of VIP wasn't something I was totally comfortable with, as yet, but I thought I was doing quite a nice job of settling into it. I hoped I wouldn't be let down by the receptionist, as that would mean an unpleasant and humiliating end to her worst day ever. Still, I'd put up with worse.

Throwing on my old jeans and sweater after showering and shaving, I packed my bags and left them on the bed. Checking that I hadn't forgotten anything before closing the door of the room, I walked the familiar route through the town centre and towards the laboratory complex. Once there, I entered without as many of the usual security checks. The ORB security team obviously knew Steve Barratt. As indeed did a lot of the people who I'd passed on my way. It had been interesting to watch their reactions as they recognised me, some were simply courteous and deferential as they nodded to me, but others looked on in awe as I passed. They were all cautious as it was not ORB's policy to identify their operatives, but in truth, the people in this closed world talked and many things were known that wouldn't be admitted to. Added to which, I could almost smell the pheromones being excreted by the ladies who stopped and gave me their coyest smiles. I tried my best to be humble in all this, but it wasn't easy. And anyway, why should I be? I'd earned my place in the highest ranks of ORB and their adulation and respect was my reward.

The feeling I'd got from this taste of fame had been enjoyable. So enjoyable in fact that I'd ended up taking a much longer route than necessary to the labs. I tried telling myself that this had been my way of loosening up with a decent walk, who was I kidding?

At James's old lab I stopped and noticed that the door was open. I went in and saw that the place was pretty much as I'd last seen it, although devoid of my ex-technician. Having put two and two together, I'd come to the conclusion that he was at best, being detained whilst ORB decided what to do with him, or, at worst, was no longer a living James. There had to be repercussions for the failure of the virus and, although James was not the sole creator of this weapon, his name was firmly on it and it was he who had supplied me with it. I felt a bit sorry for him. Not in any sentimental way, but simply because I understood how hard he would be taking the failure of the virus. Socially inept, badly dressed, overweight and with a body odour problem, he had a lot of weaknesses, but in his field, he was more than a genius. To have failed so spectacularly must have hurt him.

His notes lay strewn across the workbench as they must have been when he left the lab for the last time, but after flicking through a few pages I realised that whatever they related to it was beyond my comprehension. I picked up his pencil and pocketed it. A memento? Or something more. The door behind me creaked open.

"Kingfisher?" the voice of a young man asked.

"Steve Barratt," I replied coldly.

"Sorry man," he said, "my bad. Look, I'm Adam, here's my ID."

I looked at the ID Card and checked him over. The photo of a long-haired, pseudo-biker in a brewery t-shirt and with more metalwork on his face than I felt was safe, matched the person who stood in front of me.

"Okay Adam, not a good start," I told him, "Whatever you may be used to and whatever you think, only you and I officially know the alter-ego. Things have got sloppy round here and that stops now. You with me?"

"Er, yeah, sorry man," I could see him trembling as I reached out my hand to shake his which was damp and clammy.

"You alright?" I asked.

"Yeah, sure," he stumbled on his words, "erm, it's just that, man, I can't believe I'm here with you. The Kingfisher. Man, this is such an honour."

"Thanks," I said, "but less of the drooling please. We've got work to do and I need your immediate attention. You sure you're up to being my support?"

"No problemo, man," he snapped back into efficiency mode, "I used to work closely with James so I know a lot of what he was working on. Bummer about that virus thing, hey? Man, he must feel like pure doggy-doo just now."

"Yeah, well it happens," I told him, "just make sure that it doesn't happen to you. I need gear that works, is that crystal clear?"

"Sure man," he answered, "so what can I help you with?"

We talked about the things that I needed, some of which were repairs to existing equipment, including my suit and the animals that had been fried by Amy. We left James's lab and went to a separate building where Adam had his base, and where he had had the foresight to have installed a filter coffee machine. He poured us a cup each and told me that the repairs could be done by tomorrow. He also showed me a second suit that James had completed as a spare and which would be sent back with me.

"Doing your sort of stuff man," he laughed, "I guess there are times you need a change of clothes!"

I didn't share his laughter and he looked out over his workbench embarrassed. His eyes landed on something and he seemed to forget that he'd been babbling on too much.

"How about this?" he held up a wrist cuff that seemed, on first impression, to be made of solid, iridescent metal, "I was working on it with Amy but when I knew I would be working with you I tweaked it a bit. Got the colours to match your suit and this is just one of a pair."

"And it does just what?" I asked him.

"Well, man," he smiled again, unable to stop being his usual jocular self, "I could tell you that it looks way cool. Cos it does, right? But, apart from that, and man, you are going to love this, it also does this."

He slipped the cuff over his wrist and pointed it at an easel over on the far side of the lab. I watched as he made just the slightest movement, then stepped back as a bolt of lightning seemed to emerge from the cuff and vaporise a plastic Star Wars figure that was fixed to the top corner of the easel.

"Oh, man, not Luke!", he shouted, "I was aiming for the other side."

"I guess Snoopy lives to fight another day," I was laughing now, seeing the figure that sat on the opposite corner of easel, "Seems like the force wasn't with your friend. Still, quite impressive."

I had hoped that he'd recover quickly from his mistake but I was disappointed when he went over to the melted blob of plastic and seemed crestfallen by its demise. What he had just shown me was incredible and I knew that it would be a welcome addition to my kit, if also a reminder of how Amy had nearly beaten me.

"Man, that was an original," he whispered, "I'll never get another."

"Collateral damage," I said, taking the cuff off him and fitting it to my own wrist.

He showed me how to work it and by the end of our first session together, the figurine was forgotten and we were enjoying challenging each other against a hastily drawn target scratched onto a sheet of steel. It was honours even by the time we finished and I left him to sort out the rest of my gear.

As I was leaving the labs, a trio of porters came in wheeling two large trolleys laden with a sumptuous buffet. Standing in their path I rooted through the offering, challenging the porters to stop me.

"Sorry," I told them, looking at my watch, "you're a bit late. Take it in anyway and let the techs have a bit of a feast. Decent enough spread though. Well done."

They muttered something as I left. Maybe one of them even contemplated arguing the time with me, as my watch clearly displayed 13:00. My thoughts were elsewhere, although the buffet had looked so good that I did briefly consider turning back and grabbing a handful of food to keep me going. But that would have been a retreat. That was something Steve Barratt didn't do anymore.

Chapter Fifty-Four

The artificial sunshine invigorated me as I took a stroll around the market place at the centre of the underground town. At times, it felt like I could be anywhere in England although this illusion was periodically halted by the functional stuff of the ORB operation. One such example was the shining reception desk that stood out in the far corner of the small market square, just beyond the pub that I was heading towards. As I walked nearer, focused on the pint ahead of me, a voice hailed me:

"Mr Barratt?"

Stopping and turning around, I saw the receptionist at the desk waving at me. I walked over to her and was on the verge of asking how I could help, when she pre-empted me and told me that she was sorry to disturb me but she had the keys for my new apartment.

"I was just about to send them via messenger," she said, her voice recognisable as the same as the one I'd spoken to this morning, "then when I saw you passing, I thought it would save you time. We've found you a suite in the Presidential enclave. I hope that's alright?"

"That's great," I smiled my thanks, "I appreciate it."

"It's my pleasure," she purred, "and can I say what an honour it is to meet you. If there's anything, and I mean anything else that I can do for you, you only have to ask."

There was nothing that I needed just then, but I wasn't so daft as to not be able to read the undertone in her offer. One which made a bit of a mockery of the engagement ring on her finger and one which promised untold pleasure. Of course, there would then be the complications, which were always more than the brief fling was worth. It was nice to be wanted, but that side of things was low down on my agenda. Funny really, as in the past I would have been straight in there but now, it almost seemed as though I was above such base satisfaction. Thanking her again and promising that I would call if I needed anything, I left her to her fantasies and headed off to my new rooms.

Although I remained impressed by what had been packed into this underground complex, I realised on this visit that the Tardis-like dimensions of the place were a lot like those of a narrowboat: everything was there, but the actual footprint was smaller than you would believe possible. This meant that my walk to the Presidential enclave, which was on the other side of the town, took me less than ten minutes. I wanted to have a bit of a chill out and I wanted to change my clothes as well. If Steve Barratt were to be seen out and about, his current attire didn't really do him justice.

Access to the restricted President's area was to the side of the centre's premier restaurant which was a fusion of English and French cuisine overseen by a Spanish Michelin starred chef under the Baltic name of 'Grigori's'. Previously I'd only eaten the wholesome but fairly basic fair of the town but, as I approached the security desk that barred access to the enclave, I decided I'd book in here this evening. A decision that I soon found out that I needn't have bothered to make.

"Mr Barratt, Sir," the guard waved me through, telling me to take the first left and I'd find my apartment to be the third along the pathway.

I found the place easily enough, slipped the key-card into the door and entered a palatial suite of rooms better than anything that I'd expected. There were two bedrooms, a bathroom with a sunken whirlpool bath and sauna, as well as a lounge that led onto a balcony with views over a small garden with a fountain in full flow. Everything was above five-star standard and the rows of books, the well-stocked drinks cabinet and the racks of DVDs showed me that every need of whoever occupied this place had been catered for. After spending the majority of my time on the boat, it was a nice change, but more than that, the sheer opulence of this apartment spoke volumes about my elevated status within the Order.

The master bedroom had a giant four poster bed in the centre around which were various armchairs, settees and tables bedecked with fresh flowers. My new clothes were on the bed, neatly laid out, pressed and ironed where necessary, and every item to my taste although way, way beyond my usual budget. Next to this stack of designer gear was an envelope with my name on it. I opened it and read the card inside. It was an invitation from the President to meet me for dinner that evening at eight. The reservation had been made at Grigori's. I turned the formally printed card over and read the hand-written inscription on the back:

'Steve, so pleased we are both on site at the same time, please do me the honour of joining me. Looking forward to meeting you again, J'

Okay, so now she was no longer Madame President and I was plain Steve. I was definitely beginning to enjoy my new found status.

The hours before this appointment disappeared in the laziest way as I flitted between the sauna and the steaming bath, working my way through a perfectly chilled bottle of bubbly that accompanied a collection of John Wyndham short stories. The bath was big enough for three or four people, but, after a few unfortunate slides across the water, I managed to find a way to balance myself comfortably. So comfortably that I thought I could have stayed there all night. Needing to stave off my hunger and soak up a little of the alcohol, I floated a bowl of Japanese rice crackers in the tub, which I ended up refilling several times. With the bath massaging me gently through the finest of jets whilst I continued reading, I remember thinking to myself that I could get used to this sort of life.

Come evening, I dressed in the smartest of the outfits that they had provided, opting not to wear a tie though as that would have felt too formal and because I wanted to push the boundaries a little in the degree of respect afforded to my illustrious leader. The clothes were all off-the-peg, designer items, but I detected a couple of tweaks that had been made to them to make them bespoke to me. Looking in the mirror I was pleased with what I saw.

"OK," I said as I left the apartment, "Let's see what you've got to say Madame President."

She had already gone through to the private dining room that had been booked for us. A waiter led me to the door which was opened by a matching waiter on the other side, just as we approached it. She was seated on the far side of a longer than necessary table that was set with the finest and most exquisite silverware. I recognised her from our last meeting, but these circumstances were different and that difference was reflected in appearance. An off the shoulder satin dress clung to her surprisingly shapely body, whilst her hair, that had been tightly clasped into a bun at our last meeting, now fell loosely in all its glory, sparkling with strategically placed jewels.

"Madame President," I said, taking her hand and giving it the lightest kiss.

"Please, Steve," she laughed, "let's not be too formal. It's Joanne. Now, do take a seat."

I sat myself down opposite her, waving the overly attentive waiter away in order that I might be able to put the chair where I wanted it. Things had not started as I'd expected, but I remained wary.

"Thank you," I said as I settled into place, "This is all very civilized. I'm just wondering …"

"Don't worry," she interrupted me, "the catch, that you were going to ask me about, doesn't exist. I would say that it's a figment of your suspicious mind, but I can understand why you might be a tad wary. The simple fact is, yes, the Council is interested to know how you feel after your last mission and I have told them we will talk about it, but we're here now, in this rather special location, because I happened to be around, you arrived and I thought it would be nice to move on from the challenging circumstances of our last meeting and seek to generate some more pleasant memories."

"Okay," I said, "well, to get the formalities out of the way then, you can report back that I feel fine. In fact, I feel better than I've felt since starting to work for the Order. Does that surprise you?"

"I little," she smiled, "especially after the concerns you raised last time we met. So, no concerns at all then."

"I didn't say that," I replied, "but before we talk anymore, perhaps we might place our orders, and start working through the wine list."

We made our selections from the menu and ordered a bottle each of red and white wine. More precisely, I allowed the President to order the wine, explaining to her that I was a budget supermarket plonk fan and would appreciate it if she could select something of an appropriately solid and unfussy bouquet. She recommended the soup as a starter, which I was happy to go along with as a prelude to a decent slab of rib-eye that promised to come with 'home cut' chips. I was keen to see how this would compare with the offerings from the various pubs I frequented, given that the decimal point here was one step further along in the price column.

"You mentioned reservations?" she asked.

"Yes, I did," I paused, wondering how hard to push this one, "You see, the thing is, we can't clear the air after the Amy affair until we've discussed the … how shall I put it … the less than perfect legacy of that affair?"

"Go on," she stared at me with piercing eyes.

"You're probably expecting me to express a little concern about the collateral damage that we are all aware of. But the truth of the matter is, I'm past all that now. Personally, at least. My concern is with ORB's failure to support me properly. How the hell did that virus ever get passed by you guys?"

"It was a mistake, I agree," her response was clear and calculated, "We do everything we can to provide you with the tools that you need and we test them thoroughly to ensure that they do what we tell you they will do. With the virus, something went wrong. What's frustrating is that we still can't isolate why some of it worked and some of it didn't. The journalists never recovered. Believe me, we feel bad about that, and we may not be through the woods yet as a relative of two of the victims is somebody who has a connection with our organisation. But, let's hope that comes to nothing. No, we can't understand why we're getting the reading we'd expect from the virus implanted in the CEOs and we have no concerns about it lying dormant if required. We have James in isolation just now, along with a couple of other technicians, trying to give us answers. If it was their error and, I personally think that one or all of them may be found to be at fault, then we will take the necessary action. Whatever happens, we will find the cause and have already put in place extra levels of checks on all new weapons."

"A little late," I said, starting on the soup that had been placed in front of me, "and not particularly reassuring from my part. I am out there doing a job for the Order and I expect the correct level of backup from HQ. Amy was a cock-up to start with and the whole thing just got worse and worse. Last time we spoke, I said I had reservations about the work I was doing for ORB. Those reservations are now gone. I've decided where my future lies and I am all out for this now, but, I will not tolerate shoddy support from you guys."

She seemed taken aback by the genuine anger in my tone.

"It's nothing personal," I continued, "but, as President, you need to hear this and report back. The 'New Franciscans' and 'The Order for Restoring Balance' may have been a lot simpler centuries back, before the power of technology shifted the whole dynamic, but it needs to move with the times and make sure that it remains ahead of a very fast-paced world out there. The core of the injustices may be the same, but they are happening in a very different world and unless the level of collateral damage is contained then ORB becomes as guilty as those it pursues. That's not what I signed up for but, whereas last time I was questioning whether I wanted to be a part of it, now, I know that I need to be a part of it. I believe in what we do and I will fight and fight in whatever way necessary to drag this Order into the present time. You made me what I am, now I am demanding that the person you have created is allowed to fulfil his proper destiny, without the distraction of failures."

"You make a fair point," she said, "and I apologise on behalf of the Order for the difficulties we may have created for you. I will report back what you've told me. Now, let's start doing justice to this food and drink and move onto less hostile ground."

She came around to my side of the table and poured me a taster of the red wine.

"Please," I laughed, "you should know me better than that. Just fill it up."

She smiled as she topped up the glass before returning to her seat and settling herself with her own glass. Although I tried to shake off the feeling, putting it down to the alcohol, I couldn't convince myself that there wasn't a tangible sexual tension rising between us. It was all I could do to dismiss the unwanted thoughts that were creeping into my mind. As soon as the mains arrived, she dismissed the waiter, leaving us alone in the room.

"I may have been a little dishonest," she said, "when I told you that there was no hidden agenda to our meeting. There are a couple of things that I want to discuss with you, both in some way related. But before I mention them, tell me more about the Amy affair, it fascinates me seeing into the other side of our operation."

I talked through the whole of the main course, detailing the planning and execution of the demise of the Angel of Mercy, before drifting into similar details of other operations. She asked sensible questions and seemed genuinely interested in what I had to say. It was nice for me to be able to share my thoughts and my experiences with somebody else and with someone who I thoroughly enjoyed sharing them with. As I sat back in my chair, having cleared the food and the first bottle of wine, she pressed a button on her chair and the waiter reappeared. He cleared the table, then returned with a platter of fruit, cheese and biscuits.

"I didn't have you down as a fancy desserts man," she said, "I trust this will be okay."

She picked off a grape from the plate and popped it provocatively in her mouth.

"That's fine," I replied, "and I'm sorry that I seem to have done all the talking. So, tell me a little about yourself. I presume you have a proper life outside these subterranean walls. What makes Joanne tick?"

"Oh," she said, "compared to your life, it's all very traditional and, if I'm honest, a little unexciting. I am Lady Joanne, the title coming from my now-deceased husband. Yes, I come from a top drawer family and yes, I do what the upper-middle classes do with their time. I live a life of leisure now that I am in my twilight years, doing the charity circuit and making sure the estate runs smoothly."

"If you're in your twilight years," I taunted her, "then that dress is telling some awfully big lies."

"Thank you," she smiled and gave me a wink, "you're right, perhaps I do myself an injustice. There may be some life in the old girl yet!"

"And what about hobbies and interests?" I asked, steering the conversation to safer ground, "Am I stereotyping by guessing at a bit of riding, some genteel gardening and perhaps a role in village life?"

"You must think that I am something out of an Agatha Christie novel," she laughed, "but actually, you're spot on with the hobbies. That's why ORB is so much a part of my life. I like the challenge and I like being able to make a difference. But the action and adventure also do it for me. Dare I say that they arouse me in a certain way?"

"That's a strong word," I said, "perhaps not appropriate."

"You may be right," she stood up and came around to me, "come on, let's relax by the fire. Whisky?"

We moved to the far end of the room where a fire blazed in the grate and two armchairs were positioned opposite each other but a little too far apart to be described as intimate.

"Spill the beans then," I said as we settled down, "you said you had an ulterior motive or two. What's that all about?"

"Okay," she seemed to lose ten years as she leant towards me, "firstly, the most important one. I have plans for you. In fact, I intend to nominate you to be promoted to the Council when the next opportunity occurs. We've never had an operative move from the field to the Council but you're different. Everything we've discussed tonight confirms my gut feeling. We need somebody like you on the Council. Somebody with balls. And somebody who is prepared to challenge the status quo. You're right, ORB is a little too set in its ways but with you on board, we can work together to bring the necessary changes about."

"Quite a turnaround", I said, "from our last meeting. I'd be honoured. In fact, I'll do whatever is necessary to make it happen. And the second thing?"

"It's related in a way," she leant a little closer then changed her mind and stood up, "you see, I want us to be lovers."

The alcohol was working through my blood stream quicker than I'd expected and for a moment or two I wondered whether she'd spiked my drink with some date-rape drug.

"It's as simple as that Steve," she continued, "I may be a tad older than you but I've never felt as horny around somebody as I do around you. Please, just tell me no if it's a definite rejection, but otherwise give me a chance. We could have some fun together."

"Beginning tonight?" I asked, unsure exactly what I would say if she agreed.

"Unfortunately not," she sighed, "you see, it just wouldn't do for me as President and a member of the Council to take an operative as a lover. I know it's all old fashioned but aside from the principal of it, there's a practical issue to."

"Which is?"

"Which," she told me, "is that you would not enjoy being too close to me just now. You see, I am protected from you by the Order. You remember the headaches you had when you were near to Jean? Well, that same implant has the DNA of all of your senior colleagues in it, meaning that if you were ever to turn against us you wouldn't be able to get too close for too long. That's why there has been a certain distance between us tonight, with the table being bigger than necessary and these chairs being a little further apart than we would both like. We can make the briefest contact, but that's all. However, if you become a Member of the Council, well, that all changes. The implant goes. So, I give with one hand but seem to take with the other. I hope not for long though."

"Joanne," I smiled, "you really couldn't make a lot of this up could you? I'm interested in both parts of the offer. You are a very attractive and very sexy woman. More than that, I actually enjoy your company. I'm game for both. Let's hope it happens sooner rather than later."

Once these unexpected revelations were out, the evening seemed to come to a natural end. We talked a little more and drank another drop or two, but within the half hour we were bidding each other goodnight and going our separate ways. I had enjoyed the evening. The food and drink were superb, the company more than pleasant and the promises made, beyond my wildest dreams. I slept very contentedly that night.

Chapter Fifty-Five

Needless to say, the spring in my step was springier than ever the following morning as I toured the ORB facility, now with an eye to the changes I might be able to make when I was on the Council. People nodded to me as I passed them, and the receptionist I'd seen yesterday smiled at me in a way that dripped sexual arousal. It was a shame that that was a no go. Not now that I was destined for bigger things. Still, it was nice to get the attention.

The door to the Assembly Hall was open. There was the sound of a cleaner vacuuming the carpets in the ante-rooms upstairs, but otherwise the place was deserted. I walked the long walk down from the entrance to the stage, still set with the heavy oak tables that had been placed there for the members of the ORB Council. Climbing the steps at the side of the stage I walked behind the tables and found myself looking out over the main arena. In a short time, I would be here by right. It would be my voice that echoed around the chamber and it would be my face that the assembled crowds looked on with adoration and respect. What was the point of being just another ORB operative? I needed to be the Number One, the first among equals and the one that made the transition from the shop-floor to the management suite.

"Soon," I whispered to myself, "Soon."

Leaving the theatre, I made my way to the lab complex, having decided in the early hours of the morning to stir things up a little down there. James' lab remained unlocked and unguarded with the residue of his abandoned workload laid out and gathering a thin layer of dust. Checking that I wasn't being observed, I pocketed a couple of the ion spheres that had been left behind. A high degree of trust had been placed in me, now that I was positioned as a firm favourite of the President, but I saw no harm in cadging a few bargaining chips should the tide change. With my treasures tucked neatly away, I used the desk intercom to call for the Head of Security to come immediately.

"Yes, Sir?" he was breathless from running the short distance from the lab entrance.

"What's the meaning of this?" I asked, pulling no punches in my tone.

"I'm sorry, the meaning of what?" he squirmed as he spoke.

"This lab should have been secured," I shouted at him, "The technician who used to work here is being detained, pending an investigation, and anybody can just swan in here and help themselves to anything they want. Get it sorted. And get it sorted now."

"Yes, Sir, sorry Sir," he called for another guard and I supervised as they inventoried the contents of the lab before sealing the door and locking it with a heavy duty padlock.

"Don't ever let me see such lax procedure again," I said to him, fingering the items that remained in my pockets.

He mumbled an apology as he left and I could see the whole of his team spreading out across the lab complex and taking up positions outside each of the units. When I had more influence, this section of ORB, more than any other, would be secured tighter than the Royal Mint. No wonder the Order was slipping. Centuries of complacency were revealing themselves in the cracks all around and I wondered where else the place might be leaking from.

"Mr Barratt," a familiar voice called to me from nearby.

"Morning Adam," I said as I walked across to his container, "how's everything going with my gear."

"We're pretty much sorted," he told me, "just a few minor tweaks but you'll need to let some of it settle for a few days. Man, I ain't gonna let anything out that might come back and bite me. Is that okay?"

"Sure," I told him, relishing the fact that I would have to keep my luxurious accommodation for a few more nights, "as you say, we need to make sure things do what they're supposed to do."

"Tell me," I continued, "how much contact do you have with the other techs.?"

"Well," his answer was slowed a little by a hint of suspicion about my motives, "we all know each other and we socialise a lot outside of working hours. Sometimes we work together on projects, when our individual skills are needed to help things along, but most of the time we stay tight-lipped about exactly what we're doing."

"The reason I ask," I reassured him, "is that I want to know if there's anything out there that might be of help to me. I don't just want the things I ask for, or the things that fit properly with the Kingfisher. I want to be able to cherry pick the best of the best. How easy is that to progress?"

"Man, you don't take any prisoners do you!", he paused and thought, "We could walk the labs now and ask the guys what's happening. We've moved away from letting too many people share too many things just recently, but, if it's at your instruction, then I guess you'll take the flack if there is any. Wouldn't want to get on the wrong side of the current President. Man, is that one cool bitch."

"That cool bitch," I told him, "is your boss. A little more respect in future."

He mumbled an awkward apology.

"But", I continued, "you don't need to worry about her, I don't think she'll cause us a problem."

We started at the first container in, before working our way through all of the other laboratories. It took us the rest of the day to do this and there was only one laboratory whose technician simply wouldn't grant us access. I made a note of the lab number and the technicians name, passing it on to the President's office via the Security Head. As Steve Barratt, the Kingfisher, I couldn't have a lowly tech tell me what I could and couldn't look at. His secrecy had also whetted my appetite about what he was working on, so I needed access to that lab as soon as possible.

Of the other labs, most of what was being worked on was very specific to the individual operatives concerned and a lot was simply a derivation of the same technology that I was using in my gear. ORB was now extremely protective of the nature and identity of its operatives, but that hadn't always been the case, so there was a lot of information in the public domain. This reassured me that I would be able to find out enough about my fellow operatives even if that meant keeping this knowledge to myself until I was installed on the Council. Beside which, I was able to deduce an awful lot about them and what they were like, simply by looking at the equipment they had made for them.

At the first lab, under a thin silk sheet, I spotted a very standard looking car that I was certain was as powerful and well-equipped inside as my own very standard looking boat. In another I saw the top half of a flaming orange suit that spoke of an operative who would make a powerful adversary, and in another I saw a two-foot-long glistening eel-like creature that made me think that I was not the only operative to use the water as a cover. This latter object intrigued me and the technician who was working on it agreed that it was something that I could probably use. I told him to get me one ready as soon as possible and if he needed to check he could go to the President. I wasn't sure that she would agree but I was pretty certain that he wouldn't even ask the question.

"What's it secret?" I asked him.

He gave me a demonstration. The eel was remotely operated and powered in exactly the same way as my own flying and scurrying animals were. He set it moving in the Perspex tank that took centre-stage in his lab, then I watched as he put it through its paces. It was only an eel in its static state and I was amazed to see it transform itself into numerous other fish and underwater creatures. After showing us these shape-changing characteristics, he proceeded to demonstrate how it was able to spread itself as thinly as its outer shell would allow, widening itself to cover the base of the tank with what appeared to be a thin, green film.

"That last move," he told me, "got our operative out of a really tricky position last time he used it. Their target fell into the water and couldn't swim. The operative slid the eel under him and wrapped him in its shell as a kind of blanket. Lifted him out of the water and then took him away to where his punishment awaited. But it also does this as well."

I watched as he dropped a small goldfish into the water and saw the eel consume it. Then it released the fish which swam away as if nothing had happened.

"What's that all about then?" I asked.

"The goldfish," he told me, "isn't a goldfish anymore. Look."

He played with a few dials and took control of the goldfish.

"You see, the eel takes in living creatures and replicates them to act as assistants."

"That is so cool," Adam blurted out, "we should work together man, I could use that sort of a thing on some of my stuff. Seriously, that is way radical, man, think about it, self-replicating creatures, they might even do us out of a job."

We carried on our tour of the labs and I picked up a few more tools. I wasn't ashamed to be asking for extra help like this, and if the others weren't pushing the boundaries like I was, then that wasn't my problem. We broke for a brief and very late, lunch, after which we spent the late evening in Adam's lab, fine-tuning some of our existing kit. I asked him what the best tracking technology was and he showed me a new homing beacon that he'd been working on, an item that was an extension and development of my original spiders. It was, to all intents and purposes a wood louse. Ugly as nature's original, it didn't use the legs that shimmered underneath it to work, but instead floated just above the ground.

"New tracking technology in this," Adam explained, "means that wherever, and I mean wherever this beasty is, you can get a fix on it. Not as versatile as some of the smaller ones you use but it is the most powerful that we have ever made. Absolutely nothing can stop this baby's signal. You can bury it a thousand feet deep and still know where it is, or you could put it way out in space and still be able to lock onto it. Not the prettiest I know, but man, is she powerful."

"Is it ready for the field?" I asked.

"Sure man," he replied, "I'll load you up with a few."

"I'll take one now please," I said, "I want to play around with it later tonight. Truth be told, I need to be certain after recent events, that it does what you say. That okay?"

He hesitated before handing it over to me with an earnest plea that I return it to him first thing tomorrow morning before anyone found out I had it.

"Adam, man," I put my hand on his shoulder, "you know you can trust me.".

That evening I used the grim looking insect to do what I had wanted to do from my first day in this underground cavern. It told me where I was. Coupling it with the ion sphere that I had taken, I was also able to use it to give me detailed co-ordinates of all the key points of the ORB secret bunker, which wasn't quite so secret anymore. This was information that I felt might come in useful one day. Information that made The Kingfisher just that little bit more powerful.

Chapter Fifty-Six

There is a place and time for everything. For me, the place of luxury might vary but its time must always be for a brief period. A few days of pampering and relaxing in an artificial world of pure indulgence is a delight. When it becomes a lifestyle however, such a lifestyle's maintenance demands outweigh the benefits. So it was that I enjoyed the many and varied comforts of my suite in the President's enclave but always with an eye to the reality of my life in the outside world.

My choice of public persona was to be, like so many others on the cut, comfortably enjoying an independent life in a very small home. To be a small fish in a very big pond, even if that pond was manmade and more accurately described as a long, thin, ditch. In both Summer and Winter extremes of weather, my home was too hot unless I'd neglected the fire and had to brave the chills of an undefended frosty morning. Mod-cons were few and far between and the opportunity for sprawling out in a wide space was very limited. But still, I loved it and wouldn't choose any other lifestyle. Granted, I now had certain commitments that intruded on my freedom, but I could still choose between the inner city or the deep countryside as my location, I could still enjoy the free pleasures of nature or the small indulgence of an afternoon in the pub. Beyond this, and as a function of my alter ego, I could also choose between exploring complex research objectives on the internet or spending the days wallowing on the towpath with an easy-read detective thriller.

I wasn't alone in this choice. My fellow boaters had made the same decision. They also enjoyed the occasional delve into the luxury of hired apartments or spa hotels, but they always returned to their boats. We were half a world away from the madness of mainstream modern living but we were better placed than any to truly appreciate the benefits of the prosperity that few who were in the midst of it ever recognised.

These were some of the thoughts that filled my head on my first night back at the boat, as I relaxed over a glass or three of single malt and let the strains of Beethoven take me to that place of relaxation one step removed from sleep. I hadn't realised how untidy I'd become until I returned to the boat to find that it had been serviced both inside and out by a team from ORB. The upgrades and additions to my toolkit had all been hidden away on board, the drive system tweaked and tuned, the exterior resealed and polished, and the interior scrubbed and tidied up. That's one of the things that I liked about ORB; they knew the challenges we faced out here and they were there to support in ways that you didn't always feel that you needed support. That said, it was a sign of weakness for me to have to be bought back into line by a maid, so in future I would put a little more effort into domestic affairs.

Winter was now starting to come to an end, with the last of the frosty mornings still visible but beginning to have to fight against the unstoppable approach of Spring. For a number of years now, the weather had been kind to us over the Winter months and Christmas was more likely to bring floods and unseasonably warm weather than any sort of Dickensian snowfall. Still wrapped up in my layers of warm clothing, I made a point of venturing out into the cold and waking myself with a brisk run along the solid and crunchy towpath. I ran to keep fit and I ran to think. That first morning back in the wider world, I thought a lot. I thought of the past and the different life that I had lived seven or eight years ago now, and I thought of the new life that I had been blessed with. I thought of the peace that I enjoyed in my little metal box on the water and I wondered about the lives that were lived in the houses I passed, all with their boilers still steaming away to fend off the touch of nature. And I thought of the future and the transition that I had made from trainee vigilante to the promised position of a place on the ORB Council.

A long shower after this run, followed by breakfast, saw me settled in for the day, although I had noticed a rather quaint pub that would be perfect for an evening stroll. The boat had been taken down the Wolverhampton flight, which was a mixed blessing as I enjoyed the challenge that had been denied me, but nevertheless, appreciated the labour it had saved. Whether they were unsure about my return date or simply because they wanted to ensure the boat's security, they had paid a local boatyard to look after her until I came along. Because I knew that ORB would have paid over the odds for this service, I planned to stay there for a few days before heading back out. It was a nice location and gave me the choice to stroll up into a city if

I so desired, take a train anywhere in the country, or strike out the other way, either up and along the Shroppie in one direction or on the Staffs and Worcester in the other.

When I eventually moved, I winded the boat at Autherley Junction and opted to head towards Stourport, remembering that this was a route that I'd always planned to do but had never got around to. It would lead me to the link with the River Severn and I still hadn't put the boat through her paces in a proper stretch of water, so that gave me something of a reason for the journey. Of course, instructions from ORB made any planning a tad superfluous, but then again, I was now better placed than ever to operate from wherever I chose to be. I was also keenly aware that the tracking facilities of the Order were beyond comparison and felt sure that they allocated missions as much to accommodate the location of the operative as their skills.

It took me a few days to get down to, and through, the Bratch Locks, one of the most picturesque parts of my journey so far, after which I pulled in at the first mooring behind a freshly painted boat that had a look of familiarity about it. Having tied up and, as per my new resolution, tidied up a little inside, I stepped off the deck to have a closer look. The rear doors of the boat were open and what I saw made me almost faint. They were adorned with two carved panels that I had last seen as they left my workshop on the way to Jack and Elaine, oh so long ago. As I moved closer to inspect them, Jack popped his head out and gave me a cherry hello. Now, I knew that he wouldn't recognise me, but I was shocked that I barely recognised him. All the worry lines had left his forehead and his smile was no longer forced.

"Aye up lad," he said, "are you alright."

"Sorry," I replied, "I was just admiring those carvings."

"Aye," he said proudly, "you'll never see anything like them again. They were done special for us and, I'm sorry to say, the artist isn't with us anymore. Boat fire. He was a fine lad."

"Elaine," he shouted down into the boat, "what were the name of that artist did these carvings?"

"Oh, Jack," she laughed as she joined him on deck, "you can't really forget Zipoly now can you! Zipoly Hardacre."

She paused and I was shocked to see the beginnings of tears in her eyes.

"Such a tragedy," she continued, "not long after he'd posted these to us, his boat went up in flames with him on it. He was more than an artist though."

"Oh? I asked.

"Elaine," Jack interrupted, "the lad must be freezing and you need to make that Skype call to Rebecca. Tell you what lad, are you going to be in the pub later?"

"Well, I can be," I smiled as if the thought had never crossed my mind.

"Good, then we'll meet you there. Say about seven-thirty. We'll tell you the story then. But we've got to go now, our daughter's in Australia, been settled there for a year now and doing very well for herself. If we don't catch her now she'll be impossible to reach for another week. See you later."

He closed the doors and I walked away, remembering the events of that early mission that I had set myself and pleased to hear that Rebecca was making a new life for herself. I carried on walking the towpath to the pub, treated myself to a pre-dinner pint, then returned to my own boat where my favourite tinned pie and mushy peas would soon be on the table.

The pub was busy for a midweek evening, but then again, it was a perfect canal side haunt and clearly a place that was respected by, and therefore well used by, the boats that moored nearby. Everybody looked at me as I entered, checking me over before marking me down as a fellow boater by the high-vis jacket that I wore and the leather hat, both of which were respectably dirty and worn. I nodded to other boaters as I headed towards the bar and was just about to order a pint when I heard Jack shout across to me.

"Over here lad!"

"What are you drinking?" I asked

"We're working our way through the last of the Christmas Ale there, thanks."

I ordered three pints and went to join them.

"Glad you could make it," Elaine said, giving me a too-friendly hug.

She too had changed a lot since I had last seen her. Her features were no longer gaunt but had filled out into a proper matronly sturdiness more conducive with her age and personality. And she was full of smiles as well. With them on the table were another couple.

"Oh sorry," I said pointing to the three pints, "I didn't realise there was anyone else here."

"That's no problem," the male half of the couple said, "we're on wine. We've only just met Jack and Elaine as well; this is the only table free. Look, we can move if you need us to."

"Not at all," said Jack, "everyone's family as far as we're concerned and anyway, we met this lad only today and still don't even know his name."

"Steve Barratt," I smiled and shook hands with everyone at the table.

"I were just telling George and Helen here about my home-brewed wine," Jack said, "I have to be careful not to upset the Landlord here, but I can't keep my recipes a secret now can I? Tell you what I'll do George, I'll drop by the boat tomorrow with some notes."

"That'll be fine," his wife replied for him, "I'm not sure I want George to be able to make the stuff if it's anything like what you say."

"I'll bring you a bottle tomorrow, love," Jack laughed, "then you'll change your mind."

We settled down for the evening and talked boats, canals, pubs and a bit of politics, with a lot of points in between, then there was the necessary silence for Elaine to say her piece.

"The reason we invited Steve here," she said, "is to fill him in on the guy who did our door panels on the boat. Zipoly Hardacre."

"Wasn't he," George thought hard about the name, "…yes, wasn't he the guy they suspected of being that vigilante…the righteous something."

"Corrector?" I offered.

"Yes, that's it. The Righteous Corrector."

"Well," said Elaine, "we'll never know that will we, but let me tell you our story and then you can make your own minds up."

It was over an hour later that she finished up her tale, by which point a number of other customers had joined our table and were listening eagerly.

"So," she concluded, "now we have our money back, our daughter back and life is good again. Plus, we have the finest boat doors on the cut. As to whether Zip was more than just a carpenter, who knows. It just seems too much of a coincidence don't you think? Oh, what a loss he was."

From my side, it was strange to hear myself being talked about in this way and with nobody else around the table having any idea of the true nature of the person who sat with them. They were days of crude works by myself, although I acknowledge that the carvings were damned good. But they had delivered a result and it was so reassuring to hear how all those involved had been given their lives back. A strange silence followed Elaine's final words, but the mood was soon broken.

"Come on then," a Black-Country voice from the other side of the pub rang out, "let's get this party going."

We all turned just in time to see a rough and ready local donning an accordion, break into the first of what would be a lot of jaunty songs that evening. Conversation stopped as he was joined by a ukulele, a piano and a guitar. I left them just before midnight but they showed no signs of stopping at that point. If I hadn't left then, I was in danger of embarrassing all concerned with a rendition or two of my own favourites, which, given that my voice was not particularly tuneful, saved them an ordeal and me a big hangover.

Arriving back at the boat, I poured a small whisky to see me to bed and was settling down with that when I noticed the message light blinking on my communications console. I pressed the button and the screen filled with a new mission. Oh well, the break had been nice while it lasted.

Project: Philip Rivers
Operative: Kingfisher
Status: New – Active Immediately
Notes: Prisoner AO9634/M, HMPYOI Worcester, Cell 17A/U. Please make contact and advise that ORB are close to resolution on sentence, release imminent.

As always, ORB were sparing in their details, although in this instance they did have the courtesy to attach a plan of the prison and a scanned newspaper clipping detailing Philip Rivers' transgression and imprisonment.

He was seventeen now, but at the age of sixteen, whilst the brief outbreak of riots that had occurred last year in Birmingham had been in full flow, he'd been stupid enough to post a message on social media asking others to meet him at a well-known spot where they could all 'join in the fun' as he'd put it. I remembered the riots vaguely, something to do with an Asian youth being shot by an armed police officer and this situation then being used as an excuse by members of his community, other activists and of course, every low life and criminal in the area, to launch a series of attacks that soon blossomed into full scale riots. There was a lot of damage, mainly to looted shops, but the whole thing had blown over within forty-eight hours. Even still, the public mood was against the local youths who you would think, by the press coverage, were responsible for not only the damage done here but also every other failure and breakdown of modern society that plagued the nation today.

It was this mood swing in public opinion that led to Rivers being found guilty of incitement to cause a riot and being sentenced to five years in prison. The public had its whipping boy and the establishment could breathe easy again. But five years for a sixteen-year-old kid who didn't really know what he was doing and who hadn't actually got as far as committing the crimes he dreamed of? A little over the top, I thought. Clearly ORB agreed.

Chapter Fifty-Seven

The combination of the alcohol, the late night and the work I'd done travelling through the locks, should have been enough to put me fast asleep and quickly. Added to which, the report on Rivers mentioned nothing of any major urgency. But sleep eluded me and I lay restlessly in my bed, my body craving the nocturnal nothingness that my mind refused to give it. Something deep inside of me was urging me to immediate action and no amount of ignoring it could ease its persistent nagging.

At two thirty a.m. I clambered out of bed, loaded up my control computer and keyed in a code that opened one of the hidden panels in the boat's walls. Inside, tucked away in a bespoke compartment that both protected and recharged its energy cells, lay one of the newest additions to my gang. I took the box to my desk and opened it up, removing a thin layer of fine tissue wrapping to see the first of my kingfishers.

Until I'd seen my first live kingfisher darting through the undergrowth beside me as I travelled along the canal, I shared what I believe is a popular misunderstanding about the size of these most beautiful creatures. Artwork, photographs and all many of other reproductions seem to create an impression of size that belies the truth. This may be because it's a bird that is best seen in extreme close up, or it may simply be because it is a creature whose blue-green perfection implies a greater mass. The kingfisher that I now held was life size, small and delicate between my fingers and a testament to the craft and skills of Adam. He had packed as many features as he could into this robotic ally of mine, but he had also advised me of the limitations that he simply couldn't overcome due to its size. I knew therefore that it could fly long distances, given its combination of anti-gravity streamlining and micro-fusion power cell, but that it couldn't do as much as one of my owls or eagles once it reached its destination. At this stage that wasn't a priority for me. I needed something fast tonight. There was something happening with Philip Rivers and I needed to know exactly what it was.

Given that I wasn't planning on leaving the boat, I synched the bird with the mini tablet that was easier to use than the wrist pad I used when out on missions. I programmed in the location, keyed in its start-up code and released it through the hatch over the rear doors. The distance wasn't great and was covered promptly by the bird which sent me an ever increasing series of repeating bleeps to indicate how far it was from the target. When the bleeping was almost a constant hum, I switched to visual and watched as the bird scooted over the prison walls and then slowed to hover by the primary housing block. Checking the blueprints and information that ORB had sent me, I directed the bird to Rivers' cell and watched as it approached. The light was on. That was unusual. More unusual though was the shadow that was playing against the window pane. It was a slow swinging motion. I knew exactly what it was and, more importantly, I knew exactly what I had to do.

The bird's beak fired out a jet of laser light that melted a hole in the glass small enough to allow it to enter the room. Rivers was hanging from a light fitting, his body swaying gently in the night. Another jet of laser light burnt through the rope that held him and he fell to the floor. I listened intently as the bird came to a rest beside the body. There was a faint sound of breathing. Then there was a cough and a splutter and Rivers came to, trying to understand first, where he was, then second, why he had failed in his attempt to take his own life. He muttered an audible curse.

"Philip", I whispered through the Kingfisher, "please listen."

"Who's there?" he mumbled, looking around the dimly lit room then seeing the bird, "What the …"

"Philip," I spoke through the bird again, "I need you to listen. There is nothing to be afraid of. Are you okay now, or do you need me to call the doctors."

"No," he whispered, "not the doctors. I'm okay. Don't call anyone. They hate me. No doctors."

"Okay," I said, "now I know this is all a bit weird, but suicide isn't the answer. You need to know that there are people out there working for your release and it will be soon. You're not alone."

"Who are you?" he asked.

"We are your friends," I said, "and no, we are not talking birds. This is a robot, but I can see and hear you through it. But it's not the best way that we can talk so I need to ask you, if I leave you tonight, can we talk more tomorrow, in a closer way?"

He paused and rubbed the welt marks on his neck. The rope he'd used was an accumulation of scraps of any cord he had been able to pick up on his travels and as such had been course and fine enough to break the skin in a few places.

"Yes," he said, "I don't know what's going on but what does another day matter. They lock us in at eight-thirty. I'll be alone from then."

"Does the window open at all?" I asked, unable to get a view of the workings of the small opening that hid behind a steel grille.

"I can open it about six inches," he replied.

"Okay, do that, and see if you can cover up the small hole that this bird made. I'll be back at eight-thirty tomorrow. Please remember, there are people on your side and I'll make it more clear to you tomorrow."

I saw him nod as I raised the bird off the floor and back through the window. The kingfisher did what it needed to do but its speech capacity was limited. Tomorrow I would send in a different creature and spend more time with him, but tonight I was reassured that at least there was a person left to comfort.

As the kingfisher returned to base and I was able to shut the console down, sleep finally caught up with me and I took myself straight off to bed. Whatever happened from now, and yes, I was terrified that I wouldn't have the chance to take this mission further, at least I knew that I had done what I needed to for that night. Not only was I the high-powered operative that did the dirty work for ORB, Steve Barratt had also been reminded that he retained a heart, of sorts, and that this work wasn't always about death and punishment.

When I sent the red-tailed kite out the following night, I sent it with a supply of additional supporters clutched in its talons. Before visiting Rivers, I used its ability to take in a lot of data from a high altitude and located a spot where it could hole up when not in use. It was a powerful piece of kit and had a lot of energy stored within it, but this particular bird also had solar cells incorporated into its wide wing span and would therefore be able to charge during the day. There were multiple niches among the eaves of this late Victorian building and I selected one that looked to have not seen human feet for many a year but which caught a fair amount of the sun.

At precisely eight-thirty I flew the bird into Rivers' cell, seeing the look of surprise on his face as it landed on his bed.

"Thanks for waiting," I said, tipping the bird's head to make it a little less intimidating, "please, sit down and I'll tell you a little more of what this is all about."

Thus began a three-week series of meetings in which Philip Rivers poured out his heart to an animatronic bird, and in which I spoke words of encouragement, support and, as necessary, rebuke. My role in this was to see the injustice of his sentence resolved, but that didn't mean that Rivers was guiltless in the whole affair. This was made clear right from the start and, to be fair, he took it on the chin.

"Look, I know I was wrong," he told me, "It was stupid and it was criminal and yes, if others had responded then we would have gone out and looted with the rest. But I just got caught up in things and I didn't have anything else to do. I couldn't believe it when they locked me up though, and then to be given five years."

We talked about the night that I had found him and the bird had cut him down.

"I'd just had enough," he said, holding back the tears, "and I looked at the years ahead and didn't think I could see it through. This is a youth prison and I can't cope here. What will it be like when they transfer me to an adult one?"

He shared his experiences behind those walls and I did what I could to check up on the facts and see how much of what he was telling me was based on facts rather than his own sense of anger and persecution. Sadly, too much of it was true. From the warden, through to the officers, down to the youths who were top-dogs in that place, corruption, abuse, violence, drugs and rape were part and parcel of everyday life.

Rivers came from a poor family but his parents and siblings had a strong moral code and had never been in trouble with the authorities. This left Rivers vulnerable in his naivety but he had been smart enough in his registration to advise that he was HIV positive. Somebody had shared this tip with him when he had been in the holding cells of the court, and it had saved him from the worst of the sexual excesses that others fell victim too. It hadn't saved him from bullying though. He had had all of his very limited possessions stolen in the short time he had been there and complaints to the warders fell on deaf ears. He had also succumbed to the lure of drugs, just prior to his suicide attempt and was beginning to gain a reputation as somebody who might be useful to the pushers over time.

"I saw where I was heading," he told me, "like you hear about alcoholics just having that one extra little drink and that it won't do any harm. And I couldn't see a way out. They don't have any counselling that's worth talking about in this place, as far as the law is concerned we're scum. I could feel myself starting down the slippery slope and I didn't want to become like the ones I'd seen here. The worst of them are injecting their eyeballs to get a hit. It's sick. I'd rather be dead."

The catalogue of wrongs that I became aware of through Philip surprised me. I knew that we still had a long way to go as a nation to make prison more effective in reducing recidivism, but the bottom line seemed to be that, in places like this, it was still simply a case of offenders being better off out of sight and out of mind. All well and good, I thought, for those who deserved to be punished, but who made the rules on that? At what point do good people who have done bad things, turn into bad people? And the teams in this prison were very clever in what they did. Anything that transgressed legal boundaries was perpetrated by, or positively attributed to, other inmates. Those things that transgressed moral boundaries were seen as simply a fact of life, a mechanism for the staff to stay distanced from the inmates and prevent them from going native.

When I considered what Rivers was in for, and compared it to the institutional abuse that he was being subjected to, I despaired at the failings of a system that I knew was doing great things elsewhere. For that reason, I spent my days whilst waiting to speak to Rivers, investigating alternatives and putting together a dossier for ORB. They didn't have to follow my lead, although I wasn't going to give them much choice in the matter. I believed they would agree with me though, and that they would see that the work I was doing would further their own cause.

Rivers was advised of his early release on the 26th March 2023. He left custody that day and returned home to try and rebuild his life. I had every hope for him and believed that he could get back on track with the help of his family. He wasn't the same person who had entered that prison. In that respect, imprisonment had worked. Had he been forced to see his original term through, things might have been very different and the world would have welcomed him back only briefly as he began a revolving-door life in the justice system.

HMPYOI Worcester was evacuated in the early hours of the 27th March 2023, as cells began to smoulder during a bizarre and still unexplained electrical event, the like of which had never been seen before. Cables, pipes and all the periphery of systems required to support modern living were all destroyed by the blue fire of electricity that sparked from cell to cell. However, not a single person was injured and the fabric of the building remained intact.

A week later, a development proposal was submitted to the Ministry of Justice and supported by a number of senior and well respected members of the establishment. The building and land that the prison was on would be sold for the princely sum of £15.65 million pounds, and a much needed housing estate would be built in its place. At the same time a new Young Offender's Institute had been budgeted for, along the lines of a revolutionary Scandinavian model, at a cost of £15.675 million pounds. On the day that both plans were approved, an anonymous donation was sent to the Department responsible to cover the £25,000 shortfall.

Chapter Fifty-Eight

I wasn't concerned about the feedback that I got for the Rivers affair, although ORB scored the whole thing highly, reserving judgement over the events that had surrounded my role in the mission. Since I had submitted video, audio and written evidence to back my actions up, I think they were content to let things lie and move on to new things. As was I.

+++

'The New York Enquirer', 12th April, 2023
'Ghost in the Machine?

Police in Worcestershire, England, have requested help from the NYPD in order to understand the contents of CCTV footage retrieved following a raid on a house that was being used to distribute child pornography.

The images captured at the scene by a low tech series of security cameras, appear to show a 'ghost' move around the building before exiting from an upstairs window. A spokesman for the local police department explained that the quality of the images was particularly poor which is why the NYPD have been asked to give advice on cleaning up the pictures. Since the terror attacks of 2001, the NYPD has developed systems that are world-beating in terms of image enhancement and this request by an English police department is only one of many that they receive each day.

Having seen the first screen-shots from the footage, sources close to the Video Enhancement Unit based in central Manhattan say that they are excited about the prospect of discovering more detail which may, or may not, confirm some sort of supernatural activity.

Eight individuals were arrested when police raided the property in a quiet riverside location near the city of Worcester, and a further half dozen are assisting police with their enquiries.

See the first exclusive images from this haunting video on page seven of this edition of The Enquirer.

+++

'The Telford Telegraph', 14th April, 2023
'Radical Cleric Submits to Voluntary Deportation'

In a surprise U-turn, Abu Hadadi, the radical Muslim preacher who was in the process of suing the UK government for wrongful imprisonment and breaches of his human rights, has submitted to be voluntarily deported. In a telephone call to the Immigration Service late last night, Hadadi, 46, and three of his supporters advised officials that they had changed their minds about their actions and would be happy to leave the country at the earliest opportunity. They are wanted on terror related charges in their home country of Iran and have always maintained that their lives would be at threat if they were forcibly repatriated.

It is uncertain as to why the cleric has changed his mind although it is believed that his change of heart may be a reflection of what he has called a 'new and insightful vision of the true nature of the Prophet Mohammed'.

+++

'BBC Wales Today', 13:00, 26th April, 2023

In other news, a local restaurant owner has been fined by Llangollen Council for multiple breaches of environmental health protocols. Harry Freeling, who has run businesses in and around the area for many years, was one of the areas most respected catering operators who regularly scored full marks on inspections.

It is understood that Freeling volunteered information to the Council regarding some of his practices and this voluntary approach was reflected in the reduced level of fines imposed. Following this case, two members of the local environmental health inspection team have been suspended pending further investigation.

+++

March and April were steady months for operations and gave me a chance to try out some of the new tools that I had been given, or that I had borrowed from other operatives. Hadadi was an interesting one because it was extremely sensitive for the Order and required a careful approach. In strict, legal terms, the actions being taken by Hadadi and his team of advisors were acceptable, exploiting as they did the long and extensive reach of UK, European and Global protocols. Ethically though, the guy was using safeguards that had been put in place for sound reasons and making a mockery of them. This both threatened their long term sustainability and also the public confidence in protocols that were important in that they reflected a global common humanity. You only had to look back at the hysteria that saw the UK leave the EU five years ago to see the harm that this sort of abuse caused. Mind you, things were settling now after our humbling return.

Free of the restraints that the rules imposed on those opposing Hadadi, I formulated a plan whereby he could leave the country voluntarily and retain credibility in his faith, but be under no illusion that if he stayed he would be hurt, humiliated and persecuted far more than the punishments that he faced if found guilty in his home country. I wasn't too proud of my methods, but once I had established his weak points, ensuring his compliance came easily. Interestingly, threats to his family and friends meant absolutely nothing to him. I genuinely believe that I could have maimed, mutilated, raped or even killed his wife and children and he would have only been pleased to add this to his own case for being wrongfully treated. However, once I tapped into his pride and made him aware of how I could destroy his reputation as a respected Muslim cleric he caved in. He would rather die in the vanity of his own twisted interpretations of Islam than be humiliated and rejected. He was a very sad and lonely man I realised but the choices were his. I didn't rate his chances much in his home country.

Prior to this of course, I had been in Worcester and had worked on eliminating a computer scamming outfit that wasn't quite the sordid enterprise that it was reported as. The set-up was operating out of an old Vicarage situated next to the river in Worcester and was using highly skilled computer technicians, smuggled in from Asia, to phish for data from vulnerable individuals. Even I had had the phone call on my supposedly high security mobile, advising me that the caller was from ComputerWeb, the multinational software giant, and that my computer was 'at risk'.

This was a relatively low level 'nuisance', but it had the potential to do a lot of harm to an individual's home computer equipment, to fleece the unsuspecting of decent sums of money and even to cause immense anxiety and stress to those less able to cope with such emotional challenges. More important than all of this though was the simple fact that the operators were lying. If they could claim to be 'David' or 'Jemima' and blatantly lie their way through a conversation with a stranger today, what would they be capable of doing tomorrow? This was pre-justice justice and it was a form of justice that remained secret but had a powerful influence on the future.

The building was falling into disrepair and I first used a travelling rat to check the place out, feeling that this was most in keeping both with the surroundings and the mission at hand. It drew me a layout of the place, including the locations of all the operators and the mainframe drives that were in use. I saw the CCTV but wasn't too concerned about it as it was linked to old VHS video recorders and had clearly seen better days. The important aspect of this case was that I had to catch each of the operators at work simultaneously and disable them swiftly enough that nobody in the building could eliminate evidence. That's why I decided to try out the 'Auto Track' system that I had borrowed from another ORB operative. In my time probing the activities of the other ORB operatives, I had been made aware that there was one called 'The Cipher' out there, who worked almost invisibly as a miniature stealth bomber, targeting a variety of cases but always unseen and barely recognised.

On the day of my mission I sent out a handful of ion driven spiders to set the points of the Auto Track, and made sure that they were all in position ready for my afternoon assault. All the operatives were in full swing at two thirty p.m., at which point I braced myself and triggered the Auto Track release. At a sickening velocity the system picked up on the drives in my boots, gloves and belt and flew me through all the locations that had been pre-set where, at each, I barely had time to administer the paralysing drug before being catapulted to the next one. All eight operators were out of action within one minute, after which I was ejected through a window to land in the river. My suit sealed and I was transported back to the boat several miles away. From the boat I hacked into the mainframe, first by sending a message to all of the operators who I knew were sitting, fully conscious of their surroundings but completely unable to move. They would all have been watching their screens as the message came up:

"Hello, this is Jeremy speaking to you from ComputerWeb. How are you today?

The reason I am contacting you is that your system is at risk and you need to take urgent action.

What? You can't move? Oh, dear me.

Never mind, help will be on its way soon."

I then wiped the screens and all the hard drives before loading in the filthy, repugnant data that ORB had supplied me with. This transformed that small scamming operation into the hub of a major child-porn outfit. Once the files were loaded and I could sense the look of horror on the faces of those who sat watching their screens in helpless horror, I made a call to the police. They arrived ten minutes later.

Needless to say, the liars were silenced and would be silenced for a good while yet. What was most amazing though, was that in that short space of time before the police were able to disconnect the computers from any outside server, enough data had been received by ORB relating to users of this disgusting material that they were able to clear up a number of other injustices that were outstanding.

Which leads me finally to explain the issue with the restaurant owner. The truth is, I had a bad meal there. I suffered badly on my return to the boat and, believe me, there is one place that you don't want to be suffering sickness and diarrhoea and that is on a narrowboat. Granted, I did want to check out another of The Ciphers tricks though, so it wasn't all just petty vengeance.

Freeling obviously had an unnaturally strong relationship with the local health inspector which, it later transpired, was due to their connections within both the counties most respected golf club, and its less well publicised swingers club. He was good at what he did but he was the sort of person who felt that he could bend the rules because he was slightly above them. Inspections that were supposed to be unannounced were prepared for meticulously, but at other times, like the night I was there, staff who were not trained in the basics of health and hygiene passed on their diseases to me.

The Cipher had a natty little gadget that was able to identify and act on a multitude of the commonest bacterium. It transformed them from their natural state into mini electrical fields in their own right that could be used to travel to required destinations at the speed of light, or alternatively, eliminate themselves. It was the sight of his kitchen alive with this dancing and dangerous blue energy that made Freeling understand that his standards were maybe not as high as his paperwork indicated. I let the energised germs circle him and threaten to invade him, before destroying them and leaving the building. He cleaned up his act the next day. I was still cleaning up mine a week later.

At which point I had done my Worcester trip, had travelled back up the Shroppie, every day purging my body of its illness and losing over a stone in weight. By the time I was fully recovered, I was back at Gailey Wharf, moored just below the round house and settled for a few weeks of being stationary now that the Easter break was in full flow. The popularity of canal holidays seemed to waver but that year was one of the stronger ones. The previous year had produced an exceptionally mild Spring with near tropical sunshine at certain times in April and this had led to a rise in the number of boats on the cut this year. With Easter being at its latest date possible, it all looked very promising, but the rains fell harder than ever and I can't help thinking that some holidaymakers may have been disappointed. Throughout those last two weeks of April, the heavens opened. Temperatures were up where they should have been, maybe even a bit above average, but the constant fall of water didn't seem to let up and the skies barely offered a glimpse of anything more than a dull, depression-inducing greyness.

Moored where I was, I was in the mainstream, but was able to keep my own company for most of the time, watching through the boat windows as the hire boats and their bedraggled crews slugged towards the next lock. For most, the weather wasn't a major problem; they hadn't signed up for a holiday in the sun and there was always something primordially satisfying about tying up at night and drying off over a drink or two. I did feel sorry for the families with young children though, as a narrowboat isn't really the best place for youngsters to be cooped up in whilst weathering a storm. That said, the little ones seemed quite resilient and I saw quite a few of them battling to open lock gates in defiance of the constant showers.

My only excursions out were my early morning and late evening runs along the towpath, few of which resulted in the customary pause at a pub since I was trying to detox and therefore avoided temptation when I planned my routes. As there was only a garage for supplies, and I didn't really want to drip my way on public transport, I was also forced to thin down the stores in my kitchen cupboards. Mind you, there was still probably enough there to feed a family for a month, as long as they were happy to get by on cheap Chinese noodles, tinned pies and a bit of old potted beef. Okay, I agree, it's not the healthiest of fares and it certainly didn't compare to the riches I'd indulged in on my last trip to ORB, but I enjoyed myself immensely working my way through these basic offerings.

Before settling down to moor here, I'd stocked up on plenty of reading as I'd passed through Audlen and had been fortunate enough to find the one Dickens that I was missing, The Old Curiosity Shop, as well as a number of quick reads by some of my favourite crime writers. The Dickens in particular kept me busy for that first week and I'm not ashamed to say that I cried a few times. Although fiction, I knew that much of what I was reading was based on facts and it made me appreciate anew just how fortunate we were to be living in this age of prosperity where our worries and concerns were centred on the most trivial of things. This led me to think about the unseen role of ORB during the Victorian era. Aside from their own admission about Jack the Ripper, I knew little about the historic activities of the New Franciscans as they were then known. I guess it was easier to operate covertly in those days, and yet, that ease of operation would have been tempered by the crude technologies available for their operatives. Swings and roundabouts I suppose, but give me today anytime.

About halfway through the week I met another Steve. He moored up behind me in a beautifully maintained boat that was no more than a year old and I gave him the usual greeting but nothing more as I had him pinned as another of the 'shiny boat brigade'. This was a derogatory term that was used, mostly unfairly and usually due to jealousy, about the boaters whose vessels were always as polished as precious gems, but who often gave them another wipe and polish after a day's cruising (and often, before it as well). Of course, as I had spent more time on the cut, I was less and less moved by these sort of prejudices and kept an open mind on most of the people that I encountered. At least, I tried to. I'd pigeon-holed Steve without thinking about it and was therefore very surprised when I got a knock on the boat that evening.

"Hello mate," Steve smiled as I opened the door, "wondered if you fancied a quick snifter?"

I wasn't doing anything that evening so I agreed that I wouldn't mind, but that the pubs nearby weren't really worth the trip.

"No problem," he said, "I was thinking about a drop or two on the boat. Truth is, I've got more whisky on board than I'll ever get through and I thought we might have a tasting session."

Without too much hesitation, I followed him onto his boat. This wasn't particularly unusual for life on the cut, but it was a little more forward than most times. Still, I wasn't going to turn down the chance of a few decent whiskies and it would do me good to have a little company and a break from my self-imposed exile.

"Come in, come in," he ushered me into an immaculate lounge and, after removing my shoes and clambering on board, I settled on one of the long couches that lined the walls.

"Hope you don't mind me asking you over," he said, "'cos some people are a little wary about that sort of thing. I guessed you were on your own though and thought we could try and shake off some of the grumpiness that this weather brings in. Anyway, I'm Steve."

"Me too," I laughed, "well, I guess we won't forget each other's names in a hurry."

"This is a beautiful boat," I continued, "how long have you had her?"

Thus began our long and increasingly drunken introductory session. Steve had lost his wife to divorce just over a year ago, not because of anything that he had done, but because she'd wanted a change in her life. With the proceeds of his half of the family house, he'd decided, on a whim, to buy a boat and had been able to move onto this one almost immediately as it was a cancelled order.

"Not sure what happened to the first buyer," he said, "but I snapped her up and got her at a great price since the boat-builder already had a wad of cash that had been paid in a deposit. I took it as an omen that this was how I was meant to live. And I've never looked back."

We talked about children and families, and we talked whisky and boats. The time flew by and the alcohol smoothed things along. About halfway through the evening, I noticed a guitar hanging on the wall and asked Steve if he played.

"A little," he said, lifting the guitar down and strumming a few chords, "what sort of music do you like?"

I told him that, aside from Johnny Cash and a few other country and western classics I was open to his choice, at which point he reeled off some of the oldies, amazing me not only with his playing but also with his singing voice.

"This is one I've written myself," he said, closing his eyes and breathing deeply as he began to play. Now, I'm no music expert, nor am I qualified to comment on the quality of song lyrics, but what he played that evening just blew me away. The song was about loss, as so many are, but it was tinged with moments of the deepest sadness set against those of enormous hope.

I closed my eyes and sipped at the single malt, allowing my mind to drift off in the moment and enjoy this impromptu concert. This was life as it was meant to be. This was the epitome of canal life and a moment in time that had to be savoured as one that would never be repeated. Steve would never be a pop star, nor did he have ambitions to be one. In fact, he was more than happy in his role as a medical embalmer, although that particular career choice did nothing for me. And Steve would never be rich, nor famous, nor showered with honours. Yet none of that mattered. He was one of the many billions of people who walked this Earth and played their part in an anonymous way, but who could change lives by his friendliness and humility. It made me think about my own position. What exactly drove The Kingfisher and why did I think I was something special? The days of my regrets were over but that didn't mean that I had to reject the wider world completely.

That night with Steve went on into the early hours. I was humbled by his playing and by the lack of any positive contribution that I could bring to the evening's entertainment. As I staggered back to my own boat, stumbling down the steps as I clambered in, I felt honoured and privileged to have shared that time with Steve. We lived very different lives and would likely not see each other again for a long time, if at all, but he had touched my life in a special way. This was canal life at its best. This was the reason why I knew that whatever the future would bring I would be found living on a narrowboat and keeping my mind open to the myriad new experiences that openness, niceness and sheer unadulterated basic humanity would offer up to me.

When I woke up at lunchtime, I poked my head out of the hatch at the rear of the boat and saw that Steve had already moved on. As I made a cup of coffee and scraped butter onto slightly burnt toast, I felt in my pocket and found the lyrics he'd written down for me. A tear welled in my eye as I read the lines that had so moved me the evening before, "I look in the mirror and the face that I see, so often not one that I think can be me, but the eyes cannot lie and through darkness and joy, I see in them something that life can't destroy."

Chapter Fifty-Nine

The message came through just as I was filling up with water at Penkridge. There was to be a conference call at two p.m. that afternoon. That left me just time enough to get the essentials out of the way, drop down through the lock and demolish a speciality house burger at the pub after mooring the boat. Fortunately, the rain had eased up that morning and the warm sun that followed it had lifted my spirits as I'd sat in the beer garden and watched the world go by. I had been planning on a few more beers but that obviously wasn't meant to be. This was the first time that ORB had called me in on a conference call and I knew that it would mean work for me, and work that needed to be started soon.

I'd just got myself back on the boat and seated myself with a cup of coffee in hand as I waited at the computer console when the message came through from Adam five minutes before the conference call was due to start. It said simply, "Ready?" to which I replied "Yes.".

I watched as the wall opposite my computer console changed before my eyes. The traditional wooden panelling dropped away and in its place were several flat panel screens, folded and stored one behind the other. They began to separate and with just the slightest buzz unfolded themselves to form an arc of six screens before me that spanned the width of that section of the boat. I hadn't done a conference call before and I didn't even know that these screens existed. The boat continued to surprise me.

They flickered into life and there, laid out as clearly as if I'd been in the same room as them, were the twelve members of the ORB Council, with the President seated in the middle. At precisely two o'clock she started the meeting.

"Thank you all for attending this call," she said, looking at me and then around the room to the various monitors that I now realised contained images of the other Council members who, despite the impression on my monitors, were actually scattered about the country, communicating in the same remote way.

"This is a very important meeting," the President continued, "and one that will have significant implications for the future of the Order. The details of what I am about to communicate to you are naturally of the highest sensitivity and only for the ears of the members of the Council and the chosen operative, Kingfisher. Can I please have your written understanding of this now."

I watched as the other Council members signed what appeared to be an invisible piece of paper, then looked at my own desk where a similar object had appeared. I 'signed' it, and it was no longer there.

"Thank you," the President leaned closer to the camera that was capturing her and I saw something in her eyes that I had never seen before. It was only later that I realised it was genuine fear, "now to business. As some of you may be aware, the recent situation that occurred in Birmingham with the failure of the Nanovirus used, has had some repercussions that we had hoped would go away. Two of the journalists who lost their lives were the daughters of Jason King. We knew that King would investigate, but it appears that he has now put two and two together and knows that his children died at the hands of ORB."

Every face on those monitors stared intently as the members of ORB began to digest what was being said.

"At present," she continued, "we have no indication as to what King will do. Our source of information is deep undercover on King Island and confirms that King's investigations were only completed yesterday. With the process of grieving and our knowledge of his penchant for meticulous planning, we believe that this gives us a brief time slot in which to act. That action is why we are convening today. Very simply, Jason King must be eliminated. I need confirmation from the eleven of you that this is an agreed course of action, however regrettable it might be, and I need to know that you, Kingfisher, are up to this task."

There seemed to be a protocol to the procedures at this point and I listened as each attendee confirmed that they agreed with the course of action. Only one member, Tom Anderson, hesitated and was reluctant to give an immediate answer.

"Madame President," his thick Lancashire accent resonated through the boat, "this is terrible news and the call is for drastic action. Can you clarify why we are so certain that King knows ORB's culpability."

"Tom," there was a strained tone to the President's voice, "I would have hoped that my word would be enough. However, if you must be reassured, I can tell you that King employed Howard Investigations to do most of the legwork. Their communications system is one which we monitor closely and have access to through Howard's partner who is one of us. We were unable to intercept him before he presented his findings to King, but he followed up with a written report that we have here. Dare I ask you if you need to see that report?"

"No, thank you, Madame President", he answered, "and thank you for your clarification. I agree with the course of action proposed."

Once everybody else had replied, I knew it was my turn to respond.

"Madame President, Council members," I made sure my voice was bold and respectful, "I am willing to take on this task and the Order can be assured that I will do whatever is required to bring this to a swift resolution."

"However," I continued, silencing those who were trying to speak to thank me, "I need some time to plan this and do not want to be out there alone this time. I therefore respectfully ask that we reconvene tomorrow when I can lay out my plan, discuss the equipment that I need and, most importantly, get a unanimous vote of confidence in my proposals from the Council."

There was a pause and the images disappeared from my monitors. This, I understood, was the Council talking amongst themselves and agreeing on a unified response. After a couple of minutes, the images returned as the President answered me:

"We agree, and will reconvene tomorrow, same time. Thank you all."

The system shut itself down and the monitors folded themselves back into the wall. I took a long drink of the coffee that I hadn't touched since making it and then span round in my chair and booted up my computer. This was the big one for me and, even though it hadn't been said, this was the one that I was sure would get me onto the Council. And, judging by the President's manner towards Anderson, it seemed likely that a vacancy would soon open up for me to fill. I had to get it right.

Although I'd had very little sleep, I was pumped and ready to go when the conference call started on the following day. I had a plan and a plan that I couldn't wait to present. At two o'clock, the monitors buzzed into life again and it was as if the past twenty-four hours had not existed. Once she had confirmed everyone's presence, the President simply turned to me and said:

"Kingfisher, begin."

I laid out my plans in detail and answered every question that they had. I never claim that I am perfect in my work and there were a few useful suggestions that I took on board in refining the detail of what I would be doing. Half an hour after the start of the call, the Council had given me their total support and the call ended. At least, I thought it had ended but I was confused because the monitors didn't retract. As I looked at them, I found out why.

"Steve," the President was alone in front of me.

"Joanne," I smiled.

"You do know that this is the one," she said, leaning closer to the screen as she spoke, "if you crack this, then we can move forward with your place on the Council and the other things we discussed."

"Madame President," I replied, leaning closer to her face on the monitors, "I understand exactly what my rewards will be. And can I say how much I am looking forward to receiving both."

"Good luck," she whispered, then her screen went blank.

Within an hour of the call ending, I was in an unmarked car and heading to Manchester Airport. My flight to King Island, First Class, naturally, was scheduled to leave at nine that night which left me plenty of time to research my destination in the lounge at the airport. I scanned the official information that filled the guide books that I had purchased, then I surfed both the public web and the ORB data network for any supplementary details I needed to know. This was a fast-moving mission that would normally have required months of planning but, given the urgency of the matter, had to be completed in a few days. On top of that, I had to ensure that my cover story was secure and that I was familiar with the personal details of Martin Jefferson whose identity I had been handed along with his flight reservations and hotel bookings. The passport was waiting at the airport, where the genuine Mr Jefferson was apprehended and escorted quietly away for a spell off the radar in accommodation that would be a little less luxurious than he had been expecting. King was too close to ORB for them to risk my using one of my other identities and the logic of hijacking a passenger was perfect, as it would divert any suspicion on King's part to those who were only now booking tickets. The subterfuge was at Anderson's suggestion which amused me as his eagerness to ingratiate himself with the President was only helping me in my bid to take his place.

King Island was, until late 2008, the Kingdom of Tupanau; a collection of four main islands and about half a dozen atolls in the South Pacific. In that year, the reigning monarch died without leaving an heir and the Kingdom was plunged into a non-aggressive, yet still divisive and disruptive, period of civil unrest. At the same time, Jason King, having sold his majority stakes in a number of hugely successful computer and internet businesses found himself sitting high in The Sunday Times' Rich List with a disposable income of near on ten billion pounds. ComputerWeb (the genuine article) and Anonymous Images were just two of the many businesses that King had developed, and his interests and activities spanned the globe making him one of the world's most successful businessmen. However, Jason King was not a proud man, nor was he under any illusions that the success he had enjoyed was not in proportion to his brilliance or worthiness; he knew that he had been fortunate to be in the right place at the right time and that with this vast wealth that he now enjoyed, there came an enormous burden of responsibility.

That said, his humility had boundaries and he had always had a weakness, born out of his rejection by his peers at school and growing stronger as his solitary career took off. He had always wanted to live up to his name and be an actual king. There was an element of vanity in this, but he was no power-crazed dictator looking for a channel for his passions, nor was he some sort of arrogant colonialist hankering to be the Great Lord of a subject people. He just liked the idea of being a monarch and felt that he could do some good in that position.

The fates collided when he'd opened his newspaper to read about the ongoing problems in Tupanau that were covered under the predictable headline, 'Trouble in Paradise'. Something clicked in him and within a couple of days he had found himself exiting his helicopter on the hot and stunningly beautiful shores of this nation. Having researched its history and discovered that it had changed monarchical lines several times in its recorded history, including a spell under Her Majesty, Queen Elizabeth Second, he'd been encouraged to progress with his plans. Surely he had as much right to reign over this nation as she did? Furthermore, if it had historically had such a flexible approach to monarchy, then he had believed he had more than a fighting chance of being able to achieve his goal.

His crew had off-loaded a Land Rover from the helicopter and driven him into the town centre of the capital city, Ericstown, the name reflecting a period of still barely explicable Swedish rule. The fabric of the city stood in stark contrast to the natural beauty of the islands. Crumbling buildings, decaying infrastructure and pitted roads met his sight and everywhere he'd looked as they'd driven slowly to a grand but decaying parliament building, he'd seen throngs of unemployed workers, picking their way through mounds of discarded rubbish. Crowds had begun to form and follow them, such that they had soon been swamped by a sea of dirty faces peering in at the windows. Eventually, this had halted their progress so they had had to walk the last hundred yards, with King leaving an armed guard to protect the vehicle.

Having entered the building, the doors had closed behind them and they found themselves in an eerily silent place made all the stranger by the chilled, air-conditioned atmosphere that contrasted so sharply with the tropical heat outside. A solitary receptionist had been seated at a mahogany counter and had stared challengingly at them in a bid to confront these foreign strangers who had dared to come without an invitation. One of King's party introduced them in the local language.

"Please," the receptionist had said, "though we welcome the courtesy, we can speak English. It will be much less time consuming."

Having established a little of their purpose, they'd been invited to meet with the leaders of the two opposing factions on the island, neither of whom had been democratically elected and both of whom seemed to be completely out of their depth. The upshot of that meeting was that King had reached an agreement with them, to be put to the vote of the people the following day. Since few of the inhabitants were constrained by work commitments, there was a near hundred percent turnout for the vote which saw King Island created out of the fractured pieces of a once-proud Tupanau.

King was vilified by the world's press for his actions and marked down as a neo-colonialist, a power hungry Westerner, and given any manner of other disparaging titles. But the reality that he knew, and which the islanders were attracted to, was that he had been more than fair in his proposals. He had effectively purchased the kingdom for a sum that wiped out its national debt and which accrued a sum to each inhabitant equivalent to four year's wages at current rates. On top of this, he allocated one of the islands for housing and promised to deliver to the locals what the Victorian Quakers in England had done when they built new and respectable towns around their factories. He also set out plans to move this tropical paradise into the twenty-first century with a blueprint for the economy based on tourism and sustainable agriculture. Over and above all of this though, and probably the most important element of his vision, he promised that on his death, the kingdom would cede back to the islanders as a parliamentary democracy, with or without a monarch as they chose.

Debate still raged in the press and in the sheltered world of academia about the rights and wrongs of King's monarchy, but nobody could fault him for his record of achievement in making his plans come to fruition and in restoring this nation's sense of pride. The nation and its monarchy was recognised by the United Nations and its wealth was growing exponentially each year as it became the most fashionable travel destination for those who were lucky enough to be able to secure a visit there. Since it was a place of finite size and since King wanted to maintain the quality of life there, tourist numbers were restricted and passenger flights closely matched to hotel availability. But paradoxically, King ran the airline at a loss to ensure that the treasures of his domain were not only available to the super-rich. That had been why Anderson's suggestion was so beneficial to me, you couldn't just book a ticket to King Island whenever you felt like it.

The approach to the airstrip offered an incredible view of the islands in all their isolated beauty, surrounded as they were by crystal clear waters and glistening white beaches. Anyone privileged to see this sight could understand immediately why King had wanted to own and to save this special place. From the air I was also able to make out the elements that formed this new nation. There were four main islands that King had chosen to name as Islands One to Four. I suppose that kept things simple. Island One was the mainland, Island Two, linked by a new road bridge, was where the locals lived, and Island Three was used for agriculture. Island Four was rarely seen in detail by the general public and was where King had his home, and the place where employees of ORB were allowed to enjoy their holidays. King had first come across ORB when his personal power an influence had been established and they had asked him to join the Council. He'd bought into what the Order was all about, but hadn't felt himself to be up to the responsibilities of being a Council member. Instead, he had helped bankroll its operations and had set aside the island as a retreat for ORB staff. Aside from these islands, there were a number of atolls but these had been handed over in perpetuity to one of the global environmental charities who managed them with funding from King.

The plane touched down smoothly and taxied to the terminal building. As the only commercial flight booked in for that day we disembarked promptly and were led by a team of smiling locals into the building. As we were about to enter, the air around us thickened and started to thud as a helicopter came into view and landed on the roof of the terminal.

"Ladies and Gentlemen," one of our guides announced proudly, "you are privileged to have seen our king arrive. I apologise that he will not be able to greet you personally as he has recently suffered a terrible bereavement. Now, please follow me."

I expected the usual airport processing to be a smooth process but was shocked when we all backed up and came to a halt just inside the doors. Chaos seemed to have descended on operations here and even my First Class status could do nothing to get me moving through.

"What's going on?" I asked a fellow traveller.

"Somebody said that their computers have gone down," she replied, "look at them all flapping around. We could be here for hours."

Just as she said this, the door leading to the roof of the building opened and a stocky man in suit and tie and dashed through and down to the where the gates were heaving with disgruntled passengers. This was my first sight of Jason King. I watched as he spoke to his staff and then as he ascended the steps again to take up a higher position.

"Welcome to King Island," he shouted down from his position high above the concourse, "I am so sorry but things have gone a bit floopy here with our computers and we can't seem to get them going again."

The crowd of travellers looked up at him as he continued.

"It's baggage that's the real problem," he said, "so can I propose that we get you all through the system smoothly and away to your hotels, where we will bring your luggage on within the hour. Please spread out along all the gates and we'll have you through as soon as possible."

I watched in amazement as every available member of staff opened up a new gate and started to see passengers through. What amazed me more though was that King himself manned a gate and worked alongside his staff. Within ten minutes we were all landside and being fed into taxis and out to our hotels. King hadn't processed me, but I had been in the line beside him and, as I heard him chatting away and working to clear the backlog, I couldn't help but understand why he was revered by his subjects. My admiration was all the more because I knew the terrible emotional burden he was carrying. Had I not been hardened to my task, I might have been inclined to let my conscience trouble me, but there was no going back now. It seemed such a shame that such a nice guy was living his last days on Earth.

Chapter Sixty

My hotel, or should I say, the hotel that Martin Jefferson had decided to treat himself to, was the finest on the Island. It had a central complex with the usual assortment of luxury shops and spas, all wrapped neatly around a clear and clean swimming pool, but its main attraction was that the accommodation was all in beachside huts. It had been this factor that had made Jefferson the perfect candidate, but when I say huts, I do them an injustice as they were as luxurious as any five-star hotel suite I had ever enjoyed.

Because of the shift in times zones I didn't get to see much on that first day. Having settled in to my cabin I poured a few glasses of complimentary cognac and sat on the terrace to watch the beginning of the sunset. Then I erred on the side of caution and took myself to bed. I woke up on day two, much refreshed and called through to have my breakfast delivered to the room. I didn't have any plans for that day that involved me leaving my hotel, so instead I spent the morning relaxing on the beach, with a session in the afternoon in the swimming pool and gym to shake off the last of any travel tiredness. I had to be back in my room for five p.m. local time to see if things continued to go according to plan. At precisely five, I saw the private jet swoop down towards the runway, close enough for me to read the call sign on its side, ORB3. It was tempting to take a walk to the airport, but we would meet again shortly. For now, I was confident that James had arrived ready for his meeting with King tomorrow.

My alarm woke me at eleven forty-five that night and I stepped out onto the beach behind my cabin, scuffing gently through the sand towards the sea. There was no sign of any activity but this didn't concern me, in fact, it reassured me that we were on track with the next key stage of this mission. I settled myself in the lounger on the back porch and watched the point where the waves were breaking onto the sand. Just after twelve, there was movement in the water and two giant turtles began to lumber their way up the beach. This was a feature of the Island, heavily promoted by the tourist brochures and it was especially pleasurable for me to see. I watched as they slowly made their way up the beach, seeking a spot to lay or retrieve their eggs. The two that were coming towards me were oblivious to my presence and continued their lumbering march until they stopped beside the porch. After a brief pause they resumed their journey, moving around to the side of the decking that backed onto undergrowth.

I walked behind them and played with the controls on my watch. The turtles stopped, their shells lifted from their bodies and I reached in to grab the two bags that carried my essential supplies. Hoisting these onto the patio, I pressed a couple more buttons and the turtles returned to the sea. There was no way that I could arrive with the stuff I needed in hand luggage and we knew that the air and sea space around the islands was heavily monitored. But who would ever suspect a giant turtle of being in league with the monarch's assassin? I smiled to myself as I remembered the moment that I thought of this solution to a problem that had nagged me for all that night after the first conference call. With this delivery, I now had all that I needed to continue with the mission and so, very pleased with progress so far, I took myself back to bed awaiting tomorrow's action.

My plan had been very simple. Since both James and King were problems for ORB, it made sense to use them against each other. For that reason, at noon on my third day on the island, James was being buffeted against the waves in a launch that would take him from the mainland to Island Four. At one o'clock he would be meeting King as the official delegate from ORB, there to present an apology and discuss a solution to the crisis that the death of his daughters had created. Donned in my full Kingfisher outfit and armed with the necessary tools, I would also be at that meeting. For which purpose, I was currently deep under the water and lost to sight in the wake that the launch was making. I clambered out of the water a good distance from the jetty where James was landed, choosing to negotiate the jungle surrounding King's house rather than take a direct approach. We arrived at roughly the same time. James was deposited at the front door of the villa, looking a little lost and extremely nervous, whilst I was working my way through the foliage of a tree that afforded me more than enough of the view that I needed.

Setting my helmet camera to record, I watched as James rang the bell and was ushered into the house by a classically dressed butler. The thermal image showed his passage through the property, which I followed by using the suit to fly me from room to room. I was fortunate that King's study was fronted by a heavily-planted balcony. As I sat on the roof, I programmed a large spider to crawl down and positioned it with an unobstructed view of the room, checking the audio feed was working, just as James entered and the door was closed behind him.

"Please come in," I heard King say, his back was to the window.

I watched James try to make it to the desk without stumbling, and saw the relief on his face when King invited him to sit on the chair in front of him. The attaché case that James was carrying rested at his side as he took deep breaths and tried to calm himself.

"Now," King said, "I understand that you have word for me from ORB. Looking at you there and, forgive me if I am blunt, but I presume that you are more of a courier than an experienced representative of the Order."

"Yes, yes, …. Sir," James's social skills never being very good were now being severely tested, "I have a package, an envelope for you. You are … please…if it's okay…can you read it?"

He reached down and opened the case, removing a thick envelope and passing it to King.

"You look terrified," King said, "please relax, do you want a drink?"

"No thank you, Sir," James replied, "but, please, … if I may, do you have a toilet I can use?"

I watched as King pointed to a door off to the left, then sat back in his chair and began to read the document. As he read, he became engrossed in it, barely acknowledging James' return to the room. He read it once quickly, then again at a slower speed, scribbling notes as he went along. Then he looked up at James.

"You've got some nerve," King's voice dripped with venom as he addressed James.

"Sorry?" the bewildered reply.

"You really are either the dumbest of the dumb," King continued, "or the most insensitive of the insensitive. You do know what's in these documents don't you?"

"A little Sir," James's reply was barely audible, "I understand that it is an apology from ORB and some explanation as to how the situation happened."

"Let me quote a few things to you," King stood with the document in his hand and began to pace around the room, "Yes, here's the apology, 'on behalf of everybody involved with the Order we apologise unreservedly for the loss of your daughters and express our deepest condolences to you', and then more and more of the same. Meaningless as far as I'm concerned.

But then it goes on to explain a little of the detail. Let me quote again, '…as you are aware we rely on specialist teams of technicians to provide the equipment that our operatives need. In the case of the virus, one of those technicians developed a product that was not properly tested but was released by him nonetheless. Whilst ORB accept responsibility for the overall execution of this operation, we felt that you should be aware that the technician, James, who is sitting in front of you now is directly responsible for the faulty equipment that he allowed to be used on your daughters…', do I need to read on?"

James was too shocked to say anything. He mumbled some rubbish that was unintelligible and then to make matters worse began to cry and shake uncontrollably.

"You are nothing more than a pathetic little runt!", King screamed as he came up behind James and locked his hands around his throat, "how dare you sit there sniffling and shaking after what you've done? You. Yes, you, according to ORB, are the murderer. Now I know why they sent you. You're not leaving here alive. I'll deal with ORB another time but for now, every moment of tearing pain that I have had to endure having lost my beautiful daughters is coming down on your head and I am going to wipe out that pitiful life of failure that should have been ended before you even dropped out of your mother."

His grip tightened on James's neck and I couldn't help smiling to myself to think how easy it had been to absolve ORB whilst getting King to do the clean-up operation himself. Then something changed. I saw a different look in King's eyes and watched as he released his grip and let James fall, gasping, to the floor.

"No," he whispered, "No. Not like this. I won't be like them."

He reached down and helped James up into his chair.

"I'm sorry," he said, "I'm sorry. They nearly had us then. This isn't the way. If you got it wrong, I forgive you. It's just that I miss my daughters so much."

As they collapsed in tears into each other's arms I used the opportunity to fly down and into the room, slamming the balcony door shut and sealing all exits with a bolt of energy that I shot from my cuffs. This was 'Blue Light', my favourite adaptation of the cuff that Adam had supplied me with. The bolts I fired lingered on their target and rendered whatever they had a grip on untouchable. They'd stay active until after I left.

"That's enough of the blubbing," I muttered, "now both of you, over there on that sofa and sit down and shut up."

They moved towards the sofa and complied immediately.

"I'm sorry you didn't have the balls, Mr King," I said, "We thought that this would be the easier way but you've failed us. Now we have to follow plan B. And, just so you are aware, there is no tomorrow for either of you."

"I'm not going to draw this out too long," I continued, "although it does give me a certain amount of pleasure to have the upper hand against you, James, my ex-supporter who royally messed up with the viruses, and you, Mr King, with your threats to bring ORB down. You may be monarch of all you survey here, but ORB is bigger than you'll ever be and I'm here to show you what happens when the big beasts feel threatened."

I shot them both with nanobots that injected them with a mild sedative.

"Here's the scenario," I told them, "Young James here is allowed in to see His Highness for reasons we don't know. He carries with him a case that the king authorises to be admitted into his presence without inspection. What could be in the case, I wonder? Your choice, Majesty. Porn, drugs or weapons?"

"No," King said, "I won't play."

"Okay," I said, "then drugs it is. That should discredit you enough."

I set the dial on my wrist and a beautiful parrot, native to this island, flew into the room and transformed into a block of pure heroine. The outer shell was programmed to disintegrate into its composite atoms, leaving only the drugs behind. This saved a lot of clearing up later. I picked up the block and placed it on Kings desk.

"So," I said, "the deal goes wrong and James gets greedy. Thinking he has the advantage, he draws on King and fires a fatal shot to his heart."

"But," I continued, reaching around to the back of King's desk and removing the weapon that I knew was kept there, "James doesn't know that King is armed and able to fire off a shot in his death throes."

I wasn't sure how much of this they were taking in since James seemed to have retreated into that catatonic realm that he had first found when the bullies attacked him at school, and King sat expressionless watching me.

"You're the best they have to offer?" he sneered, "And you think that this is the sort of justice that ORB was founded to deliver. Go ahead. Do what you have to do."

So I did.

+++

'Global News Agency', Worldwide Telecast, 7th May 2023
'Tragedy on King Island: Jason King Dead'

Authorities on King Island, the independent state in the South Pacific where Jason King, the internet billionaire, became monarch in controversial circumstances, have confirmed that he was killed today in what seems like a drug deal that went wrong.

Sir Carlos Magnusson, Chief of Police, has confirmed that shots were heard from King's office at approximately two p.m. this afternoon. A team of officers forced entry to the room and found King slumped across his desk having been shot through the heart. It appears that his assailant was, in turn, shot by King before his death as another body was found in the middle of the room, apparently having died from blood loss in an attempt to escape.

When asked about rumours of these events being drug-related, Magnusson replied simply that these were early days and they were keeping an open mind.

King's death marks the tragic end of a family that until recently was the envy of the world. His wife succumbed to cancer three years ago, whilst his two children died earlier this year after contracting the Birmingham Mystery Virus.

According to local custom, the bodies of the deceased have been cremated, although police continue to seek to identify the other person killed, whom they know only to have been called James.

+++

I transmitted all the footage to ORB as soon as I arrived back at my hotel room, then enjoyed a couple of days on the island, soaking up the sun and relaxing. The atmosphere in that country was not particularly conducive to boosting my holiday mood, but to have left immediately might have attracted some suspicion. Like most of the tourists who were there on the day, I even took time out to watch the funeral procession pass by. However, I was also able to use the disruption of the tragedy that had occurred as my excuse for cutting the holiday short a day or so after the cremation. This meant that, as I was one of many early-leavers, there were no suspicious glances as I boarded the plane home. Had it all gone wrong, we had a contingency plan in place, whereby I would let the suit take me out to a waiting fishing vessel and so be transported home by sea. It was nice that the First Class flight option remained, it was a much more refined and comfortable way to travel.

Chapter Sixty-One

My absence from Penkridge was for less than a week. The boat was securely moored where I had left her and the computers inside advised me that she had remained untouched whilst I'd been away. Easter was now over and the waterways were quieter, although I saw a lot of familiar faces passing by now that I was in what I referred to as my home territory. Yes, I hankered to move about the whole network, but this particular inverted triangle, centred on Great Haywood, remained, and will remain always, my chosen place to be. Though now a very different person to the one who first took to the water with an old wreck of a boat and a family in tow, I still felt a sense of comfort knowing the memories that these canals had for me.

With no pressing commitments, I decided to do all the old places again and see how they'd changed. If I wanted to I could divert away further afield, but since the weather was now extremely favourable and the days were that bit longer, I saw no reason why I shouldn't treat myself to a bit of nostalgia.

As I was preparing to set off, a message came through from ORB:

Project: King
Operative: Kingfisher
Status: Completed
Notes: King Island authorities confirm death and cremation of both King and James. Inquests to be held in next few months. King Island to be ceded back to locals, but proviso has been made in King's Will for a previously unknown relative, believed to be a cousin.
Rating: 100%
Feedback: Excellent work again. Special thanks from Madame President. Look forward to seeing you at base soon.

That was another perfect score for The Kingfisher and a very nice way to start the day. How long it would be until I got that call to fulfil my destiny as a member of the Council I couldn't say. I wasn't in too much of a hurry, but knowing the President's feelings, I felt sure that it would be sooner rather than later.

Dropping down through Longford Lock, I remembered how Fran and I had invented one of our particularly stupid towpath games here. We'd moored above the lock and as we'd watched the motorway madness of the M6, one hot and drunken Summer afternoon, the game came to us. The object of the game was to spot a lorry with a name beginning with every letter of the alphabet. Three days later we were still looking for a Q! This inevitably led me on to thinking about the kids and some of the other games that we had played whilst driving about the country. There was the caravan game where the name of the next caravan that you passed was converted into a score. And there was the increasingly annoying, 'Eat that bridge!' when they were younger. What an irony it was that they had lost their lives to that same stretch of tarmac that had once been such a source of fun.

Some people grieve for their whole lives. As I slipped under the motorway towards Teddesley Lock, I thought about how I had responded to my own loss. It had hurt more than any pain that this body would ever know, but it had had to end. There was always a little bit of the hurt that remained inside me, but creating a new life for myself and particularly in the manner that I had, had allowed me to lock that pain further away. Some might say that this was cold and callous of me. I don't know. All I do know is that I believe that Fran and the kids wouldn't have wanted there to be another victim of that tragedy and that I almost owed it to them to make the most of the brief spell of life that I still had left to enjoy. Nothing could change what had happened, so why should I let it drag me down for the rest of my days? It was this ability to stand above emotion that had also helped me cope with my duties as The Kingfisher. The body count was racking up but, in my heart, I still did not consider myself to be a murderer.

I stopped at the chandlers after working through the lock, picking up some bits and pieces and taking longer than I expected when I came across a whole display devoted to Boat Space Solar products. It was comforting to know that Zipoly had left something behind and that this was a positive gift from ORB. There would be more, I was sure of it, but I understood why so much of the technology that I enjoyed wasn't ready to be shared with the world yet. Either it had potential to cause damage on a wider scale, as with the telecoms system, or it was simply a step too far and too radical a leap for the world to bear in one hit. Whilst I knew that the ion-drives and the hints of success about fusion would be of massive benefit to the world, I was also conscious that many of ORB's sponsors and Council members had vested interests in the existing technology. The world would have to wait a little longer for some of the gadgets that I took for granted. As to the weapons that I now enjoyed, I hope that they never make it out of our very closed circle.

Mooring for the night opposite the Moat House Hotel, I sat on the deck with the boater's essentials – a pint, a sandwich and a good book. There was a wedding in full swing and the party spilled out onto the canal side gardens. A number of times I waved at the guests and wondered at their conversations as they looked across at me. To anyone who has lived on a boat for any length of time, boaters are ordinary people living a slightly less ordinary life, but to the majority of the public, we are a mysterious breed. I've lost count of the number of times people have said how much they envied my lifestyle and wished they had the guts to do the same, to which my normal reply is simply that they should go for it. That said, the dream doesn't suit everybody. Losing a lot of mod-cons and living a much more basic lifestyle, means some hardship beyond what many want to endure. Still, it was always fun to share a little in the new life of those newlyweds and to be a part of a day that I hoped would be the start of something special and long lasting for them. Thinking about this, I worried that I might be softening a little in my old age. Either that or I was getting back to normal and starting to relax and unwind again. Funny really, but nobody who passed would have guessed that just a few days ago I had been enjoying tropical sunshine whilst generating the events that had been extensively covered in the nation's press. That's what I love about the canal, you never really know the details of the lives of the people who live in those slim metal cans.

At Great Haywood junction I flipped a coin as to which way I should head. It sent me right, and I cruised through to that old favourite spot at Wolseley Bridge. Treating myself to a slap up pub meal, I stumbled back to the boat at closing time, taking it easy on the following day and deciding to wash and wax the boat, which was something I rarely got around to doing. The next day saw me at Handsacre, home to the best chip shop on the network, the presence of which was the nearest I came to a reason for being there. And was the nearest to any firm destination that I had in mind for this trip as anything. In the end, I had to stay there for a few days in order to work my way through the menu and ensure that kebab was balanced with fish and chips. To make matters worse, I discovered the pub that was a short walk from the canal and revelled in their proper, homemade food and very special beer offer. Comfortably sated and rested, I moved on, through Fradley Junction and into Alrewas.

Alrewas is a nice village with decent moorings and a place that I enjoy staying, but Fradley is the place where you go when you feel like a bit of company. For too long now, I had been on my own in my own world and a conversation with a stranger or three was in order. There was nothing happening to make demands on my time, so I settled into a mooring spot that allowed me to stay a fortnight in the town if I so chose. With the 'mucky duck' pub in walking distance, I was confident that I would have a few days in the sunshine and in good company. It didn't let me down and every day I was able to sit outside, watch the fun and games on the water as boat after boat took multiple revolutions as the wind hampered their efforts to make the right angle turn. The joy of this cabaret was enhanced by my working my way through the ever-changing guest ales.

Each time I visited, a new memory was stored for me. I met regulars that I had spoken to in my old identity, including the young lad who worked at the piggery and who could talk you under the table in his excitement about his work. We'd first walked past him as he fished on the towpath with a can of lager in his hand and yes, Fran and I had given him a wide berth because he looked a bit dodgy. It was the same with the young guy who'd seen us through Meaford Locks many years ago and who we were terrified to moor next to. That same lad had turned out to be a brilliant artist (I still have one of his watercolours) and a born-again Christian. I think the expression goes something along the lines of, judge not, lest you be judged.

It was on my last day at Fradley that I met Karen and Dave. They were on holiday with their two young children, staying in a friend's caravan on the park behind the pub.

"We were so lucky," Karen said, "because we would never have been able to afford a holiday if we didn't know Terry and Ellie."

It turned out that they had lost all their money defending their Father's will against a malicious step-brother who ended up with the bulk of the estate after employing some dubious tactics.

"He should have just been happy with half," Dave told me, "after all, he was only a step-son and probably didn't deserve that. But he wanted it all and he made some nasty claims about our relationship with Dad. With hindsight, we should have just walked away but we wanted to see justice done and we hadn't banked on the depths that some solicitors will go to earn their blood money."

The case had taken months to settle and, with the help of some letters that had a dubious provenance but which were supposedly written by their step-mother, the house, which was pretty much the only thing of value in the estate, had been allowed to pass to the step-brother.

"The little we got," Karen continued, "was a hell of a lot less than the costs we incurred. We reckon it'll be another five years before we clear the debt. Still, we've got the kids and a clean conscience, but that doesn't pay the bills does it."

They gave me a few more details and I listened intently. Quite a crowd had gathered around us by the time she'd finished telling her story, and a few of the other drinkers joined in with their own tales of loss at the hands of injustice. The mood was good despite the pain of some of the stories and it reminded me of the great gulf that appeared to separate our society, between those who were nice, good-natured, human and stoical people who could overcome troubles and still evade bitterness, and those for whom self and wealth were the driving force. Fortunately, these were the sort of people who were too tight and too insular to want to drink in a pub, so they were rarely encountered in places like this. But their influence still managed to put a dampener on so many lives.

That night, I did the necessary research and made an unofficial visit to a very nice house in a supposedly secure, gated location. A search of the house yielded all that I needed and it was with a real sense of satisfaction that I woke the owner and asked him to do what I wanted him to do. If the fear and the threat weren't enough, the neatly documented file that he had stupidly kept and which mapped out his scam from the beginning, would certainly do the job. On top of that, if he still refused to follow things through to their conclusion then he would have to carry the small limpet that was fixed to his leg for the rest of his life. Sometimes, if the conscience is missing or simply not strong enough to remind an individual of their moral duty, then a more tangible reminder is necessary. Once I had confirmation that everything had been settled in this case, the limpet would fall off and disintegrate. And nobody would ever know for sure that it was me that had moved this one along. The beauty of a busy pub is that I was only one of a number of people who heard about this problem. They might suspect, but they would never know for sure.

I thought of Karen and Dave as I untied from my moorings in Alrewas and headed towards Burton, the home of British brewing, just as my authorised mooring period ended. By now, they should have a cheque in their hands that would help them enjoy a slightly more luxurious holiday in the near future. They would have to wait a while for the balance as the property market always moved slowly, but I made sure that I kept tabs on what was happening and saw, that evening, that the house was up for sale.

Justice may fail occasionally, but I can't let its failures slip by when there is something that can be done. Of course, I need to make sure that I am not creating new injustices, but in this case, a full confession was forthcoming from a very confused and deservedly frightened man who hadn't banked on their being a force for good that far outweighed his own evil.

Chapter Sixty-Two

Somewhat akin to Stone, Burton-Upon-Trent is a historic, canal side town that doesn't quite make the most of the unique place it has in British history. Aside from being the generally acknowledged home of brewing in the nation (although many would dispute this, particularly from South of Watford Gap), it is also the home of Marmite. Yes, that Marmite! That black stuff we all grew to love or hate as youngsters and which is so uniquely British. The two histories, of course, are interlinked: Marmite being a by-product of the beer brewing process. Added to which, Burton is the next stop along the road from Branston. Think pickle. And yet, today, Burton is more mainstream shops and a bypass than it is a historic town. It's a shame, but not something that was going to stop me having an enjoyable time there. Enough of the pubs keep going to make it a place worth visiting, including one that has a tap connected directly to a brewery, and the canal walks are interesting.

My itinerary remained fairly loose, but I thought it would be worth carrying on to the end of the Trent and Mersey and drifting on towards Nottingham as this was another route that I still hadn't done. Sadly, I wasn't to do it that time either as, on my fourth night in Burton, and for the life of me I can't remember how I filled up so many days in that one place, I received the message that I had been waiting for and was called back to base. Before responding to acknowledge receipt, I had a few little projects that I had to complete. When these had been done, I hit the reply and waited for ORB to spring into action.

They sent a crew for the boat as it was in a place where mooring was restricted and security quite minimal, picking me up in a very nice black Mercedes, the pleasures of which I was barely able to experience before the gas came through the vents and I was fast asleep. When I woke up, I wasn't surprised to find myself back in that most luxurious suite that I had enjoyed on my last visit, nor was I surprised to find a porter at the door with that most classic of dishes, the ORB Full English breakfast. Not a bad way to start the day.

After finishing breakfast, I dressed and, in the process, found a sealed envelope addressed to me. It contained an agenda for my stay:

Monday: R&R
Tuesday: Technical support
Wednesday: Presentation Gala and ORB Council Meeting
Thursday: R&R
Friday: R&R
Saturday: Return to field.

Alongside this information was an invitation to the Presentation Gala, which I was pleased to note was gilded and identified me as a VIP attendee. The agenda was a little vaguer than I had hoped for and certainly a lot more time consuming, but I still held out the hope that I would be there on the Council by the end of the Wednesday. This was a hope that was added to by the post-it note that was stuck to the back of the invitation: '*Steve, everything going to plan, drop by for a quick catch up. J x*'.

This was more encouraging. I did as I was asked and, on my way to check out the latest developments in the labs, I called into the President's Office. The guard informed me that Madame President was not to be disturbed, but I pulled rank and asked him to check anyway. He came back a short time later and advised me that the President could spare me five minutes. My heart was racing as I walked down the thickly carpeted hall and knocked at the door.

"Come in."

I opened the door and both the President and I smiled at each other with schoolchild enthusiasm.

"Steve, come in," the President came around from behind her desk and gave me a lingering handshake, "glad you could pop by. Take a seat."

I sat in front of her as she settled at her desk.

"I'm sorry we can't spend a lot of time talking today," she said, "I'm really snowed under, but I wanted to see you about a couple of things."

"Promotion?" I asked.

"Let's just say that I can't say anything," she paused, "but that you won't be disappointed."

"Thank you," I replied, "you're delivering on your side of the bargain. You happy with the last mission?".

"I'm not sure happy is the right word," she smiled as she spoke, "more like ecstatic. It worked a treat. Two birds with one stone, as they say. Brilliant. You deserve everything you're in line for."

We chatted a little more, then I knew the interview was coming to its conclusion.

"I've arranged for a new suit for you," she said, "so if you want to pop to the tailor's, they have your details. Need you to look your best on the big night."

"Thanks," I answered, realising that this dug me out of a hole, as I didn't really have the clothes for a gala evening, "but there is one last thing, if I may."

"Go ahead."

"I think that I am right in saying," I chose my words carefully, "that we are both looking forward to the changes that we see in the near future. But, and maybe this is me just planning that bit too much, I'm thinking about that night itself. Once things have changed, we're free to carry our other ideas further. I mean, once the barriers are down, how can you stop the flood?"

"Go on," she smiled at me with that hunger in her eyes that I had seen not so long ago.

"Well, I'm thinking about practical issues," I said, "and I don't want to have to wait, if you know what I mean. There would be nothing worse than us getting together after the presentation and finding that my headaches stop us in our tracks. Does that make sense?"

She sat thinking about what I was saying, the answered me.

"Of course, I hadn't thought. Your implant."

"Would make sense to lose it before the big night, don't you think," I said, "one less thing to worry about?"

She stood up and walked across to the wall safe that was set into the brickwork beside the fireplace. Without saying anything, she opened the door and removed a small headset.

"I agree," she said, coming over to where I sat and placing the headset over my ears, "so, if you'll just sit still, we should be able to fix that."

She sat back at her desk, typed some instructions into her computer and I felt the earpieces of the headset warming up. As she hit the Return button, a piercing pain shot momentarily through my brain and I almost blacked out. Then the President was in front of me again and removing the apparatus.

"It's as simple as that," she said, removing the tiniest piece of equipment from the left hand earpiece and crushing it under her heel, "do you want to see if it's worked?".

Before I knew what was happening, she had straddled me and we were locked in a long and lingering kiss, desperately probing and searching into each other with our tongues. As promptly as she'd started, she stopped.

"No headache?" she asked.

"None at all," I smiled as she tried to make her way to the door in as demure and innocent a way as possible.

"Good," she held out here hand, "then until Wednesday night. Adieu."

As I left the office, I wiped my mouth with a handkerchief and looked at the residue of lust induced lipstick and saliva that it contained. My self-control was nothing compared to the President's and I was still struggling to walk when I passed the guards station.

"Everything alright, Sir?" the guard asked.

"Never better," I replied, "never better."

Before going back to my suite, I walked the short distance to the tailor's shop and picked up the suit that had been ordered for me. Back in my room, I tried the black tuxedo on and realised that no expense had been spared in the preparations that the President had made. I looked pretty good. No wonder she had been happy to make sure that I was able to perform on the night.

After a light lunch in the suite I headed off to the labs and spent the afternoon with Adam catching up on any new ideas he had been working on. I wasn't sure how this Council membership worked, or whether I would be allowed to carry on working in the field, but I still wanted to make sure that The Kingfisher was the best prepared of all the ORB operatives.

"Kingfisher, man," was the greeting I got from Adam.

"Hi, Adam," I embraced him as an old friend, "look, if we're gonna make this work, can you drop the 'man' thing? It's just a bit too much sometimes."

He laughed and promised to do his best.

"Good," I continued, "because today we are going to have some fun. I want to catch up with you on the latest stuff but then I need a blowout. You up for a bit of fun tonight?"

"Sure thing, m..., sorry," he smiled as he answered, "I'll try and drop it, but man, it ain't easy!"

"Guess it'll take a while," I sighed, "anyway, to business. I know it wasn't long ago that I was here so don't worry, I'm not expecting any miracles or anything major. I've had an idea though, and want to run it by you. Oh, by the way, the Blue Light is superb, love it. Cipher not too hacked off that I borrowed it?"

"No, course not," Adam laughed, "anyway I gave him some of your stuff, so you're about quits now."

I told him what I wanted from him. We talked about the fine details and he told me that it wouldn't be a problem.

"I need it pretty soon though," I said to him, "in fact, I want it for the Awards Night. Thought it might be a bit of fun, you know, just in case I get called up for an award or something else."

"Hell, man, if anyone deserves an award it's you. Of course I'll get it done. Should be able to put it together today. There's some stuff one of the other guys has used that I reckon we can adapt. You know the Professor?"

"Who?".

"He's one of you lot, an operative," he explained, "but then again, he ain't like you at all. He's smart, real smart."

"Cheers," I laughed.

"No man, I don't mean that," Adam struggled to defend his comment before realising I was joking, "no, he's like, you know, Uber Smart. IQ in the two hundred's and eats and breathes mathematical equations. He doesn't use many weapons, but they sent him out on a mission a while back and there was no way he was gonna be able to do it on his own. His projects all get resolved without face to face interaction. Imagine, right, you have to fix a problem. Okay, the rest of you, you go out there and do what needs to be done by confronting the person and fixing the physical side of things. Well, the Professor, he'll study the problem and break it down into numbers and formulae and all that stuff, then somehow, he sets in motion a chain of events that get the job done. It's like that thing about a butterfly flapping its wings in Ecuador changing the weather in Liverpool."

"So why did he need a weapon?" I was intrigued by this guy.

"Well, thing is, he had to get out and into someone's house to start the chain reaction," Adam explained, picking up a pad to show me how things had worked out with one of his doodles, "Right, here he is, and there's the target spot. It's Winter, and I'm just getting familiar with your stuff via James. And man, I can't believe that guys gone. Such a shame."

"Yeah," I murmured, "carry on."

"Right, here's the target zone. Here's the Professor. He has to get this dose of chemical into this little corner here. Something about the target's cat has to carry some spores, they get transferred and the rest of the plan drops into place. So, we use a big fly. And I mean a big, big fly. It goes in, sprays the room and then it's away."

"Sounds perfect," I said, "so, crack on with it."

We talked some more then I arranged to meet up with Adam that evening for a blow-out. If I was to be changing my position, it was unlikely that I'd have the chance again and we'd not fully pushed the ORB facilities to the limit.

"Meet you at 'The Scales of Justice' at eight?" I asked.

"Sure man," he replied, "looking forward to it. I'll introduce you to the gang. I pretty much know everyone down here."

We parted and I took a leisurely stroll through the town, making contact with as many of the people I passed as possible and, in my head, starting the process of being more than just an operative. I had to make sure that people began to see me as a leader. And I wanted to gauge the general feeling in this isolated spot. ORB got the job done, but change was needed. I had ideas but the best ideas were usually other people's, so the more of them I had, the more I could get done.

At the burger bar I stopped for a quick cheeseburger. Not something that's too easily available from the towpath and not something conducive to helping me stay fit. But something I hankered for just then, and something I was going to have. The girl who was waiting tables was only young. She can't have been more than twenty, and, as I was the only customer in the place, I spent some time chatting with her. I was keen to know how somebody so young arrived at a spot like this. The story that she told me made perfect sense.

"ORB picked me up when my family were killed," she told me, "I was only fifteen, but they did what they had to do with the authorities and I was released to their care. At the time, I was just happy to be getting away from all the rubbish out there. My Dad had been some sort of engineer and it was some sort of political hit, but, to be honest, I've never been that bright with things like that. I can cook though. I love it. This burger place is only a stepping stone for me until I can move to one of the restaurants. Mind you, I can make a difference here."

As I ate the burger, I understood what she was saying. I've had a lot of cheeseburgers in my time but this was the best ever.

"You see," she explained, "you've got to love what you're doing and love every bit of food that you put out there. My Mum and Dad taught me that. Whatever you are doing, you're making a difference in some way. So, you do the best you can."

I asked her what her plans for the night were, and as I finished the last of the fries, we had arranged for her to join us at the pub later. I wasn't thinking about myself. Adam and her would go well together and boy, did he need someone who could look after his culinary needs. I headed back to the suite and smiled as I realised that I had now added 'matchmaker' to my CV.

The Scales of Justice was the closest thing to a real pub that ORB had been able to cobble together in this underground city. It wasn't a new build by any stretch of the imagination and parts of it dated back to the beginnings of the town back in the late eighteenth century. Since then, it had resisted most of the makeovers that had so damaged the atmosphere of pubs above ground, although it was a few steps removed from its spit and sawdust origins.

Adam joined me at eight and Charlotte, the burger queen, a few minutes later.

Chapter Sixty-Three

Since my Damascene conversion, following the virus debacle and the death of Amy, to the new relationship that I now had with ORB, it would be fair to say that very little that Steve Barratt did could be taken at face value. It seemed to be paying dividends so far, and that night at the pub was no exception. If I was to be the future of vigilante justice I needed to soak up as much as possible from as many sources as possible and, with their guards down after a few pints, the gang poured out information to me all through that night.

One of my concerns with ORB was that it was slipping in its standards. This was reflected in the supposed anonymity of its operatives. I revelled in the fact that everybody knew me as Steve Barratt, but that they also knew, despite it being something they couldn't acknowledge, that I was The Kingfisher. None of them would admit it openly, aside from Adam who, as my technician, was in on my identity. But people knew. As they also knew the identities and some of the characteristics of the other operatives. By the end of that night at the pub, I knew them too. I wanted to know them but understood that we had to be unaware of each other's existence out there in the real world. The risk was too high that we would start working together and that our relationships would undermine ORB's authority. Amy was a good example. Had I known her, my willingness to extinguish her life might well have been less.

So it was that I found out more about The Cipher and The Professor. I felt I knew a little about them already, having mined their resources for my own benefit, but the guys at ORB knew the people behind the masks. The Cipher kept himself very much to himself. He worked like a ghost and preferred to live that way too. The Professor however was a little more gregarious, although like James, his social skills were limited. I assumed that they would be at the presentation event and looked forward to seeing them, even if we could not acknowledge our respective roles.

The new people that I learnt about completed my knowledge of the full set of the field team. The Banker focused solely on financial justice and was the only operative to operate across continents when required. His armoury was small, but, like the Professor, he was able to effect huge financial movements through generally peaceful means. Amy had been the operative recruited after the Banker, and there was an awkward silence as she was discussed in the group. Yes, these people knew that she had made her own bed, but they also knew that I had been responsible for terminating her. They swiftly moved on to the last of the current operatives, described by Adam as Wino Willy, but who preferred the title of The Indigent. As I was a nomad of the waterways, he was a nomad of the streets. He was the person that you would be most likely to meet, as he was friendly, gregarious, outgoing and he operated as a bold and brassy homeless person out there on the streets of the country. He was a regular in the ORB centre, as much because he had limited means of carrying his supplies and needed to come back often to replenish them. As a proper people person though, he also loved to be in this place to share with his friends the things that he couldn't talk about up there. He was, by his own definition, the chief defender of the poor and the downtrodden. His background had been one of privilege reduced to vagrancy and he had been picked up by ORB when, like me, his attempts to affect a little change had led to his appearing on too many official radars.

Having this knowledge boosted my confidence. I knew what was in store for me and now had a more holistic view of the whole ORB operation. But that night also brought me invaluable knowledge about the characters and the motivations of the people who worked behind the scenes for the Order. The technicians I knew fairly well, but in finding out about Charlotte and the many others who joined us for a drink, I discovered a real passion amongst the team, albeit one that was being frustrated by some of the operating practices. I probed for more detail and was given plenty. The Council very rarely asked for the opinion of the troops on the ground and this had created a sense of isolation amongst them. This feeling had been further exacerbated by the denial of any errors that may have been made and a culture in which questioning the power of the Council was not only frowned upon, but also felt to have led to the disappearance of one or two members of staff.

"It's not that we don't have the highest respect for ORB," Charlotte said, speaking for the group, "it's just that sometimes we think that the current generation of general staff members, like myself, are treated as though we should be eternally grateful for what the Order has done for us. They train us well, and I'm now loving the cooking as much as I loved working in the administration team, but they don't seem to know us as people."

"She's right," John, a middle-aged housing officer added, "you see, we talk, and we all know that ORB took us away from a place that we didn't want to be in, but that doesn't mean we can't add value to the Order. I wanted some minor changes made to make the standard accommodation that bit more comfortable, and they wouldn't even meet with me to discuss it."

Whilst there was little sense of rebellion amongst the staff, there was certainly a current of dissatisfaction and one which I could relate to. It all poured into me and I determined that I would not be a part of the old Order but would be a part of a new future. It accorded with Madame President's vision and I was now armed with enough information to secure me as her right-hand man.

As I returned to my suite that evening I had a lot to think about. I was far too inebriated to plan anything in detail, but I had a vision of what needed to be done and a passion to effect change. Nobody had spoken to me as anything other than an operative who might be able to pass on some information. Had they only realised my true agenda, they might have been more forthcoming, or they might have reported me to their minders. Either way, I was alone again and happy that the place I wanted to be was within sight. It had been a hard few months and had taken its toll on me, but the winning post was within sight.

The following day, my last full rest day before the awards event, was a busy day for me. I wrote and shredded multiple documents and I put in place things that ORB should never have allowed me to do. They were slipping in their standards and they were slipping in their vigilance. All of which was to my benefit. I was prepared and ready for Wednesday night and I no longer felt as alone as I had. There were people who would move forward with me and I seemed to have the support not only of the President, with whom I was looking forward to a very special relationship, but also with the guys on the ground.

When I was summoned to a meeting with two of the senior Council Members on that Wednesday morning, I went with the bounce of arrogance in my step and with the idea that this was to prepare me for elevation. Things didn't quite turn out that way. The Council that I believed to be a solid and secure group of individuals appeared to have as much division in it as the rest of the Order. I was asked to meet with two Members whom I had seen but never spoken to, and requested to keep the meeting quiet. We met in an office that seemed to have been covertly created and which was invisible behind the gates of the main refuse disposal centre. Despite this, it was furnished with the best furniture and the arrays of monitors that covered the walls told me that this was no overnight construction. I knocked confidently on the door, straightening my tie as I did so and brushing down the expensive new suit that I wore for the occasion.

"Come," the high pitched voice was a surprise to me.

Entering the room, I saw the voice's owner, a frail and elderly man, seated behind a desk, accompanied by a younger and stockier colleague.

"Please sit down, Mr Barratt," the younger man said, "we haven't long and I'm sure that you have things to do to prepare for tonight."

"You know us by face, Mr Barratt," the older man said, "but we should formally introduce ourselves. I am the Right Honourable Gregory Hounds QC and this is my associate Lord Wilkins. You can call us both Sir."

"Yes Sir," I replied

"Good, now to business," Hounds sat up in his chair and stared straight through me, "You need to know that not everybody is in support of your impending promotion. I shan't beat about the bush and I will tell you that neither myself nor Wilkins here are, shall we say, fans?".

"Okay," I felt my forehead begin to prickle with sweat.

"The bottom line is that we have concerns about your loyalty," Wilkins spoke this time, "although we still retain every respect for the work that you have done. There were four of us on the Council of twelve with these reservations, but with the likely departure of Anderson, that will be down to three. This means that, as you seem to have the full and, may I say, the almost fanatical support of our dear Madame President, we are powerless to stop your elevation. But that doesn't mean that we will let you have an easy ride of it."

"The Order," Hounds intervened, "is older and bigger than any of us. It is more than the sum of its parts. It is, to put is as plainly as possible, a creature that has a life of its own and that we, as Members, work with, rather than against. It is a force for justice with a beating heart but no physical core. It is a belief set, a faith if you like. And one man cannot be allowed to try and rein in or tame what is an untameable beast."

"I have no intention of trying…", I started to reply.

"Please," Hounds continued, "we are not here to listen to you or to hear your pleadings. We are not stupid and we have eyes and ears in places that you could never guess. This meeting is fully deniable by us both and is for us to tell you where we are coming from. It is not a negotiating platform. Are you clear on that?"

"Yes," my voice was remarkably subdued and I felt like a schoolchild in a Headmaster's office.

"Good," Wilkins took over the conversation, "now, we admire a lot about your work, your principles and your ruthlessness. In a way, if anyone deserves to be promoted then it is you. But, Hounds, myself and a few others don't wholly get this Steve Barratt thing. There's something there that doesn't ring true. We can't put our finger on it, but you are asking too many questions. The other night at the pub, you were not the impartial observer we believed you to be. Yes, we know that you have got wind of the changes afoot for you, but we can't believe that there isn't something else there. Are you one of us?"

"Of course," I replied, "I am ORB. This is what I am. And to be frank, you say that you don't want me to justify myself, so I won't. You know what I've done for the Order. You know how I have played my part. I have become what you needed me to be and I have chosen my path."

"Listen to me and listen well, Barratt," Hounds rose unsteadily to his feet, "I have put many years into the Order and a little humility on your part might not go amiss. Of course, we need new blood, but you are not the man that you think you are. I'm sorry that you feel that we have made you more than just another cog in the machine, but that's what you are. You are expendable, you are not infallible and you need to understand that it is you that needs to change and develop, not the Order."

"We've seen this before," Wilkins too rose to stand, "before our time, when Victoria was on the throne. An operative challenged the Order. They thought they knew best and they fermented revolution. Do you want to know what happened to them?"

I said nothing.

"They were terminated," Hounds answered his own question, "not in a nice way, but in a very public way and as a lesson. We can still do the same, and believe me, we will if you try and upset things. Mark our words. The Order is more than you."

"Thank you for coming," Hounds dismissed me just like that.

Looking them both in the eye, I thought about what to say but chose to remain silent. I gave them a look that was ambiguous and saw it register with them. They may have had a point or they may have been simply confirming to me that I was right to be a part of the future. I let the door close softly behind me and, processing these events in my mind, allowed myself a smile. Perhaps the Members of the Council weren't all as detached from reality as I'd first thought.

Chapter Sixty-Four

I left my arrival at the gala dinner to the last minute, gauging my time so that I was just that side north of fashionably-late that would ensure that I minimised the dead time waiting for things to get going. It also meant that I increased the air of expectation about my arrival. The meeting with the unhappy ORB Council Members had done nothing to quell my excitement about this evening. If anything, they'd actually made me more hopeful that the event would be one that was remembered for many years to come. Yes, I was cocky. And yes, I strutted into that room with my head held high, looking and feeling like a million dollars in my beautifully tailored evening dress.

Perhaps I imagined it, but when I arrived and was announced it felt like the whole room seemed to pause and take a breath as every eye was turned to watch me enter. Feeling that there might be some substance in what had been said to me earlier that day about humility, I tried hard to play down the effect that I was having as I joined the party. It wasn't long though before the first glass of red hit the spot and I began to revel in the attention that I was receiving. The food was an exquisite buffet that captured the full range of the underground town's catering abilities, displaying dishes that I had grown up with alongside rare delicacies that I was unlikely to see again. The buffet format meant that eating was a lot more casual than I had anticipated and I made the most of this by moving through the guests, meeting and greeting as many of the varied attendees as I could.

At precisely eight o'clock, a bell rang and we were all invited to move through from the room where we had been dining into the more formal surroundings of the adjoining function suite. Rows of chairs had been set out in this room, enough to accommodate the five hundred or so people who made up the entire ORB population. The stage was set with the same top tables that I had slipped behind when wandering through this place at an earlier date, but this time, they were occupied with the Council members flanking the President who sat in the centre. In front and to the side of the assembled leaders, a glass podium awaited its first speaker, whilst on the opposite side a table had been laid out with an assortment of gold figurines and framed certificates. Looking closely, I could just make out that each of the figurines was a miniature representation of the statue of Lady Justice that sat atop the Old Bailey.

"Quaint," I thought to myself.

Once everyone was seated, a row of guards, twelve each side, lined up along the outer edges of the assembly. They wore a standard and well recognised outfit but their identity was hidden behind full-faced helmets. This was the accepted practice in ORB. Guard duty was rotated amongst the inhabitants of the town in order to ensure that everybody understood the role and duties of those who kept order, whilst helping to prevent any potential force for rebellion growing up. I looked closely at the guards and particularly at the two senior leaders who stood at the front of each line. They had a slight variance to their outfit and I could see straightaway that they were armed more heavily than the others. Perversely, this made me feel a bit better about things.

"My Lords, Ladies and Gentleman," a disembodied voice echoed out of the speakers that filled the auditorium with sound, "pray silence for your host tonight, your current President, Lady Charnford."

A round of applause filled the room as the current ORB President took her place on the stage and stood behind the podium. She beckoned for silence.

"Thank you. Thank you," her voice was strong and powerful, "Can I just say, how honoured I am to be here tonight on this most exciting and very special of evenings. And how good it is to see you all assembled here."

"You know," she continued, "that we very rarely meet as a group like this. But that doesn't mean that you don't all play an important part in the work of the Order. This is the one time of the year that is your night and I ask you please to set aside any thoughts of your own position within the Order and simply enjoy yourselves and have a great time."

A loud cheer and another round of applause filled the room.

"As you will know," she continued when the noise had abated, "this annual gala evening traditionally begins with a speech by the current President. I intend to continue that tradition, but promise not to ramble on for too long."

She waited to let the ripple of laughter die down.

"This year has been an interesting and positive year for the Order. We have maintained our role in the delivery of justice to our beloved nation and have moved forward in some dramatic and exciting ways. When you return to your homes you will all be able to access the full report of this year's activities which will be on your home computer terminals for one week, as is the usual protocol. Please take the time to read this document as it will show you just how important the Order remains and the extent of our work in a world that is increasingly challenged with new injustices."

She paused and her tone and facial expression moved into a quieter form.

"Of course, there have also been some difficult times. We have slipped up on occasion and, for the first time ever, have lost an active operative. Let us be under no illusions that we have some lessons to learn and that our next year needs to be one of increased vigilance."

She turned and looked behind her at the other Council Members.

"My friends on the Council are as committed as I am to ensuring that the Order continues to evolve and develop in tune with changes that are happening in the world. Your Council is not, nor do we want it to be, a homogenous group of people in constant agreement. We have our differences at times, with some preferring to raise the flag of tradition, whilst others wish to promote a more modernising agenda. However, I believe that we are a broad church and you can be assured that we welcome diversity and I, for one, am happy for members to say how they feel we should act."

"Provided," she paused and looked behind her again, "they agree with me."

She left it a little too long to smile but when she did, the audience went with her and realised that this was her idea of humour. As the room filled with laughter, I noticed that not all the members of the Council joined in.

"So," she continued, "we move to tonight's awards ceremony. You have all worked very hard this year and these awards should never be seen in a negative way as, in many ways, you all deserve one. But, we have always recognised outstanding work and this year we will do the same. The winners of these awards have not only done a great job, as you all have, but they have done an outstanding job and gone way beyond the call of duty in their work. Now, because you are all sick of hearing my voice, I would like to hand you over to Jack Plato, our regular awards MC who is much better at this sort of thing than I am. Jack."

She waved her thanks to the audience and took her seat behind the long table with the rest of the Council. They could be seen muttering thanks and congratulations to her, but there remained a couple of faces fixed straight ahead. They were the ones that I knew to be against me and suspected were also against their President.

"Evening, evening, evening," Jack Plato danced onto the stage in a glittering suit, "how are we diddling?"

The audience mumbled a reply.

"I said, how are we diddling, are we good?" he urged the audience on to a heartier response and, because they all knew that they couldn't escape this part of the evening, they dug out their best pantomime responses.

There then followed an entertaining and, at times, quite witty period of jokes and banter as a dozen or so awards were presented to smiling recipients. The awards ranged from the more serious, 'Best Technological Breakthrough', to the flippant, 'Year's Worst Dresser'. I laughed as Adam received the latter and made a point of fitting the word 'man' into his acceptance speech as many times as possible.

"And finally," Plato concluded the awards, "we save the best until the last. This is the award that everybody strives for and one which is the pinnacle of any ORB associate's career, the award for 'First Among Equals'. Or to put it in more easily understood terms, 'The Best in Show.'"

He laughed louder than anyone else at his own joke before continuing.

"This year, that award goes to somebody who has delivered an outstanding performance in his role and who has done so, in innovative and exciting ways. On top of that, he has become, in a short space of time, something of an institution within the Order and somebody I can safely say is loved by everyone. Ladies and gentlemen, you know I can't say what he does, but I give you, Steve Barratt."

The last time I'd won an award was at a primary school sport's day and it is almost impossible for me to describe the feeling that flooded over me when I took to the stage and looked out on the cheering audience standing upright and clapping me loudly. I was buzzing with pride, but I also felt remarkably and genuinely humbled by the whole thing. My acceptance speech contained the usual platitudes and thanking others, but as I was finishing, I felt a hand next to mine and turned to see the President beside me. She moved past me and called for quiet as she stood before the podium.

"Ladies and Gentlemen, I too would like to congratulate Steve. This is a well-deserved honour. But, if I could have silence for a minute, I would like to say a few more words."

The room gradually assumed the silence that she called had for.

"Thank you," she paused before looking to me and to the audience, "now, as you will be aware, the Council is your body of elected members, consisting of the twelve good people and true who direct the operations of the Order. It is with great regret that I inform you today that, for health reasons, we are to lose a Member of the Council. Please be upstanding in your gratitude to Mister Tom Anderson."

The audience rose and Anderson stood up and bowed to acknowledge their applause. He managed to look dignified in this most humiliating moment, made all the more so by the President's deliberate emphasis on Anderson's lack of a title. He looked across at me as he took his seat again, and that look will stay with me for years. Previously, only my ex mother-in-law had been capable of delivering such a powerful, withering look. The difference was that, whilst hers could shrink me for hours, Anderson meant nothing to me, therefore his stare was quickly forgotten.

"Of course," the President continued, as the hall quietened down again, "this means that we now have a vacancy and need to find a suitable replacement for Mr Anderson. Tonight, I am delighted to inform you that the Council would like to offer that vacant position to Steve Barratt and ask that he do us the privilege of accepting this role. Steve?"

The audience rose again and repeated their loud applause, making more noise than I thought possible. As I stood in front of them, I tried to give my humblest look, but a glance across at Madame President turned that look into a full Cheshire-cat grin. I knew I had to make an acceptance speech and positioned myself beside the podium to do so, but, because of the audience's excitement it was a couple of minutes before I was able to begin. This was now my moment. This was what it had all been leading up to. I took a long drink of water, raised my hand for silence, and addressed the crowd.

"Madame President, Ladies and Gentlemen, friends and colleagues, this is truly a great honour," I paused to let a late wave of applause die down, "And, I can honestly say that being here, now, is the greatest moment of my life."

I waited while the audience settled and looked out across the sea of faces as I drank more water, composing my words carefully.

"The Order for Restoring Balance," I began, "snatched me from impending disaster and I know that it has done the same for many of you here this evening. Since the day it saved me and I was inducted into the Order, I have witnessed some amazing things, and I have seen the best of things."

Seeing the captive look on the audience's face, I paused again to compose my thoughts and make this my most memorable moment.

"I have seen justice delivered," I continued, "in ways that defy imagination and in places that often defied understanding. And, I have been privileged to be a part of that process. I have tasted the best of the innovations of your hands and have enjoyed the highest levels of hospitality and support. I would like to thank you wholeheartedly for all of that.

The Order is an amazing institution. It is as old as recorded history, yet, almost timeless in its purpose, and it is an organisation that seems to transcend the routine operation of day to day life. It has been described to me as something that is beyond the sum of its parts and that has a life beyond the temporal."

"You," I let my eyes roam across the sea of expectant faces, "as the heart and soul of the operation, need to be recognised for the great people that you are, making a great contribution in your own ways. Whether that is leading the Order, creating impossible solutions to problems, or indeed, cooking the best burgers I have ever tasted. You deserve to have the support of a Council worthy of your endeavours and your dreams. For your sakes alone, I would be honoured to be a part of such a Council."

A tangible air of expectation filled the room as I hesitated a beat before continuing:

"However, it is with a heavy heart that I feel that I must concur with our own Madame President's assessment, that this year has seen some challenging circumstances. We would be foolish to deny that mistakes have been made. Mistakes that might have been avoided. Mistakes that have been compounded by an air of complacency that seems to have permeated this once great Order."

I paused to let my words sink in, looking back at the Council members seated around the table, focusing on Hounds and Anderson, before turning away and moving away from the podium. Walking slowly to the front of the stage, I continued my speech.

"You have all afforded me the highest respect since my arrival here," I looked closely at the faces looking up at me, "and so I reciprocate that respect by asking that we all be a bit more open about things tonight. Let's be honest, you are not supposed to know who I am and what I do, but you know I operate out in the field and you are all aware of the activities of The Kingfisher. Well, let me tell you, I am proud to bear that name."

Once again, the audience erupted in cheering and, despite my raising my hands for silence, I could do nothing but wait for it to fade away.

"Yes," I raised my voice in politician style, "I am proud to be The Kingfisher. Proud, despite what our President describes as some of the challenges that I have had to work through in my role. It was I who had to take the life of the Angel of Mercy, or Amy, or Janice, depending on how you knew her. It was I who watched as her life slipped away in my hands. By my hand. Of course, she should never have gone rogue. But, she should never have been put into a position that encouraged and allowed her to go rogue. And I, should never have had to be put in the position of having to clean up the mess made by the Order's complacency and errors."

Out of the corner of my eye, I saw the two lead guards take an interest in what I was saying and move their hands just a little closer to their weapons. But nobody was going to silence me now.

"Let me tell you something," I effected my best emotional voice, "As the light of existence faded from Amy's eyes, I didn't see hatred, nor did I see regret. What I saw was relief. I truly believe that Amy was relieved to be free of the burden she carried as an operative for the Order. We need to learn from this situation and understand that justice requires a degree of freedom. This is not a prison. This is not a dictatorship. And, contrary to what has been said to me by certain members of the Council themselves, the Order is not bigger than its constituent parts. To say that it is, sounds too much like a way for us to abdicate responsibility for our actions. To say that it is, denies our right to exercise our own choices and judgement. To say that it is, displays weakness."

I turned and looked directly at Hounds and Wilkins, challenging them to silence me. They simply turned to each other and whispered.

"So," I resumed, "as somebody who has set their individual self aside to serve the greater good of the Order, today, I am honoured to be offered a reward for that service. I believe that the Council needs somebody like me and I believe that you, as the heart and soul of the Order, need somebody like me to represent you at its highest levels. The days of complacency and mistakes and arrogance must end and a new day of freedom must be welcomed in."

The room erupted in applause, allowing me the time to assess the stance of the guards and to glance briefly at the President who lifted her hand to encourage me to wind things up.

"But," I waited for silence again, "can I be confident that change will happen? Do you know something? I don't believe that I can. Has the Order reached a low point from which it cannot recover? Sadly, I believe this may be the case. Let me demonstrate."

Lifting the arms of my tuxedo to reveal two gleaming silver cuffs, I fired a bolt of Blue Light that encircled and trapped the Council members as it snaked around the table they occupied. Another few bursts of fire saw every exit sealed behind a swirling circle of the same Blue Light.

"Complacency," I shouted, "the same complacency that has allowed me to enter this room armed in this way. Is this the way that the Council handles its responsibilities?"

As I paused to watch the looks on the faces of my audience, the first two guards on either side turned and fired a stream of nanobots. They hit their spot and along each wall, the other guards fell unconscious.

"What is this?" the President rose and shouted, "Barratt, what are you doing?"

"I think Madame President," I said coolly, "I am refusing your offer of a place on the Council. What is more, I am taking this opportunity to resign from my role. I can no longer be a part of ORB."

"Oh, it's not that easy," she replied, scanning about the room to identify supporters, "Cipher, Banker and the rest of you, take him out."

As she made this appeal, I reached into the inside pocket of my jacket and removed what looked like a large handkerchief. Throwing it in the air, the audience gasped as it transformed into what looked like a giant moth and flew rapidly around the auditorium. As I watched its progress, I scanned the room trying to identify the other operatives who I had never seen face to face. Once the moth had done its job, it wasn't too difficult for me to see who they were. They were the ones trying to rise but doubling over in pain and holding their heads. Their implants were responding to the President's DNA, DNA that I had taken from her kiss and that Adam had so kindly replicated before supplying me with the means by which I could saturate the room with it. The moth poured out a steady stream, invisible to the eye, but enough to cripple those who carried the same implant that I had, until Madame President herself had been kind enough to remove it.

I nodded at the two remaining guards who shot each of the operatives with a tranquiliser. They fell asleep instantly and were probably glad to do so. I'd felt the pain of that implant before and I wasn't going to make them suffer for too long. If there had been a less painful way for me to identify my colleagues turned adversaries, then I would have chosen it but I needed a quick resolution. There were still things that I had to say to the rest of the assembly. The guards then came to join me and stood side by side with me on the stage.

"The problem that I have," I held up my hand for silence, "The problem that I have is that complacency and mistakes are manageable. But the issues that pervade ORB go way beyond that. We have a President who is simply not fit for purpose. A President who has allowed her own rampant hormones to colour her vision and who thinks that feelings and love can be bought by honours. We have a Council that dips in and out of the Order in a self-righteous way, led by their lust-driven leader, but all believing that they can do anything they like and be exempt from any moral responsibility because the Order is something that transcends humanity.

Well, I'm sorry, but you are wrong. Justice and righteousness may well exist beyond the lowly realms of mankind but the Order is of this Earth. The Order is a man-made institution that has grown and developed out of the very human desire to correct injustice. A worthy cause and a necessary one, in its time. And yes, there remain injustices out there, so there remains a need for some form of organisation to restore the balance. But the Order, as it exists and operates today, is not fit for the job. The world out there has changed and with that change comes a need for the Order to change."

I paused to take stock of what was happening, confirming that the Blue Light was holding and that, aside from the slumped operatives, the rest of the audience was seated safely. I checked too, that the guards who flanked me were happy with progress, then I continued:

"I was called to do some dirty deeds for the Order. I complied and I understood that they were necessary deeds that did indeed restore the balance of justice. But, when sixty-seven innocent victims died as a result of a faulty virus produced by ORB I was forced to rethink my position. You saw me return from that mission a changed man. You saw a newly confident and assertive operative who seemed to live and thrive by working without any emotional ties or moral concerns.

Well, I'm afraid that that persona was something of an illusion. I'm not sorry to tell you that, yes, I was a changed man, but not changed in the way you may have believed me to be. I am not a cold-hearted, ruthless avenger, prepared to bow down to the great Order and do everything and anything that it insists I must do. I am not a vain, loveless killing machine. I am a human being. A human being who knows the limits of his conscience and when I read about the wives and husbands, the sons and daughters, the cousins, uncles, parents and friends that had died at my hands, I could no longer buy into what I was doing."

There was a small commotion at the back of the room as somebody tried to slip out of the hall, only to be stopped as they were propelled back by the Blue Light that kept us in that place.

"Please," I said, "I don't want anybody here to be afraid. Granted, this is not what you expected but can I ask that you hear me out. I promise that my intention is not to harm any of you. You're the good guys. My issue is with this lot."

I waved my hands behind me to indicate the Council.

"Let me show you now some more tangible proof of my intentions," I continued, "As you know, the response of your Council to the Amy situation and the 'collateral damage' that occurred was not to fall on their swords. This was just something that had happened. But they needed a scapegoat to appease their consciences and, rather than seeking to see if they were in any way at fault, they singled out a technician, James. James was just like any of you. He served ORB as best he could and played his part. The failure of the virus was not James's fault. It was the fault of the complacency and arrogance that is rife in today's Order. Nevertheless, I was charged with killing James. Cutting out the weak link. Sacrificing an innocent to the sacred cow of the Order.

And then, to compound the issue further, I was asked to also take out Jason King. Why? Because he was against the Order? No. Because he wanted to bring ORB down? No. I was asked to kill Jason King because, as the father of two daughters, killed by the Order, killed by me, he wanted some answers. That's where today's ORB finds itself. The Order is making mistake after mistake and reaching depths of injustice that negate any good it does by covering up those mistakes. I decided that I could not let this downward spiral of murder and mayhem continue. For that reason, I chose not to complete my last mission. Jason? James?"

The two guards beside me removed their helmets. Jason King was on my right and he smiled and waved at the crowd who broke into spontaneous applause. James stood on my left, tears streaming down his face. It took a full five minutes for the room to quieten down again, but I still had more to say.

"Madame President, I have charged you with being unfit for your role," I looked at Joanne and received a killer stare back, "and is this not proof of that fact. Your complacency has allowed me to bring outsiders into this centre. Your complacency has allowed me to fix this centre's location and arrange for a fleet of helicopters to land outside the entrance. Your complacency has put the Order in a position where it cannot defend itself."

"I could take this whole centre out if I wanted to," I turned back again to the main audience, "But that's not what I intend to do. Jason, James and I will be leaving shortly and will not be returning. You will be left with the Order intact, but, I'm afraid, in tatters. I call on you, you, the people who are the true lifeblood of ORB, you, the ones who are passionate in your service for justice. I call on you now to take control back and bring the Order back to where it should be."

I had to stop again as another round of applause broke out, during which, Adam rose and climbed the steps to join me on the stage, whispering in my ear. I held my hand up again for silence.

"The question has been asked," I said, "as to whether I might be the person to lead this revolution in ORB. Well, let me answer that. I could have chosen to seek to destroy ORB but it is true that this Order is bigger than me. One man cannot bring it down. Nor can one man take it to where it needs to be. ORB is nearly one thousand years old in one form or other. It is a righteous organisation at its heart. It needs to exist. But I am not the man to take on that role. Nor do I believe that any single person can lead the Order effectively. ORB needs a group of dedicated individuals, good people who can lead it. And, I am confident that, as the current Council departs, you can find those people within your own ranks.

I am not the man for the job. I came here on the back of a personal crusade to make righteous corrections to injustices. That's where I am comfortable. I'm too selfish, too proud, too much of a loner to be a part of ORB. It needs humbler, more loving and more caring people at its helm. For that reason, I will be returning to a life of anonymity where I can affect the small changes that I, as one small man, believe that I have been called to make. Jason and James will support me and yes, I'm afraid to say that we will be borrowing a lot of the tools and the technology that you guys have supported me with.

I'd be daft not to. We have, in our new home base, enough capacity to take anybody here who would like to join us and embrace a higher degree of freedom than the Order has allowed them. That base will be somewhere in the vicinity of King Island where life is quite relaxed and the climate is extremely favourable. I know that not all of you are enticed by sun, sand and sea, but we could certainly use as much help as possible."

I explained the process by which we would bring people across to us, emphasising that now was not the time to make that decision. Requests would go through the new Council who we trusted would be elected to take ORB forward. The days of total isolation for the Order had to end, but we would not be a part of the structure.

"And so," I concluded, "with a slightly heavy heart but with a passionate belief that you can bring the Order back on track, we shall now take our leave."

James pressed a series of buttons on a console in his hand and the side door of the theatre opened to allow a cart to roll in, a large white sheet covering its cargo. James and King stood in front of me as I slipped off the tuxedo and the rest of my formal suit and put on the trappings of my alter ego. They stood aside to allow me one last look at the audience who, in turn, were able to see The Kingfisher before them in work mode. With a last wave, I pressed the necessary buttons and the three of us rose slowly before allowing the boots we wore to take us on a pre-marked route out and away from the meeting, our exit coinciding with the Blue Lights fading to nothing.

The Tracker Bots led us to the front entrance of the centre, where a luxury helicopter waited to collect us. Boarding this, we seated ourselves and King gave the pilot a thumbs up. As the helicopter roared away, the innocuous police station that was the unseen and unknown entrance to the ORB facility, deep under an equally innocuous village in the Yorkshire Dales, faded away and became a mere dot before becoming a memory.

"Well," I said when we were safely in the clouds, "I think that went alright, didn't it?"

We laughed as the champagne cork popped and we began the renewal of our acquaintance.

Chapter Sixty-Five

As we flew towards King Island, we recalled how easy the deception had been. I'd already apologised to James that I'd let King get close to killing him, but I would never have let it reach its conclusion. It was necessary for me to see the real Jason King, but I had always been confident that he was no murderer, despite the depths of his grieving. Our time had been limited on that first evening and, after going through the most difficult part of my plan, I had had to explain the next steps very briefly to the two of them and ask them to come up with the cover story that would surround their deaths. As King owned the Islands, this wasn't difficult and had been achieved with only a couple of people being aware that Jason King was not dead, nor was his intruder. King was now his own cousin, looking surprisingly similar, whilst James had been welcomed to the Island as a visiting technician.

The Order had gone too far for me. When I understood how coolly I had dealt with Amy and the pain that I'd caused in delivering that virus, I'd known that I couldn't work for them anymore. The play-acting had been a strain, but it was worth it because now I was free to play my part as I was intended to. It was this lack of freedom that had niggled at me with ORB. Of course, I understood that there had to be secrecy, but I almost felt that the town's inhabitants were like caged animals. Hopefully, this would change. The underground city and the organisation it supported remained and would remain for another thousand years, provided the Order grew into the age it now operated in.

During the first few weeks when we were settling ourselves into the Island, we monitored the Order and were advised of the changes that had gone on there. The Council had all resigned and a new Board of twenty Members had been elected. The key difference was that every mission was now voted on by everybody in the town. It seemed to have done the trick but these were early days.

Charlotte opted to join us, partly because she'd liked my comments during my speech but primarily because Adam had made the same decision.

This meant that King Island had not only the best technicians to add new innovations to its daily life, but also that you could now get a decent burger on Island Four. I was secretly pleased that only about another dozen or so people had made the choice to join us. We could have used a few more but, with the majority choosing to stay with the Order, there was a vital retention of many years of knowledge and experience where it needed to be. We had no intention of being another, rival Order. In truth, I just wanted to get back to my boat.

My transition away from ORB had not been as easy as I first thought it would be. Once the helicopter was in the air and I had time to relax, my body simply gave in and I'd drifted into a deep, almost comatose sleep for several days. King had arranged for Doctors to come, but they had simply put my state down to nervous exhaustion and, it transpires, they were right. On the fourth day I woke up and felt better than ever. This meant that we could have that catch-up that we'd promised each other, and I for one was keen to know what had been happening from their side of things.

"So, how did you get on with my boat?" I asked.

"What boat's that then?" King replied.

"My boat, Kingfisher, she's alright isn't she?"

"No," King smiled, "no boat of that name. Mind you, I've got one just the same!"

"Yeah, right," I laughed, "you dream on and get your own boat. No, seriously, how was it."

"Fantastic," King replied, "absolutely amazing. Everything you said about life on the canals is so right. I love it."

"Yeah, but it wasn't an easy start was it?" James said.

"Oh, yes, I forgot," King chuckled at the recollection, "I thought it would be cool to arrive by helicopter. You know, you get used to travelling that way. Anyway, we landed in the playing fields next to the leisure centre at Burton and I swaggered out and off to the boat. By this time, your boating buddies were giving me a strange look and I explained I was looking after her for a few days. The chopper hadn't impressed them. 'Aye,' says one of them, I think his name was Tom, 'well now, if you can't get the engine started or you need a bit of help with the first lock, you give me a shout'. I'd smiled in a patronising way, but then the following morning had made a complete mess up of the lock process. Tom stood by chuckling, but he still came to help us through. It's a great leveller is the water isn't it ?!"

"Too right," I agreed, "not a space where people are that impressed with ostentatious shows of wealth. Did you get settled alright though?"

"After a few days," King said, "I almost didn't want to come back here. Weird isn't it. There's just an atmosphere on the water you can't describe, pure peace, relaxation and just a happy state of mind."

"I did everything I needed to, though," James intervened, "just as we agreed. She's now entirely yours and they'll struggle to find her again."

It had been agreed that, whilst they waited for my calls from ORB, they would move the boat as far south as possible, whilst James tweaked the communications to make sure it could no longer be tracked. Naturally, this meant that I would be losing some of the mod cons, the gadgets and the gizmos that ORB had supplied, but I could live with that.

"Do you want to tell him the rest?" James asked.

"Oh, I guess you'll find out sooner or later," he told me, "but let's retire to the veranda and have a few sherbets."

We sat out on the terrace of his home and watched as the tropical sun descended on another perfect day in paradise.

"Let me start at the beginning," King said, "from the moment that Jason King died. I knew that I had to see the thing through with you, in honour of the girls as much as anything else. And I knew that this meant ceding the Island to the natives. I could live with that, after all it had been a successful project but I realised it had been a bit of vanity on my part. Nothing like being dead to concentrate the priorities, eh? Anyway, we'd devised the cousin plan so that all went through smoothly and yes, it was a bit of a cheap stunt on my part to keep the name, but I didn't think I'd be able to pull off a full change of identity. Besides, it's not unlikely that my Dad and his brother both liked the name Jason is it? With that in place, I reached an agreement with the islanders and we took out a hundred-year lease on Island Four, which is now King Island. The others are reverting to a new name but haven't decided on that yet."

"I helped sweeten things a little as well," James said, "by tweaking communications on the islands so that now everybody has free internet access and telephone calls. It's routed through ORB, but if they ever find out I'll be able to move it somewhere else easily enough."

"Yes," King continued, "so it was a smooth transition. Then we heard from you and came over to the UK until we were ready to act. We had to move the boat and James needed to make the adjustments, so we had a little cruise. I tell you, I can't remember when I last had such a good time.

There was I, a multi-billionaire, struggling to peg in, with the wind and rain soaking me to the skin. By the time we'd got to the pub, I realised that it's not the money that makes the man."

He paused and took a long drink from the elaborate cocktail he'd insisted on making for us all.

"And I saw what attracted you," he continued, "in the people who live on those stretches of water. It's easy to be patronising and say that they're good, honest, simple folk, but it's more accurate to describe them as people who have tasted life in the mainstream and have opted for a less complicated lifestyle. I knew that I wanted, in some way to be a part of it, so I read all the magazines and papers and asked a load of questions as we travelled down south. Oh, and in answer to your question, she's moored at a boatyard in the Midlands just now."

"In your boatyard, you mean?" James interjected cryptically.

"Ah, yes," King clapped his hands, "of course, my boat yard. I couldn't help it. The guy was struggling to make ends meet, the developers were circling, wanting to turn it into apartments and everyone in the pubs was up in arms. So I bought it."

"Okay," I said, "guess that saves me mooring fees. Smart move though. I could use a base now that ORB's gone."

"Exactly what I thought," King said, "and I've started work on it already. You'll have an underground workshop there. The old boy who was running the yard was only hanging on to stop the developers, so he's about to retire and I'm putting in a new Manager. Nice guy, you'll like him."

"Something tells me he's not a stranger," I laughed.

"Well, actually, now you mention it," King was loving this, "you see I didn't just buy a boatyard, I bought a marine supplier as well, a company called Boat Space. You heard of them?"

I smiled as he acknowledged my recognition of the name.

"Tony's married now and they've got a little one on the way," King said, "so I thought I'd help them along and get myself a partner."

"Bottom line is," James said, "that we are all now partners in a few waterways businesses and at last count have about thirty boats on our books. Should keep you busy out there."

They filled me in on more of the details. The underground laboratories they were building were in recognition that any future activity we got involved in wasn't really suited to the initial plan of basing it on King Island.

"We started off thinking that the Island was the best place," King explained, "and that its location would be an attraction. Seems that I was wrong in this. ORB employees may have enjoyed the escape to the sun, but they had had such a sheltered upbringing that they prefer the idea of being in the UK. That's fine with me and, in reality, it works better. We're not global crusaders, if crusaders we are. No, a little piece of England will do for now. The wider world can look after itself."

It would have been a logical conclusion to decide that my identity as Steve Barratt was no longer viable. I liked it though. ORB would always be able to track us down and they team knew me as Steve. In the end, I was given multiple identities to choose from, which I still use to this day, but Steve Barratt is the name I defer to. Same old name but a new role as a partner in King's venture that had, almost overnight, snapped up anything that was for sale on the canal network. I was so grateful to him for this. Not only did it keep me on the water but it also gave me a purpose in my working life. I had the money to retire and take it easy, but I craved the sense of achievement that conventional employment used to give me. With the facilities I now had access to, I could earn my keep in building a better future for the waterways, whilst having the freedom to work in my less well known role. Steve Barratt may have been officially retired but The Kingfisher was going nowhere.

"Which pretty much brings us up to date," King concluded, "provided, of course, that ORB leave us alone."

"I think they will," I said, "and I think it will work out okay. There are forces at ORB, behind the scenes, that we will never know about, but I think that we got the workforce on board and it'll be a while before it's allowed to go rogue again. And I don't know how practical it would be for them to try and build a new facility without anyone knowing about it. Only we know the location. That knowledge is worth a lot to ORB and they won't mess with it."

We spent a few more days relaxing on the island but I wanted to get home and, despite the baking sun, free drinks, beautiful women and sparkling beaches, I hankered for the chill of the cut. They flew me back to Heathrow at the end of that first fortnight and I hopped on a coach to Stafford. The boat was in the water at the yard, Stan was finalising the handover to Tony and his wife, and I was welcomed as a stranger and given the keys to my home.

The following morning, I headed away with no particular destination in mind, revelling in the freedom that I now enjoyed but still hankering for the opportunity to work out my purpose as a small part of the work of rebalancing of justice.

Chapter Sixty-Six

It took me three weeks to cruise from the mooring, down through Oxford, along the Thames and back up the Grand Union towards the Midlands. During that time, I had no contact with the outside world other than my daily chats with fellow boaters, towpath visitors and shopkeepers where necessary. I switched my phones off, put the web dongle away in a drawer and only allowed myself half an hour of BBC News on the radio every evening. I had to do this. I had to do it for two reasons. Firstly, to get back to the life that I had made for myself and which had to be the core of my existence over and above anything else, and secondly, to remind myself that I was not some great and important avenger of justice, without whom the world would be lost.

The journey worked on both scores. London had its own charms I suppose, but my real pleasure was in the journey either side of that great City. Week one was a slow trip down the Oxford Canal and onto the Thames, taking in the natural beauty that surrounded me, staring in wonder at some of the stunning homes that I passed and simply drinking in the atmosphere of the waterway. Pubs were a nightly treat, one which I paid for in the weight I managed to put on, but worth it nonetheless. People however were, as always, the number one delight. Not that I sought them out or really craved to be with crowds. No, it was more a natural merging of different lives that touched together as they meandered along the slowest highway in the nation.

The canal was now my home and wherever there were navigable waterways, that was my locality. After leaving ORB, I never intended to stop doing what I could to correct injustice, but I had resolved that I would keep my involvement local. Despite the incredible benefits that came from new technologies and social media, they came with a significant drawback in that the local was forsaken for the national and global. Eyes were lifted up to the stars and away from the doorstep. There were times when this helped bring about change, as multiple opinions formed a greater force for good, but for the most part, it meant that people were lost in a fantasy world that came at them from their phone's screen, denying them sight of what was happening beside them. Change may well happen globally, but local change is where lives are touched on a daily basis. Simple acts, small deeds, unknown interventions at a local level are where needs are met. If the local is forgotten, then the issues multiply and become national. We are all small people standing in a local place. This was my view anyway, and the reason that I had determined to focus on local issues as I became aware of them. That said, I was very fortunate to have over two thousand miles of water to call my locality.

Whilst I was out of the loop, King continued on his spending spree, bitten by the canal bug and chomping at the bit as he waited for the opportunity to come over and have another cruise. I caught up on all of this when I finished my sabbatical period and booted up my computer for the first time. There was none of the stress that I used to feel when returning from a break previously, as I knew that nothing important would have been sent to me. I had requested e-mails strictly on a FYI basis and, to be fair to King and the team, they had respected this wish.

With another boatyard on his books, a small marina and a chandlery, King had just completed a deal to buy a boat-builders in Cheshire. This had been a suggestion of mine as I had a vision that he could help fulfil. Tony's wife, Kate, was proving to be the star of the show, despite being nearly full-term with their baby, and had drawn all these businesses together under one umbrella group. King was on the paperwork somewhere in the background, as indeed was I, but the day to day operation of all of these businesses was in the hands of Tony and Kate, although each one retained its original staff for now. It was early days, but the finance was there to support these various concerns and I was confident that King knew what he was doing. The canals had a future and were more popular than ever, but the shift in public attention had been to their use as a recreational centre for walking, canoeing and cycling. King was passionate about the water being the primary focus, both for recreational and business use. He had even started buying up land to reinstate some derelict waterways and had floated again the notion of a Grand Canal to sweep through the heart of the nation and provide both a glorious and impressive waterway as well as a means of both diverting floodwaters and averting the problem of droughts. Granted, he was a little bit of a very rich kid with a new toy, but something told me that he understood what the canals were about and that this was no passing fancy.

For my part, I had drawn up a design for a new steel boat that would be affordable as both a leisure cruiser and to live on. It was over fifty years since Sam Springer had changed the face of the waterways with boats like the one that Fran and I had started on. Now, the opportunity was ripe to do the same again. Housing was at a critical level and the cut was becoming a little too much of a rich man's playground. James was to design the detail of the vessel with only two elements that had to remain in his brief: that it be cheap and that it be solar powered. The rest was up to his imagination, although I did hint that it would be nice to put the Springer 'moustache' on the front.

The boat-builder had been instructed to start recruiting new apprentices and I was delighted to find out that he had been able to track down and secure Philip Rivers as one of the first of these. Rivers had struggled since being freed from prison and, despite going back to college to resume studies at night, employers simply wouldn't give him the chance. He had committed himself to a life of honesty and wasn't prepared to lie his way through interviews. Sadly, such high morals are rarely rewarded.

The apprentices were all given homes in a coral of old boats that was being added to daily on the hard-standing at the rear of the boat yard. These boats were all habitable, just about, but as they were offered rent free, they were snapped up quickly. The idea was that as the new apprentices cut their teeth, they would renovate their own and each other's boats, eventually seeing them returned to the water. The boat would then be gifted to them on successful completion of their term as apprentices. Although nobody was rejected off-hand in their application, King and I had agreed that priority would be given to young offenders. It was the first intake of these workers who came up with the name of 'Second Chance Boats' for the business. We liked it and it stuck.

For my part, I would have some input into these businesses and, as a silent partner, be allowed to use them on my travels. My savings and accrued finances were locked away in one of King's investment accounts and I chose to live on only my earnings as a supplier of carvings and other woodwork. This meant clearing out some of the ORB technology from the boat to create a workshop at the back, but James and Adam came over and did this for me, carting away the stuff that they could use and making sure that I had enough for my needs in each area of my life. The pod stayed, as much because it was hidden away. The multiple computers and monitors, along with most of the animatronics went. A simple bench with simple tools replaced my old workstation and the moment I put that first chisel against a block of Ash, I knew I'd made the right decision.

That visit from Adam, James and Charlotte, who had never even seen a narrowboat before and who was now a firm fixture in Adam's life, was a long weekend of alcohol, laughs and memories.

"Man," Adam said, "I can still see Madame President's face after you left. She looked completely broken. I'm not sure whether it was the looks from the other Council members, your attack on them all, or simply the realisation that she wasn't going to get laid that night!"

"Come on," I said, "it was never really going to happen. Although, we got a bit close. What I don't get is how easily she fell for it."

"Love," whispered Charlotte.

"Sorry?" I asked

"Love. That's what she wanted and why she fell for it. She had everything, the power, the position and the money, but she didn't have love. That's what she saw in you."

I thought about it and realised that she was probably right. Beneath that cold exterior there may have been a heart after all. That I'd broken it, wasn't going to give me sleepless nights, but I wished her well regardless.

"So what exactly happened after we left?" I asked

"Well," Adam replied, "it was like this man. The Blue Lights disappeared and the guards came to. The other operatives were out of it until the next morning. Then we all sort of started to drift away. It wasn't like the storming of the Winter Palace or something like that, we just left the room, mingled a bit in the restaurant, mopping up what was left of the booze, then headed off in small groups back to our houses. It was the next day when we really got a feel for what was happening. Man, had they moved quick. There were to be elections to the Council to be held the following week and there was no mention made of the other Council members. They just disappeared although I think that a number of them helped secure a plan for a transition before they left. Anderson was definitely there. After the elections, and yes, I did think about standing myself, but hey, my mind was already made up about what I was going to do, well, they gave us all the choice to stay or leave. That's when we arrived at the island."

The conversation then moved to lighter topics and we ended up sleeping where we sat and regretting those last whiskies for all of the following morning.

Aside from this visit, I remained on my own, enjoying again the circuit that I had first known so long ago around and about the junction at Great Haywood. Moored at Wolseley Bridge, I sat on the towpath and was reminded of the various different people that I had been over the years sitting in this virtually unchanging spot. A lot had happened but there was still an awful lot to do. Tomorrow, I'd test my new workshop and do a little carving.

+++

'The Stone Courier', 10th September 2023
'Problem Tenants Move On'

The self-proclaimed 'family from hell' who have made headlines in this paper many times over the past few months, have moved on voluntarily from the two houses they rented from Stone Council.

It is unclear what has happened to them or where they have gone, but neighbours are said to be delighted that they are no longer around. It was only two weeks ago that Jack Mackey, the head of the family, taunted reporters with documents that he had received confirming that his application to the European Court of Human Rights had been accepted and that breaches of his human rights would be investigated.

Mackey and his family are alleged to have made life hell for other residents of the flagship new estate in the town's Eastern District having moved in to two properties on the estate. Loud parties, rubbish mounting in the garden and continued abuse of anyone who asked them to toe the line, are just some of the reports filed against them. Until their disappearance, Council officials had repeatedly voiced their frustration that they were unable to evict these tenants.

It is not believed that they will return to the properties as they left behind walls painted with both apologies and mysterious slogans, one of which referred to 'The Spiders'.

Once cleaned up, the properties will be offered to two local families who are currently on waiting lists.

+++

'Mid-Counties News', 23rd September, 2023
'I Lied About Abuse'

In an emotional press conference, called at short notice by Vaughan Ellis, the out-spoken atheist, he confessed to having made up claims that he was abused by a Roman Catholic priest thirty years ago. The priest, Father Michael O'Connell died last year in prison whilst serving a four-year sentence.

Before handing himself in to the police, Ellis called the press conference as a way of ensuring that the public fully understood his level of guilt in this affair.

"I don't know how it got as far as it did," he told reporters, "but I know I could have stopped it. I don't blame the lawyers who urged me on, or the numerous supporters who made me into something of an idol. It was my action and it was driven by my hatred for the church. If there was any way to turn back the clock, believe me, I would do it. As it is, I am prepared to accept the consequences of my confession and will take whatever punishment is deemed fit for me."

Asked why he had decided to come forward, Ellis simply said that he had experienced a crisis of conscience that he could not live with. A close friend of Ellis who wishes to remain anonymous has told this reporter that in the days prior to his confession, Ellis seemed more and more disturbed and had made comments about 'a bird' and 'hidden documents'.

Police are expected to charge Mr Ellis in the next few hours with perverting the course of justice.

+++

'The Sunday Herald: News Review', 14th October, 2023
'Return of the Righteous Corrector?'

Following the appearance on e-bay of a previously unknown carving by the self-styled vigilante, the 'Righteous Corrector', speculation is mounting that a new copycat operator has taken over this mantle. It is widely accepted that previous actions against injustice that were identified by a wooden disc carved with the logo 'RC', were the work of somebody who lived on a boat until they died when that boat went on fire. We are unable to name this person for legal reasons.

However, the appearance of this latest carving, an exact replica of the originals, has led to a number of experts raising the possibility that the Righteous Corrector was not in fact killed and has now resumed his work.

+++

Chapter Sixty-Seven

The details of my operations don't really matter. You know now how I operate. I can tackle the big stuff and the small stuff, depending on what calls me. Now that I'm free of ORB I have to spend that bit more time investigating and checking all my facts, but that isn't an issue. The freedom is priceless to me. And now that ORB no longer dictates what I do, I have to take the full responsibility for my actions. I'll always identify my work because I want my victims to know that their suffering is justified. I hadn't expected the Mackey gang to put the token on e-bay, but I guess they needed every penny they could get. I won't say I didn't watch how much it fetched. Seems there's quite a demand for them though.

I make no bones about what I am. I am a murderer, a mutilator, a terroriser and a thief. Should I ever have to appear in court and face the numerous charges that could be raised against me I would almost certainly spend the rest of my life in prison. But when the law fails, for whatever reason, then, in my view, and in that particular instance only, the law is not binding. Can't believe I'll ever find a sympathetic judge to agree with this though, so let's hope it never gets to that stage.

We're coming to the end of my story now. It seems fitting that it should end where it began, with Fran and the children. I'm writing this after a visit to the church in Weston where Fran's family had put up a memorial plaque. It's been a hot and tiring day, but I am at peace. The church is set just off the canal and has a section of the graveyard set aside for bargees from the past. It's also just a short walk from the Saracen's Head where I confess I'd partaken of a little Dutch courage.

As I'd stood before the memorial, a small metal plaque on which are inscribed the names and dates pertaining to my family, I thanked Fran's family for keeping it up to date. My own details had been added underneath. Fran and I had always said that we didn't want to be buried and that we should never be under obligation to remember each other in too sentimental a way when we had passed. Still, I couldn't be accused of being a regular visitor to this place and this wasn't about misplaced emotions. This was about closure. About remembering what I had been and what had motivated me to change. And about what remained as a permanent foundation on which I was to build my future.

A door closed behind me and a soft voice spoke in my ear:

"Good afternoon, Sir, visiting old friends?"

I turned and saw the Vicar, dressed in a black shirt and dog collar despite it not being a Sunday and despite the cold weather.

"Yes," I told him, "I was very close to the family. A great shame."

"Death always is a tragedy," the Vicar replied, "but in this case, it's one where even the most ardent of us can question God's Judgement."

"You think so?" I said, "Don't worry, I'll not tell your Bishop on you."

He laughed and drew closer.

"I guess," he said, "that you knew the father too. This Zipoly?"

"Quite well," I told him truthfully, "we were like brothers almost."

"They say," the Vicar leaned in to me conspiratorially, "that he was this Righteous Corrector fellow, you know, the vigilante."

"Do they?" I feigned surprise, "Still, losing his family like that. It's got to affect you somehow."

"Does it justify vengeance though?" he asked, "Isn't forgiveness the better way?"

"To be honest," I answered, "I don't know. Would you be able to forgive in his circumstances? And even if you did, wouldn't you feel compelled to act to make sure that it didn't happen again?"

He thought about this and seemed undecided about how to answer.

"I don't know a huge amount of religion," I continued, "but doesn't God say that vengeance is His?"

"He does."

"Then, what if He uses people to affect that vengeance? Is that such a far-fetched idea?"

"I suppose not," he conceded, "and from what I've heard about this Zipoly guy, it may be the case. God is Just. And yes, it might freak us out if we saw bolts of lightning smiting every deserving creature on the planet, so yes, he could use agents. But then we have to ask the question of how that person would know that God directed him to breach His Own Commandments. Then of course, it begs the question, what is justice? Is it more than the law? Is it a force that we tame with the written word, but which must always remain, somewhat like God Himself, too big to be framed by man? It's all quite tricky, isn't it?"

"It is," I agreed.

He asked if there was anything he could do for me but I thanked him and told him, no, I needed to get back home. We parted with a handshake.

Which seems like the perfect note to end on. That question will always be unanswerable as the complex interactions of weak and imperfect people continue to affect each other in a myriad of unpredictable ways. I have made my choice to do what I do. I am still around. You won't know my current name and please, don't knock on every boat you see called Kingfisher as I may well have changed that name as well.

As to the morality of what I do, that's for others to discuss and debate. For me, the option to sit on the fence just doesn't present itself, but the truth of the matter is that I still don't know whether what I do is right or wrong.